# The Secret Life of Evie Hamilton

# The Secret Life of Evie Hamilton

CATHERINE ALLIOTT

MICHAEL JOSEPH
*an imprint of*
PENGUIN BOOKS

MICHAEL JOSEPH

Published by the Penguin Group
Penguin Books Ltd, 80 Strand, London WC2R ORL, England
Penguin Group (USA) Inc., 375 Hudson Street, New York, New York 10014, USA
Penguin Group (Canada), 90 Eglinton Avenue East, Suite 700, Toronto, Ontario, Canada M4P 2Y3
(a division of Pearson Penguin Canada Inc.)
Penguin Ireland, 25 St Stephen's Green, Dublin 2, Ireland
(a division of Penguin Books Ltd)
Penguin Group (Australia), 250 Camberwell Road, Camberwell, Victoria 3124, Australia
(a division of Pearson Australia Group Pty Ltd)
Penguin Books India Pvt Ltd, 11 Community Centre, Panchsheel Park, New Delhi – 110 017, India
Penguin Group (NZ), 67 Apollo Drive, Rosedale, North Shore 0632, New Zealand
(a division of Pearson New Zealand Ltd)
Penguin Books (South Africa) (Pty) Ltd, 24 Sturdee Avenue, Rosebank, Johannesburg 2196, South Africa

Penguin Books Ltd, Registered Offices: 80 Strand, London WC2R ORL, England

www.penguin.com

First published 2009
2

Copyright © Catherine Alliott, 2009

The moral right of the author has been asserted

Set in 12.5/14.75 pt Monotype Garamond
Typeset by Rowland Phototypesetting Ltd, Bury St Edmunds, Suffolk
Printed in Great Britain by Clays Ltd, St Ives plc

A CIP catalogue record for this book is available from the British Library

ISBN: 978-0-718-15360-1

www.greenpenguin.co.uk

Penguin Books is committed to a sustainable future
for our business, our readers and our planet.
The book in your hands is made from paper
certified by the Forest Stewardship Council.

For Anna with love and thanks

# I

Just recently, and it's hardly even worth mentioning except perhaps as a reproof to myself, I find that whenever I enter a church, not only does my heart sink, but I'm invariably late. Today was no exception. As the sorrowful aroma of beeswax, stone and candles contrived to lower my spirits, so the shrill tones of the female vicar, welcoming the congregation, confirmed my bad timing.

As I crept in, a few heads near the back swivelled to smile sympathetically. I made to slide in amongst them, whispering apologetically, 'Sorry, sorry . . .' but my sister-in-law up near the front was having none of it. Her pointy features, flushed, irritated and rotated at a hundred and eighty degrees, were hard to miss.

'Down here,' she was mouthing theatrically, beckoning me on like an Italian traffic policeman. She even had the white gloves. White gloves!

Dutifully I gathered my hymn book and handbag, and hastened, head bowed, down the aisle. As I hurried along, I inadvertently looked up and caught the eye of my brother in his rather too tight hound's-tooth-check suit, up by the altar, in his occasional capacity of church-warden. He rolled his eyes in mock horror and gave me a huge wink.

'We were worried about you,' Caro hissed as I squeezed

in beside her. Everyone in the pew shoved up a bit. 'You're so late!'

'Sorry,' I muttered. 'Traffic was horrific.'

'On a Sunday?'

I shrugged helplessly as if to suggest I could hardly be held accountable for the vagaries of Oxford's one-way system, and craned my neck past her to greet the rest of my family, such as it was. Beside Caro, my mother and stepmother had both leaned forward to smile: Felicity, my stepmother, elegant in a taupe chenille jacket and vanilla silk skirt, and my mother, startling in leopard-print leggings, a pair of tangerine trainers and matching headband. She blew me an extravagant kiss.

'What's she come as?' I muttered to Caro as I sat back.

'Don't,' she moaned, closing her eyes. 'I swear she does it on purpose. I told her it was smart but casual, as in "no hats", but she looks like she's out on day release. As if the minibus has just dropped her off!'

I suppressed a smile and turned my attention to the vicar, visiting for the occasion: not the village's usual, but very enthusiastic, and, despite a telltale flush up her neck, really getting into her stride, encouraging us in carrying tones, to support these young people before us today, to applaud them in this, their momentous decision, to foster their faith.

I smiled. Jack, my nephew, one of the six or seven teenagers in the front pew, the sun from a stained-glass window shining through his ears, making them glow pink, his red hair dishevelled and hanging over the collar of an uncharacteristic tweed jacket, had the grace to turn and flash me a grin. When he'd cycled into college one day to see us and I'd casually enquired as to his motives, he'd replied in surprise, 'Oh, you get terrific presents. Hugo Palmerton got a diving watch, and his godfather gave him a digital camera.' As I'd raised faintly startled eyebrows he'd rushed on, 'And obviously I believe, and all that stuff. And it's a good idea if you want to get married.' He nodded sagely. 'Saves a lot of hassle.'

I had an idea he was confusing confirmation with baptism, but grasped the general sentiment. He was getting something under his juvenile belt, another notch on his list of 'must dos': get GCSEs, play in the cricket team, snog a girl at a party. Getting confirmed, whilst not necessarily up there with the snog, was still a rite of passage to be doggedly manoeuvred. He was at a particular stage on his greasy pole, as I, I supposed, glancing around, was on mine. There was a time when I used to go to church for weddings, Saturday after Saturday, and then christenings, Sunday after Sunday. Now, with unerring regularity, it appeared to be first communions. Next, I imagined, with a jolt of surprise, it would be . . . yes. Well. After all, there'd been one of those already, hadn't there? Dad's. One box ticked. One box that had gone up the aisle, containing a supposedly hale and hearty man, a florid-faced, larger-than-life man, in this, our village church, whilst we'd all sat in this family pew, hankies clutched to mouths, shocked and silent: the remains of the Milligan family.

Family pew. An anachronism, of course, but one that Caro maintained rigorously, referring to it loudly, as Mum and Granny never had, as if we were the ancient descendants of some aristocratic lineage, instead of impoverished

3

farmers who'd managed, by the skin of their teeth, to hang on to a certain amount of dubiously infertile land and a crumbling old farmhouse.

Caro leaned in to me now. 'No Ant?' She glanced around, as if perhaps expecting him to slide in, having parked the car. I swallowed my irritation.

'No, I told you, he's taken Anna to a clarinet exam.'

'Ah, yes,' she said vaguely. She had a faraway look in her eye, as if in some dim, distant conversation I *had* mentioned it, when in fact I'd made a point of ringing her and apologizing profusely, knowing what store Caro set by family occasions.

'Does she still enjoy it?' she whispered incredulously.

'Loves it,' I hissed back, as we were enjoined, at that moment, to get to our feet and sing hymn number 108.

Yes, that was always the implication, wasn't it, I thought as I added my low warble to Caro's reedy treble and joined the debate as to whether those feet really did walk upon England's mountains green: that my overstimulated, hot-house flower was wilting under the pressure of academia and music exams and pushy parents, whilst her 'brood', as she always referred to them – as if three were a cast of thousands, for heaven's sake – got out into the fresh air and had a 'proper childhood'; as if, somehow, Anna's was *im*proper. My blood simmered away for a bit, but then, as the hymn came to rest in a green and pleasant land and we were bidden to pray, I tried to, not have green thoughts, but pleasant ones.

After all, she was not only my sister-in-law, she was my oldest friend. I was guiltily aware that at one point 'oldest' would have been substituted by 'best'. Certainly

4

years ago, at school, when we were pretty much joined at the hip and lived in each other's houses. Which was probably where the trouble had started. She'd taken one look at my rambling old farmhouse in its idyllic riparian setting, the river threading through the willows in the bottom pasture, observed the big family meals in the farmhouse kitchen, the laughter, the noise, the sense of history, and thought: I want some of that. I can almost remember the look in her eye as she'd stood at the kitchen window one day after lunch, watching Tim, huge, burly and kindly, with his father's shock of red hair, bowling at a tree stump in the back garden. She'd wanted him too, and she'd got him. And if I'm honest, I thought, gazing down at the pattern on my tapestry kneeler, I'd looked at her orderly family, her punctual meals in the uncluttered town house with its state-of-the-art appliances, its colour TV and microwave, her quiet, professional, teacher parents, and thought: and I'll have some of that. Of course, I didn't marry her brother – that would have been too neat, and apart from anything else she didn't have one – but my eyes, shall we say, were opened: to an urbane, civilized lifestyle. One that revolved around restaurants and concerts and political debate instead of wheat yields and set-aside and crop rotation. I was smitten.

When, some years later, I'd met Ant, tall, tousled, slightly myopic in his John Lennon glasses, an academic I'd found in a bookshop I was working in, I knew it was a blueprint I'd been working to. And so everything slotted into place. Caro got her heart's desire, and I got mine. In fact, Caro, even more so, because when Dad died, suddenly, unexpectedly, not in a tangle in his combine, as some farmers do, but just quietly in his sleep and, it transpired, intestate, Caro got the farm too. She almost hadn't, actually, because everything naturally went to Felicity, but Felicity wouldn't hear of it. No, no, the house and land should go to Tim. It was what Dad had always wanted, she insisted, what he'd *said* he wanted, what would have happened if he'd flipping well bothered to write it down. Felicity took sufficient from the estate to buy herself a small house in town, and left the bricks, the mortar — the acres — to Tim and Caro.

I wouldn't say Caro moved in with indecent haste, but it must have been a relief to leave the dismal white bungalow in the village and hustle her children into their bedrooms under the eaves, with the playroom downstairs, family kitchen and rambling back garden. The fact that the roof leaked like a sieve and the winter months were spent running from room to room with buckets whilst the damp galloped gaily up the walls was neither here nor there. She'd got her farm, her land, the whole bucolic bit.

As I'd got my bit, I thought, as I watched Jack come back from the altar, fresh from taking his first parish communion, cheeks flaming, eyes down, collar too tight, looking so impossibly like Tim at that age. I'd got my academic: my sensitive, clever Ant, who duly went on to become a don, making me, nearly bursting with pride, a don's wife, and all at the tender age of twenty-nine. Ant, not me. We had a house in college, in Balliol, one of those dear yellow stone terraced ones, looking out onto the grassy quad complete with gates and porter; we had like-minded friends on our doorstep – dons' wives with babies, with whom I pushed prams. Life was sweet.

But then Ant had gone one step further. He'd written a book. Not a dry, academic tome, but a rather accessible biography of Byron, about whom he was a bit of an expert and whom he regarded as a bit of a dude. Which was how he'd portrayed him. As a legend. A modern-day lyricist, a good-looking, aristocratic, floppy-haired, druggy poet with supermodel girlfriends, in an accessible way that had caught the public's eye, and, more importantly the eye of a daytime television programme, which promoted him. Almost overnight, he became something of a success, and Anthony Hamilton, obscure English professor from Oxford, became Anthony Hamilton, best-selling author. Which wasn't entirely in the script, as far as Caro was concerned.

Oh, it wasn't the fame she envied – I knew she got a vicarious thrill out of being his sister-in-law; broadcasted it loud and clear at the slightest opportunity – no, it was the money. Not a great deal, but enough for us to move out of the college house, which, whilst sweet, was tiny, to a large Victorian villa on four floors with high ceilings and sash windows in that academic Mecca, Jericho. Bills were paid, credit cards sorted, and Anna's school fees, which frankly we'd struggled with, became a doddle. And Tim and Caro couldn't even afford school fees. There was no money in farming now, not unless you had a thousand acres or a private income, and even with the extra Caro made from holding wedding receptions in the garden they were still very short. So they'd had to send their three to the local comp.

I shifted in my pew. Yes, their three. To my one. After all, I'd been quite good about that, hadn't I? Quite grown up. We all had our crosses to bear. OK, not in the early days I hadn't been good. Not when Jack had been swiftly followed by Phoebe and Henry, and Anna by not a sausage. The despair, the sadness, the seething jealousy had threatened to overwhelm me then, but later . . . well, later, Ant and I accepted it. And she, Anna, was so lovely.

I remember once, standing at the window at Church Farm, watching her play with her cousins in the garden. Jack and Henry were fighting as usual, Phoebe was petulantly splashing in the paddling pool as Anna patiently tried to fill her doll's teapot from it, and I was reminded of an Aesop fable. The one about the vixen, surrounded by her swarm of cubs – seven or eight – counting them loudly, taunting the lioness beside her, who only had one. 'Ah, but mine is a lion,' the lioness had replied with a smile. In a guilty, secret place in my heart I felt that; felt that every scrap of Ant and my energy, every ounce of excellence from the collective gene pool, had gone into creating not a scrappy load of cubs, but a tall, blonde, clever, brave lion.

'Are you going up?' Caro nudged me and I felt a rush of blood up my neck. How awful. To be considering her children so. In church!

'Sorry?'

'For communion. Are you going?'

'Oh. Yes – of course.'

Our pew was filing out from the other end and I got up and followed Caro, Mum and Felicity, pausing to greet Henry and Phoebe on the way, who, yet to be confirmed, were staying put. I felt even *more* guilty as they smiled shyly but delightedly up at me. Sorry, God, I muttered, as I crept towards the altar. They're lovely. Of *course* they're lovely. How *awful*.

Up on the rostrum, Tim was dutifully helping with the communion wine, there being quite a congregation today, offering the chalice to Felicity as she knelt. The vicar, meanwhile, was offering hers to Mum.

'No, thank you,' said Mum, firmly.

'Oh – but I thought . . .'

'I'll take it from my son.'

The vicar cleared her throat. 'The thing is,' she murmured embarrassed, 'we've got quite a lot to get through this morning, so—'

Mum's voice became ominously loud. 'I will take the blood of Christ from my son!'

Caro shot me a look of horror and, after some hasty eye contact, Tim and the vicar switched places. As Mum stood up and I went to kneel in her place, she hissed, 'I will not take the Holy Sacrament from a woman!'

'So you made crystal clear,' I muttered back.

Tim's eyes, though, were sparkling with amusement at the diversion, and as he approached me with his chalice I felt those terrible church giggles I'd felt years ago; every Sunday, in fact, in this church, as Tim did his damnedest to make me laugh, seeing how many coughs or farts he could get away with during prayers, deliberately singing off key in the hymns, making my father lean across to swipe him as I shook with mirth beside him, my fist in my mouth. I determined not to look up at him now. As he put the cup to my lips, he affected a thick Irish brogue.

'De blood of Christ, my child,' he wheedled softly.

No. I would not lose it. And I was fine, actually, until, as I sipped, Tim whispered in mock alarm, as if I'd taken a huge gulp, 'Steady!'

Doing the nose trick with the communion wine is pretty unforgivable, and as I returned, chastened and wine splattered, to my seat, Caro was frowning darkly. I knew she thought I was a bad influence on her husband. 'Tim seems to revert to childhood when he's with you!' she'd trill gaily, and I just knew she meant, behaves like an absolute oaf. As I bent my head to pray, I recalled a friend's comment when Caro had married Tim. 'How lovely, so you're gaining a sister.' Why, then, years later, did I have a sinking feeling I'd lost a brother?

Shocked for the second time by my impure thoughts, I resolved, as we all filed out ten minutes later into the sunshine, congratulating the young people as they stood about awkwardly, to be more sisterly. More . . . supportive.

Caro turned to me, a defensive look in her eye. 'You're coming back to the house?'

'Of course,' I smiled.

'Good,' she beamed, clearly imagining, I realized with a jolt, that I might not. 'We haven't done much in the way of catering, just a glass of sherry and some sandwiches.'

'Lovely,' I said faintly, knowing the sherry would be sweet and the sandwiches curly, and wondering how Caro had got so determinedly stuck in the 1950s when she hadn't even lived through them. Why she was so determined to be a parody of a landowner's wife.

'Of course, we would have done lunch,' she said, peeling off her gloves – Granny's gloves, I realized with surprise – and scurrying down the path, 'but it gets so expensive, doesn't it?'

Ah, there it was: the first reference to penury. Plenty more where that came from. She hurried up the lane to the farm where our land – her land – adjoined the churchyard. Stick thin as ever, bent at the waist as if against a howling gale, she bustled along and I followed, just as I'd followed her to lessons or PE, always with that same steely determination; always needing to get on.

In my not terribly strenuous efforts to catch up with her I passed Mum and Felicity, loitering by the church gate, looking furtive.

'Coming?' I called cheerily.

Felicity glanced over her shoulder. 'Er, no.'

'No?' I stopped in my tracks.

'Well, the thing is, Evie, we've got tickets – have *had* tickets, for ages – for a choral concert at Christ Church. Tom James is the soloist, and we told Caro at the time, when she arranged this, that we could only come to the church, but you know what she's like.' Felicity looked genuinely fearful, whilst Mum grinned, eyes rolling, enjoying herself hugely.

'Oh, I think we just tell her to piss off, don't you?' she said loudly, puffing on a ciggie. 'After all, it's Jack's party, and he's not fussed, are you, darling?'

'Go on, you ravers, off you go.' Jack appeared behind us, putting an arm around each of their shoulders, hustling them towards their car. 'Off to your gig. Your guilty secret is safe with me. Like the leggings, Granny.'

'Thank you, darling.' She struck a pose. 'I thought if

I wore skin-tight Lycra I wouldn't be so tempted to throw my knickers.'

This was baffling even for Mum, and I wondered if she'd got Tom James muddled with an ageing crooner from Wales. Two hours of Fauré's *Requiem* might come as a bit of a shock if she was expecting to punch the air to 'Sex Bomb'.

'Well, you look terrific,' said Jack, unfazed. 'Got a fag, Granny?'

'Yes, darling.' Mum went for her handbag. 'Here, I —'

'No she *hasn't*,' hissed Felicity, staying Mum's hand and glancing round tremulously. 'Caro will freak. Now come on, Barbara, we're in enough trouble as it is. Let's get going.'

Jack and I shielded them as they hastened to Felicity's old green Subaru, and then, as they drove away, we turned to join the straggle of people making their way down the lane to the farm.

'I've got half a mind to go with them,' Jack said gloomily, pulling a butt out of his jacket pocket and attempting to set fire to it. It was doomed to failure but he persevered. It always amused me that he deemed me the *laissez-faire* aunt, the one he could smoke in front of. Or perhaps he was testing me.

'Oh, come on, Jack, your mum's gone to a lot of trouble.'

He frowned, considering this, his freckled face upturned to the sun. 'Yes, maybe that's the problem. It's always trouble. Never fun. Oops, talk of the devil.' He tossed the butt in the hedge as Caro, having gone round the back of the farmhouse, flung open the front door from inside.

'Come on, Jack, you're supposed to be welcoming everyone!' she yelled across the yard.

'Coming,' he called. Then, softly to me: 'Might just go for a whiz in the hydrangeas first, though. Got a bit of an experiment going. Did you know if you pee on a pink one, you can turn it blue?'

'I didn't, but thanks for sharing that with me.'

'It's the acid, I suppose.'

'I suppose,' I agreed, as my favourite nephew – although of course one shouldn't have favourites, but the most like Tim, at any rate – slunk off around the side of the house, shoulders hunched.

I, in turn, squared my own as I went through the sagging, five-bar gate hanging limply on its hinges at the front. I could already see a gaggle of people through the sitting-room windows: old friends, family friends, neighbours from the village, no doubt. People who'd tell me they didn't see enough of me these days. That I spread myself too thinly. Maybe even Neville Carter's parents, I thought with a pang. That rocked me for a second; made me hold the gate. Then I took a deep breath and picked my way in my heels through the filthy yard, which periodically, Tim got the local pikies to tip a load of shingle over. But no amount of shingle could stop the mud seeping through, just as – I paused and glanced up at the modest stone farmhouse – no amount of time could stop the seep of memories.

# 2

'Evelyn! Oh my God, I haven't seen you in ages.'

I'd just taken the few steps required to cross the narrow
flagstone hall and duck under the low door into the sitting
room, when the hated name rang out and my arm was
seized. An overweight woman in tight white trousers,
tight pink sweater, and an even tighter perm, beamed
delightedly at me, her face glowing. She reminded me
vaguely of a girl I'd been at school with, Paula someone.

'It's Paula! Paula Simons, remember?'

'Gosh. Of . . . course. How are you?'

'Really well, thanks. Have you brought your husband?'
Her eyes roved past me, hopefully.

I smiled. 'No, he had to take our daughter to a music
exam, I'm afraid.'

'Oh, shame.' Her mouth drooped. 'I brought a book
for him to sign. You should have taken her!'

'Who, Anna?' I was startled. 'Yes, I suppose . . . but
then Jack is my—'

'Hey, Kay. Kay, look, it's Evelyn *Hamilton*!'

Another pink-faced middle-aged woman materialized,
and this one I really didn't know except . . . oh heavens,
Kay Pritchard. Suddenly I was nine years old again in
the school cloakroom, giggling hysterically amongst the
hats and coats. Our teacher, Mrs Stanley, had just told us
that one of our classmates, Debbie Holt, wouldn't be

coming in that day because her mother had died in the night. In the stunned silence that followed, Kay and I had dissolved. Not tears, giggles. Nerves, I suppose. We'd been sent out, but to our horror, couldn't stop, even in the cloakroom. Later I'd been mortified and it had haunted me for weeks. I wondered if she remembered. I also wondered if I was as changed as Paula and Kay: so . . . old?

'Oh, *Evelyn*! Oh God – is he here?' She glanced around excitedly.

'He's not, I'm afraid. Will I do?'

'Oh.' She pouted. 'Well, you'll have to, won't you?' She gave a tinkly laugh. 'But I want to hear all about it. Did he really go to bed with a different woman every week?'

This, a reference not to Ant, but a Georgian dramatist, whose biography he'd just written and which was currently being serialized, pre-publication, in the *Daily Mail*.

'If that's what it says.' I smiled thinly.

'You haven't read it?' Kay's eyes were huge.

'Er . . . not that particular one.' I'd read most of the Byron, and I'd started the one Ant had done on Kilvert, which hadn't been such a success, but not this one, the one Ant referred to disparagingly as his 'Bodice Ripper'. The whole thing made us cringe a bit, actually. After all, he was a serious biographer, it wasn't usually the sort of thing he did, but the publisher had offered a big advance for something a little more spicy, a little more Byronesque, a little less Kilvert – no more dreary parsons, please! And to be fair, there was really only one steamy chapter, which, naturally, the *Mail* had chosen . . .

'And you're living in Jericho now, I gather?' Kay's face

was flushed, either from the warmth of the room or her sherry. Her eyes were bright.

'Well, on the edge.'

'Yes, but *still*.' They looked at me admiringly. 'And what are you doing now?' demanded Kay, rather pointedly.

'Oh, this and that,' I said uncomfortably. 'What about you, Kay?' I said quickly. 'Still, um . . .' I mentally scrolled down my school-leavers archive, 'nursing?'

'Yes, but not in hospitals any more. It doesn't really work with kids. I'm a practice nurse. You know, in Ludworth?'

The next village. So perhaps I should. Perhaps Caro should have told me. When I'd asked. I smiled nervously. 'Right.'

'And I'm on the Parish Council too,' she informed me. 'For my sins.'

'Sounds fun,' I said politely.

She made a sour face. 'Think *Vicar of Dibley* without the humour.'

I laughed, and through the years caught a flash of wit I'd enjoyed when our desks had adjoined long ago. I wondered vaguely what they were doing here, these women, then remembered with a jolt they were also Jack's godparents. It occurred to me that none of Anna's godparents stemmed from my school days. They were all friends Ant and I had met together. Well, not quite true. They were Ant's friends, from Westminster, or Balliol. Not Parsonage Road Comprehensive. I wondered, un-easily, what that said about me. That I'd simply moved on? Or reinvented myself? Didn't sound very nice.

Across the other side of the room I noticed Tim standing awkwardly by the fireplace, resting one leg, his hand gripping the mantel. He'd had a hip replacement a couple of months ago after years of pain, which was supposed to make a new man of him. I thought he looked worse. I'd have loved a quick chat, but Caro, looking harassed, swept by with a plate of egg sandwiches and I realized I should offer to help. But that would mean circulating, and I'd already spotted Neville Carter's parents in the other room, which would mean talking to them and . . . oh, for heaven's sake, Evie.

I seized the plate of sandwiches from Caro's startled hand and marched across the hall into the small magnolia dining room. It doubled as the children's homework room, and had been hastily cleared of files and papers, which were stacked in a chaotic fashion by the piano, the table requisitioned for drinks. I'd briefly glimpsed the Carters in here earlier, before Paula had claimed me. They were clutching an orange juice apiece and still had their coats on, looking rather temporary. And so *old*, I thought with a lurch as I greeted them. To my relief, Mrs Carter smiled.

'Evelyn.' Her face relaxed. 'How are you, dear?'

'I'm fine thanks, and you? Hi there, Mr Carter.'

He nodded wordlessly at me, shaking his head as I offered him a sandwich. Much less friendly, I thought, my chest tightening.

'Oh, you know, we keep busy. Our Eileen's married now, of course. She's pregnant too. Expecting in March, did you know?'

'I didn't! How marvellous.'

'And the garden keeps us very busy.'

The garden. Yes, away from children and on to flowers. Good idea.

'Yes, Caro says you had a terrific display of bulbs this year,' I blurted. She hadn't, but bulbs were safe, surely?

She frowned. 'Oh, no, we just did primulas this spring. Perhaps she meant the snowdrops?'

'That's it.' I faltered. 'Snowdrops.'

'The garden's been a great comfort to us,' Mr Carter said quietly.

'Yes.' I caught my breath. 'I can imagine. Although,' I went on bravely, 'no, I can't really imagine at all.'

There was a silence. Mrs Carter put a hand on my arm. 'Well, you had a sadness too, dear. You lost your dad.'

I smiled, acknowledging her graciousness. Losing a parent was ghastly, of course it was. But it wasn't the same as losing a child.

Happily Mrs Pallister from next door approached and I took it as my cue to remove myself, and my plate of egg sandwiches, from the Carters' presence. There. I'd done it. I felt a wave of relief. Then shame at the relief. And instead of going back to the sitting room I went down the passage to the kitchen, ostensibly to refuel my plate, but actually, to take a moment.

The kitchen still looked pretty much as it always had done, which was a comfort: cheap laminate flooring had replaced the black and white checked lino, and the walls, once cream, were now lilac, but the old range was still in situ, the oak table still sat squarely in the middle, and the station clock Dad had salvaged from a disused railway yard ticked on above the window seat I used to curl up on with my books. Right now it was fairly chaotic: the table was littered with empty plates and hastily removed bits of tin foil, and a rather cloying, eggy smell prevailed, but it had always been my favourite room and I felt better for being here. I went to the window seat, kneeling on the faded chintz cushion, leaning forward to rest my hands on the sill as I gazed out.

The bumpy, erratically mown lawn, perhaps an attempt by Jack for some extra pocket money, tumbled down to the river at the bottom: in the paddocks beyond, Caro's pink and white marquee, a permanent fixture after months of haggling with the local council, flapped prettily in the breeze on the other side. Sheep were encouraged to graze around it and the huge oak tree spread benign limbs above it in the sunshine.

It all looked desperately idyllic, but I knew the reality. Knew about stumbling out there in January, across the stepping stones in a dressing gown and wellies, slipping on mercilessly hard ground, stumbling over frozen ruts to crack the ice on the troughs for the sheep, the wind stinging your cheeks as it whipped across the Vale. Knew that, just yards from this window, behind that barn, rusting old machinery, not good enough to sell and too expensive to remove, lurked menacingly, like sleeping dragons, camouflaged by weeds and grass, ready to trip the unsuspecting. I knew where the wheel-less Jeeps and tractors were parked on bricks; knew, if you found a length of barbed wire sticking out of the ground, not to pull it or a whole line of broken fencing would emerge like an earth monster. I knew the Steptoe and Son side of farming; all of which was kept from Caro's brides, of course. They saw none of this as they tripped prettily down the lane behind the hedge, fresh from the church, the congregation following on foot – no cars, that was the draw – through a pretty white gate, and straight into the bottom meadow. From that vantage point, as they sipped champagne amongst the buttercups, Church Farm was just a hazy blob on the horizon: small, compact and Georgian. You wouldn't know the masonry was crumbling, the sashes in the windows broken, or that the gutters leaked huge incontinent stains down the brickwork.

'Bucolic Betrothals' Caro advertised as in the local paper, and then some blurb about experiencing olde worlde charm and dipping into England's rural past, which was where all this belonged, of course: the past. It should have been sold years ago, the farm, when Dad died. Not that I'd wanted any money. I agreed with Felicity: it was Tim's inheritance, as it had been Dad's from his father, and as it was with all farming families, from father to son. But Tim could have bought himself a little business, set himself up. Keeping it was like hanging on to the trappings of an empire, for all the wrong reasons.

Ant would be kinder, I thought, as I heard Paula, roaring with laughter in the next room. I straightened up from the window seat. 'They can't sell it, it's part of them,' he'd say.

'Well, it's part of me too, and I had no problems leaving.'

'Ah, but you always had your head in a book. Never looked out of the window, let alone went outside. Never let it get to you, the land. That's what it's all about, you know. See the Romantic Poets on this. Wordsworth, Blake – they'd have plenty to say on the subject.'

It was true, I thought as I picked up a fresh plate of cocktail sausages and made to go back. I'd never really troubled the great outdoors. Too busy trying to leave. All that fresh air and I couldn't breathe. I'd always felt a great affinity with the Mitford sister who'd hoarded running-away money; had even started a collection myself. Although, as it turned out, I hadn't needed to run; I was rescued.

As I left the kitchen, I paused a moment at the door at the end of the passage. Through the leaded lights I could see Jack, Henry and Phoebe, plus a few friends, on the trampoline. Too cool to bounce, they were lying on it, chatting and laughing in the sunshine. I smiled. Anna would have liked that. Suddenly I wished she hadn't had the clarinet exam.

Unsettled, I made my way back to the sitting room. Paula and Kay had clearly worked up quite a head of steam and were shrieking and hooting, glasses recharged. This was obviously a big day out for them. I tried to skirt round them to Tim, who was bustling around with a bottle being mine host, but my arm was seized by Paula.

'And you're so *brown*. Have you been away?' Her eyes were squiffy, accusatorial.

'Only to Italy.'

'*Only* to Italy,' the pair of them mimicked.

I flushed. 'Ant and I just went for a few days.'

'Whereabouts?'

'Um, Venice.'

'Oooh,' they cooed, like a Greek chorus.

A man had joined them now, small and wiry, blinking behind his spectacles. Oh God, *Kevin Wise*. Again from school, and – yes, of course, Caro had told me. He and Kay . . .

'Kevin and I go to Cornwall, don't we?' Kay regarded him sourly. 'Every year, to the same grotty bungalow.'

'Cornwall's lovely,' I said encouragingly.

'Not where we go. And his parents come with us, sadly. His mother's a witch.'

Crikey. 'Ant and I like Helford,' I managed.

'Ant and I, Ant and I,' mocked Paula. 'Anyone would think you were still in love with your husband!' She threw back her head and cackled. Then her head snapped back abruptly. 'My husband won't make love to me any more,' she announced in a loud voice, clearly spectacularly pissed. 'He says he doesn't find it stimulating any more. Doesn't—'

'Evie.' Caro plucked at my sleeve. 'Have you had one of these?'

Never had I been so delighted to see my sister-in-law brandishing a plate of vol-au-vents. 'I have thanks, delicious.' I took her aside. 'But listen, Caro, the thing is, I'm going to have to dash quite soon. Ant and I are going out to dinner tonight. His publishers are—' Shit. Ant and I *and* the publishers. I held my breath.

'Don't worry,' she said gently, to my surprise. 'I know how it is. We all have commitments, and these summer weekends are a nightmare. Everything seems to come at once, doesn't it? It was sweet of you to come.'

'Thanks, Caro,' I said gratefully, remembering why we'd been such friends. *Were* such friends. Why, at school, we'd stuck together so firmly, amongst the Kays and the Paulas. 'I'll just say goodbye to Tim.'

'Oh, don't worry, I'll tell him you've gone. And I'd better escort you out,' she said, taking my arm. 'Your fan club will never let you go, otherwise.'

'I don't know about fan club,' I said nervously as we skirted the room. 'I get the feeling they're muttering: "Thinks she's something special".'

'They're just jealous,' she said, seeing me to the door. 'They know we all left the starting blocks together and they want to know why they haven't gone as far, that's all.'

I shot her a grateful look as we emerged on the doorstep together in the sunshine. Suddenly I remembered my promise to Anna; wondered if this was a good moment. I hesitated.

'By the way, Anna's got a bit of a bee in her bonnet about riding at the moment.'

'Oh?'

'She's had quite a lot of lessons now and I just wondered . . . well, she's terribly keen to join the Pony Club.'

'The Pony Club?'

'Yes, and you're on the committee, aren't you? So I wondered . . .'

'But she doesn't live round here. It's all done locally, Evie. Neighbouring farms, that sort of thing.'

'I know, but I thought she could cycle.'

'Where?'

'Um, here. It's only about twenty minutes – well, half an hour. Or she could get the train. At weekends. Not every weekend, obviously.' I was rapidly losing my nerve.

My palms felt a bit sweaty. 'But now and again I thought she could, you know, come across. Have some fun with her cousins.'

Caro folded her arms. Her chin retracted slowly back into her neck. She surveyed me through narrowed eyes.

'Right,' she said thoughtfully. 'So you want me to pick her up from the station on a Saturday morning, take her to the rallies, give her a bed for the night, and then drop her back at the station the next day?'

I flushed. 'Well, no. That sounds—'

'You want to cherry-pick your bits of country life for her. You don't actually want to live here, but you want her to reap the benefits. Is that it?'

I stared at her, horrified. Suddenly I saw red. 'Caro, I did live here, remember? This was my home. And no, I don't mean to pass the buck. I'll come across, do my share, take the children to shows or whatever.'

'Oh, really?'

'Yes, of course.'

'OK,' she said suddenly, 'you're on.'

'What?'

'Yes, fine.' Her eyes glittered. 'You tack up the ponies, muck out the lorry, drive it to shows in the pouring rain – splendid. I'd like to see more of Anna. And you too, Evie. You're on.' She challenged me with her eyes.

'Right.' I caught my breath, taken aback. 'I will.' I swallowed. There didn't seem to be much more to say. After a moment I turned, somewhat shaken, and walked uncertainly across the yard to the gate.

'But don't forget,' she called sweetly after me, 'she can't come to Pony Club unless she has a pony!'

I stopped a moment in the muddy yard. Blinked rapidly. Then I took a deep breath and marched on as best I could, hobbling in the shingle in my heels, knowing she was watching me, a smile on her face.

I turned up the lane, fury mounting. She had to spoil it, didn't she? Just when I thought we were getting on so well, she had to go and muddy the waters. Get all chippy again. And, boy, was her resentment close to the surface. Scratch it and – *whoosh* – did she erupt. Because that was what it was, I decided angrily as I stalked on to the car. Resentment. And envy. Anna had her cool town life – plays, concerts, friends nearby – and she should jolly well stick to it. Her kids didn't have any of that, so she was damned if Anna was going to have a bit of something hers had in spades.

Well, we'll see about that, I thought as I marched round the church wall to the car. I got in, slamming the door behind me. It created a breeze and sent a shopping list on the dashboard fluttering into my lap. I snatched it up irritably. Eggs, butter, dishwasher powder . . . On an impulse I plunged my hand into my bag, rifled fruitlessly for a pen, found an eyeliner instead, and in black, sticky and appropriately childish letters scrawled 'PONY' underneath. I gazed at it a moment; felt a tiny bit better. Then I turned the key in the ignition and sped off.

# 3

'She's infuriating!' I stormed to Ant the next morning, chucking bowls in the dishwasher and tossing cereal packets back in the cupboard. 'One minute she's nice as pie, and the next she's morphed into Anne Robinson!'

He smiled into his *Independent*. 'Only if you know which buttons to press.'

'I didn't press anything *deliberately*.' I flicked the dishwasher door shut with my foot as I passed. 'I thought she'd be pleased, actually, to have Anna around, have her more involved in the farm. I certainly didn't think she'd jump down my throat like that.'

Ant folded up his paper calmly. 'Now why do I suspect you're being slightly disingenuous?'

'What d'you mean?'

'Surely you knew there was every possibility? Caro is one of life's throat jumpers.'

'Yes, but why?' I wailed. 'She never used to be.'

'Because she's sensitive. For obvious reasons.'

He stood up and drained his coffee, tilting back his head. 'And tackling her in the middle of her party was perhaps not the most subtle of manoeuvres.'

'It wasn't the middle of her party, it was at the end, when she was being uncharacteristically sweet and understanding and I was stupidly lured into a false sense of security. Oh, *morning*, sleepy-head. You're cutting it fine.'

26

Anna had slipped into the kitchen via the basement stairs and slunk into position at the table, shoulders hunched, eyes half shut.

'Not really, there's no assembly this morning. Miss Braithwaite's got clinical depression. Who was being sweet?'

'Caro,' I said shortly. 'At Jack's party.'

'Oh. Did you ask —'

'Darling, how was the exam?' I said quickly. I hadn't had a chance to talk to her last night: Ant and I had gone out for supper soon after I'd got back and she'd been asleep when we'd got in.

'Fine.' She yawned widely and shook some Golden Nuggets into a bowl. She sloshed milk on top and began mechanically scooping them into her mouth, crunching hard. As the sugar kicked in, her eyes opened a bit. She gazed blankly out of the open French windows to our stretch of parched lawn, fringed by dusty laurels. 'I was a bit nervous in the Schubert, though. Probably played a few bum notes.'

'Didn't sound like it from where I was sitting.' Ant crossed the kitchen to put his mug in the sink.

'Could you hear?' She turned to look at him.

'The walls at the Royal College are notoriously thin. Granny always used to listen to me.'

'Oh.' Her eyes widened with interest. 'So what about the Beethoven? A bit too slow at the end?'

'It's supposed to be slow. It's a moody old piece by a moody old bugger contemplating slitting his throat. You had me reaching for the Sabuteos when you launched into those last arpeggios, I can tell you.'

She laughed and I glowed as I cleared up around them, enjoying the musical banter. It was all Greek to me, just as it was when they talked poetry and Latin and, well, Greek.

Anna got up to put her bowl in the sink and I watched as they leaned languidly against the stainless steel together, chewing the academic fat: both tall, fair-skinned and blond, Ant's springy curls turning slightly grey at the temples, Anna's hair much straighter, more flaxen, and tucked behind her ears. Athletic, their figures might be described as, not small and solid like mine, and they both had fine features, straight noses, and wide-apart eyes, which gave them a faintly startled look, although Anna's weren't quite as blue. She'd got his temperament too – calm, unruffled – and definitely his brain. So what had I brought to the party? You might well ask. Ant would be kind enough to say, amongst other things, an impulsiveness to temper his natural caution, his reserve. I might say, not a lot. I smiled as I tossed a fork into the cutlery drawer.

As I popped a slice of bread in the toaster, half an ear on what they were saying about Schubert not being as religious as he made out and just laying it on thick to get in with Beethoven, I marvelled how, even though my subconscious must absorb a certain amount, I never really made sense of it. If you asked me in ten minutes if Schubert had been the religious one or Beethoven I wouldn't have a clue. But I enjoyed listening. A culture vulture, my father used to call me, when, instead of watching *Grandstand* with the rest of the family, I'd catch a bus into town and go round the Bodleian, or be found lying on my bed with my nose in a book whilst Tim helped with the lambing. Not the sort of book Ant and Anna read, I might add, but a light romance — very light — possibly a clogs-and-shawls saga from the mobile library that used to stop outside the farm. But any sort of book was highbrow to Dad, and the fact that I read all day persuaded him I was clever. That I then messed up my A levels and ended up going to secretarial college was therefore a bit of a surprise all round. Not that he minded. On the contrary, he was pleased I was doing something practical, 'acquiring a skill,' he'd say proudly, something I could use afterwards. But I hadn't used it, had probably known I never would, and had gone straight into Bletchley's Books on the outskirts of town as a sales assistant. Dad wasn't convinced about that, but I loved it. Loved the feel and smell of the books — which in my department were way beyond me — loved the people who used to come in and pore over them with their long scarves and their owl glasses. One of whom, of course, was Ant, who'd lost his copy of *Sir Gawain and the Green Knight* and had come in to replace it.

'*Sir Gawain and the* what?' I'd said, scrolling down the list of titles on my computer.

'*Green Knight*?' He'd swivelled round to look at the screen and I remember our heads were quite close.

'Is it a fairy tale? Maybe in the children's section.'

He'd laughed. 'I wish it was. No, it's like deciphering Chinese.'

Later, when I'd found it in the storeroom and boggled at the hideously difficult Middle English, I'd blushed. But it was all part of the learning curve. And after all, that was what I was doing here: learning the way of life, acquiring the habits of an undergraduate, without actually doing any hard graft. I took the *Coles Notes* approach to Oxford; I didn't actually study the text, but, boy, could I wing the lifestyle. Naturally I had a bike, and long dark hair, and a scarf of indeterminate origin with the stripes going lengthways, and I'd cycle round the city with a basket of books on the front, hoping the gaggle of Japanese tourists on Magdalen Bridge would think I was the real McCoy. I'd once – laughingly – said as much to Ant, and he'd roared.

'Oh, no, no one would ever take you for one of those St Hilda's girls.'

'Why not?' I'd said, hugely offended.

'You're much too pretty.'

I didn't quite know if I was mollified. Probably. A bit. But I wouldn't have minded being both. Like Anna. Pretty and clever.

I watched now as she scooped up her GCSE coursework folder with one hand and took the piece of buttered toast I proffered with the other.

'See you,' she called as she went through the open French windows, pausing to stroke Brenda, our West Highland terrier, who was asleep on the lawn, then going to the wall at the far end where her bike was parked. When she'd dumped her books in the basket she clamped the piece of toast between her teeth and went to wheel her bike through the garden gate to the street. She turned back suddenly. Removed the toast.

'So what did she say?'

'What?'

The washing machine had embarked on its final spin behind me.

'Caro. What did she say?'

I caught this, but shrugged and cupped my ear, pretending I couldn't hear over the noise, which she acknowledged with an impatient shake of her head. I watched as she swung a leg over the saddle and pedalled off down the road in her dark blue Oxford High uniform.

'She wants to get her ears pierced,' I murmured to no one in particular, but I suppose to Ant, who was also gathering books and papers, making final debarkation noises, patting his pockets to check for wallet, glasses.

'There, on the dresser.' I pointed to his ancient spectacle case on the top shelf.

'Thanks.' He reached up. 'Well, I suppose if that's what all her friends are doing,' he said vaguely. 'But she's a bit young, isn't she?'

'That's what I said. I said, what about next summer, when she's fifteen?'

'And she said?'

'Fine. It was almost as if she felt she had to ask, but was quite relieved when I said no.'

We exchanged smiles and I knew we were silently congratulating ourselves on having a daughter who didn't actually want every orifice pierced, or a tattoo on her bottom, like Jess next door; who thought smoking was sad, drink to be sipped cautiously, and who wanted to get ten A stars in her GCSEs, and looked as if she was going to.

'See you later.' Ant kissed my cheek.

I leaned on the open frame of the French windows in my dressing gown and watched him go: crossing the garden to get his own bike, head slightly bowed, in the manner of a very tall man. Yes, we didn't do too badly, Ant and I. When friends complained about their bloody husbands, or their bloody marriages, I found myself keeping quiet, or even making things up. 'Yes, desperately untidy,' or 'No, never remembers an anniversary,' I'd sometimes contribute. I remembered Paula's accusation, yesterday – 'Don't tell me you're still in love with your husband!' Well, I was, actually. And he with me. I knew that, not smugly or sloppily, but just with a thumping great visceral certainty: knew we were in this for the long haul. Lifers.

As he went through the back gate he met the postman and took the letters from him, brandishing them at me to let me know he'd got them. I smiled and nodded back. These days they were nearly all for him, anyway. Not just the bills – I could barely manage the milk bill – but readers' letters too. When the publishers had sent the first few – which invariably began, very sweetly, 'I've never written to an author before but I just had to congratulate you . . .' – Anna and I had hooted with laughter.

'Fan mail!' she'd spluttered. 'My God, Dad, like a pop star. They'll be wanting a photo next.'

And the very next one had asked for just that. Ant had declined, writing back saying he was terribly flattered, but really, he was no oil painting, which was why there was no author photo on the dust jacket. But it gave us a flavour of things to come, of the number of people who'd come to listen to him give a reading in New College and the sheer volume at the reception in the adjoining room afterwards, as we'd stood clutching glasses of warm white wine: quite a lot of dusty academics – colleagues, many of them – but also plenty of perfectly normal people too, and that was the clincher. To be celebrated amongst one's peers, the people Ant respected, was crucial, but to have gone over the wire, to have breached the gap between these hallowed, honey-coloured walls and entertained the man on the street, the woman in Tesco's, to have reached the *real* world, was something else. Joe Public's recognition was secretly craved by the high-minded, for only that brought fame and fortune.

And I'd been so proud, *so* proud, standing there beside him in my new wraparound dress, Anna, stunning in a Topshop number, laughing later with Ant as I recalled how someone had approached me and asked politely, 'And what do you do?' and I'd replied thoughtlessly, 'Oh, nothing.' 'Nothing will come of nothing,' the bearded cove had murmured before moving on, and I'd shrugged, used to quotes being flung at me in this city, used to people being surprised I didn't teach, or paint, or write, secretly knowing Ant did enough for both of us. 'Should have told him to sod off,' Ant had said, annoyed, but I'd just laughed.

But there'd been jealousy too, at his success. Intellectuals, despite, or perhaps because of, their brains, can be a mean-spirited bunch, and there'd been those who'd said Ant had sold out, been too commercial, betrayed Byron, in his flagrant depiction of him as a 'yoof culture' figure. But as Anna said, it was all bollocks, because if Byron had been alive today he'd have loved it. Would have turned up the collar of his leather jacket, flopped down on the sofa in his stately pile with his babe and given an interview to *Hello!*, unlike Wordsworth, who'd have headed for the Lake District in his anorak. And herein lay the rub. The fact that Byron would have been cool and Wordsworth a geek came as no surprise to anyone in the English Department: it was that someone had thought of saying it, of stating the obvious, that they didn't like.

So we'd been careful, in the face of this potential envy. Or rather, Ant had been careful. I, on the other hand, had gone shopping. House hunting, to be more precise. Recalling that, I cringed now as I wrapped my dressing gown around me and scooped up my breakfast tray, making for the stairs. Oh, we'd agreed we were *moving*, that much had been discussed – the college house was only rented and we needed to buy – but what we hadn't quite established was where. As I nipped up the stairs now to the ground floor, balancing my tea and toast, I passed the double doors into the drawing room – drawing room, God, we never thought we'd have one of those – following the curved, French-polished rail up to my bedroom. But this wasn't the house I was cringing about, no. It was the one off the Banbury Road, the one in Westgate Avenue with the six bedrooms, the acre of garden, the music room, the – God help me – orangery. I remember looking round it, excitement mounting, following the estate agent as more and more spacious rooms unfolded, and then the next day, breathlessly dragging Ant and Anna there, verbally incontinent with excitement. I explained, as I hustled them up the crunchy gravel drive, that it was just down the road from Grant Marshall's house – Grant, a medic, having also recently made it over the wire as a television psychiatrist – and his famously snooty wife, Prue, and that I simply couldn't *wait* to see Prue's face!

In the event, Ant's face had been more interesting. He'd stood on the terrace overlooking the vast, manicured garden, thrust his hands in his pockets and jingled his change nervously.

'For just the three of us? It doesn't seem quite right.'

There was a silence as I digested this.

'It's too far from where we've come from,' Anna, young, but terrifyingly articulate, had commented at length. She'd picked a scab on her knee and frowned, as if she wasn't quite sure what she meant by that. But I knew exactly and I felt ashamed.

Ant cleared his throat. 'I'm just not convinced it's sort of . . . us.'

'No, no, you're right,' I'd said quickly. Meekly. 'Quite right.'

Suddenly it was as clear as day. This house took us out of quiet, muted, university-professor land and into loud, cushy, fat-cat suburbia. Suddenly the wall-to-wall white carpets were vulgar, the four bathrooms flashy, the orangery a joke. And I hadn't known. Not immediately. It had had to be pointed out to me by my intrinsically tasteful husband and child.

We'd headed straight back into town, and then the following day had seen this place. Tall, terraced, with a little iron balcony at the front, still central, still close to our friends, still built of mellow Cotswold stone, still with integrity. I paused at the landing window now, looking out at our long, slim walled garden, elegant and leafy, sandwiched between two similarly elegant and leafy enclosures, belonging to a chemistry don and a journalist. Yes. It suited us, I thought, going on to my bedroom. Was right up the Hamiltons' street.

I smiled and hopped back into bed with my toast and the papers.

When Ant and I had been married only a few months, he'd left for work one morning then popped back ten minutes later, having forgotten a student's essay. He'd found me back in bed with a box of lime creams, a cigarette and *Cosmo*. I'd been as mortified as if he'd caught me with a naked man, but Ant had roared with delight.

'It's why I love you,' he'd said, leaning over the bed to kiss me. 'Because you're not up and dressed, hair scraped back, beavering away trying to write the next *Madame Bovary*, like everyone else in this city. You just enjoy yourself. You embrace pleasure.'

I seem to remember we'd embraced a bit more pleasure that morning as one kiss had led to another and Ant was late for his tutorial, and I remember wondering if the student waiting patiently for him to arrive had any idea that the flushed young professor, who eventually appeared waving the forgotten essay, had just achieved bliss in the arms of his wife, on top of a box of lime creams. Probably not.

These days my tastes had changed, and tea and toast accompanied the *Daily Mail*, but I still read the important bits: the 'Femail' section in the middle, the diets, the detoxing, the fashion – I didn't skimp. This being Monday

I also shimmied through the local paper too, glancing, out of habit, at the houses at the back, then the furniture for sale — we were vaguely looking for a baby grand piano for Anna — when an ad in the livestock column caught my eye.

For Sale. Beautiful grey Connemara pony, 14.2 hands, 6 years. Very willing, a great character. A teenager's dream. First to see will buy. £1,000.

I stared in disbelief; read it again. Oh. Oh, how marvellous! Right here, in front of my nose. It was fate. I just knew it was. And I also knew, from listening to Anna, that 14.2 was about the right height. And a thousand pounds, I was sure, was pretty reasonable too. I feverishly read the address. Parkfield Lane. Which was off the Woodstock Road. Minutes away!

I straightened up in the crumpled bed, retying my dressing gown, lips pursed triumphantly. Never in a million years had Caro imagined I'd actually *buy* a pony when she'd sent her taunt sailing across the yard, and never in a million years had I imagined I could. She knew I didn't know a thing about horses, knew she'd clean-bowled me right through the stumps, and yet . . . what could be so hard? I peered at the ad again. 'A teenager's dream.' Well, I had a teenager and she had a dream – perfect. My hand was already straying across the duvet towards the phone on the bedside table when it stopped. Hang on. It was one thing to sit up in bed full of bravado, and think, I'll show her, and quite another to march into her farmyard leading a horse.

I swallowed; saw my nerve rapidly disappearing down the plughole. Well, OK, I'd talk to her, I determined. She'd probably calmed down a bit by now, as had I, and we'd sort this out like . . . like friends. Like sisters. If Caro really meant Anna needed a pony for Pony Club, then fine, we'd get one, but if she'd meant over her dead body, we'd forget it. Anna would understand. I quaked, remembering her eager little face at the gate this morning.

On the other hand – I leaned forward, dissecting the ad minutely – this pony might go quickly. It was clearly a winner, and my sister-in-law was a busy woman. She never answered her mobile and I'd have to go to the farm to track her down, and whilst I was canvassing her opinion in a pigsty, or sucking up to her whilst her head was down her Portaloos, she'd say she'd think about it and get back to me, while in the meantime some other lucky teenager would have bought it. Whereas if I just presented her with a *fait accompli* . . . In another moment, and with that famous impulsion Ant was so fond of, I'd plucked the phone from the bedside table and dialled the number.

'Hello, yes, I've just seen your ad in the local paper . . .'

Ten minutes later I'd agreed to meet a man in a stable yard off the Woodstock Road, who'd promised me a mare to die for: a horse so serene the Queen herself would be proud to be seen on her, so quiet she'd take a sugar lump from your head without harming a hair, and so well trained she'd wandered into his kitchen only yesterday, quiet as a mouse, without him even noticing.

I'd had a rather unsettling vision of a horse, perched on a stool at my granite breakfast bar, legs crossed, calmly reading the paper and demanding cereal, but agreed that my daughter and I would most certainly be there on Saturday morning, early, to meet this equine paragon. Then I put the phone down and flushed with horror. Lord, what had I done?

I quickly dialled Caro's number. Tim answered.

'Oh, Tim.' I flooded with relief. 'I was, um, ringing to thank you both for yesterday,' I lied. 'Such a lovely day, and all that delicious food!'

'Well, it was good to see you. How did Anna get on?'

'Oh, fine. She said it was easy. I mean – not bad.'

'Grade seven, Caro tells me!'

'Um, yes. Tim, is Caro around? I wouldn't mind a word.'

'She's not at the moment. She's down at the yard with Harriet.'

'Harriet?'

'The blind pig. She has to hand-feed her or the others don't let her get a look in.'

I blinked. The paradox didn't escape me. Caro was already up and hand-feeding her blind pig, whilst I was sitting up in bed in my Cath Kidston nightie.

'Right. Yes, well, speaking of animals, Tim, I just wondered . . .' and off I skittered, it all coming tumbling out, ending up with '. . . I mean, we obviously haven't got anywhere to keep it, so I just sort of wondered—'

'Course you can,' he boomed, interrupting me. 'God, we've got too much grass here for our own horses, one more won't make any difference. And if it lives out it's no trouble at all. No mucking out stables and all that malarkey.'

39

'Well, that's what I thought,' I said eagerly. 'And obviously I'd pop over and – you know – check it occasionally.'

'Oh, Caro can do all that. She has to sort out the others, she can cast an eye.'

'Oh, no, I don't want Caro doing anything,' I said quickly. 'It's my responsibility. But I just wondered, if it needed – I don't know – its feet picking out or something and I couldn't get there, maybe you, or Jack . . . ?'

'Well, not me, obviously. I don't know the first thing. Dangerous at both ends and uncomfortable in the middle, as far as I'm concerned, but Jack's your man, or Phoebe. And how lovely to see more of Anna. The kids will be thrilled.'

I knew he was genuinely pleased. There *was* a bit of a gap, socially and intellectually, between Anna and her cousins, and Tim and I had been so close.

'Caro too,' he added.

'Er, actually, Tim, she wasn't.'

'What?'

'Thrilled. I sort of broached it with her yesterday, and she was a bit . . . you know.'

'Was she? Well, yesterday was a stressy day, Evie. But don't you worry. You get your horse and we'll give it a home. Anna can come at weekends, get the train over. Caro will pick her up. I must fly now, hon. Got to see a man about a bull.'

I opened my mouth to protest, but he'd gone. I put the phone down guiltily. I'd gone round Caro, hadn't I? Gone straight to Tim. But not deliberately, I decided. I'd actually rung to speak to *her*, to thank *her* for yesterday, seek *her* permission. It wasn't my fault Tim had answered, was it? I got out of bed and reached for my clothes. I'd ring her again later. When Tim had already broken it to her, told her it was a *fait accompli*, I realized with another guilty pang. Oh dear. But actually, Tim's response was the more natural one, I decided as I buttoned up my new Joseph shirt. The more mature, friendly response. And I'd do the lion's share of the work – I pulled on my jeans – of course I would. I'd enjoy it. I needed a project. I wouldn't ride it or anything, but I could – you know – lead it. In my mind's eye I was already strolling down a country lane in a spriggy summer dress and a straw hat with an old grey mare, flowers in its hair. The old grey mare, not me. And the old grey mare was the horse not—Anyway. Lovely.

Right now, though, I thought, darting round the room, popping in some sparkly earrings, finding my Italian mules, I needed to hustle. Maria would be here at ten to clean and I hated her to find me in bed. I had to get Ant's suit from the dry cleaners and pick up that clarinet music Anna wanted. I had a busy day ahead and I needed to get on.

# 4

Days passed and Friday found me cycling to meet Ant for lunch, under a cloudless sky, treats from the deli for the weekend safely stashed in my basket, long dark hair streaming out behind me. I'd suggested cutting my hair recently – shoulder length, I'd thought, in a bob – but Ant had been horrified.

'Why?'

'Because I'm too old for long hair,' I'd protested.

'Don't be ridiculous. It's you.'

He'd looked so upset, I'd left it. But perhaps I should tie it up, I wondered as I cycled behind a lady of a certain age with an elegant grey chignon fastened to her head with pearly combs. She turned left under the arch into Trinity and I smiled to myself. That was what I loved about this city: you never quite knew who you were cycling behind or sitting next to on the bus; a scientist working on the next cure for cancer, or an astrophysicist sending rockets to Mars?

'Probably some poor devil off to restock the KitKats in the staff canteen,' Ant would scoff.

'Nonsense, you can tell. They have that vague, eccentric look, like they don't know what day it is.'

'Ah, like your mother.'

He had me here. Mum rarely knew what day it was, sported a wispy grey ponytail and a charity-shop wardrobe, yet didn't have a scholastic bone in her body. Felicity, on the other hand, my stepmother, looked like she'd just stepped off a yacht in St-Tropez and was, in fact, a biology professor at Keble.

'I rest my case,' Ant would say smugly.

I smiled as I neared the end of their road: Mum and Felicity's. Not that they lived together or anything, but when Dad died, Mum had told her about a house that was coming up at the end of her street. Felicity, grief-stricken, and for once needing a bit of help and guidance, had looked at it and bought it immediately. Yes, odd, I mused, turning into it now as a short cut, how that had worked out. No one had been terribly surprised when, after Tim and I got married – and I do think she'd hung on until then – my mother left my father. They rowed pretty much constantly and had always had a tempestuous relationship, but the marriage really came to a head when, on one memorable occasion, empty gin bottles were thrown, of which, as Tim commented later, there were not a few. Mum had come to loathe the farm: the mud, the wet – which was rich, my father would snap, when she'd married a farmer – and Dad hated what he called her spiritualistic crap; her cod medicine.

Mum, a self-styled free spirit, was heavily into alternative remedies. Reflexology, aromatherapy, you name it, she'd tried it, her latest obsession being reiki, of which, after a startlingly brief training period, she claimed to be a qualified practitioner. The final straw for Dad had been her plan to set up a practice at the farm, transforming one of the barns – with a few pink towels and some womb music, he'd snort – into a holistic medical centre.

'I'm not denying there's something in all this alternative bollocks,' he'd roared. 'What I *am* denying is that your mother is in any way, shape or form qualified to administer it!'

One unseasonably clement day in October, after just such a heated exchange, Mum took her beloved Cairn terrier, Bathsheba, and walked all the way into Oxford – no mean eight miles – to visit her sister. She telephoned Dad to say that since it was so far, she thought she'd stay the night. The following morning she rang to say she thought she'd stay a few days, because Cynthia, her sister, was under the weather. A few days had turned into a few weeks, and then a few months – and then she never came back. If Tim or I enquired, Dad would say vaguely, 'Your mother? Oh, she's still at Cynthia's.' And if we rang Mum and asked when she was thinking of returning, she'd say, 'Oh, when Cynthia's a bit better, I expect.'

The truth was it suited them. Mum was back in the city where she belonged, and Dad was happy with the farm to himself, remote control in his hand of an evening and no frustrated housewife wanting him to light candles and sit cross-legged listening to his inner music. Dad lived like a slob, wore the same clothes every day, ate baked beans from the tin and left washing up in the sink in a tottering pagoda. Periodically I'd despair to Tim, who'd say – who cares? He's happy. Let him be. And he was. They both were, in fact, for the first time in years, and life became remarkably peaceful.

Inevitably, though, as time went by, they both became lonely and then came what Tim and I nervously referred to as 'the courting phase'. Mum embarked on a series of jaw-droopingly unsuitable boyfriends – some half her age, one a student, for God's sake, one a busker she'd found in an underpass, all of whom predictably came to nothing – and Dad moved in Felicity.

I have to say, in the beginning Tim and I were slightly wary of Felicity, simply because she was so palpably not Dad's type. He'd met a few women through Rural Relations, a country dating agency – primarily rosy-cheeked women with trousers held up with binder twine – but Felicity was tall, slim, ravishingly good-looking and highly intelligent.

'What does she see in Dad?' I wondered rather disloyally to Caro over a cup of tea in her bungalow. She'd bristled slightly, Tim being very like his father.

'Well, he's tall, good-looking and not entirely impoverished, with a farm and three hundred acres – what's not to see?'

'I suppose,' I'd agreed, suitably rebuked.

Some weeks later Dad had invited us all to Sunday lunch, to meet Felicity properly. We'd tried not to boggle as we spotted napkins on the table and a vase of flowers in the middle, and then sat down to a starter – a starter! – with Dad at one end in a freshly laundered shirt, Felicity at the other, looking nervous. And actually, because of her slight unease, I'd warmed to her instantly. We all had, even Caro.

'She's just what your father needs,' she'd declared when she'd rung me later for a post-match analysis. 'An intelligent woman with a no-nonsense approach to lick that farmhouse into shape.'

45

'Mum was intelligent,' I'd countered loyally, but I knew what she meant.

'Yes, but she got so distracted. Felicity has such a clear vision of how that farm should be.'

It was true, Dad and Felicity were a brilliant team. In no time at all she'd cleared the house of clutter, redecorated, and even attacked the garden, so that although we all still knew the place was falling down, cosmetically it looked a lot better. And she was fun to have around; pleasant, friendly but didn't try to ingratiate herself too much, just cheerily invited us to lunch most weekends, knowing Tim, especially, still regarded the farm as home. She'd click around the kitchen she'd repainted a sunny cadmium yellow, in high heels to Classic FM – whilst Mum had shuffled in moccasins to Cat Stevens – served delicious food with vegetables and herbs she'd grown in the garden, and then excused herself after coffee, ostensibly to disappear to work in the study but perhaps to let us chat. Dad adored her, absolutely adored her, his whole, astonished, wide-eyed demeanour saying, *Look! Look what I've got! Bloody hell!*

In time, Felicity included Mum in her invitations too, asking her first one Christmas, for lunch.

'So that everyone can be together, and you and Tim don't have to flit from house to house?' she'd asked me anxiously, soliciting my opinion first, when we'd met for lunch in Browns. 'What d'you think, Evie?'

'I think it's a brilliant idea,' I'd said. 'If she'll come.'

To our surprise, she did, and a surprisingly jolly Christmas Day was had by all. The first for many years, I'd thought as I'd caught Tim's eye over the turkey, wondering if he remembered the one when Mum had chased Dad round the table with her Christmas present to him, an electric carving knife.

And Felicity had a way of getting the best out of people: of getting Dad to be garrulous and genial, Tim to be amusing and a chip off the old block, Mum not to be too embarrassingly wacky but charmingly eccentric, and even Caro . . . Caro I'd looked at with new eyes that Christmas Day as she'd recounted losing her shoe in Cornmarket, putting it on again and getting home to discover she'd got one blue and one brown. 'I swear,' she'd insisted, wide-eyed around the table as we'd all roared with laughter in our paper hats, 'I'd got someone else's shoe!' I'd remembered what fun she could be and had caught Tim looking at her too, remembering why he'd married her.

Yes, Felicity had been the cement our family needed, no one doubted that, and no one had been surprised when she and Dad eventually tied the knot. Even after he was married Dad couldn't stop parading her like a prize heifer; proudly showing us the new research book she'd written, pointing out the letters after her name, teasing me that I wasn't the only one in the family married to an academic. He'd happily host faculty dinner parties for her too, pulling corks and grinning benignly as molecular science chat went on around him.

'Mum would have loved all that,' I'd said wistfully to Ant in the car on the way home from one such dinner. 'All she wanted was a bit of culture in the house.'

'That's not culture,' he'd smiled. 'That's scientists.'

I'd dimly grasped the distinction, but all clever people were cultured to me. I think of all of us, though, Ant had been slightly suspicious of Felicity to begin with and I'd wondered if there'd been a tinge of rivalry, both coming from the same University pool. In time, though, he'd warmed to her too, seeing what a profound difference she made to Dad, who bounded around the farm like one of his young calves, like a new man. Which was why, one bright August morning, it was such a shock that he was a dead man.

Grief-stricken as we all were, we knew immediately it was Felicity who needed help. After the funeral she retreated to the farmhouse, pulling up the drawbridge, putting the answer machine on, hunkering down for days. We'd worried and rallied, Caro and I bringing lunch to the farm on Sundays, which she usually cooked so effortlessly, trying desperately to keep some semblance of normality going, some cheerful banter as she sat, toying listlessly with her food, or not sitting at all, shuffling around in the background as we ate – no clip-clopping now – sifting through letters of condolence, looking pale. After a few months it was no real surprise when, one Sunday, she announced the house was too big for her and held too many painful memories and that she was moving to 47 Fairfield Avenue, down the road from Mum, who, at number 16, had inherited Cynthia's house when she'd died. They weren't necessarily soul mates back then – Mum was just doing Felicity a good turn – but over time, proximity and a shared past – after all, they'd both been married to the same man – they forged an unlikely alliance. Tuesday nights found Mum in Felicity's sitting room at the backgammon board, where gin and tonics were served promptly at six; they took it in turn to provide the sandwiches. Thursday night was book club night, and on Sunday's, if they weren't with Caro or me, they lunched together in town. Oh, and some mornings had coffee too.

I smiled now as I cycled passed Mum's little terraced house at one end and pedalled towards Felicity's more substantial property at the other. Were they there today, I wondered. If Felicity wasn't teaching, in all probability yes, but I wouldn't stop. I glanced through the heavily draped sitting-room window. I was five minutes late as it was, and coffee with those two only led to drinks. I wouldn't get away without joining them for a hefty sharpener.

I pushed my bike through Cornmarket, pedalled on down St Aldates, calling out a cheery hello to Ron, who'd been our porter at Balliol but was now at Christ Church, and who was patiently trying to explain to a group of uncomprehending Chinese that they couldn't simply step over his chain and stray into his quad. He shrugged despairingly at me and I grinned back. There were tourists swarming everywhere at the moment, particularly in the main streets, but not down here – I swung a left, free-wheeling down a little alleyway – not in the tiny trattoria Ant and I favoured, slightly crummy but off the beaten track, and only really frequented by staff and students; the *cognoscenti*.

How lovely, I thought, to have a husband who still wanted to have lunch with me. For years, on alternate Fridays, because he only had one lecture, I'd cycle in and have a bowl of soup with him at Lorenzo's.

'I might even catch the end of your lecture,' I'd called

49

this morning as Ant, as ever, took the letters from the postman as they passed at the back gate. 'Although if it's as steamy as the last one I'll be under the seat with embarrassment.'

I'd crept in a couple of weeks ago when he'd been lecturing on Lawrence, or, more particularly, the sex in Lawrence, and been quite shocked to hear him spelling out the finer nuances of fellatio to a hall full of wide-eyed first years.

He'd laughed. 'Prude. And, anyway, it's Joyce today, so no chance of that. Poor devil was desperately repressed. See you later.'

I hadn't made it, of course. Too busy making huge decisions at the cheese counter and Ant was already at our favoured table when I arrived, the long, communal one along the back wall. He was reading as usual, I noticed fondly as I wove my way through the steamy room, waving at Carlos, who ran the place, as I went. When I'd first known Ant and we'd lunched in here, he'd invariably be reading a slim volume of poetry. More recently it was an essay, as he tried to catch up with some marking, and I saw him tuck just such a paper hastily inside his jacket pocket as I sat down opposite him. I loved the fact that he still wore an old corduroy jacket as true academics should, and that he smelled of fresh air and books as I leaned across the table to kiss him.

'Must Try Harder, or See Me?'

He gave a weary smile. 'Oh, I dare say I'll trot out the usual encouraging platitudes, just as they trot out theirs about courtly love. I might have to confiscate *The Chaucerian Legend* by A. J. Holmes from the library.

See how they get on without it. See if the cogs still turn.'

'They'll only find it on the Internet, and anyway, you can hardly blame them. Surely everything there is to say about Chaucer has already been said. You lot have had twelve centuries to get to grips with him, they've only had a term. They're hardly going to come up with something earth-shattering like – I don't know – *The Nun's Tale* is actually an allegory for a frustrated lesbian, are they?'

'Might make for more interesting reading. Would also give Lucian Bannister the final nail he needed to bang in my coffin, though. Convince him my lectures are way off beam.'

Lucian Bannister was the faculty head, a dinosaur with conformist views, who regarded Ant as something of an upstart. They didn't necessarily always see eye to eye. Ant took off his glasses and massaged the bridge of his nose with his thumb and forefinger and I thought how tired he looked. Not for the first time I decided the end of term couldn't come quick enough. I folded my arms on the table and leaned across.

'Just another few weeks to push and then you can tell Lucian Bannister to shove it. We'll head off to the sun. Tuscany again, perhaps?' I looked up at him under my eyelashes, fluttering wantonly.

He gave me an odd, tight little smile and replaced his spectacles, and I experienced a mild inner panic, rather as I had done when I'd shown him the house off the Banbury Road.

'Or Devon,' I said quickly, sitting up. 'Only joking. I just thought we'd agreed Anna might like San Gimignano, the churches, that sort of thing. Decided she was old enough to appreciate a bit of—'

'No, it's not that. I think it's a good idea, she would. No, it's . . .' he licked his lips, 'something else.'

My stomach lurched. Suddenly I realized he didn't just look tired, he looked white. White and stricken. Oh God, was he ill?

I reached across the table and took his hand. I was vaguely aware that the elderly couple beside us had paused in their conversation; lowered their knives and forks tremulously.

'Ant?' I could hear the fear in my voice. 'Ant, what is it, darling? Tell me.'

I saw him swallow. Then his eyes met mine, which I realized they hadn't done, not properly, up until now. Those kind blue eyes. They looked scared.

'I had a letter this morning.' He reached inside his jacket. Took out the piece of white paper I'd just seen him tuck away. 'You'd better read it.'

I took it from him, mutely. Sat back in my seat and opened it out. It was handwritten in an immature hand on plain A4 paper with no address at the top; just an email address.

*Dear Professor Hamilton,*

*There is no easy way to tell you this and I don't mind telling you I've written and rewritten this letter loads of times. Each time, though, it always seems to say the same thing, so I've decided to keep it short. OK, here goes.*

*Many years ago, you knew my mother. You met her in Oxford and had a relationship with her. She didn't live in*

*Oxford, she lived here, in Sheffield and after a while, she came*
*back. I was born in September 1990.*

  *As I said, this is not an easy letter either for you to read, or*
*for me to*

I looked up. Felt my mouth open, the blood desert my
face. I stared at Ant's face, also bloodless, his eyes lowered
to the table. For a moment my thoughts were scrambled
then – no. My head screamed *no*. But I couldn't speak. I
glanced back down. Dumbly, found my place.

  *. . . for you to read or for me to write. But I knew one day I*
*would, when I was seventeen, which I'm about to be.*

  *If you would rather not reply to me, I understand. I know you*
*have a family. But if you would like to meet me, I would really*
*like to meet you. I could come to Oxford, if you like. I have*
*enclosed my email address, but not my home address, because I*
*still live with my mum and it wouldn't be fair on her. She does*
*know I've written, though.*

  *Yours sincerely,*

  *Stacey Edgeworth*

I looked up aghast. Found myself staring at the crown of
Ant's head. It was in his hands.

# 5

It was some moments before I found my voice. When I did, it sounded strange; unnatural.

'A child? You have a child?'

I stared at him, stupefied. He was still cradling his head, but he raised it now to look at me, his fingers dragging down his face as it emerged. His blue eyes looked pale. Washed out. He shrugged hopelessly.

'I don't know. No, I didn't think so. But you've read the letter.'

I stared at him. Couldn't speak.

'And – you know, I was young. One had relationships. Sometimes brief. I just don't know . . .' He waved his hand vaguely at the piece of paper I was holding. He seemed dazed.

I licked my lips. Tried to think straight. 'When did it come?'

'This morning. I met the postman.'

Yes. Yes, he did.

I looked down at it again. The words blurred before my eyes. A child. He had a *child*. By someone else. My head spun.

'So this – this name – Edgeworth. Do you recognize it?'

He shrugged helplessly. 'I'm not sure.'

'You're not sure?' My voice was shrill now.

'Well, yes, vaguely, I suppose. I used to drink in the King's Head, and there was a barmaid there. Blonde. Quite attractive. One night we all ended up down by the river, pissed, and I walked her home. We . . . ended up in a field, somewhere.'

I stared at him. Pissed. In a field with a strange barmaid. This didn't sound like Ant. But then, as he said, he was young. He looked young now, blinking behind his spectacles, just about meeting my eye. Young and frightened.

'Ant,' I cleared my throat, 'it's one thing to remember being pissed and falling around in a field, but did you make love to her?'

His eyes widened as if registering the enormity of this. 'Yes, I did.'

I took a deep breath. Let it out slowly. Right.

'And so then,' I was thinking aloud now, feverishly trying to assimilate facts, 'then you didn't see her again, and she went back to Sheffield—'

'And then, years later, I get a letter from someone who says she's my daughter!' he blurted out, wide-eyed. 'I mean, bloody hell!'

We stared at each other over the checked tablecloth. I was dimly aware that the elderly couple beside us were horribly gripped, risotto congealing on their plates, but I was beyond caring. The ramifications were slotting firmly into place – clunk, clunk, *clunk*. A child: a daughter: *another* daughter. This scrappy piece of paper, this slip of Basildon Bond . . . Suddenly I felt my blood rising. Oh, no. Over my dead body.

'Oh, it's a nonsense,' I said wildly. 'An absolute

nonsense. Some . . . some girl comes down from the north to work as a barmaid in Oxford, gets a summer job, gets laid – a lot, probably. Christ, probably shags no end of students – and then, years later, with a child to support, gets her to write to you, that's what this is all about. This is – oh!' A light bulb went on in my head suddenly. 'Oh, Ant,' I gasped, 'it's the books!'

'What?'

I reached out. Seized his hand. Shook it.

'The books. She's seen them in the shops! She looks at the name, reads the fly leaf, and then – yes – then sees you on telly, of course!' Ant had been on a daytime television programme recently, much to Anna's and my amusement, promoting the latest book. I pressed my fingers to my temples to help the imaginative flow: shut my eyes tight. 'Yes, there she is, doing her ironing in the front room, telly on, and there *you* are, chatting away to the interviewer, and all of a sudden, she thinks, hang on a minute. I remember him. That's the bloke that used to drink with his mates in the King's Head when I was pulling pints. Pulled *me* one night, if I remember rightly. Famous author, eh? Anthony Hamilton . . . *Oi! Stacey!*' I cocked my head up some imaginary stairs. '*Get down 'ere!*'

'Well, wait,' said Ant nervously. 'I'm not so sure. I mean, what if she's *always* known, and now that the child's grown up they've decided to—'

'Quite a coincidence, don't you think?' I squeaked. 'You were only on the show last week!'

He gazed at me a minute, then inclined his head, admitting as much. 'Yes, but still . . .' He swallowed.

Fear was gripping me too. I was bloody scared, but

I wouldn't have it. Wouldn't. Another daughter? Anna's sister? My husband with two children? My throat was tightening. Oh, no.

'Look,' I said fiercely, warming to my theme, 'we don't know anything about these people. We just get a letter one day, it drops out of the clear blue sky and we're supposed to jump? This has opportunism written all over it, Ant. This is a scheming adventuress after—'

'What?' he blurted suddenly. 'After what, Evie?'

'Well . . .' I flustered, 'after money!'

He slumped back in his seat. Looked sick. 'Come on. We're not that rich. And I'm not that famous.'

'But if she slept with you on a one-night stand she probably slept with twenty others! The child could be anyone's daughter, anyone's!' I swept my hand around the restaurant to demonstrate mass culpability. A hush fell. I had a pretty captive audience.

'Come on,' he muttered, getting up, 'let's go.'

'Don't you see? It could be any number of men in Oxford,' I persisted, seizing his hand and pulling him back down again. He resumed his seat tentatively. 'Or even back in Sheffield! She doesn't exactly give precise dates, does she?'

'But what if it's not?' he hissed, leaning over the table towards me. 'What if she's mine?'

Mine. That word pierced me. His eyes were wide: in my face.

'DNA,' I said suddenly. 'That'll settle it. Let her come, Ant. Let – let Felicity, or someone who knows about that sort of thing at the University, sort it out. Bring it on, I say.'

He looked startled for a moment. Then nodded. 'Yes. Yes, you're right. Of course. And Felicity would know someone. Know the right people.'

You bet she would. Someone in her department would help. At the back of my mind I also knew that this mother-and-daughter team would have worked that out too; would know that we'd do that. Which meant they had to be fairly sure of themselves. I caught my breath. I knew Ant was thinking it too. And if Felicity gave us the news, then everyone would know – Mum, Tim, Caro . . . my chest tightened. My family. Another child? At Sunday lunch – oh, by the way, Ant has a child.

'Or – or perhaps someone we don't know could do it,' I said quickly. Ten minutes ago I was meeting my husband for a bowl of soup. Now we were deciding who would or wouldn't tell us about his illegitimate offspring.

I looked at the letter. I wanted to burn it. Pretend it had never happened. Rewind my life to ten minutes ago. We sat in silence, our bowls of minestrone, which Carlos had gingerly placed in front of us before legging it, cooling undisturbed.

'You're right,' Ant said at length. 'It's probably a mistake.'

'Of course it's a mistake!' I seized his collaboration swiftly. 'God, Ant, why hasn't she contacted you before? Why now?'

'But, Evie, if it turns out . . . if . . . you know, Stacey is my daughter—'

*Stacey!* I took a slug of wine at the very *name*. It went all down my chin. As I seized my paper napkin and mopped furiously, my neighbour's liver-spotted hand crept out to reclaim, what was, after all, his glass of Chianti.

'I mean, if she is,' Ant went on, anguished, 'then obviously . . . obviously I'll have to acknowledge her. It's only right.'

'Of course,' I said brightly, screwing the paper napkin in my lap into a tight ball. I began to shred it into a million pieces. 'Of course, my darling, we both will. Both . . . acknowledge her.'

I cycled home in turmoil, my mind racing. Oh, it was preposterous. Preposterous. It couldn't be true. Just couldn't. I pedalled numbly, realizing vaguely I had to be careful because I was in shock. Had to watch the traffic. It was as if I'd used up all my powers of persuasion, my energy, in rubbishing the very idea to Ant, and now I felt like a wrung-out dishcloth, clinging to the handlebars, my feet, somehow going round and round, I knew not how, as I cycled through the city centre, mouth dry with fear.

As I turned left into Jericho, I passed a friend's house in Worcester Place: Shona, a lovely Irish girl, married to a medic, who'd been horrified to read, a few months ago, that children conceived by anonymous sperm donation now had the right to discover who their fathers were. Years ago at medical school, her husband, Mike – along with countless others – had been quick to donate to what was universally known as the wank bank, in return for a few quid to buy a round in the Students' Union.

'Mike donated so much bloody sperm he could populate an entire village!' Shona shrieked, waving *The Times* at me when I'd popped round for a coffee. 'Who knows how many little Mike Turners there are out there, and now they can all beat a path to my door. Every time I open it there'll be another one on the doorstep!'

When I'd got home, Ant and I had rolled around laughing. Mike was very tall, prematurely white-haired, and had an odd, bouncy walk. The idea of all these gangly, snowy-haired clones of Mike, bouncing down the Banbury Road to the Turners' house had us in fits.

I wasn't in fits now, though, I thought, freewheeling down the back alley behind our house and walking the bike in quickly through the back gate – flinging it against the wall in the manner of a woman who's definitely reached her journey's end – not if she was beating a path to my door. This was about the unfunniest day of my life. I glanced round warily at the house. Might she just turn up? Don't be silly, Evie. I crouched down and put the padlock on my front wheel, trying to cling to normality, but knowing my hands were shaking as I twisted it shut. But . . . it could happen, couldn't it? I straightened up. There could, one day, be a knock at my door, and there she'd be: this teenage girl, telling me she'd come to see her father. Artificially straightened hair sprang to mind, along with heavy eye make-up and rotating jaws, gum visible.

'Yeah – me name's Stacey. I've cum for me da'.'

I froze in horror. Then reached up and shot the bolt across the garden gate before snatching up the bags from the basket and scuttling down the garden to the French windows. I let myself in and shut them very firmly behind me – locked them too. After all, there was practically a veiled threat at the end of the letter – 'I could come to Oxford, if you like', as in, Watch Out!

I fluttered around the kitchen, wiping already clean surfaces, realigning chairs, putting things away, but when I'd put Ant's newspaper in the fridge, I stopped, sat down, knowing my legs could support me no longer and I could flutter no more. I gazed dumbly down the garden. It should be a riot of colour at this time of year, but for some reason I hadn't quite got round to getting the bedding plants in. Hadn't had time. Ant had said we should go for perennials, which apparently came up every year – as the name suggests, he'd added drily – but I hadn't got round to that either. Shrubs, then, prevailed, mostly evergreen, and consequently rather dark and dull, and of course the ubiquitous trampoline, which took up at least a third of the lawn, and where Anna bounced higher and higher, up into the branches of the laburnum, until I'd fling open the window and yell, 'You'll hit your head!' It stared back at me now, like a huge, knowing eye. A Cyclops. Anna. My chest tightened. Oh God, don't go there. Don't. Don't imagine her shock, her disbelief, her incredulity. A daughter? Dad's got another child? And fortuitously, I didn't have to, as the phone rang, breaking into my ghoulish thoughts. I snatched it up gratefully, but my voice wouldn't come.

'Evie?' It was Caro. 'Evie, are you there?'

'Yes,' I managed. 'Hi, Caro.'

'God, you sound awful. Have I caught you at a bad time?'

The worst.

'No, I was just – eating. Went down the wrong way.'

'Oh, right. Well, listen. Been meaning to phone you all week. Tim tells me you're dead set on getting this horse, so to avoid any misunderstandings I just wanted to set out a few ground rules.'

I leaned my elbows on the breakfast bar and sank my head into my hand, massaging my temples, cradling the receiver with the other. Caro's voice was brisk, combative, rehearsed. I could tell she'd been working up to this call; might even have a piece of paper with bullet points in front of her.

'Well, no, not dead set, really,' I mumbled. 'It's probably not such a good idea. Too much trouble for you.'

'Nonsense, one more mouth to feed won't make any difference. I did a quick head count this morning and d'you know, including the chickens, we've got one hundred and eleven beating hearts, so what's one hundred and twelve, I ask myself.' She was clearly gagging to adopt the martyr's crown. 'And anyway, Tim informs me it's a *fait accompli*,' she finished crisply.

I massaged harder as I dimly registered the row they'd no doubt had, the stand-up-knock-down in the kitchen: Caro shrieking that she was rushed off her feet as it was; my brother, firm, as he could be occasionally, taking a stand, talking of family, duty, of helping his little sister. Normally I'd be falling over myself to apologize, to rectify the situation, say it was a big mistake, that Anna had gone off ponies, wanted to be a gymnast, anything, but I just nodded mutely into the receiver, imagining Ant going to a tutorial, his heart heavy; the letter like a lead weight in his breast pocket, burning a hole in his heart.

'So if Tim says it's final, it's final, so there we are.

Contrary to popular belief we all know who *really* wears the trousers in this house. Now, for God's sake don't go and buy one on your own. Take someone to see it, OK?'

'OK,' I muttered dumbly.

'I'll come, if I can, but my caterers have let me down *again* and the marquee's got a hole in it where someone's clearly had fun with a cigarette, and the next few weeks are jam-packed with weddings, so God knows when I'll get away. But for heaven's sake, if I'm not there, make sure it lives out so we don't have any mucking-out to do, and that it's good in traffic. And even *more* importantly, make sure it's got a snaffle mouth. You don't want some Arab in a gag, do you?'

A white-robed sheik, staggering, bound and gagged through the desert, sprang confusingly to mind.

'No,' I agreed.

'So steer well clear of anything in a pelham or a curb, or she'll be carted into the next county. Just make sure it's safe, OK?'

Safe. Safe sex. Always wear a condom. Or not, as the case may be.

'And don't look at anything described as a "fun ride" – that's shorthand for goes like a train – or "a proper character" – which means it bucks. But as I said, I'll come with you in a few weeks' time. Just as soon as I can get away from this sodding wedding fiasco.'

I remembered my manners. Cleared my throat. It was remarkably dry. 'Um, how's it going, Caro?'

'Oh, swimmingly. I've got potential brides bowling up my drive at an alarming rate, wafting around my kitchen wanting to discuss canapés and flowers and whether or not they can tie the knot under the willow tree. They can, believe it or not – can get married where they like these days, in the bloody bog if they so wish, as long as I've got the licence. And their ghastly mothers are all gimlet-eyed and never missing a trick. *They're* the nightmare, incidentally, the mothers. Last week we had one who discovered the groom's family had invited more guests than her side *and then blamed me*. Said I should have spotted it! I kicked her in the end, had to pretend I had a twitch.

'Good, good,' I said distractedly.

'I mean they're not *all* ghastly, don't get me wrong. The Asians are heaven, lovely big families all nodding and smiley and *so* well behaved. Never any fornicating in the bushes, and never any sick to clear up, either. *God*, I love the Asians.'

'Um, look, Caro, I'd better go, but thanks for . . . you know.' What? I tried to remember why she'd called. Oh, yes. 'The pony.'

'Well, you haven't got it yet, and I'm not entirely convinced you know what you're letting yourself in for. Just for pity's sake be careful and don't look at anything under eight that hasn't been there, done it and got the T-shirt. But at the same time you don't want too many miles on the clock.'

She was talking a different language now, but no matter: I'd long since stopped listening because, actually, I'd just thought of something. Realized something. While she'd been prattling on I'd been thinking about the letter and about the girl being seventeen. I'd done the maths instantly, of course I had, and felt safe. I hadn't known Ant then. But that distracted me from when the child had

64

been born – September 1990. She was still very much sixteen, wouldn't be seventeen till later this year which meant – and here I got to my feet, slowly replacing the receiver as Caro said goodbye – yes, of course. The child couldn't be Ant's. Simply couldn't. Because if it was her seventeenth birthday in the autumn, she'd been conceived – I did some rapid mental arithmetic – the previous January: which meant I'd been going out with Ant. Going out for some time. Not only that, we'd been engaged.

# 6

I'd had to order Ant's copy of *Sir Gawain and the Green Knight*. We didn't stock such esoteric titles in Bletchley's: this wasn't spacious Waterstone's, or even academic Blackwell's. We were just a tiny independent, albeit on three floors, but each the size of your average front room connected by rickety stairs. It was all very charming and Dickensian, and appealed to my romantic notion of how a bookshop should be, even down to the musty smell of Jean's cats, who slunk down from her flat upstairs and stretched out on shelves or in pools of sunlight, adding to the ambience. I think the customers bought into the whole nostalgic bit too, liking the fact that they could settle down in a faded armchair with a book and not be asked to move on. Comfy chairs were a rarity in book-shops back then, and in a way it put us ahead of our time, even if the reality was that they were there for Jean, our fifteen-stone manageress, who liked to pause mid-floor for a breather. A couple of other things gave us the edge too: we were on the fringes of the city where a lot of students lived, we had a larger than average art and architecture section, and also a contemporary music sec-tion, which was popular. We stocked the usual fiction, of course, and pretty much all the classics, but not, as it happened, Ant's request.

'They usually get that from the university bookshop,'

Jean told me as she overheard me ordering it on the telephone. 'Who was it, a student?'

'He looked a bit older than that.' I glanced down at the name I'd scribbled on a pad, even though I knew it by heart. 'Anthony Hamilton? With a local number.'

She peered over my shoulder. 'Oh, *Doctor* Hamilton. One of the youngest dons in the English Department. On a bit of a meteoric rise, by all accounts; shooting to stardom. Well, he must have dozens of those in his stock cupboard. I can't think why he's getting it from us.' She pulled an incredulous and not altogether friendly face. 'Perhaps he fancies you.'

'I doubt it,' I said quickly, knowing any single man who came in here had to fancy Jean. Ant was over eighteen and therefore ripe for the cull. I could feel myself colouring, none the less.

'Well, he's terribly attractive, don't you think? I certainly wouldn't say no.' She rolled her eyes and pouted provocatively. 'Wouldn't mind getting stuck in the stock cupboard with *him*.' She shot me an arch look before sauntering off to the staffroom on her thick calves, ample hips swinging, a pile of books in her arms.

Jean, a divorcee, who bore an uncanny resemblance to Sybil Fawlty, had a slightly desperate air and a *double entendre* for every occasion. She had to lower the tone, didn't she? I thought as I watched her go.

Nevertheless, I spent the next few days pouncing on every parcel that came in, just in case Jean or Malcolm should get to it first, and practising exactly what I would say on the telephone when it did arrive. In the event, of course, it was desperately prosaic.

'Oh, hello, Doctor Hamilton?'

'Yes?'

'It's Evie here, from Bletchley's Books. Just to say, your copy of *Sir Gawain* arrived this morning.'

'Oh, thanks very much. I'll pop in and get it.'

'Okey-doke, bye!'

'Bye.'

As I put the phone down a hot flush swept over me. Okey-doke? When had I ever said that? That hadn't been in the script. But at least I'd got my name in – all part of the plan – and I'd nonchalantly shortened the title too, omitting *the Green Knight*, as I gathered those in the know did. And what a deliciously deep, modulated voice he had. 'Thanks very much. I'll pop in and get it,' I purred.

'Get what?' asked Jean, appearing at my shoulder, frowning.

'Oh, nothing,' I flustered, hurrying away.

Over the next few days, I hardly left the shop. Whenever the door opened my head pirouetted, and I spent a lot of time in Health and Harmony, which was right at the front on the ground floor, with an excellent view of the street.

'Having trouble breast-feeding?' enquired Malcolm, my lovely gay colleague, who, on one of his rare forays down from Art and Architecture on the first floor – 'lovely sensitive types you get up there, nice hands' – was watching me dust Miriam Stoppard's *Pregnancy and Birth Book* for the millionth time.

I giggled. 'Not, as such.'

'Something more serious?' He raised an eyebrow as *The Pain of Infertility* was flicked over now.

68

'How would I know?' I sighed, resting my feather duster a moment. 'I could be as fertile as the River Nile or as barren as the Gobi, I've no idea. No one's ever tested my tubes. I do know this, though, Malcolm, my biological clock is ticking loudly and there's no one to hear it but you, Jean and the cats.'

'What about Steve, the surfing dude?'

'No ambition. No . . . direction.'

'Except the beach, perhaps?'

I flicked him an unworthy-of-you look and resumed my dusting.

'OK, well, that other chap then,' he persisted. 'Neil, the sarcastic book rep?'

'Too chippy. He kept calling me a glorified shop assistant and waiting for me to rise, which I didn't.'

'Not enough glory, that's why. Commandant Sybil sees to that,' Malcolm jerked his head towards Jean, who very much ruled the roost here, overseeing any events in the shop and generally not letting us have a look in.

I sighed wearily. 'Actually, I'm thinking of joining that new dining club at the Poly. Meet a few more people.'

'Well, as long as you're not hanging around here waiting for blue eyes,' he said gently, 'because I'm afraid you've missed him.'

'Oh!' I swung to face him.

'Came in ten minutes ago while you were in the loo. I was all for running to get you, but Jean blocked my path and served him herself.'

'But she knew—'

'Of course she did, but she doesn't want her pretty

69

young assistant being chatted up by one of the dons, does she? Here, my sweet,' he delved into a shelf and plucked out a copy of *Anger Management*. 'Read and learn. You'll last longer. I have.'

He sauntered away. Bitterly disappointed, I dusted on in silence. Later that morning I slipped to the café next door to drown my sorrows in cappuccino. When I came back, Malcolm ran up, eyes shining.

'Good news or bad news?'

'Bad.'

'He's been in again, and you missed him.'

'Damn!'

'But the good news is, he's coming to the poetry reading on Saturday night. Took a leaflet and everything, and – get this, poppet – asked if we all had to be there.'

'Oh! D'you think he meant—'

'Well, he surely didn't mean *moi*, munchkin. I'd have known.' He tucked his silky blond hair neatly behind his ears. 'And I really don't think he meant, that . . . that thing . . .' His eyes widened in mock horror as Jean, half-way up a ladder at the top shelf, hitched her skirt a bit to scratch her pantyhose. Malcolm shuddered.

She turned to frown at us. 'Come on, you two. Less chat.'

'*Jawohl, mein Führer*,' muttered Malcolm under his breath.

'Oh, and, Evie, your don came in.' She grinned at me over her shoulder. 'I'm afraid you missed him.'

'Yes, Malcolm said.' I smiled sweetly back.

Malcolm gave me a huge wink as he sauntered away, pretending to shake Jean's ladder as he passed, then breaking into goose steps and a Nazi salute when he was out of her sight.

Saturday couldn't come quickly enough. Normally I avoided readings like the plague. Being only a small bookshop we didn't attract the likes of Jeffrey Archer or Jilly Cooper, rolling up in their chauffeur-driven cars with their glamorous publicity girls; instead, some unknown local author would shuffle in off the street in a duffel coat, their book in a Tesco carrier bag. Given the spotlight, though, and the evening, these usually timid souls would become expansive; droning on and on, reading reams and reams of interminably dry stuff, which Jean, being a pseudo-intellectual, would smile knowingly at, head on one side, stifling her yawns, whilst Malcolm and I whispered in the corner about how much better we could do it if we were in charge, at least asking thriller writers, or romantic novelists, and perhaps three or four, not just one.

Poetry readings were the worst. Some bearded type would read banal or incomprehensible verse, as everyone sat around in hushed, respectful silence, nodding off. The audiences were generally embarrassingly small too – the poet's girlfriend, his mother, and a cluster of loyal friends – although we did try to fill it out with a few locals, bribing them with drinks.

This one looked like being no exception. The poet was female, and although I don't think I've ever seen a picture of Joan Baez, I imagine it's what she'd look like. A scrubbed face and humourless brown eyes stared at me through a curtain of long dark hair as I was introduced to her. She took my hand limply, murmuring something that sounded suspiciously like Emmylou Harris.

'Evie Milligan,' I smiled back, determinedly upbeat, and determinedly miniskirt-clad too, with sparkly earrings and lashings of lip gloss.

My job had been to arrange a not too intimidatingly large circle of chairs around a solitary 'throne' where she would sit and recite, and to which I led her now.

'Is this all right? Or you could have it a little further forward if you like?' Some authors preferred a more intimate circle.

She frowned. 'I think I'd like everyone sitting on the floor.'

I blinked. 'Right . . .'

I wasn't sure how this would go down with any elderly matrons who occasionally popped in to relieve a lonely evening, but I supposed I could grab them a chair, and half an hour later Emmylou was sitting cross-legged on a beaded cushion – model's own – surrounded by twenty or so similarly intense-looking supporters – not a bad turnout, actually.

'They're all girls,' I hissed to Malcolm, one eye on the door. Doctor Hamilton had yet to appear.

'Oh, yes, didn't you know? She's one of us. Well, one of them,' he added sniffily. 'I prefer my gay female friends to be of the lipstick-lesbian variety, glamorous, sharp-tongued and witty. This is the other end of the spectrum. The hairy-toed right-on brigade.'

'Oh.' I looked around with interest. They were all earnestly studying the text.

'All of them?'

'Well, I don't know empirically which church they go to, Evie. Some will be lucky to get serviced at all, by the look of them, and some might turn out to be common or garden feminists who failed to notice bra-burning and emancipation happened twenty-odd years ago with Marilyn French at the helm. Eh up, here's the Führer.'

Jean, flushed and slightly tipsy – she was always in charge of the warm white wine – was making her way centre stage, clapping her hands prettily as if the place was humming with lively chatter, instead of hushed whispers. Her pink face clashed violently with the startling purple crepe trouser suit she'd chosen to sport for the evening.

'Ahem! Good evening, ladies and gentlemen. Well . . . ladies. Lovely to see so many of you here, and may I say how delighted we are to have Mary-Lou with us tonight. Emmy . . . lou, as many of you know, is a local poet, and winner of the Banbury District Award for Young Talent.'

A ripple of applause followed and Emmylou nodded gravely around, accepting only what was her due.

'And now I hope you'll listen quietly –' what were we, six? – 'as Emily reads from her latest collection entitled *Women in Chains*.'

'Oh my,' groaned Malcolm in my ear, before sliding away to hide behind Crime and Thrillers, the better to roll his eyes at me and make me laugh. I determined not to look at him, but actually, even if I did, I knew I was too disappointed to laugh. After all that, after all my devotions to hair and make-up, not to mention a new skirt and chain belt from Dorothy Perkins, he hadn't turned up. And now, now that the reading had started, twenty minutes late, as it happened, he probably wouldn't. I listened miserably as Emmylou's shrill, reedy, self-important voice rang out strident and forceful. No nerves, it seemed, which didn't endear her to me. I was naturally suspicious of anyone who wasn't permanently covered in confusion.

It began like a rallying cry to slaves in the 1800s.

> Rise up!
> Rise up and speak of the tyranny of machismo,
> The unequal struggle,
> Of weary loins and sagging dugs,
> Of flesh parting company with bones—

It was intensely irritating, dated stuff, and I took to pushing back my cuticles, whilst Malcolm, out of sight of Jean, leaned back on Wilbur Smith and shut his eyes. He stuck his fingers in his ears too.

She paused after poem one, and Malcolm removed his fingers and looked hopeful. But it got worse. From nowhere, Emmylou produced a wooden block, which she kneeled on. She then proceeded to blow into what looked like a home-made recorder. She caught my eye and I gave her a weak smile, just as, at that moment, the door opened and Anthony Hamilton, tall, slightly shambolic, and with just the right amount of confusion I require my friends to be covered in, came into the shop. He glanced around apprehensively and, it seemed to me, the whole place lit up as he found my eyes and smiled. I instantly blushed from top to toe.

Jean, all jangling bosom and flapping jewelled hands, was advancing fast, whispering, 'Dr Hamilton!' and bustling to find him a seat – not cross-legged with the squaws,

I noticed, but on a plastic chair at the back. He looked uncomfortable perched alone and aloft beside Jean, the two of them like a couple of proud parents at a children's assembly, particularly since a few heads swivelled, as children's heads are inclined to. I squirmed for him.

Emmylou, meanwhile, had abandoned her whistle and was back to the poetry, her voice shrill and declamatory, deep in menstruation. Why? I couldn't look at Anthony, so I concentrated instead on the carpet and getting to the end of the poem, which, at length, we did. A ripple of heart-felt applause rang out, until I realized I was the only one clapping. Ah. Right. Not at the end of each verse, perhaps. I caught Ant's eye, which was amused. Well, better than bored or livid, I decided, as the poem finally ended, and now please, *please*, could we have one about daffodils? Or trees?

'This next poem,' Emmylou informed us gravely, tossing her dark head importantly, 'is called "Maud and Diana".'

Well, that sounded all right. A bit like Thelma and Louise, or perhaps Hinge and Bracket? A couple of maiden aunts. Except it wasn't maiden aunts and it wasn't all right either, because Maud and Diana were a couple of little minxes who couldn't keep their hands off each other. My face got pinker with every toe-curling line. 'Enough!' I wanted to cry. I risked a glance at Malcolm, who, jaw slack with delight, looked highly diverted, whilst Jean patted her perm nervously, blinking rapidly, trying hard to look like a broad-minded woman who was used to poems of this nature being read in her shop, instead of a lonely, frustrated one who simply worked in a bookshop to meet men, as, I realized with a jab of horror, I did, and as I knew Malcolm did too.

Emmylou's eyes were bright, her cheeks flushed, as she glanced up from her text to recite the last lines from memory.

'Diana and Maud found their epiphany that night,' she declared to the assembled throng. 'Hearts sang. Minds rejoiced.' Her eyes roamed the room and found mine. 'Vaginas throbbed.'

In the startled silence that followed all I could think was, *why is she looking at me?* It was too much for Malcolm. He gave a snort of derision and legged it, body at a forty-five-degree angle, to the fire escape. I'm ashamed to say I followed hot on his heels. I bolted through Horror – appropriately enough – around the table of drinks, and out through the heavy black fire door at the back. On the wrought-iron staircase, overlooking the rooftops, in the cool night air, Malcolm and I clutched one another, hiccuping, snorting; even Anthony forgotten.

'You pulled!' gasped Malcolm.

'No!' I shrieked back. 'D'you think?'

'Oh, for *sure*, hon. She wanted you. She's hot for you.'

'Oh, please.'

'No, no, that's her line. Please, Evie, *please*. She wants her epiphany.'

We dissolved into giggles.

'But, Malc, that's not poetry, is it?' I said, wiping my eyes, recovering a bit. 'Aren't you supposed to leave something beautiful behind on the page? I mean, when you've finished?'

'Rather than something yucky, I agree.' He lit two

cigarettes and handed me one. 'Here, hon. Suck on this.'

'And did you see, Jean?' I took a drag.

'Little Miss Liberated?' Malcolm mimicked Jean's furious blinking, sucking in his cheeks, patting his hair.

We dissolved into hysterics again, just as the door behind us opened.

'I take it this is where the staff take their ciggie breaks?'

I swung around to see a tall, quietly amused figure, tapping the end of his own cigarette on a packet of Rothmans.

'Oh.' I struggled for composure. 'Well, not really. It's just – you know – a bit hot in there. But we must go back.' I stubbed my cigarette out hurriedly.

Doctor Hamilton lit up and blew the smoke over my head. 'I wouldn't worry. She's paused for a breather. I think everyone needs a drink after that.'

'Has she finished?'

'Apparently.'

'Well, thank the Lord,' said Malcolm with feeling. 'I'd better go and charge the Lambrusco glasses. Lovely to meet you, incidentally.' He extended a hand and flashed a dazzling smile. 'Malcolm Harding.'

'Anthony Hamilton,' smiled Anthony, shaking hands.

'I'll cover for you, angel,' breathed Malcolm as he went to go in. 'You catch your breath.'

'What *is* going on out here?' The fire door swung back and Jean appeared, looking like Brünnhilde, glowering furiously. 'Malcolm! The white wine, please. And, Evie, what on earth are you doing luring our guest out here?' Oh, she *had* to be vulgar, didn't she?

Malcolm came to my rescue. 'Evie doesn't feel very well. She was getting some air.'

'Well, she'd better go home then, hadn't she?' Jean snapped sourly. 'Go on, Evie, go and get your bus. Malcolm and I will manage tonight. Doctor Hamilton, shall we?' She opened the door to usher him back in, Uriah Heep-style, bending low, pussycat smile in place.

'Actually, I ought to be going too.' He turned to me. 'If you're not feeling well, I'll give you a lift. You don't want to get a bus. Where are you going?'

'Um, just past Magdalen Bridge,' I stuttered.

'Oh, perfect, I'm at Balliol. Just round the corner.' Nowhere near. He smiled at Jean. 'Thank you so much. It's been a very enjoyable evening and, um, very ... informative too. The small amount I caught of it. So sorry I've got to fly.'

Jean looked ready to spontaneously combust. Malcolm ushered her away like a nurse with a mental patient, pausing only to turn and flash me a meaningful, delighted grin.

'I'll just get my coat,' I muttered to Anthony as we went back through the shop together. I lunged to grab it from behind the counter, avoiding Jean's furious eye, then scampered to join him as he waited for me at the door.

My heart was pounding, and naturally I couldn't think of a thing to say as I walked with him to his car, a beaten-up old Citroën parked down the road. Happily, his *savoir-faire* gene was more developed than mine.

'Feeling better?' he enquired as we got in and put our seat belts on. He flashed me a knowing smile as we pulled out into the traffic.

'Much,' I grinned back. 'I'm afraid poetry readings tend to have that effect on me.' I couldn't believe I was in his car. I looked around greedily, knowing I'd want to remember later. Polos on the dashboard; papers strewn in the back; nicely messy.

'You're not a fan then?'

'What? Oh, no, I love poetry. It's just . . . not that particular type.'

'Oh, right. What type d'you like?' I realized he was interested. Damn. But luckily I knew the names of some poets. Crikey, I lined up their volumes often enough. I threw some out.

'Oh, you know, Keats, Sylvia Plath, Pam Ayres, that sort of thing.'

He smiled. 'Fairly eclectic.'

'Oh, yes, I like the Eclectic Poets.' Possibly a group, like the Romantic Poets, whom I'd heard of.

He laughed. Why? No matter. Here I was in his car, snuggled up in my coat beside him, looking at his terribly attractive square profile. Heaven.

'You must be in clover then, working in a bookshop. Ample opportunity.'

To pick up square-jawed men? No. Perhaps not. 'Well, *quite*,' I enthused, coming to. 'I'm always reading. I read copiously.' Good *word*, Evie.

'Novels?'

'Oh, *novels*,' I gushed. 'Can't get enough of them.' Now I really could be honest. 'All the time, actually – well, when Jean isn't looking, obviously.'

'Obviously. And what d'you like?'

'Anything I can get my hands on.' I flushed. Golly. That sounded a bit . . . you know . . . back to the square-jawed men. 'I mean – any books.'

'Of course. Classics?'

I took a deep breath and wondered, fleetingly, if I could bluff my way, literary speaking, for the next ten minutes or so. Happily some invisible divinity whispered sense in my ear and I decided against it.

'Actually, I prefer more modern books. Contemporary fiction,' I added quickly, remembering that tag. 'I'm a big fan of E. J. McGuire.'

'I'm not familiar with him.'

'Her,' I corrected, twisting in my seat to face him. 'Oh God, she's terrific, you must try her. She does these brilliant sort of thriller things, really tense and creepy, and you have absolutely no idea how it's going to end up or who's done it.'

'Sounds like Poe.'

Like . . . poo, did he say? I blinked. 'Well. Obviously it's not to everyone's taste,' I began, 'but—'

'Edgar Allan. You know, Victorian melodrama.'

'Oh! Right. Yes, well, maybe. And actually it is quite melodramatic, now you mention it. But I quite like that. And there's always a terrific twist at the end, which you don't see coming. Oh, and she does romances too. Quite often they're set in a hospital so, you know, you get the doctor/nurse thingy going on, or sometimes it's some-where hot and sultry so there's safari suits coming off all over the place. Well, not right off. And not too steamy. Not steamy at all, in fact.'

'I must look out for E. J. McGuire. Left here?'

'Yes, then down on the right.' He stopped the car. I turned to him, flashed a winning smile. 'And I must look out for Poo. Poe!'

He laughed; turned in his seat to face me, his arm crooked over the back of it, eyes shining right into mine. Wow. I took a deep breath. Lost my nerve.

'Jane Austen's wonderful too, isn't she?'

He laughed again. 'She certainly is.'

Well, at least I was making him laugh. Clearly on cracking form, Evie. Laugh him into bed, why don't you? No! Just like Jean. Not the laughing bit, the bed. And that wasn't what was called for. I'd just met him, for heaven's sake. He really was terribly attractive, though, all twinkly-eyed and smiley beside me. Another deep breath.

'Would you . . . like to come in for coffee?'

It wasn't coffee time at all, more like supper time, more like nine o'clock time, but he wasn't offering anything else – quite thin, I noticed, so perhaps he didn't eat much, and hell, these intellectual types needed a bit of encouragement. He looked at me: an amused, evaluating look. I flushed.

'I'd love to,' he said quickly, before I could open my mouth to retract it. 'Or maybe even a drink?'

'A drink!' I said joyfully as if he'd hit on the Holy Grail. Too joyful. Calm down, Evie. I got out of the car. 'But I have to warn you,' I prattled on nervously as I led him down the street, 'I'm three storeys up, so you might need oxygen rather than vodka by the time you get there.'

'I stand warned.'

'And I don't know if my flatmate's in, either. I mean, she never normally is, but—'

'Would it matter if she was?'

'No. Of course not. I'm just saying she . . . you know . . . gads about.' As if I didn't.

Happily further talk was made impossible, as for the next few minutes, we struggled up six flights of steps. Lesser Romeos had been known to stop for a breather on level four, or even level three, but this one had stamina, I noticed. I led on, wishing my skirt wasn't quite so short and hoping I didn't have a ladder in my tights.

I was rather dreading our entrance to the flat. Health and Safety hadn't thus far been alerted, but I fervently wished I'd had a quick clear-up before I'd left. But then again, I hadn't really envisaged bringing him back; had, at the very most envisaged a drink, or – and we're talking wildest dreams here – a pizza. Yet now, here he was – my heart pounded as I put the key in the lock – following me into what would doubtless be a fairly revolting . . . oh . . . my . . . God.

The kitchen, which one encountered fairly promptly, given that the hall was the size of a napkin, was spotless.

I spun round in surprise. 'This is unreal. Someone's tidied up!'

No piles of washing-up tottered precariously in the sink, no midden of newspapers obscured the table; no broken cupboard doors hung open spewing forth cartons of soup, pasta, Pot Noodles. The two tiny work surfaces were clear, the stainless steel sink shone, and all rickety doors were wedged tightly shut. The lino wasn't sticky either, I noticed, testing it tentatively with the soles of my shoes. Suddenly, the sitting-room door opened and a blonde in a pink dress flew out.

'Oh, Ant. This is my flatmate, Caro.'

'Hi.' She looked flushed and anxious, and shot him only the briefest of glances. 'Evie, my mother's here!' she whispered in terror, pointing back over her shoulder at the door she'd slammed.

'Oh, *no!*'

Christ, no wonder she'd cleared up. Caro's mother was a terrifying woman, formidable, critical and probing, the headmistress at the local high school. I didn't relish the usual inquisition about what I was going to do with my life as she fixed me with a fishy eye. 'You can't go on working in that bookshop for ever, Evie.' Or, when introduced to Ant, '*Another* boyfriend, Evie?' hanging – hopefully unspoken – in the air. Oh, no, this particular foursome was not going to work.

'We'll go,' I said quickly. 'Grab a drink in town.'

'Good idea.' Caro hustled us towards the door.

'Oh, but surely . . .' Ant looked perplexed.

'She's a Buddhist,' I told him firmly. I wasn't quite sure what this was, but I was pretty sure they were teetotal. 'Doesn't approve.'

'Doesn't touch a drop,' agreed Caro. 'And really hates anyone who does.' Her hand was already on the doorknob. She swung the door wide and ushered us out.

As she went to shut it behind us, though, I stayed it with my hand. Peered back round. 'You washed up,' I said in awe, marvelling at the sparkling sink. 'Must have taken hours.'

For weeks now, Caro and I had blithely skirted the remains of a particularly gruesome dinner party – casseroles burned black, mashed potato caked onto pans, all growing penicillin, forcing us to fill the kettle at an excruciatingly awkward angle.

'I threw it away,' she confided softly, glancing over her shoulder in case her mother heard.

I giggled. 'You *didn't?*'

'I bloody did. I couldn't face it. It's all in the dustbins outside. You can get it out, if you like,' she added with a defiant grin. 'See you.' And with that, she shut the door.

'Is she serious?' Ant asked as we tripped down the stairs.

'Oh, definitely. Caro and I have a very simple approach to clearing up. Most of our stuff is shoved under beds, or even . . . damn.' I stopped. 'I need some ciggies. Won't be a mo.'

I bounded back upstairs, fishing the key out of my coat pocket. Opening the front door and darting through to my bedroom, I hissed '*Fags!*' at Caro, who was still in the kitchen. She was bending over the tiny table, which, I noticed, was laid for two, lighting a candle. I stopped in surprise. Turned. Her pink dress was very short and her thick blonde hair tumbled over her shoulders into, what I now realized, was quite a spectacular cleavage. As a blast of Rive Gauche rocketed up my nostrils, I was aware of Ant, appearing in the doorway. He'd followed me up the stairs, perhaps for a second look. Caro straightened up; seemed caught. I folded my arms. Cocked an eyebrow.

'Your mother?'

She flushed. Blew out the match. 'Ah.'

'Hasn't she bloody gone yet?' boomed a familiar voice from behind the sitting-room door.

I froze. Then my head rotated slowly towards it. In

another moment I'd crossed the kitchen and flung the door wide. An arresting sight met my eyes. A naked man faced me, stretched out on the goatskin rug in front of the two-bar electric fire, hands locked behind his head. Although the face was very familiar, it wasn't one I was used to seeing round these parts. Neither were his parts. He sat up languidly, casually flipping a corner of the rug over to cover them.

'Oh, hi, Evie,' he grinned. Then he looked around me. 'Who's this?'

'This is Anthony,' I said evenly. 'Anthony, this is my brother, Tim. We pretty much like to keep it in the family.'

## 7

Chronologically speaking then, we all by and large leaped off the starting blocks together, Tim and Caro, Ant and I. All got away at the same time. Tim and Caro, as we know, had a minuscule head start, but it didn't take Ant and me long to catch up. Ant, being a gent, went through the motions of buying me drinks and suppers, but under my guidance quickly dispensed with formalities and we soon ended up in bed, where we stayed for the next few weeks. Ant occasionally got up to give a lecture, and I occasionally got up to work in a bookshop, but as a rule, we were horizontal. When we eventually emerged from base camp, sated, smiling foolishly, and blinking in the sunlight, it was to find Tim and Caro waiting for us.

And from the word go, it was a success. We made a good team, the four of us, a good posse. We drank in pubs together, cooked suppers together, went bowling, saw films – three of us knowing each other from the year dot, one of us a new boy, never having heard the jokes, but roaring dutifully, his eyes opening to the lighter side of life.

Ant's background, I discovered, was subdued. The only child of a widowed mother who'd 'given in rather gratefully' – Ant's words – to a bout of pneumonia four years ago, assuring her son it was time she went to see his father, he'd had, not an unhappy time of it, but a quiet one.

Tim and I, on the other hand, came from a long line of practical jokers, and Tim was the biggest. He was forever organizing parties at which Ant and I were the only ones to arrive in fancy dress, whilst everyone else was in jeans. We'd walk in and Tim and Caro would shout 'Surprise!' and fall about laughing, and I'd fall about too, as Ant stood blinking behind his specs in nothing but a sheet and a crown of thorns. We introduced him to flaming sambucas, setting fire to his coffee beans and roaring when he predictably burned his lips on the glass; we taught him to drive the remains of the car Tim had written off, and which had pride of place in our sitting room; how to take imaginary bends making screeching tyre noises, to have a snog on the back seat: he loved it. He bought into the frivolity, finding it a refreshing change, I think, from tedious faculty drinks parties at the University, where he had to nurse a glass of wine for hours, and where everyone vied to be cleverer than anyone else, whilst the Milligans vied to be sillier.

The only practical joke he did draw the line at was when he went for an interview for Provost at Balliol, and before he went, found a note on his desk saying 'Don't forget to take your urine sample.' Off he went and, at the end of the interview, when asked if he had any questions, produced it from his pocket saying uncertainly, 'Um . . . what shall I do with this?'

On the whole, though, he found us entertaining. We raced around town in his terrible old Citroën, and even went on holiday in it together, Ant driving, Caro navigating – naturally – through the Dordogne and right down to the coast, whilst Tim and I giggled in the back. Ant, hunched over the steering wheel, would search myopically for signs, as Caro, leaning out of the window, waved down passers-by and asked directions to the beach.

'*Garçon! Garçon!*' she called imperiously on one occasion. '*Ou est votre bêche?*' She received a horrified stare and a Gallic shrug as her man walked on.

'You just called him a waiter and asked him where his spade is,' Ant informed her.

'Yes, but he got my drift, for heaven's sake,' Caro muttered, rolling up her window.

It was on that holiday that Tim asked Caro to marry him. I remember them coming back from the beach one day, when Ant and I had been to see a monastery; Tim looking sheepish, Caro pink, keeping it to themselves for a bit – well, like ten minutes – before Caro, unable to resist, blurted out, 'We've got something to tell you.'

To this day I can remember my heart dropping like a brick through water. My best friend and my brother – of course I was delighted, of course, but . . . it wasn't me. I hated myself, still do, but even as I was rushing off to get the champagne with Ant – terrible cheap stuff from the local shop – and coming back brandishing it joyfully, I was aware of a nasty sicky feeling inside me. I happen to think it's a fairly primeval urge women have, after about the age of twenty-five, to get married, and our biggest drawback as far as men are concerned. It's almost better to say you've got VD than to say you want to get married.

But we can't help it, and I had a lump in my throat as we toasted their happiness.

'How exciting! Oh, I'm *so* pleased!'

And the thing is, even as I was gushing, I knew there was a bit of Caro that knew what I was thinking, because we'd known each other for donkey's years and talked about boys and weddings and what our bridesmaids would wear and what our children would be called, and all the silly things girls aren't supposed to talk about as they're doggedly pursuing their careers but do. So as she's telling me breathlessly about the village church, and the marquee at the farm, she knows too that I also want the village church, and a marquee at the farm. She knows my hopes and dreams, which is the good thing about a best friend and also the bad, so she knows my insides are curdling, but she can't help it. Can't help it, and why should she? She's getting married, she's first, she's won. And her eyes, when they look at mine, are full of happiness and shame. Happiness and shame. And I'm galvanized. I will be next, I will!

Ant wasn't stupid. Far from it. The four of us had been hanging around together for some time, and now two of our number were going it alone.

That night, after we'd made love, in that sticky, rather exciting way one does in hot villas, in our little whitewashed room with the crucifix over the bed and the view of the bay, the waves rushing up the beach, he held me close.

'Lovely for Tim and Caro,' I murmured into his shoulder.

Yes, I know, a bit obvious, but as I said, it's primal. And actually, it would have been odd *not* to mention it.

'Hm,' he murmured sleepily. Then, after a moment, 'They'll be good together.'

My heart flipped at this. Did that mean . . . he thought we wouldn't?

'Yes, they will.'

Silence.

'They're quite different,' I ventured, wanting at all costs to prolong this line of chat.

'Hm.'

'Don't you think?'

'You mean, Tim's easy-going and Caro's a control freak?'

I laughed. 'I suppose. But actually, Tim probably needs a bit of control. Needs . . . I don't know . . . gripping.'

'Hmph.'

Silence. I took a deep breath. 'So . . . how d'you think we'd check out? As a team?' Blimey, Evie.

We'd slipped apart now, on account of the heat, and were lying side by side, the sheet thrown off: the over twenty-five-year-old girlfriend and her man.

After a moment, Ant rolled over on top of me and propped himself up the better to look at me, his elbows either side of my head. The moon, through the open window, lit up his face. Thoughtful. Sincere. My heart began to palpitate. Oh my God . . . this was it. *This . . . was . . . it!* His eyes searched my face, my hair, then—

'*Got it!*'

He thwacked the pillow, spun round and sat up, showing me a squashed mosquito in the palm of his hand.

'I've just saved you from certain pain. This blood-sucking parasite was about to take a slurp from your cheek.'

I sat up beside him and, using the wrong muscles, grinned gamely at his hand. Wanted to bite it. 'They always go for me.'

He kissed my cheek. 'Sweet blood, that's why. They like that. Night.'

'Night.'


Tim and Caro got married in the autumn. And it was lovely, of course it was. Heaven. It was in the village church, naturally, right beside our house, on a fine October day, and I was chief bridesmaid in a midnight-blue velvet dress, very sophisticated and without a hint of meringue, and Ant was an usher, devastatingly handsome in a morning coat. Caro looked radiant in ivory silk, with tiny blue velvet bows sewn just above the hem – I know you need to know this whether you're over twenty-five or not – and velvet ribbons hanging from her bouquet, which was cream rosebuds. Mum looked very pretty in her hippyish way, in a long flowery dress and a floppy straw hat, hair right down her back in those days, and she and Dad – still together then, albeit tenuously – put aside their differences and their gin bottles for the day, and beamed and looked proud. The reception was held in a marquee in the garden, with lashings of pink champagne, and then a rather pissy disco, before the happy couple went off on their honeymoon.

And then the next weekend, while Tim and Caro were still in Venice, Mum and Dad, having surprised themselves by making peace for the wedding, or at least an armed neutrality, decided to have a break from the farm, and go on holiday to Crete, where they had an almighty row in a taverna and were thrown out but that's another story. The one you need to know is that Ant and I moved in to look after the farm for them that weekend, and that was the weekend Neville Carter died.

Seventeen years ago, on 12 October 1989. And seventeen years later, here was I, in my basement kitchen in Jericho, having just had lunch with my husband, who'd just received a letter from a girl purporting to be his daughter. I gazed out of the window to Anna's trampoline, knowing I had to remember. Knowing it was important.

The Carters lived across the road from us and, knowing I was house-sitting at the farm, had popped by.

'Evie?' It was Mrs Carter who'd opened the front door, as people did in our village. She called up the stairs, 'Evie, are you there?'

I'd run down, flushed, from the bedroom, pulling down my T-shirt. 'Oh, Mrs Carter.'

'Evie, would you mind, dear, only I've been called into work,' Mrs Carter was a district nurse, 'and I wondered, could you have Neville for me? I'll only be an hour or so.'

Damn, I remember thinking. 'Of course, Mrs Carter.'

'He'll be no trouble. He can play outside, if you like. If you're busy.'

'Yes, yes, fine.'

'Just keep an eye.'

And Neville, narrow, weedy, pinched-faced, not an attractive boy, and not popular with the village children either – a sneak, by all accounts – had sidled inside, biting his nails. He was eight, not a baby, not necessarily needing to be watched all the time, and – oh, I didn't want to remember any of this, but somehow I knew it was important – and I'd said, 'Neville, will you really be all right in the garden?' when she'd gone.

'Yeah.' Not looking at me. Uncommunicative, shifty.

'Or d'you want to do some colouring? Look, we've got these.' I hustled him to the kitchen, rifled in the dresser drawer for some felt pens and sat him down at the table with Mum's kitchen pad.

He shrugged. 'Don't mind.'

'Well, have a go, hm?'

And back I'd leaped up those stairs, to Ant, in bed, leapfrogging on top of him with a shriek, pulling my top off again, no bra, and Neville had wandered off: first to the swing – I remember glimpsing him out of the window, on the old tyre that Dad had hung on a rope for us – and then out of sight, to that bit of the stream we'd all been warned about as children, where the water flows much faster, darker, and you can't see the riverbed and oh ... so ghastly. So ghastly later. Ant, ashen-faced as he and Maroulla, the wife of our farm worker, dragged him out: me, weeping, shrieking on the bank, the parents, Mr and Mrs Carter, arriving. Oh, no. Mustn't remember the parents. My parents then, getting a flight back from Crete, pale beneath their tans, shaken: the screaming, the rows, Mum good, Dad not so good. Telling the truth, *hav*ing, obviously, to tell the truth, about where we'd been, what we'd been doing, in the spare room, the horror on my father's face, the shame on Ant's; his gentle, kind, intelligent, wouldn't-hurt-a-fly face that had killed a child.

And afterwards, we'd cried together, huddled together, cringing, guilty figures at the funeral. Tim and Caro were back now — not a nice homecoming — and the whole village was there, everyone I'd known and grown up with, looking at me, who they knew, with a mixture of pity and surprise, and looking at Ant with mistrust. The man she'd been with. The man they didn't know, who she'd been upstairs with.

Ant had taken time off work — his college had been kind — and we'd drunk in pubs on the outskirts of the city: anonymous pubs where people didn't know us, drinking too much, always there for last orders, our guilt and our shame binding us. And then one of those nights, walking back, full of alcohol, he'd asked me to marry him.

I looked up from the slate work surface I was gripping fiercely now, and down the garden again, to the laburnum tree. To give me my due, if I was to be afforded any, I'd said no. No, I said, we were too highly strung and emotional right now. Not in our right minds. Let's wait. But he'd insisted. Said it was all he wanted. And, let's face it, he knew it was all I wanted. Knew that that day, as we'd been fooling around in the spare-room bed, in the farmhouse, as Neville had quietly padded down to the river, I'd been angling again, not in a crass, unsubtle way, but still . . . Saying how lovely Tim and Caro's wedding had been, how beautiful the church was, how happy they'd looked.

I felt the blood rush to my face now as I gazed at the

wisteria on the garden wall, my bike propped beside it. Well, if that wasn't crass and unsubtle, what was? And, whilst I was angling, Ant had – I forced myself to remember this, as I never had before – looked awkward. I felt a jab of horror. Had gently – and was this after we'd made love, or before? – gently untangled himself and said, 'Evie . . . I'm not sure.'

I shut my eyes. Well, lots of boyfriends weren't sure. Said they weren't ready. Needed time. And I hadn't pushed it. I opened my eyes. Hadn't said, but, Ant, we've been going out for months now, as long as Tim and Caro, and I badly want a baby and she's going to beat me to it, and all our lives we've been competitive, all our lives it's mattered, to Caro and me. No, of *course* I hadn't said any of that, and only even fractionally thought it. It was only because I was forcing myself now, years later, to be so ruthlessly honest that these thoughts were surfacing. I was probably *forcing* them to surface, like squeezing a spot that wasn't quite ready. But now, now this letter had come and was making me think, what if Neville hadn't died? I knew it was important; knew we'd become closer, but had never allowed myself to think . . . had it changed *every*thing? Had Neville dying changed the course of my life? Surely it was always on a trajectory to marry Ant?

I felt panicky, leaned heavily on the work surface, hands clenched together. And now – a child. By another woman. Conceived around that time. A barmaid, he'd said, a passing fancy, but nevertheless, a release from me. From my nagging. I pressed my fists to my temples. The demons were crowding in on me, making me think the worst of myself. Making me think, what goes around, comes around, Evie. A child. Two years older than Anna. And so – and this I had to really make myself do – and so think back. Think back to the moment before we'd heard the scream from Maroulla, who'd found Neville floating face down; think back to what Ant had said a few seconds before the scream had changed our lives.

'Evie . . . there's something you need to know. Something I've got to tell you.'

Up to now, it had been ruthlessly erased from my memory. I'd never said – weeks, months later – what was it, Ant? What was it you had to tell me? That was my shame. That I'd pretended he'd never said it. Or that I'd never heard.

I let go of the slate worktop. Took a deep breath. Exhaled shakily. But as I went to leave the room, I looked around. Wondered what else I'd pushed. He hadn't really liked that Welsh dresser I'd found in the antique shop in Woodstock; had thought it olde worlde, cutesy. But there it was. Hadn't really liked the yellow walls, thinking them too bright, a little challenging over the morning paper. But there they were. Hadn't really liked the watercolour of the milkmaid and the chickens above the sink – too twee, too whimsical. But there it was. And here I was too.

I bowed my head and left the room.

# 8

'Mum! There's a guy on the phone wanting to know if you're coming to look at his skewbald!'

I sat bolt upright in bed. His what? I hadn't slept a wink until about four in the morning, when I'd finally taken a pill, so now, here I was groggy, swaying and full of toxins.

'Oh,' I croaked. The horse. I swung my legs out of bed. A mistake. I sat on the edge, holding my head. 'Tell him we're on our way.' I quavered to the carpet.

Ant's side of the bed was empty, I noticed. I got up tentatively and tottered off to find my clothes, fumbling around the bedroom like a blind woman, listening to Anna's voice on the phone, downstairs in the hall.

'Yes, I'm so sorry . . . oh, did she? Oh, my mum's *hope*less, yes, we're on our way!'

She mustn't know, was my overriding panicky thought as I pulled on my jeans and grabbed a T-shirt. She mustn't know that this was anything other than a normal day. I clutched my T-shirt to my breast and sat down suddenly on the edge of the bed, remembering last night. Last night, when Ant had come home, quite late from an evening meeting in college – and late was normal, but not as late as this – I'd confronted him.

'You see?' I'd said, with a mixture of fear and triumph.

'See, Ant, it can't be your child. We were going out together, even engaged!'

And then I'd watched his face turn grey as I knew it would; watched him crumple, defeated into a chair, his gentle eyes pained. I'd listened, as he explained that yes, it could be his. That this had indeed happened while we were going out together, this thing with the barmaid – a one-off, a one-night stand – because he'd felt so trapped. Felt he was going insane.

'When, exactly?' I'd whispered, hanging on to the back of a chair. 'When had you felt so trapped? Felt you were going insane?'

'After lunch, at your parents' house,' he muttered. 'One Sunday. When Caro told us she was pregnant.'

My mind skittered back, foraging. But I remembered. Caro and Tim had been married for about three months, Ant and I engaged for one. And Ant and I had just returned from a much-needed break in Scotland, deciding, while we were up there, that our wedding would also be in the village church, like Tim and Caro's, but smaller, a more low-key affair. It was, after all, only a short while since Neville's funeral at the same venue. Ant had been quiet in Scotland. He'd fished a lot, whilst I'd walked, or read, but people were quiet when they fished, weren't they? This, then, would have been our first family gathering since . . . our first Sunday lunch for some time.

Mum, with half a bottle of cooking sherry inside her – and this would have been shortly before she left home – was on flying form: outrageous, confrontational, dancing to Fleetwood Mac in her cheesecloth dress as she stirred the Bisto well after two o'clock, Dad unamused, glaring at her. I imagine there comes a point in every marriage when what was once charming becomes intensely irritating.

I seem to remember things getting a bit tense, and Dad telling her to cut it out and get the bloody lunch on the table, when Caro announced she was pregnant. Three months pregnant, a honeymoon baby, and everyone was thrilled. Everyone forgot their irritation in that moment. Dad hastened to the cellar for a bottle of champagne, Mum hugged Caro, yes, everyone was delighted: the first grandchild, the first *Milligan*, Dad said proudly as he popped the cork, and Ant and I joined in the congratulations. And I was genuinely thrilled, because, after all, I was getting married soon, so no sicky feeling inside, not like when she'd got engaged before me, and delighted for Tim, *really* delighted for Tim, so then why, oh why, on the way home in the car, had I casually wondered what he thought of me coming off the pill? Ant? After all, we were getting married in a couple of months, so even if I got pregnant immediately, it wouldn't show. And it might take us ages; it had taken Sally Armstrong fourteen months!

Ant had cleared his throat. Then he'd reminded me, gently, that we'd thought we'd wait a year, hadn't we? Have a year of fun – which we badly needed in the circumstances – and enjoy being young-marrieds. And I'd said, yes, but, Ant, I'm not getting any younger. I'm twenty-six, for heaven's sake, and you're thirty! And Ant had gone very quiet, as if there was no answer to that, and I, well, I hadn't given up. I'd pressed it, fired up by a few glasses of wine, thinking, golly, at least I'm *asking*.

Some girls would just stop taking the wretched thing, this pill that's supposed to liberate us, give us so much freedom, although who exactly it liberates is debatable. And then finally: 'Yes, dear.'

Of course he didn't say 'yes, dear', but if we'd been a couple in the fifties, or in an Andy Capp cartoon, or Thelma and George, he would have done. No, he said words to that effect. Whatever you want, Evie. Wearily. Like a punch-bag. And then later that evening, when we were back at his rooms in Balliol where I was pretty much living, he'd gone out. For quite a long while. And I'd been a bit scared. Knew I'd been out of order. Pissed, too. And later in bed, I'd apologized.

'I'm sorry, darling, I'm going too fast. Forget it. I won't come off the pill.'

He hadn't answered. He'd turned over and we'd gone to sleep. Eventually.

'So you went out and shagged a barmaid!' I shrieked last night, like another cartoon character, perhaps the one whose ankles you see in *Tom and Jerry*, with the crinkled stockings and the rolling pin. 'Christ, Ant, how many times? Once? Twice? Or perhaps you went on a weekly basis?'

'Once!' he roared, fists clenched. 'I told you – just once!'

Ant never raised his voice. Never ever shouted at me, or at Anna, but instead of being shocked, I seized on it. I shouted back, wondered how many other bastard children he had littered about the country. Finally, Anna had burst into the kitchen in her nightie, wide-eyed and scared.

'What? What's going on?'

Ashamed, we'd simmered right down, and gone quickly to bed, assuring her nothing; scared ourselves now, in case she'd heard anything. And now, here she was again, bursting into my bedroom, her eyes like dinner plates.

'Mum! Come *on*. I said we'd be twenty minutes!'

'Right,' I agreed shortly, getting up.

I hurriedly found some shoes and brushed my teeth, then I followed her downstairs and out to the car, shutting the door on Brenda, who wanted to come with us. Anna was in her jodhpurs and boots, her hat swinging impatiently in her hand as she stood by the car, waiting for me to unlock it. My head was swimming and I felt nauseous.

'D'you know where we're going?' she asked accusingly as I got in.

'Um. No. Hang on.' I got out and tottered back inside for the directions.

When I got back, she was sitting in the front seat looking straight ahead, stony-faced. I fumbled with the ignition and off we went.

'What were you and Daddy rowing about last night?' she said, before we'd even got ten yards down the road.

'Hm? Oh, nothing really, darling.'

'Nothing!' She swivelled to face me in her seat. 'You were screaming and calling him a bastard and Daddy was shouting. I hardly call that nothing.'

'Oh, it was just . . . a silly thing. About holidays. You know I always want to go abroad and your father likes Scotland. That was all.'

'Oh.' She looked slightly mollified, but not entirely

convinced. 'Bit strong for a holiday argument, wasn't it?' she said at length. 'You were crying too.'

'Yes, well, you know, wrong time of the month. Makes monsters of us. Where is Daddy, by the way? Have you seen him this morning?'

'He's in the garden. Reading.'

'Ah.' Reading. Always his refuge. His escape. From me? I took a deep breath. Let it out shakily. Come on, Evie, get a grip. 'Now, anyway,' I turned a bright smile on her, 'this *pony*. How exciting! I wonder what colour it is.'

'It's a skewbald, he said on the phone.'

'What's that, then?'

'Brown and white.'

'Oh.' I blinked. 'I could have sworn the advert said it was grey.'

'So you do know what colour it is.' Still belligerent, accusing. Not letting me off lightly. I knew I had to raise my game.

'Oh, well, maybe it's grey, or maybe it's brown and white,' I said lightly. 'Or maybe it's grey and brown and white?'

She shot me a withering look. 'It's down here on the left, according to your bit of paper.'

'Here?' I blanched at the somewhat unpromising urban landscape.

'Yes, look, it says, "After the Shell garage."' She waved the piece of paper in my face.

We were bowling along the Woodstock Road and I obediently swung a left, down a street lined with terraced houses. I slowed down and peered at the directions as she held them up in front of me. This looked like an industrial estate. At length, though, we wiggled around a few bends and then the road petered out and we achieved a track, which led, in turn, to what could hardly be described as a stable yard. More like a collection of sheds with corrugated iron roofs, and a mobile home standing gauntly in their midst, I thought as I gazed around. There were a few scrubby-looking paddocks in the background with telltale sprays of ragwort, which Tim would have had up in seconds, none of which betrayed the presence of horses. We came to a halt in the yard.

A couple of fierce-looking mongrels bounded up to the car, barking loudly. Anna and I shrank back in our seats while they shouted at us, teeth bared, all curling lips and white eyes. Eventually a young lad appeared and dragged them both away, tying them to a chain. When we were sure they were secure, Anna and I ventured forth gingerly.

I wasn't really dressed for this, I realized, having stuck my feet into the first shoes that had come to hand: a rather expensive pair of beaded flip-flops I'd bought in Italy. I'd ruin them, I thought, as I picked my way through a mucky yard. Ruin flip-flops! I jolted with horror. My husband had a child with another woman, and I was worrying about flip-flops?

A small, scrawny man in baggy fawn trousers, braces and a flat cap slid out of a shed. He came to meet us. His eyes were small, light blue, and very quick. A practised smile revealed an unusual dental arrangement.

'Mr Docherty?'

'Tha's right.' In a slow, singsong Irish brogue. 'You'll be coming after the pony.'

'Exactly. But now just remind me, Mr Docherty, what colour is the pony?'

'What colour will you be wanting?' Quick as a flash.

'Oh. Well. It doesn't really matter, I suppose. It's just that, well, in the advert you said grey, and my daughter thinks you said skewbald, so—'

'Ah, well, you see the grey one, she was after being sold, but the skewbald now, she's a rare beast. A grand mare altogether. Pure-bred Connemara, out of Mayflower Summer by In Your Dreams, so she is. You'd go a long way to find another a mare like that, may the Good Lord crack me legs from under me if it isn't so.'

Still smiling, he jerked his head economically to the lad, who took a head collar from a peg and went sullenly towards a stable.

'I see. So . . . the one in the advert in the paper—'

'Went in moments. I have an awful high turnover here, you see, and you're lucky to be seein' the skewbald at all. I've a gentleman comin' all the way from Bristol he is, wants something special for his little gurr'l. A very wealthy businessman, by all accounts, but he's after breaking down on the M5. Rang just a moment ago, and here you are, so . . .'

'Oh! Yes, well, how dreadful. But we are here first . . .'

It didn't occur to me to wonder why a very wealthy businessman should own a car liable to break down on the M5, and feeling my luck was in for a change, I followed him with Anna to where the horse was being led out of its stable.

It was indeed brown and white, and bigger than I'd

imagined: rather thin and rangy too, with ribs I could see, and its back looked slightly humped with the tail tucked in between its legs. Was that normal? But it had a kind, somewhat sleepy eye, I decided. The mare raised her tail and evacuated copiously out of her rear end a stream of rather evil-looking green slime. Perhaps she was nervous. She wasn't the only one.

'Right. What d'you think, darling?'

Christ. In the recesses of what was left of my mind I remembered Caro telling me to bring someone along. Ant, at least. Caro, even better. But we were here now, befuddled and bemused. I deferred to my daughter.

'She's lovely,' she said, stepping forward to pat her, her eyes aglow with owning a pony – any pony.

'Yes. Yes, she is, isn't she?' I agreed, inching forward myself and tentatively laying on a hand. Awfully greasy. I retracted it. But I quite liked the idea that it was a she. Mares were more docile, weren't they? Than boy horses? This one was so docile she was nodding off.

'She'll be a bit keener when she's ridden, I suppose,' I hazarded. 'She looks a bit sleepy.'

'Ah, faith, she's aisy goin, this one is. But if it's keen you want, you won't find a fleeter mare in Oxfordshire,' said Mr Docherty, kicking her hind foot to make her stand a bit squarer.

'And does she jump?' asked Anna, shyly.

'Is it jump? Jees, she'll lep that brick wall as soon as look at it.' He pointed to a dry-stone wall behind us. 'Lept clean out of the yard the other day, right over the five-bar gate. Shown a clean pair of heels, too, eh, Barney?'

Barney shrugged and looked noncommittal as he stood holding the slack end of the head collar rope, chewing gum and gazing into space.

'But she's – you know – quiet too, is she?' I said, alarmed at the prospect of her leaping around Caro's yard. 'You know, easy to handle?'

'Is it quiet? Ah, she is that. But she's a mare, you know?' He gave me a conspiratorial wink. 'She'll not be taking any nonsense.'

'No. No, well, obviously, we won't be giving her any nonsense.' I wasn't entirely sure what he meant by that, or what I meant, for that matter. God, my head. Oh, for some Nurofen. 'I mean – we'd treat her very kindly.'

It occurred to me, suddenly, we might be under scrutiny here ourselves. A friend of mine who'd wanted to get a dog from a rescue home, and had imagined she'd been taking the philanthropic route to dog ownership, had been startled to find an earnest young woman in her sitting room with a clipboard, asking pertinent questions – and sometimes impertinent ones – about her domestic set-up: grilling her as to her suitability to own this pre- viously abandoned-by-the-roadside pup. The fact that she lived in town and was a divorced mother of three apparently didn't go down too well.

'We're married,' I said quickly. 'My husband and I.' Anna looked at me in astonishment. 'And although we live in the city, we'd keep it – her – at my brother's place. Church Farm in Daglington.'

'Caroline Milligan's place?' Some shadow briefly crossed Mr Docherty's face.

'That's it. D'you know it?'

'I do. Get that currycomb and look sharp,' he snapped irritably to the boy.

'What's her name?' asked Anna as the boy tied the mare up and began grooming her with what looked a horribly painful rubber pad with spikes. She bore it beautifully I must say, standing stock-still as he yanked the implement over her back, pulling out great tufts of hair, poor thing.

'Molly Malone. But we call her Molly.'

'Oh, sw-eet!' Anna, overcome with emotion, put her arms round her neck and kissed her. For some reason, and perhaps it was because she was unable to prevent this public display of affection even in front of this surly teenage boy, or perhaps it was because my emotions were perilously close to the surface that morning, I found this profoundly moving. My eyes misted up. A girl and her pony. First love.

'We'll take her,' I said decidedly. 'Do you deliver?'

The boy turned to hide a smile, and even Mr Docherty had the grace to cough.

'You'll be wanting your lass to ride her first? Or even the lad to hop on. Show her paces?'

'Oh. Yes.' I coloured. Anna was glaring at me, shocked. Was that how it was done, then? I'd never bought a horse before. 'Yes, good idea. The lad . . . and then Anna. Oh, and what about her legs?'

'What about her legs?'

Still smarting from my gaffe, I had a notion I should be feeling them. I hastened forward to run my hand expertly down a large hairy back one, but my sunglasses slid off my nose and clattered onto the concrete, which startled the horse, who stepped back and smashed them, as I, to avoid her rear end, stepped smartly into her slimy green poo in my flip-flops. I stared in dismay as it squelched up between my toes.

'Never mind, it's only grass,' I said quickly, seeing Anna's mortified face. 'I mean, that's all they eat, isn't it? And hay. Oh, don't worry about that, they're only Boots ones,' I said, as the boy made a pretence of picking up the bits of broken sunglasses. He promptly abandoned his efforts and deftly shovelled the evidence into a wheelbarrow.

'Her legs are clean,' Mr Docherty assured me smoothly.

'Oh, good.' I nodded, disinclined to take the investigation further.

'Tack her up then.' He nodded to Barney.

In another moment, Barney had got a saddle and bridle on her, and vaulted onto her back. After leaning down to get some muttered instructions from his father, he gave the pony a hefty kick, and a sharp flick of the reins on her neck. At this his mount jolted off at a rather unsettled pace, through the open gateway and into the ragworty paddock. We followed at a slower pace, and then leaned on the fence, watching as he went round and round in circles: first walking, then trotting, then that faster thing . . . marvellous. I felt I was on the set of *Rawhide*: just needed a cowboy hat and a piece of grass to chew. He came back and slid neatly off, handing the reins to Anna.

'All right, darling?' I looked at her anxiously.

She looked a bit nervous, but got on carefully, like she'd been taught at the riding stables, not in a leap and a bound like the boy, but holding the reins in one hand and levering herself up. I felt so proud as I watched her trot off. How brave! A strange horse! I'd no more get on that than fly to the moon. I watched her do a careful up-down, up-down trot, immaculate in her yellow jodhpurs, shiny boots and velvet hat, but I was only half watching. I'd spotted a water trough just along the fence line, and unable to bear the poo-between-the-toes feeling any longer, nipped off to dunk my foot.

When I got back, she seemed to be going quite fast, I'd say a gallop, and Mr Docherty was shouting, 'Pull her up now, gurr'll!' but Anna's eyes were shining, cheeks pink, as she careered unsteadily back to us.

'Yes?' I called up to her.

'Yes!' she said breathlessly, elated and excited.

'Marvellous.' I beamed at the man. 'A thousand, wasn't it, you said?' The boy looked astonished, and Mr Docherty anguished, as it presumably crossed his mind that he could have asked twice as much, but he was quick to point out that yes, that was indeed the price, but minus the tack.

'Ah. And how much is the tack?'

'Five hundred.'

'Five hundred!' I looked at the saddle, rather dirty and grey, and the tatty old bridle. 'Good grief. I had no idea.'

'Ah well, you see, it's all in the workmanship,' he said, sucking air in through his teeth. 'There's a devil of craft goes into it, and sure, you could buy new, but this is Molly's tack. Fits her like a glove, always has done. She'd be desperate in an ill-fitting saddle.'

'Yes, yes, of course.' Like a tight pair of shoes, I

imagined. Except with someone on your back too. Horrid.

'We'll take it,' I said firmly as the boy made an odd barking sound into his hand. 'She must have her familiar things.'

'And I'll throw in the head collar for free,' Mr Docherty assured me, kicking his son.

'Oh, how kind!' I exclaimed, but even as I was writing out the cheque, on an upturned bucket, which had been hastily provided, I wondered, uneasily, if this was rather like marvelling delightedly at the free Aga cookbook, which, as Ant had pointed out, had come free with five grands-worth of cooker.

'And did you say you would deliver?' I persisted, as Mr Docherty smartly pocketed the cheque. I really had to gain some ground here.

'Ah, we will. Wednesday morning I'll pop her in the lorry and bring her round, just as soon as the cheque's cleared.' No flies on him. 'I'll tek her straight to your brother's place, will I?'

'Yes, please. Oh, and if there's no one about – my sister-in-law's frightfully busy – don't worry too much about trying to find her. But perhaps my brother, Tim . . .'

'Ah, no need to trouble anyone. I'll keep out o' harm's way and pop Molly straight in a stable, will I?' He widened his eyes, encouragingly.

'Um, yes. Why not?' I certainly didn't want Caro disturbed and batey, and Tim would be relaxed about that. 'You can't miss the stables, they're just round the back of the large Dutch barn.'

'I dare say the boy and meself will make them out.' He

touched the peak of his cap, in a rather sweet, old-fashioned gesture, as, I felt, in a gentler age, a horse dealer might.

A horse dealer, I thought with a start as we drove out of the yard. Is that what he was? That sounded a bit — you know – dodgy. But I reckoned he was honest, essentially. And I was pretty sure we hadn't paid over the odds. And even if we had, more importantly, Anna had got her dream, a pony. And she might need a few dreams, I thought wretchedly as we drove back down the Woodstock Road. She was prattling away beside me, shiny-eyed, about Molly, about how she couldn't wait to tell Jemima, her best friend, couldn't wait to show her cousins. Yes, she might need a pony to cling to, if her little world was about to be shattered, her bubble burst.

I gripped the steering wheel, letting out a long, shaky breath as we turned into our road, then slammed my foot on the brake as a girl stepped out onto a zebra crossing in front of us. I went hot. Christ, I'd been miles away. As she walked past she glared at me through the windscreen, clearly believing I hadn't stopped quickly enough. A skinny girl, in a skimpy white halter-neck top, about seventeen. Was that her, I wondered, with a sudden stab of horror. The barmaid's daughter? I sat, frozen at the wheel as I watched her mount the pavement, then turn left, in the opposite direction to our house. No. No, of course not. I drove on, flustered.

But one day – one day it could be. One day, maybe having got no response to her letter, or perhaps some response – I'd been so upset last night I hadn't asked Ant if he'd formulated a plan, if he intended to write – she'd come. Anna and I would arrive back from the school run, or perhaps a shopping trip, to find her in the drawing room, perched on a sofa opposite Ant, cool and defiant, Ant turning wide, frightened eyes on us as we walked in.

'Won't Daddy be pleased!'

I swung around to Anna, horrified. 'Why?' I whispered.

'Well, he always says he likes a houseful of girls. And now he's got Molly too. He's got another girl!'

# 9

As we drew up outside the house, it was in time to see
Ant, not in his usual weekend jeans, but navy chinos and
a biscuit linen jacket, shutting the front door behind him.
He locked it carefully, pocketed the key, then turned to
come down the steps, pausing to pick up a large suitcase.

'Where's Daddy going?' said Anna, her voice betraying
a note of panic.

My mouth dried as I watched him descend the steps.
His head was bent and he looked purposeful, sad.

'Wait here.'

I parked chaotically on the opposite side of the road,
nose in, tail out. Then I got out and dashed across the
street, nearly getting mown down by a convertible Alfa
Romeo, with an alfa romeo at the wheel, his squeeze
beside him.

'Oh, for *fuck's* sake!' he roared fruitily, but I ignored
him, climbing over the bonnet and running to Ant.

'Where are you going?' I gasped.

He stared impassively at me. 'To your mother's.'

'My mother's?' Even in my distress it seemed an
unlikely bolt hole.

He looked at me. 'Don't you remember? We're going
for lunch there today.'

My mind cleared. 'Oh!' Saturday. Yes, of course, lunch.
'But – the suitcase . . .'

'It's not. It's that old Z-bed we had in the attic. She wants to borrow it for this reiki thing she's doing.'

I gazed down at it; saw that he was right. The collapsible bed. Which folded up into what looked like a large case. And which we hadn't used for years. I felt my heart slow down, but it had been at racing speed, so it wasn't an immediate descent. As he looked at me I realized he was suddenly alive to what I'd been thinking. A wave of shock passed over his face.

'But, it's huge,' I prattled on, trying to gloss over my horrific assumption. 'What were you going to do – drag it there or something?'

'No, I was going to put the seats down in the back of my car and meet you over there,' he said evenly. 'I tried to ring you, but your phone's off. I assumed you and Anna had already gone on. It's nearly one o'clock, you know.'

'Is it? No, I didn't.' I passed a rattled hand through my hair. 'I've lost track of time. We've been to see that pony. Anna wanted to— Oh, darling.' She'd materialized beside us. Beside her parents, talking rather too anxiously on the steps of her house.

'Look, Daddy's taking Granny the Z-bed. We're going there for lunch!' I said, as if we were off to Disneyland Paris, trying to protect her with my forced jollity, but also Ant, from knowing that she too had thought the same. But he'd seen her worried little face, and suddenly, from being the happiest family this side of the Banbury Road, we were crumbling. Ant and I rallied simultaneously.

'Right, well, we may as well use your car, now you're here,' he said. 'Bigger boot.'

'Good idea. And, Anna, you run up and change. Chop chop, Granny will wonder where we are, have lunch on the table!'

Highly unlikely, I thought, as I too raced inside to change my shoes and grab a jacket. When had my mother ever managed to get a meal together on time? So my stab at normality, normal in any other family, earned me an odd look from Anna.

I hurried back to the car, deliberately racing my daughter, to slide in beside my husband, who'd assumed the wheel.

'We must talk, Ant,' I gasped. 'This is horrible.'

'I agree,' he said quickly. 'Not fair on Anna.'

'No.'

'We must keep the peace at all costs.'

'Yes.'

But as she rejoined us and we set off, Ant and I making forced, over-bright conversation, me regaling him with the horse-trading saga, Anna, gradually becoming convinced things were OK and joining in from the back, enthusing about her new pet – 'She's s-oo sweet, Daddy, you'll love her' – I couldn't help wondering what the costs would be; what I must agree to, to keep the peace. To keep this little family on track.

Felicity was already at Mum's place when we arrived. The pair of them were standing outside the little blue house, their backs to us, looking back at the front door, which badly needed painting. I wondered if that's what they were discussing. We came up the cobbled path behind them, through a riot of cottage garden flowers.

'It's just a bit misleading,' Felicity was saying anxiously, turning as she heard us. 'I think you should wait.'

'Wait for what?' I asked.

'Your mother wants to put up a brass sign, about being a reiki practitioner,' she explained nervously.

I boggled at the little brass plaque Mum had in her hands: 'Barbara Milligan, Reiki Therapist.'

'Of course she should wait! Christ, she's not even qualified yet!'

'I'm more than halfway through,' Mum said defiantly, clutching her plaque to her breast. 'So I'm a practitioner in progress. And one woman in my class is already seeing students. At half-price, of course.'

'Well then, she's stupid,' I snapped, all the pent-up emotion of the last few days being taken out on my mother, who, if not stupid, was certainly foolish.

Three years ago it had been homeopathy, until she'd realized the course took four years and a great deal of hard work and application. Then she'd switched to aroma-therapy, and now this. I found her inability to focus on anything for more than ten minutes – and, if I'm honest, the objects of her attention span – intensely irritating, perhaps because I recognized elements of myself in her and dreaded ending up like that: inventing a spurious direction for my life, alone, as her mother had been, and my great-grandmother before that. All women who'd been left by their husbands. And even though my mother had done the walking, I couldn't help feeling this lonely, aimless life was only a mis-step away if I wasn't careful; hereditary. As a result, I was much tougher on her than I should have been, regretting it later. Who was it said we start off loving our parents, after a while we judge them, and rarely do we forgive them? Today I was more unforgiving than usual.

'It's just ridiculous, Mum,' I stormed. 'You'll be had up by the General Medical Council or something. You can't go around pretending you're a doctor when you're not!'

'Oh, now I don't think Barbara was going to do that,' soothed Felicity, seeing anxiety, always so close to the surface with Mum – not far behind her skippy enthusiasm – shadow her face, her grey eyes widening in alarm.

'Of course she wasn't,' said Anna, staunchly, shooting me a look that said, Lay *off*, Mum. 'You're just practising, as in, having a go, aren't you, Granny? For when the time comes to get some proper patients?'

'That's it, dear,' said Mum, brightening quickly, equilibrium restored – ever susceptible to flattery, I thought bitterly. 'And do you know, if I keep it up this time, in only another six months I'll be there. D'you want to see my room, Anna love? Ooh, thank you, Ant, that's just what I need. Bring it down, would you? We're in the basement.'

She wrapped her cardigan around her and turned to descend the little outside wrought-iron staircase that led to the basement. The others clattered obediently after her, Mum fishing out a key and chattering on about how marvellous it was for the surgery – *surgery!* – to have its own entrance. Anna turned at the bottom and shot me another warning glance up the stairwell: *Don't* be mean. Oh, right, so we were supposed to encourage her in this, were we? Pander to the fiction? Just as we'd all knocked back the Bach Flower Remedies and said, 'Oh, yes, *so* much better, Barbara'? I breathed deeply and forced myself to follow them down.

Mum proudly unlocked the door at the bottom trilling 'Ta-dah!' as she swung it back. We followed her inside. What had been her basement junk room, full of wicker chairs, old hair-dryers and general female detritus, had been transformed into a pink parlour. Womb music warbled low and candles glowed on every conceivable surface: all along the windowledge, on top of a filing cabinet – lit in our honour, no doubt – some just sitting in their own wax. A driftwood collage, which I recognized as one of Mum's early works, covered one wall, and on another, an Athena poster of Japanese homilies had been Blu-Tacked up. In a corner on the floor, what looked like a baby bath was full of pebbles, water trickling over them by way of a sort of Heath Robinson pump, a few ferns stuck here and there. Despite the lavender candles, which were horribly strong and put one in mind of one of the cheaper brands of lavatory cleaner, there was no disguising the whiff of damp. A blow heater going at full blast didn't do much to dispel it either. I picked up a little leaflet on the side, which told me that Metaphysical Therapy and Self-Development Counselling was also available at this establishment. I could feel myself getting crosser and crosser as the others wandered around, exclaiming and marvelling, touching the stones, reading the soothsaying, simultaneously hating myself. 'It's harmless,' Ant would say later. 'Let her be.'

'Just here, Barbara?' he was saying now, as he and Anna unfolded the bed in the middle of the room on some sort of plinth she'd knocked up from concrete breeze blocks painted pink, under a fringed lamp. Much kinder than me, I thought miserably, watching them assemble it. But then she wasn't their mother, was she? Wasn't such an accurate reflection of themselves. But surely if Felicity and Ant, both professors, could manage not to scoff, I could too?

'Looks super, Mum,' I smiled, coming across. I bent down to pat the swirly seventies print of the ancient Z-bed mattress. 'But maybe it needs a cover or something?'

'Oh, I've got one!' She instantly nipped over to collect a couple of pink towels from a pile on a chair and spread them out, detecting a hint of enthusiasm in my voice and pouncing on it pathetically, like a dog a scrap.

'Shotgun be the first patient!' announced Anna, quickly sitting on the bed. She stretched out on her back, grinning. 'Come on Granny, heal me! Reiki style!'

My mother was instantly all puffed-up importance and twiddling beads. 'Well, I'll have to have absolute quiet, obviously,' she said gravely. 'And the lights dimmed. And no audience. Go on, off you go!'

She fluttered her hands at us, cheeks pink, eyes shining.

'Yes, go on,' agreed Anna, flicking her hand at us dismissively. 'Buzz off. Granny and I have got work to do.'

As we left them alone and went to go upstairs, I shut the door behind me and glanced back. Through the little square of glass in the door I saw my mother, eyes shut, God help me, laying her hands on Anna's head and shutting her eyes. As Anna struggled not to smile, she made a sort of 'hommmm . . .' noise. I shuddered.

Ant put a sympathetic hand on my shoulder. 'It's —'

'*Don't* tell me it's harmless!' I snapped, shaking him off and pushing past him up the wrought-iron staircase.

Later, of course, after a large glass of wine, I relented and went down. Made myself available to Mum's healing hands.

'She likes you to go a bit dreamy,' Felicity whispered to me as we passed on the staircase, she having been the last patient: 'a bit spacey. Oh, and you're supposed to feel her hands go hot when she gets to the trouble spots, which of course they don't, so just pretend. I'll put the spuds on.' She nipped on up.

This only served to send my blood pressure rocketing again, so that by the time Mum – a white coat over her Monsoon dress and cardi – got to work on me, having first fannied around changing the CD in a ghetto blaster that I recognized as being an old one of Anna's, and having washed her hands very assiduously and theatrically with surgical soap, I was about to pop.

'Now, darling, just relax,' she said, in the manner of a professional soothsayer. I shut my eyes tight, knowing it was the only way forward, but not before I'd seen Mum shut hers too, and look a bit hypnotic, pretending to swoon as she stood over me. Her hands were held aloft and horizontal, hovering over me like a pair of metal detectors. The force was with her.

'Hommm . . .' she started low and portentous, like a Buddhist monk.

'Is the humming mandatory?' I couldn't resist, through gritted teeth.

'Oh, no, darling, most people don't do it. But I think it helps.' Excellent news.

'Hommm . . .' Oh, get *on* with it.

After a bit more humming and hovering, the hands eventually arrived, homing in on what she clearly believed to be my trouble spots. They came to rest on my shoulders, then slipped down my arms and over the backs of my hands, lingering on my fingers, stroking, like spiders. The temptation to shake her off was overwhelming.

'Where is the pain, my child?' she breathed gustily in her best clairvoyant manner.

'In . . . my . . . head,' I muttered back with studied irritation and in all truthfulness. I didn't need this. Really didn't need this. Not now. Not with Ant and ooh . . . Ant. Taken out of my troubles, as I had been for ten minutes by my mother's behaviour, as I remembered it rocked me like a little boat, caught in the slipstream of an ocean liner. I wobbled, a wave of sickness churning through me. Mum's hands came to rest on the top of my head. Hot hands, I thought in surprise as I lay there, slightly taken aback. Really quite hot.

'Ah, yes,' she whispered, 'it is in your head. I can feel it. Feel your pain. Can you feel the heat?'

I opened one eye carefully to look at her. Her head was thrown back, mouth slack, eyes shut, trancelike.

'Yes,' I said uncertainly.

She smiled, eyes still shut, head lolling. 'I can too,' she breathed. 'Yes. It's channelling through. Transferring.'

Transferring. Blimey.

'I feel it flowing right through me now,' she gasped.

'Where does it go?' I muttered, still eyeing her.

'I store it for you,' she gulped, wincing as if in pain. 'Take it from you, and then – out! Out! Into the ether!'

The hands were cooling now, and suddenly, her eyes sprang open. She stepped back and shook her head as if coming round from some sort of out-of-body experience. 'Phew.' She blinked. Looked exhausted. 'Better?' She peered anxiously at me.

I sat up, swung my legs off the bed and shrugged. 'So-so.'

'But you felt the channelling? Felt the transference?'

'A bit,' I admitted grudgingly.

She smiled. 'And in time, you'll feel it more. When you're a little more open-minded. More suggestible.'

'Right,' I said shortly, finding my shoes.

I watched as she bustled around the room, taking off her white coat and hanging it up, blowing out candles now that her last patient had been seen, pausing occasionally, to touch her forehead, as if still a bit weak from her exertions. Then I noticed, as she bent down to blow out the last candle on the floor, that her cardigan fell forward on one side, as if it was weighted down.

'Mum, what's in your pocket?' I said sharply.

She straightened up and swung around, her hand shooting into it protectively. She looked defensive.

'Nothing.'

'Oooh, *Mum*!'

There then ensued a rather unseemly little tussle, the details of which I won't bore you with, and of which I'm not particularly proud either, but suffice to say, moments later, as we parted, panting, I was the victor. My right hand was held aloft, as she leaped for it, like a terrier for a ball, and in it, was a warm, squidgy object, like a bean bag, which I suddenly realized was hot.

'A *hand*warmer!' I spluttered, opening my palm and reading on the side that it was intended for shooting or skiing purposes. 'Bloody hell, Mum!'

'Only to get it going,' she hissed. 'Sometimes the transference needs a bit of jump-starting.'

'*So* mean,' said Anna later, as we drove home, her eyes hot with tears. '*So* harsh, Mum, to come marching in with it, and plonk it down on the kitchen table like Exhibit A. Poor, *poor* Granny!'

She hadn't been poor so much as utterly defiant and unrepentant, I thought privately. Hadn't hung her head in shame, but had kept spouting the rubbish about jump-starting, and everyone else had soothed and agreed, and I'd been *incandescent* with irritation.

'But can't you see you're just encouraging her?' I'd spluttered, as Felicity – who always cooked, whether lunch was at her house or Mum's – put a roast chicken on the table. 'She's only going to hoodwink some poor susceptible student out of their grant – can't you see it's immoral?'

'But if they go away feeling better, so what?' Anna had demanded. 'I bet you felt better when you stood up, and I know I did. So what's the difference?'

I'd opened my mouth to protest, looked to Ant for support, but he'd just shrugged noncommittally, and I wondered if he, like me, was wondering what our very blessed daughter had to feel better about. I'd shut my mouth, impotently. Mum had looked smug, glancing around the table for more support, which didn't do much for her cause, and which happily, my family hadn't given. Felicity had swiftly changed the subject, asking Ant how his new book was coming on, if he was having to do much research, how he was finding jiggling his timetable with his writing, and whilst they talked shop and Anna joined in, Mum looked triumphantly at me, so that it was as if she *had* won, because whilst the others talked academia, I was left with her, like her, the silly ones: the one who'd warmed her silly hand, and the one who'd made a silly fuss.

That night, in bed, after Anna had sloped off to her room – no evenings for Ant and me now, with a teenager who often went to bed after us – after we'd gratefully turned in, we'd held each other close.

'We have to face this together, Evie,' he whispered. 'Otherwise it'll tear us apart.'

I'd nearly wept with relief. He was right. So right.

'What shall we do?' I whispered, hanging to that 'we' for dear life; knowing that whatever was threatening to rip us apart must surely bring us together.

'I must write to her. But I'll show you the letter first. No secrets. And, Evie, if she wants to meet me, then I have to do that. You must see that.'

He drew back on the pillows to look at me, to gauge the impact of this: his face was racked with anguish, and I thought how dreadful this was for him, and I'd only thought it was dreadful for me. Nevertheless I trembled. I didn't show it, but this coward soul of mine quaked.

'Yes,' I whispered, knowing he was right.

'She has to know who her father is. And that's all it'll be, I'm convinced. To know, after all these years. To set eyes on me. She'll have her own father, I'm sure.'

'Yes,' I said quickly. Because I'd thought of that too. Hoped that. *Clung* to that. But . . . maybe some drunken reprobate? Some unemployed wastrel who entrusted the family credit to William Hill? And maybe she'd set eyes on Ant and think – wow. Who wouldn't? Think – mm, yes please. But, then again, why shouldn't she? He was her father, after all. I dug deep for courage. Knew I was going to need it.

'But if not . . .' Ant was saying, picking his words with care, 'if she doesn't have her own father and she does want to see something of me – of us—'

'*Us?*' I gasped sitting up, unable to stop myself. 'Steady, Ant, I'm not sure I can—'

'OK,' he agreed hastily, knowing he was going too fast. Knowing it was softly-softly with me, one small fairy step at a time. That it would be a while before 'Eh up, Stepmam' was something I could hear without projectile vomiting. 'No, OK then. Just me.'

We both lay down again, uncertainly, staring up at the ceiling. Instinctively and simultaneously we reached out for each other's hands; held on tight. Later that night, we made love, and then afterwards, Ant turned over and went to sleep. I could hear his rhythmic breathing beside me, see the hump of his shoulder as it rose and fell. I lay awake for an hour, and then another hour, and finally, when I heard the longcase clock in the hall strike three, I threw another sleeping pill down my throat, knowing my mother did the same, and waited for the cosh on the head to deliver me to oblivion.

Wednesday morning at nine o'clock sharp, Caro was on the phone.

'What the hell d'you think you're playing at? I've got some strange horse in my field kicking seven bells out of the children's ponies and Phil says he saw a lad unload her from a trailer at practically dawn! Said she belonged to a Mrs Hamilton and he'd been told to deliver her!'

I shut my eyes. Shit. Hadn't I rung her? I thought I'd rung her. I'd certainly left a message on Tim's mobile and had totally meant to ring her too, but so much had been going on . . . Bugger.

'Caro, I – I'm terribly sorry,' I faltered. 'I completely forgot. I did leave Tim a message, on his mobile—'

'Which he never bloody uses!'

'No, well, clearly. And the boy was supposed to put her in a stable, not in with the ponies, but perhaps he forgot or – or couldn't find them, or—'

'So she is yours?' Caro screeched incredulously.

'Yes, Anna and I bought her the other day. I meant to—'

'You bought her on her own? Without taking anyone? Without ringing me? Are you totally and utterly out of your mind?'

Yes, it felt like it, recently, most of the time. But I wasn't having that. I straightened up in my kitchen. 'Anna knows her stuff, actually,' I said stiffly. 'She's been riding for nearly two years now.'

'Two years? I've been at it fifteen and I'm still learning. Where did you get her from?'

'A very reputable dealer, as a matter of fact. He's called Lenny Docherty, and he's got a yard just off the Woodstock—'

'Lenny the Liar!' she said with a spectacular hiss.

'What?'

'You bought a horse from Lenny the Liar? Oh God, Evie, he'd sell his own grandmother!'

'Actually,' I said testily, but trying to fend off a certain qualm, 'she has a very fine pedigree. She's out of Mayflower something-or-other and, um, In Your, whatsit. Dreams.'

'She's out of some gypsy encampment off the Highbury estate, you mean. I took one look and thought, where's the caravan!'

This was so like Caro, I thought, fury mounting, to take against her simply because she hadn't been consulted. That, essentially, was what was bugging her.

'Right, well, I'll come and sort her out then, shall I? Come and move her, if she's annoying the ponies.'

'If you can catch her,' Caro scoffed. 'Phil and I have been running round after her since seven o'clock this morning. We'll have to lasso her to bring her in. And then where am I supposed to put her?'

'Well, I—'

'Oh, for God's sake, I'll manage. Just bring Anna over here after school, OK? I want to see her on her. Make sure she can ride the wretched thing.'

'Right,' I said obediently.

I put the phone down and sank my head into my hands. Massaged my temples viciously. Oh Lord. Caro in a bate. Not ideal.

Later that day, I scooped up Anna from the school gates, having collapsed the back seats in the car so I could accommodate her bike.

'She's arrived!' Anna jumped about excitedly on the pavement as I wrestled with a recalcitrant wheel that refused to turn in on itself.

'Yes, she has. Anna, can you just—'

'Polly, my horse has arrived!' she called to a friend, running to get her bus.

Polly stopped in awe. 'Ohmygod, you're soo lucky?' She ran on, as the lucky one jigged about beside me.

'Did you bring my riding things?'

'Damn, I forgot.'

'Mum!' she groaned. 'Never mind I'll borrow Phoebe's. Does Caro like her? Molly? What does she think?'

'Um, she hasn't really had a proper look. Darling, could you just push that pedal in so I can – bugger. The chain's come off. Now I've got oil all over me!'

'But they put her in a stable, didn't they? Why hasn't she had a proper—'

'Anna, just help me with this sodding bike!' I screamed as my hand went painfully through the spokes. '*Shit!*'

'So-rry.' She rolled her eyes theatrically as though I only had to ask. Together we heaved it on board. 'Mum, d'you think you could not swear so much?' she whispered as we jammed it in tight. 'It's like you've got Tourette's or something. None of my friends' mums do.'

'Hi, Evie!' one such saintly mother, a scrubbed, unhighlighted paragon with a Ph.D. in micro-bleeding-whatever, hailed us from across the road.

I lathered on a smile as I turned and shut the boot. 'Tabitha. Hi.'

'Got the dog in there too?' she called jovially.

I laughed, but it had a hollow ring to it. This was a reference to a recent occasion, when, feeling my life lacked substance, I'd joined a few mums for a morning dog walk, something they apparently squeezed in effortlessly between dropping their daughters off at school and rushing off to split the atom at the University. Knowing they took it quite seriously I'd carefully put in floral wellies, a dog rug, a towel for Brenda's muddy paws, and driven to their habitual meeting place at Christ Church meadows. Sadly, when I opened the boot, I'd forgotten the dog.

'That's it!' I chortled now. 'Got everything in here – bike, dog, kitchen sink – busy busy busy! Must fly, Tabitha!'

Anna looked stricken as we got in the car. 'Can you not say things like that either, Mum?'

'Like what?'

'"Busy busy busy." And by the way, your jeans are way too low.'

There was no one about when we got to the farm. I opened the front door and hollered up the stairs, shouted my way around downstairs, then roamed around the garden yelling, 'Caro!'

'There!'

Anna spotted her, down by her marquee on the other side of the river. She was walking strangely, bent double like a gorilla, with a bucket in her hand. We hurried down the lawn and leaped across the stream via the stepping stones to join her.

'I'm so sorry, Caro,' I panted as we followed the grassy path through the cow parsley, carefully mown for her brides, 'really sorry. I'll sort Molly out, you just tell me what to do.' I'd already briefed Anna in the car that over-the-top contriteness was the order of the day here. 'This is all you need with everything else going on. Oh Lord, what's happened to the marquee? Here, let me.'

Caro, still bent at the waist, was working her way along the pink and white canvas, wiping it down with great sweeping strokes. I picked up the bucket to move it closer to her.

'Yuck.' I dropped it abruptly. 'Smells like —'

'Puke, which is exactly what it is.' She straightened up to look at me, hand in the small of her back. 'We had a hooray wedding here yesterday, against my better judgement, and after they'd alfresco bonked their way round the bushes, they were sick in the herbaceous borders. Some hero helpfully sprayed the marquee with it too. We didn't have to feed the dog yesterday there was so much sick about, and I'm *still* finding condoms in the bushes.'

'Oh!'

She picked up her bucket and marched off to attend to another hot spot.

'*And* there was a punch-up on the dance floor,' she said grimly. 'And when poor Tim waded in to sort it out, he ended up with a split lip!'

Why did she do it, I wondered as I turned and followed her across the stream, Anna behind us. Why did *they* do it? For the money, of course, but – was it worth it? We set off back up the grassy slope of the garden at a brisk pace.

'And now Marcia Wentworth-White at Harrington Hall has decided *she's* doing weddings too so no doubt all my lovely Asians will flock up there and no one will come here except the fucking gentiles!' she hissed.

Ah. So that was it. Might explain her bad temper on the phone.

'But surely Marcia will charge more?' Anna and I jogged up the hill after her. 'I mean, Harrington Hall and all that – you'd be much better value for money.'

'That's what I'm hanging on to,' she said grimly as we kept pace. 'That's what's keeping me sane. That they'll price themselves out of the market. We'll see. Pigs.' She stopped in her tracks

'The Wentworth-Whites?'

'No, I've got to feed them, but yes, the Wentworth-Whites are actually, especially him, no manners at all. Frightfully nouveau.' She turned and headed off in the other direction, down towards the sties.

'Anyway, I'm going for the gay market.' She jutted her chin out determinedly as she hurried on. 'Tim's a bit nervous, but I'm convinced it's the way forward. I had a lovely couple come to look the other day, Jason and Edward. They wanted to know if Edward could get married in a dress. I said he could get married in mine as long as they didn't puke and leave condoms everywhere. Here, Dolores! Here, Crackling!' She rattled her bucket at the pig pen as we approached. 'Oh, and naturists too. I found a couple on the Internet who were looking for a venue but wanted to be stark naked, and all the congregation as well. Kosher! Kosher – HERE! I said fine, as long as no one got excited during the ceremony. Imagine – with this ring, I thee – ooh, now where shall I put it?' She cracked a rare smile. 'DOLORES! COME! BOADICEA – HERE!' she bellowed.

Five enormous ginger sows suddenly appeared from nowhere and charged at us, throwing themselves against the netting. Anna and I backed away nervously.

'Actually, you can help,' said Caro.

Help? In what way? Nothing practical, I hoped.

'If you distract them,' she went on, 'I can get to their trough at the other end.'

Distract them? What – with a few songs? A dance?

She handed me the sick bucket. 'Here jiggle this.' I recoiled in disgust. 'Oh, please.'

'Don't be silly, they'll eat anything.' She threw a handful of pig meal on top. 'Just shake it, they're pretty desperate, they'll smell it.'

They surely could. The pigs were huge and threw themselves convulsively against the netting as I jiggled nervously, and as Caro ran away.

'Where are you going?' I bleated.

'To pour feed into their trough down the other end,' she shouted. 'But they tip it over so I've got to right it first. Now jiggle the bucket – that's it!'

I jiggled furiously, nose wrinkled and averted, as down

the other end of the pen, Caro, a sack of meal over her shoulder, stole over the fence like a burglar and quickly righted the trough, poured in the rations, just as the pigs, realizing they'd been had, turned and charged. Caro nipped back over the fence just in time.

'What would they do if they caught you?' asked Anna, watching, awestruck. The sows were demolishing their food with what can only be described as sensational dispatch.

'Eat me, probably,' panted Caro, brushing herself down.

'No!'

'Yes, quite possibly,' replied her aunt calmly. 'Hungarian peasants have been known to fall asleep in their pig fields, and all that's found in the morning is a pile of bones.'

Anna's round eyes went back to the grunting, ravenous beasts. 'So . . . why d'you like them?' she whispered.

'Oh, it's all part of country life, isn't it?' Caro beamed. 'And anyway, they've always been here. Granny used to have them, you know. Your mum probably used to feed them!'

I think we all knew this wasn't true. Mum had kept pigs, but Maroulla and Mario, our farm workers, had pretty much looked after them, as farm workers did back in the good old days. And anyway, they'd been miles away, in the bottom meadow. I think I can safely say I'd barely set eyes on them.

'Where's Harriet?' I asked, peering into the pen. 'The blind one?'

'In a stable next to the house so I can keep an eye on her. The others don't let her get a look in on the food front. I'll see to her in a minute. Anyway, less of the pigs – we've got other fish to fry, haven't we?' She beamed at Anna and put an arm round her shoulders. 'Now, this *horse!*'

Anna smiled delightedly back, and Caro led her off. As I followed I heard Anna telling her how Mummy had forgotten her hat, and Caro saying never mind she could borrow Phoebe's, and I caught her eye briefly, thanking her. Caro might sound off on the phone to me, but she wouldn't rain on Anna's pony parade if she could help it: she was fond of her niece, and I blessed her for that. And wasn't I doing well too, I marvelled silently as we headed back towards the house. Carrying on with life. Going through the motions. Not howling.

'Take this to Harriet, would you?' Caro paused by the back door to pick up a bucketful of soggy bread and handed it to me. 'She's in the end stable in the yard. I'll meet you at the stables when I've got Anna kitted out.

'Is she safe?' I asked nervously.

'Oh, absolutely. She's a bit listless but she still likes to potter about.'

Under the circumstances I could hardly refuse and I went off to the yard wondering if they'd say that about me when this was all over. *She's a bit listless but she still likes to potter about.* I duly found Harriet in a shed, curled up in a corner. She looked smaller and sweeter than the other honking great sows, but I wasn't convinced I wanted to feed her by hand so I opened the door a crack, popped in the bucket and, remembering the Hungarian pile of bones, bolted the door firmly and retreated.

Caro and Anna were already in the stables when I got there.

'I caught her, finally, with Phil's help,' Caro called to me from inside a loosebox; she was putting a bridle on Molly, 'so I've popped her in here. Quite frisky, isn't she?'

'Not when we saw her,' I said. 'Oh, look, Anna, isn't she sweet?' Her nose was poking over the door and I went to stroke her. 'Oh!' Her ears went back and she bared her teeth. 'Not very friendly!'

'She didn't do that when you saw her?' Caro opened the door and led her out.

'No.'

She gave me an arch look as she put the saddle on. 'Disgusting tack. Presumably he threw it in for free?'

'Um. Yes.' I flicked Anna a look.

'Hm,' said Caro, who'd seen it. 'Paid through the nose. Thought so.' She pulled the stirrup down with a snap. 'Come on then, Anna, hop up.'

Anna took the reins and Caro gave her a leg up.

'We'll take her in the sand school,' Caro went on. 'I'd have put Jack on her first, but they're not back from school yet, and – oh!'

Anything else she might have said was lost in the wind, as Molly, feeling Anna's weight on her back, stood on her hind legs in a heraldic pose, then charged out of the yard, snatching the reins from Caro's hand, heading for the wide open spaces.

'SIT UP!' roared Caro as Anna bounced around like a ball bearing in the saddle. 'Don't lean forward!'

We raced after her, my heart in my throat, as Molly put her head down and rocketed full pelt across the buttercup field, ignoring the open gate to the sand school, galloping furiously into the distant blue yonder.

'Oh God, oh dear God,' I gasped, as Molly, spying ponies in the next field, galloped towards all that kept her from their society: a four-foot hedge. The ponies raised startled heads as they saw her. Molly put hers down and judged the take-off. How Anna, who was screaming now, stayed on, I'll never know, but as Molly soared through the air, taking most of the hedge with her, she soared too, lost both her stirrups, but still landed with a thump in the saddle, which I wasn't entirely sure was a blessing.

'Bail out!' I roared, cupping my hands round my mouth as I ran. 'Get off her, Anna!'

'Easier said than done,' panted Caro as we raced after her.

Meanwhile, to our right, behind another hedge, the one that bordered the lane, the school bus had stopped. Dozens of children's eyes and mouths widened in astonishment as they watched the rodeo show unfold, Anna's cousins amongst them. Molly was now precipitating down a grassy bank, the incline of which only increased her speed, in her determination to reach her new equine best friends, who, having encountered her already today were unconvinced they wanted her company, and were cavorting around their field tossing their heads, necks arched, nostrils flared. Molly, perhaps believing this antipathy had something to do with her human baggage rather than her sharp hoofs, gave an almighty buck, as if to truly announce her presence and calibre, thus discharging Anna, and sending her flying through the air, landing with a bump on her bottom.

'ANNA!' I screamed.

Her cousins by now had descended the bus and were flying, horrified, book bags and blazers waving in their hands, across the field, to the scene of the disaster. From different points of the compass we all arrived as one, to converge around her on the ground.

'Anna! Oh, darling, are you all right?' I flew to her side.

'NO!' she screamed.

She was in floods of tears, but even I could see that the alacrity with which she stood up and brushed herself down meant, thank God, only pride was bruised, and perhaps her bottom. Other than that, she was just a good deal shaken up. I wrapped her in my arms and she sobbed piteously on my shoulder. She couldn't actually agree that anything was broken, and she didn't think she had a pierced lung, as Phoebe helpfully suggested, or that her clavicle, which Henry insisted snapped like a wishbone – and he should know, he'd broken his twice in the scrum – was impaired. We all fussed around her, patting and consoling, until at length, her sobs turned to sniffing and gulps. A suggestion of strong tea was made by Jack, and Anna nodded stoically, consenting to being led away to the house by her cousins.

'Put lots of sugar in it, Jack,' commanded his mother. 'I'll come in a minute but I need to sort this bloody horse out.'

'And whisky?'

'No!'

'Daddy does sometimes.'

'Do not!'

'D'you want me to come too?' I called after them as

138

they led her away, hoping to escape the Bloody Horse, but Anna turned and shook her head vehemently.

'You flew that hedge,' Jack was saying to her, admiringly.

'I couldn't have sat it,' Phoebe agreed. 'I've been wanting to jump it for ages, but Mummy won't let me.'

I blessed them for bolstering her. They were always thrilled to have her in their midst, and now perhaps were pleased, in the nicest possible way, to be encouraging her in something she found difficult, but they excelled at. As Anna limped off, Phoebe's arm round her shoulders, where it had never rested before, Caro strode up to Molly. She was quietly grazing nearby as if butter wouldn't melt, and consented to having her reins seized without a murmur. What, me? her eyes seemed to say. Caro gave the reins a mighty yank.

'This is *not* a first pony!' she seethed. 'I can't believe you bought her!'

'She wasn't like that!' I wailed. 'When we saw her she was as quiet as a lamb, so docile. And Anna rode her beautifully. Trotted in circles, just like she does at the stables.'

'Drugged,' snapped Caro.

'No!' I breathed, shocked.

'Quite probably.' She led Molly off across the fields and back towards the stables. I stumbled after her. 'And this mare –' she stopped abruptly to stick her thumb in the side of Molly's mouth; she jerked it open and peered in – 'is four if she's a day. Probably brought over from Ireland and very recently broken, poor thing. Badly too, and then drugged to sell. It's disgraceful. We'll send her back immediately.'

When we got to the yard she threw Molly in a box.

Then she whipped her mobile from her jeans pocket, and punched out a number.

'Mr Docherty?' Her back straightened like a poker. 'It's Caroline Milligan here.'

And she was off. Giving it to him straight, and in no uncertain terms. Letting him know he was a liar, a thief, and no judge of horse-flesh to boot, and that her sister-in-law's cheque must be returned forthwith. This, Mr Docherty clearly declined to do, no doubt informing her in slow, undulating tones that the cheque had been cleared, the transaction made, the deal struck, with both parties seemingly satisfied.

But Caro wasn't finished. 'Except that this mare has been drugged,' she hissed. 'And unfortunately for you, it shat on my sister-in-law's foot, and that shit is still on that shoe, Mr Docherty, and I shall have it tested forthwith. If traces of promazine are not found in the droppings, I shall be very much surprised!'

An equally surprised silence greeted this, as Caro, holding the phone away from her ear, triumphantly demonstrated to me, eyebrows raised. Finally, Mr Docherty found his voice. A compromise of sorts was reached: Caro agreed she would return the horse to save him the effort, and he, in turn, would return the cheque. She snapped her phone shut with a satisfied click.

'How did you know about the shoe?' I yelped.

'Anna told me, just now, when we went to get her a hat. Together with a hysterical account of you feeling fetlocks and attempting to buy a horse unridden. No malice intended, of course.'

Of course, I thought, following her back to the house,

biting my thumbnail. There never was. But why did I feel recently my smarty-pants daughter laughed at me, not with me? Smarty-pants! I'd never thought of her like that. I flushed. And thank God she *was* smart, actually, in this instance; thank God she'd recounted the story to Caro, who'd had the presence of mind – and the nerve – to use it. Otherwise I'd be one thousand five hundred pounds out of pocket, with a thoroughly dangerous, practically unbroken horse on my hands. Yes, thank God I was stupid.

The children were munching cake when we got to the kitchen. No plates, so crumbs everywhere, and trails of tea where they'd dripped one tea bag after another to the bin, like so many snails, along with pools of milk, which they were incapable of pouring without spilling. Caro pointed this out as she bustled around, putting the cake on a plate, wiping surfaces, admonishing her offspring. Anna's equilibrium had clearly returned, though, and she was laughing at Jack's impersonation of her face as she flew through the air and hit the ground. Henry was shouting, 'No – it was like this!' and pulling something even more wide-eyed and aghast, like Edvard Munch's *The Scream*. Anna and Phoebe roared with laughter, and then they all shuffled off to the playroom to watch interminable reruns of *Friends*. Phoebe wanted to know if Anna preferred Chandler or Joey: 'Anna, Anna! Chandler or Joey?' and then instantly agreeing, 'Yeah, Joey's a legend,' whilst Jack showed off, balancing a plate on the end of a hockey stick, Anna laughing and seizing the remote control, the balance of power restored.

'Nice for her to see them,' I remarked, as Caro shut the door on them and put the kettle on the Aga for us. Mum's old blue Aga: I knew the exact squeak of the joint as you raised the left lid, which no amount of oil could soothe. I'd never quite got used to Caro moving around this kitchen – cursing the way the window over the sink always stuck as she tried to throw it open, muttering about the loose floorboard – which was ridiculous, really, because she'd been moving around it for years.

'I've always said we'd like to see more of Anna.'

Damn. Quick as a flash she'd leaped on that, and I sensed that if I said, well, I'm making the effort now, here she is, she'd flash me a look that said, when it suits you. Which was right, I supposed. Suddenly I felt very tired.

'Look,' I said wearily, 'let's forget this pony business. Anna probably isn't quite up to owning one yet, and I can see it's going to be a lot of hassle for you. We'll go back to having lessons at the riding stables. She'll understand.'

'Nonsense,' said Caro, flicking through her address book as she stood with her back to me at the dresser. 'She's set her heart on it now. And anyway, you've promised.' She turned to give me a look that suggested *she* wasn't the sort of mother to go back on her word. 'You just went about it the wrong way, that's all. If only you'd listened to me in the first place, we wouldn't be in this mess. Ah, here we are. Camilla Gavin.'

Why did I let her talk to me like this? As if I was a child? Had I always? I sank into my tea, knowing she was right.

'Who's Camilla Gavin?' I asked meekly as she punched out a number.

'She's the ex-DC of our Pony Club. A terrifying woman in her day, but she's mellowed slightly, and she does have some terrific ponies. Her children move on so swiftly they're all on horses now, and Pamela Martin told me she'd be happy to let one of the ponies go out on loan.'

'On loan!' I perked up. 'You mean I don't even have to buy it?'

'No, but you have to look after it, scrupulously, which will be much harder work than that screw from Docherty's, which you could throw in a field and forget about. It'll probably be quite old, so it'll feel the cold, and it's bound to be kept in. There'll be stables to muck out, rugs to change . . .'

'Oh, but that's marvellous. If I don't have to buy it – and yes, of course I'll look after it! I'm not working, after all . . .'

I ignored her pointed, 'Quite.'

All of a sudden I was back in my original fantasy, tending to a dear little old white pony, brushing its mane as it gazed sleepily at me, giving it an apple . . . and not having to part with any filthy lucre. I sat up.

'Excellent, Caro. Definitely ring her.'

'Which is precisely what I was going to do before you went charging off to Lenny the— Camilla? Camilla, it's Caroline Milligan here!'

I sank guiltily into my tea as her voice went up an octave. She whinnied on in the secret language of horsy women, asking about laminitis, clipping, boxing, proficiency in traffic, but in the nicest possible way, of course, because this was clearly a woman Caro looked up to and respected, unlike me, who she despaired of. I watched as she listened to Camilla's responses, eyes bright, cheeks flushed, bust thrust out: almost as if she were talking to a lover, I thought. I'd seen Caro on the phone to many boys. Seen that light in her eyes.

'Oh, he sounds *orfully* sweet!' she was saying in a voice she'd never used at school. 'Yes, I *do* remember, came second in the crorss country!'

When had we become these two women, I wondered, as, phone still clamped to her ear, and in a pair of jeans she wouldn't have been seen dead in years ago, too short, too flared, Caro marched across the room to swat a bluebottle on the window with her Boden catalogue. She wiped the sink while she was there, tossing the dishcloth back in efficiently. When had we stopped throwing away the washing up, rifling through the ashtrays in our Summertown flat for butts long enough to relight? When did we start noticing the dripping tea bags, and when would they, our children, start noticing too, and become different people? Long may they drip, I thought vehemently, because if I found her so changed, how did she find me? Arrogant? Aloof? That seemed to be her constant theme.

As I listened to the gales of laughter coming from the playroom, I mourned our younger selves. When did Caro stop being the first person I'd go to in a crisis, the sort of crisis I had now? When did we stop getting so pissed we had to hold each other's hair back as we threw up, stop borrowing each other's clothes, painting false freckles on each other's noses with eyeliner, giggling over the Cathy and Claire page in *Jackie*, lying on the floor and doing up each other's jeans with the hook of a coat hanger? When did we become the sort of women who watched each other's children's exam results like hawks, wanting so much more for them than we'd ever wanted for ourselves? I longed for those halcyon faraway days, before we'd had to grow up and marry and have children and discover our husbands had . . . don't go there, Evie. Don't. I sank into my tea.

'Oh, Camilla you're a *complete* star . . . Yes, I *know* he's a poppet, I've *seen* him. Does a dear little dressage test . . . Well, that's *orfully* kind of you. Are you sure? Tack as well? . . . Shall I pick him up? . . . Golly, if you *could* pop him over . . . sooper!' I shut my eyes. Stop it, Evie, you're exaggerating. Caro laughed down the phone in a confidential whinny. 'Well, mother's clueless, orbviously – haw haw!' Thanks, Caro. 'But daughter's mustard keen . . . Yes, *really* light hands. Nice little seat too, and with a few more lessons and a schoolmaster like Hector . . . Gosh, thank you *soo* much, Camilla. *Soo* sweet of you . . . Ya, you too. Toodle-oo!'

My eye was twitching manically as she put the phone down with a decisive click.

'There. Sorted.'

Sorted. Not a word she'd use to Camilla, I'd warrant.

'She's bringing him over Saturday week and you can have him on a renewable yearly loan.'

'But why would someone do that? Why not just sell him? Presumably if he's so flaming good, he's worth a bob or two?' I was deliberately lapsing into cockney slang, now. I was Fagin, about to pick a pocket or two; either that or Eliza Doolittle.

'Because she's attached to him and she doesn't want him falling into the wrong hands. Doesn't want someone like Lenny Docherty getting his hands on him and selling him for dog meat.'

'Oh. Right.' I nodded, suitably rebuked. Just then Tim limped in through the back door on a gust of wind, hair tousled and smelling of fresh air and hay, albeit with a split lip. It was a relief to see him.

'Evie! What a treat!' He swept his flat cap off, which, like Dad, he still wore in the fields, and swooped to kiss me. I beamed. Someone was pleased to see me.

'What's Lenny Docherty got his hands on now then?' he said, picking up the fag end of our conversation and going to the sink to wash his hands. He rubbed his face vigorously with his wet hands, making it glow bright red, again like Dad, then tossed the lump of coal tar soap back in its dish. He hobbled to a chair and sank into it gratefully, lifting his leg up on a stool with both hands.

'Nothing, happily. Evie bought a horse from him, but don't worry,' she added hastily, as he turned to look at me in horror, 'it's going back.'

'You bought a horse from Lenny the Liar?'

'Well, obviously I didn't *know* he was a liar.'

'The whole of effing Oxfordshire knows he's a liar! He was a liar twenty years ago when he blagged his way into that yard, and he's been lying ever since!'

'Yes, well, I didn't know that.'

'Come on, Evie, he was dealing dodgy horses when you lived here – where have you been?'

His incredulity was quite hard to take, actually.

'Well, clearly on another planet,' I said with a fixed smile.

'Clearly!' he answered, pretty sourly for him. He balled the tea towel he'd been using to dry his hands and tossed it up on the draining board. 'I can't believe you're so stupid sometimes.'

He heaved himself heavily to his feet and left the room. I held it together until he was safely in the downstairs loo, where, in the manner of a man who could, within the hearing of his wife and sister, he embarked on a very noisy pee. And then I put my hands over my face and burst into tears.

## 11

Caro was beside me in seconds, swooping to my side, astonished.

'Oh, now don't be silly, Evie. Gracious, it's not that bad, it's only a pony!'

'I-it's not that,' I gulped, gasping for breath, 'it's e-e-everything!'

In another moment she'd kicked the kitchen door shut with her foot and in a swift, economical movement had a chair pulled up beside me and an arm round my shoulders. 'Everything?'

Was it me, or was there a tremor of excitement in her voice?

'It's Ant and Anna and – oh God – it's all such a mess, Caro! And I'm not supposed to talk about it but it all wells up inside me and sometimes I think I'm going to burst!' As I paused to wipe my face with the back of a trembling hand I saw her forehead furrow, genuinely concerned now. A bit of trouble in her sister-in-law's camp was secretly to be gloated over – Anna caught at school with a shampoo bottle of vodka, perhaps, or failing a piano exam. But a lot, a big mess, threatened the whole family.

'What?' she said anxiously. 'Evie, tell me. Is it Ant? Is he having an affair?'

I shook my head. It was full of snot and tears and felt terribly heavy, and the tears just wouldn't stop.

'No, he's not, but he was, did have one – well, a fling – and I just can't – just can't seem . . .' But it was no good. I felt my face buckle as I dissolved again.

Caro swung me round to face her, both hands on my shoulders. 'He had an affair? Ant?' I could tell she was flabbergasted. Happily we heard the front door slam as Tim exited stage left. 'But – but that is *so* unbelievable! He's just not the type! When? Recently?'

'No,' I looked up; managed to confine myself to some hiccupy shuddering. 'No, years ago. Years and years ago, when we were engaged.' I felt terribly calm suddenly, having said it. And flat. I sat back in my chair, wiped my face with my sleeve.

'Oh!' She sat back too. 'You mean – not when you were married?'

'I mean about a month after we got engaged.'

Her eyes roved back, rolling away the years, remembering. Recalling that time. She shrugged helplessly. 'Oh, well, I suppose . . . I mean, an awful lot was going on then, and he was very young—'

'Not that young, thirty.'

'No, but so much had happened . . .'

She meant Neville. And it struck me that other people had wondered at us marrying so soon after, when I hadn't.

'It was probably just a flash in the pan. A sort of desperate last sowing of wild oats, before settling down for good.'

'It was. It was a one-night stand, with a barmaid.'

'Oh, well, there you are! What are you getting so upset about? I mean, sure, it's a shame it happened a month *after* you got engaged, and not – I don't know – a couple of months before, and I can see that as far as you're concerned he's got a slightly blemished record, which is a shock and a shame, but that's *all* it is, Evie, a bit of a shame. You've got to see it in that context, not something to get worked up about all these years.'

'Caro, there's a child.'

She stared at me. Her eyes grew huge. 'A child?'

'Yes.'

'How d'you know?'

'She wrote to us, the other day. Said she wanted to get to know her father.'

She caught her breath. 'No!'

'Yes!' I wailed.

'And he didn't know?'

'Had no idea! Why should he? A quick roll in the hay, never sees the girl again – why would he?'

There was a highly charged silence as Caro digested this. The station clock ticked on remorselessly above the window. She didn't take her eyes off me. I watched them turn from horror to steel. Then: 'How do we know it's true? I mean, some barmaid from – where?'

'Sheffield.'

'Sheffield! Who gets up the duff, having slept with God knows how many men—'

'Exactly,' I said quickly. 'And sees Ant's picture on the back of his latest book.'

'Is that how she—'

'Yes! Well, no. I don't *know*, for sure, but you can imagine—'

'Of course you can!' she agreed emphatically. 'God, you can just see it, can't you? A single mother and her daughter, scheming together, writing to him, some – some Sharon—'

'Stacey.'

'Stacey! Eh up, Stacey lass, let's see if we can't get soom brass outa him.'

'You think?' I said anxiously, loving her.

'Oh, for sure! Oh, this has scam written all *over* it, Evie. I mean, why wait till now? Why not earlier? Ten years ago?'

'Because she's sixteen now,' I said, playing devil's advocate. 'She wanted to wait.'

Caro made a sceptical face. 'So she says. But it's a bit of a coincidence, isn't it? The Byron book's been out a year – the paperback's just come out.'

'The letter arrived a week after the paperback was launched,' I said quickly.

'You see! And it was all over the place. In the supermarkets even, with Ant's photo on the back—'

'Tesco's—'

'Tesco's!'

'Asda—'

'*Asda!* And she – the mother – pops her Turkey Twizzlers in her basket and thinks, I know that face . . . blimey. He must be worth a bob or two.' Caro was pink with zeal, fired up.

'Yes, I know, that's what I thought. But, Caro,' I struggled with the bald facts, 'Ant doesn't see it like that.

He thinks it could be true, that she could be his, and if she is, well then, he wants to do the right thing. Wants to acknowledge her.'

Caro's mouth contracted like a cat's bottom. 'What, bring her into the family?' she squeaked.

Anyone would think we were the Windsors.

'Well, yes. Introduce her to Anna.' My face twitched involuntarily at this.

'Christmas, birthdays,' Caro breathed, a faraway look in her eye, as both of us, I know, had a mental vision of Christmas, which was always at the farm: everyone crowded in the dining room, holly over the pictures, huge turkey, and, despite our differences, very jolly. All the cousins, Mum, Felicity, Caro, Tim, me, Ant, except now, next to Ant – a dumpy, peroxide-blonde girl, her mother too perhaps, a Myra Hindley lookalike, with hard, probing eyes, glinting as they eyed up the silver candlesticks, the crystal glasses, none of it terribly valuable, but worth an awful lot more than a few china kittens that sat in the window of their high-rise in Sheffield. Worth a bit more than the souvenir from Magaluf on the telly. And then the children's faces, confused, appalled at this cuckoo in their nest. Having to explain, nervously, to their friends on Boxing Day, at the usual drinks party at the farm, where all the neighbours congregated, that this was, um, another cousin. Anna's sister.

Caro's face darkened. 'Over my dead body!'

'That's what I said,' I gulped. 'When Ant told me. That's *exactly* what I said!'

We gazed at each other, and her eyes shone into mine in a way that they hadn't done for years, a way that reminded me of when we'd had a plan, years ago; a party to crash perhaps, a window that needed climbing into. One particular window sprang to mind, a high one, our most daring of all, at a May Ball. Naturally we hadn't been invited, being only lowly shop assistants, but nevertheless, we'd put on our Monsoon ball gowns, and after ten o'clock, when we knew everyone had eaten and the dancing begun, raced down Cornmarket, skirts lifted, giggling wildly, finding our building. Slingbacks in our teeth, Caro had shoved me up a drainpipe and I'd hauled her after me. On to the roof we'd climbed, jumping across to another, then through a skylight, recced days ago, dropping down into the ladies' loo. A few undergraduates applying their lippy in the mirror had looked up, astonished. 'Just popped out for a breather,' smiled Caro, who had all the neck, brushing off her hands. And then we'd danced until dawn. It was that same look, I realized, as we'd planned Operation May Ball in our flat in Summertown, that same steely, determined look, that she had now.

'My dead body and yours too then,' she said grimly. 'They'll have to climb over a couple of stiffs before they gain access to *my* house. Before they start believing they're one of us!'

Later, when we'd both calmed down a bit, we walked around the garden, arms tightly folded, heads bent, a couple of middle-aged women, closer than we'd been for years, discussing DNA, the fraud squad, getting them arrested, maybe even a court order to stay away.

'Deported?' I stopped. Looked at her in astonishment.

'Well, they're probably not even English, Evie! Probably – I don't know – Nigerian or something!'

I frowned. 'Wouldn't that make passing as Ant's daughter a bit – you know – difficult? A bit easy to suss?'

'Well, Poles then. God, we're crawling with them round here, picking strawberries, asparagus, wanting to get rich quick then bugger off back to Prague with their stash, feed their starving families, spread it round the bread queues . . .' Caro's grip on foreign affairs was about as firm as mine. 'Poles on the make, I bet you.'

Tim approached, loping across the lawn towards us.

'Don't tell him,' hissed Caro. 'He'll look on the bright side. Always does.'

It was true, he would. And would probably agree with Ant that she deserved to be heard; deserved to be listened to. He would be generous-spirited, nicer, as men, in my experience, often tend to be. Unlike me and Caro who'd got a sixteen-year-old bound and gagged, and in the back of a cattle truck, bouncing down a dusty track and back across the border. He looked a bit sheepish.

'Sorry, Evie.'

'What?'

'About the horse. I was a bit . . . you know.'

'Oh! Oh God, don't be silly, Tim. Couldn't matter less. Anyway, I deserved it. I'm a fool. Always have been.'

'No, that's my province.' He grinned and pulled my hair as he limped off.

I wondered vaguely what he meant by that as he ambled away. 'His hip doesn't look great,' I said distractedly.

'Never does at this time of day. He's been on it too long. Phil and I can do whatever needs doing, and I keep

154

telling him to rest it, but he won't. But it is getting better. The doctor said it'll take three months.'

I nodded. 'And he's fit?'

'Oh God, is he. Strong as an ox. Hasn't deterred him in the bedroom, either. There was I thinking, oh joy, three months off games – which was what the hospital recommended, incidentally – but not a bit of it. The moment he was out of hospital he was chasing me round the bedroom on crutches. We became very familiar with "SPOD".'

'SPOD?'

'"Sexual Problems of the Disabled", a little booklet they helpfully provide you with when you leave hospital, complete with graphic illustrations. I tell you, Evie, there are positions in that book you wouldn't attempt if you were able-bodied, let alone disabled. Forget *The Joy of Sex*, "SPOD" has opened up a whole new erotic world for your brother. He can't imagine what we've been doing for the last eighteen years.'

I giggled.

'I keep reading articles about men being too stressed and exhausted to make love to their wives,' she went on, 'and here I am, with the most stressed-out, exhausted hop-along cripple imaginable, who works from dawn till dusk, is up to his neck in debt and *still* wants to try the illustration on page thirty-two!'

I laughed. 'You'd be worried if he didn't.'

'Try me,' she said drily. 'He even tried to slip in some rodeo sex the other day.'

'What's rodeo sex?'

Caro cleared her throat and pretended to read from

a booklet. 'The couple adopt the doggy position. The gentleman then calls out an ex-girlfriend's name and sees how long he can stay on for.'

'No!'

She laughed. 'No, quite right, not in "SPOD". He found it in *Viz*. But you know Tim.' She grinned. 'Anyway, I expect you're right. I expect I'd be worried if he wasn't up for it. And Ant's the same, isn't he?'

''Fraid so,' I said quickly, forcing a smile. I felt sick at his name, and she saw and squeezed my arm. But it wasn't just that. Ant wasn't the same, these days. And I wasn't someone who talked about sex with girlfriends, never had, but Caro and I had always had a bit of a mutual moan about our over-sexed husbands and how thrilled we were when we went to stay with friends and they apologized for the single beds in the spare room. But at the moment . . . well, this was all such a shock, of course. Put us off our stride. And before that, all that fuss with the book. Too much excitement.

Nevertheless, when Anna and I left the farm with Caro hissing in my ear not to worry and to tell absolutely *no one*, and when I'd dropped Anna off at her piano lesson at the end of our road, it was still on my mind. I found myself executing my usual eleven-point turn in Little Clarendon Street, and heading back into town.

I parked in my customary high street spot, unknown to tourists and shoppers alike, and head down, collar up, in the manner of a woman on a mission, hurried towards Marks and Spencer. Up the escalator I glided, then into the requisite department. I hovered there, in Lingerie, fingering the white cotton briefs, but secretly eyeing up the black silk on the next rack. I felt furtive, like a man in a mac. Ridiculous. And ridiculous that I'd never owned any, I thought, strolling over casually to look at them. Just to flick through them. Why, even my fourteen-year-old daughter had frilly knickers, tiny pink lacy things – lingerie, I suppose – which I gazed at in wonder as I took them from the tumble dryer. Whilst I had pants, which were always white, and came in packs of three, and eventually went grey. Occasionally I bought a pretty bra, but never anything overtly sexy, just something that did the job and was comfortable and *certainly* never black, which I somehow associated with sin. A bit grubby. But . . . men liked that, didn't they? I took a deep breath.

Half an hour later, back in the safety of my bedroom, and feeling like a tramp and a whore rolled into one, I took the black lacy bra and knickers – with red bows on, for God's sake – from the bag. Too much. Oh, *far* too much. What would Ant say? Well, he'd love them, of course he would. Any man would. And it was only M&S, not Ann Summers. Oh – and a suspender belt. I'd never in my life worn one before, only tights. Hands fluttering with excitement, I whipped off my clothes and put my new purchases on; didn't actually know how to put the suspender belt on. Oh, round the waist? Really?

I tiptoed furtively to the mirror that faced the end of the bed. Stared. How extraordinary. I looked completely different. *Completely.* Like, well, like a woman in a magazine! I turned around. Lordy. And my flesh looked so . . . so forbidden, somehow. So wanton. Too much of it, obviously – I sucked in my tummy – but still . . . I lay down. Yes, I did. On the bed. Gazed sideways into the mirror. Had to shift around a bit to see, but . . . yes. Very *Playboy*. I raised one leg coquettishly in the air, rolled my eyes. Just as I was fondling the bedpost, pouting—

'Hi!' Up the stairs.

I leaped off the bed. Christ! He was home. And six in the evening was not the moment. It might have been once, but not now. He'd think it mighty peculiar to find me trussed up in black lace. I threw on a wraparound dress and was just tying it up as he came in.

'Hello, darling!' I said overbrightly.

'Hi.' He seemed almost not to notice me. He crossed the room and sat down heavily on the side of the bed.

'Ant? What's wrong?' My mouth dried. I stared across at the top of his bent head.

'Nothing.' Flatly. 'No, nothing's wrong.' He picked up the plastic M&S bag. Fiddled with it distractedly. Put it down again. 'It's just, she – Stacey . . .' he paused to let the requisite shock waves rip through me at her name, 'she emailed me. She's going to come. One Sunday.'

'Right,' I breathed. I sat on the bed beside him. All the feverish activity of the last few moments evaporated like so many raindrops on a window. The silence of the empty house closed in on us.

'She . . . emailed you?'

'Yes. We have done that, once or twice. Quicker, obviously.'

'Obviously.' Except I didn't know. Didn't know she had his email address. I knew he had hers. My heart quickened.

'She got mine from the college. Left me a message. I had to answer it.'

'Of course. Did she say which Sunday?'

'No. Just . . . sometime soon.'

He turned to me. Took my hand. His blue eyes behind his glasses were full. Deadly serious. 'Evie, you know what this means. If she's coming, if this is actually happening, we have to tell Anna.'

Do we? my head shrieked. Why can't we just tell her to sod off? Why couldn't this nightmare just go away?

'Yes,' I agreed.

'And, Evie,' he swallowed. His eyes skittered past me to the window, then back again. 'I'd like to do it, if you don't mind. Alone. I'd like to . . . find my own words. Explain to her in my own way.'

Without me. I felt my chest tighten. Felt panic rising. But, yes, of course he did. And what a relief, in some ways: leave me out of it. It was his mess, he could jolly well extricate himself. Nothing to do with me. But . . . equally, I was to be excluded. Why? What did he want to say to her that he couldn't say to me? Didn't want me to hear?

'But, Ant,' I licked my lips, 'surely this is all going much too fast? We don't know anything yet. Don't even know if she's yours!'

'Oh, she's mine,' he said quietly, but it was a quietness that chilled me. He got off the bed and walked to the window. His hands in his pockets. 'She's mine all right.'

# 12

'How do you know?' I felt faint with fear. Light-headed. A pulse was beginning to throb in my temple.

'Evie . . . I haven't been entirely straight with you.'

His back was to me. I stared at the yoke of his blue and white checked shirt. At the fair hair curling on his collar. Oh God.

'You mean . . . it went on much longer?' I whispered. 'Not just that once? That one night?'

'No,' he turned, looked surprised. 'No, that was true. It only happened once. But . . . well. She wasn't quite a barmaid. She was working in the pub, yes, for a few weeks, for a bit of pocket money, but . . .' He paused, swallowed. 'She was a student.'

'A student?'

'Yes.'

'One of yours?'

'Yes.'

A containerload of emotions hit me hard, like a goods wagon skidding off the rails, everything spilled out chaotically on the tracks. Not a barmaid. One of his students. Bright. Clever. An Oxford undergraduate, the kind of liaison he'd always, *always* frowned on, had no time for amongst his colleagues. It did happen – of course it happened – but not to Ant, not to my husband.

'How old?' I croaked.

'Eighteen.'

Eighteen. A first year. And he'd have been thirty. Questions crowded my mind. Fought to be heard, elbowing each other out of the way, like so many hands shooting up. How? Why?

'She was in my English poetry group, so I saw her – obviously in lectures – but on a one-to-one basis too, in tutorials. And that was her special interest, nineteenth-century poetry. The Romantic Poets. Byron in particular.'

Byron. His speciality. A shared interest.

'Very bright?' I whispered.

'Yes. Very clever.'

That hurt. Oh, that hurt. And there I'd been, pedalling around Oxford on a bicycle pretending to be clever. Romantic fiction of a different nature in my basket; less *Troilus and Criseyde*, more doctors and nurses.

'Pretty?'

He looked at his feet. Silly question. Gorgeous. Your worst nightmare, Evie. Ten years younger, razor sharp, drop-dead gorgeous. Big tits too, no doubt.

'Don't answer that,' I snarled. I fought for breath. Then composure.

'What happened? How did it . . . ?'

He made a helpless gesture, his arms rising then flopping to his sides. His shoulders sagged. 'How do these things happen? Slowly. Imperceptibly. It was all . . . so unspoken. So . . . pure.'

I nearly vomited; put my hand to my mouth.

'I noticed her quite soon, obviously. It would take a very unobservant teacher not to. She stood out. But not in an obvious, Hedda Gabler sort of way . . .'

I pressed my nails into my palms. Always the literary allusions. He knew I didn't know who the sodding hell Hedda Gabler was.

'More in a Jade Goody sort of way?' I snapped.

He frowned. 'Who?'

'Forget it,' I muttered. 'Go on.'

'Well, as I say, nothing happened. Nothing tangible. It was just . . .' he struggled to explain, 'well, I realized I looked forward to seeing her, to our tutorials. Began counting the days. I found myself poring over her essays when she handed them in, marvelling that her interpretation, her conceptual analysis, was so like mine . . .'

I stared at the cream carpet. This was the thing about Ant. He would be honest. I'd get it warts and all now. Except, obviously, there wouldn't be a wart in sight. About how he'd gazed at her hair – Titian, no doubt – in a dusty shaft of sunlight as he sat behind his desk, as she read haltingly from 'Tintern Abbey'. I imagined the scene: the young don, his even younger student, Ant listening as she spoke of her love for Wordsworth, nodding, smiling encouragingly as she described how she felt she was with him as he wandered the valleys of his native Lake District, how his romance with nature was her romance too. Oh shit.

'And sometimes, in lectures, I'd find myself just looking at her, directing the lecture at her, embarrassingly. As if she was the only one in the room. And in tutorials, I found I had to sit a long way away from her, over by the window, looking out at the quad to concentrate; couldn't sit too close. And then when we walked to lunch, her to halls and me to the Buttery, well, sometimes our arms would brush together and I'd feel—'

'Yes, I get the picture Ant!' I shrieked. 'You fucking fancied her!' For an intelligent man he was remarkably stupid. 'You don't have to walk me through the lightning bolt!'

'Sorry. I thought you wanted—'

'I do, but I can do without the glimpses you got of her bra as you strolled through the quad together. I can paint my own nightmarish scenes!'

'It wasn't like that. I mean, I didn't just feel a sexual desire – that's what I'm trying to explain. Well, of course I did. I did feel that, but what I felt more, was . . .'

Oh, *Ant*. I shut my eyes. Spare me. Spare me Love. He didn't even know the word he was grappling for. 'Something more cerebral,' I gabbled quickly, deflecting him. 'A higher plateau, a meeting of minds?'

'Yes,' he looked at me, surprised. 'Yes, that was it.'

No, Ant. No, it wasn't.

'I . . . couldn't stop thinking about her. I knew it was wrong, dreadful. She was so young, so impressionable, but everywhere I went, every lecture I went to, every faculty meeting, I'd look out of the windows, hoping to see her, hoping she'd pass by . . .'

I felt prickly with sweat. Damp under the arms.

'Why didn't you break up with me?' I whispered, struggling to maintain some control. 'Tell me you'd met someone else?'

He hung his head. 'I meant to tell you. To be honest with you. Not to break up with you. After all, I knew it was hopeless. She was a student, for God's sake.'

163

'So you kept your options open. You couldn't have her, so – hey, let's just stick it out with good old Evie.'

'No! No, Evie, I loved you. We were so good together, *are* good together. I was just very confused. I knew this was just a passing infatuation, I tried to put her from my mind. And once I did try to tell you about it.' He looked at me, pleadingly. 'At the farm. In bed that afternoon, just before—'

'Yes, yes, I know.' I got up quickly from the bed. He had tried. Of course he had. That terrible day. Minutes before Neville Carter had drowned. *Evie . . . there's something you need to know.*

I went to the other window in our bedroom, the pretty little round one, like a porthole, with the circle of stained glass in the middle. We'd found it in Bath, on a long weekend, hustled it home and got a builder to knock a circular hole in the bedroom wall, pop it in. My arms were folded tightly around me as I gazed out to the street, transformed to a riot of colour through the stained glass.

'And then, when Neville died . . .' Ant paused; beside me, but looking out of his clearer window.

I turned to him, incredulous. 'You felt you owed it me? To marry me?'

'No, of *course* not, Evie. But we were so . . . so in it together. And suddenly, what I felt for – for Stacey's mother – seemed so frivolous, in the light of what had happened. It belonged to another age, a carefree, care*less* age. One I no longer inhabited. It felt so wrong. I'd elevated it in my mind to something courtly and noble, and all at once it became . . . fancying a student. Suddenly

I was the sort of man who let children drown while I shagged my girlfriend – oh, and meanwhile, lusted after my pupils.' He hung his head. 'I hated myself. I took a long, hard look at myself. Walked all the way around and thought, no. It was a wake-up call.' He began to blink rapidly. 'But I didn't just marry you because it was the right thing to do, Evie. I married you because I loved you, and realized I'd been temporarily diverted.'

I stared at him. He clearly believed that. I didn't, but he did. He'd talked himself into believing this girl was all part of his shame, and being a good, nice, decent man, he believed it.

I swallowed. 'OK, Ant. Quick as you can, canter me through the next bit, there's a good chap.'

He spread his hands out, palms up, a despairing gesture. 'There isn't much to tell. You and I got engaged, and then a few weeks later I went out for a drink one night, when you wanted to watch something on television, and I went for a walk through the city and ended up at the King's Head.'

'Did you know she was working there?'

'Yes.'

'And you stayed till closing time and walked her home?'

'Yes.'

'And it was a mild night and you walked down by the river, past Magdalen Bridge – where was she, Balliol?'

'Yes.'

'And then you took her in your arms and—'

'Yes, *yes*! Stop it, Evie. I'm not proud of it.'

'I need to know.'

'Well, you *do* know.'

I breathed in deeply. Let the breath out shakily. 'Yes, I know. You felt trapped. You felt you were getting married out of force of circumstance, and you felt you had unfinished business and you finished it, in a field, by Magdalen Bridge.'

He hung his head.

'Did you feel it was finished, Ant? Is that why you never saw her again?'

'I . . . yes. I felt terrible. Worse. So I decided – we, decided, we talked about it – that that was it. I switched my tutorial with her to another student, she had another don so I didn't have to see her, and she stopped taking my lectures. Changed to Metaphysical Poets. And then a few weeks later, she just wasn't there any more. I realized she'd gone. I asked another student, a friend of hers, casually, in the cloisters one day, and was told she'd gone home. Back to Sheffield. Was homesick, or something, thought Oxford was too much for her. I hoped she'd transferred to a northern university, was reading English up there.'

'And you never checked? Never found out?'

'No.'

'And have you thought about her since?'

'No!' He turned, almost frightened. He came across the room to me, took my hands in his. His eyes were wide, pleading. 'I mean, once or twice, obviously, but no, I've been happily married to you, Evie, ever since. It was over seventeen years ago! I've never looked at another woman, truthfully, since then. Not in that way. It was something I needed to get out of my system, I suppose.' He shrugged helplessly. 'A last hurrah, call it what you will. The final nerves of a single man about to go down for life – I don't think that's so unusual.'

No. It wasn't that unusual. What was unusual were the circumstances. I took my hands from his; walked back to the bed. My legs were a bit wobbly. I needed to sit down. I ran my hands through my hair. Then I shut my eyes and covered them with my hands in an effort to think. I pressed my fingertips into my sockets. Then I dropped them, turned to face him.

'What was her name, Ant?'

As I said it, I saw something pass across his eyes. Something wary. A shadow. I watched his eyes slither to the window. Ant's eyes didn't slither about like that. Some colour rose in his cheeks. He swallowed.

'Isabella,' he whispered. 'Her name is Isabella.'

I flinched as if I'd been struck. I stared at him, horrified.

'Isabella? Anna *Isabella*? You called our *child* after her?'

I gazed at him incredulously. He looked helpless, caught.

'Evie, look. It wasn't like that. I just liked the name, I . . .'

I needed something to throw, to hurl, and I needed it quickly. I'd never had the physical urge to hurt before, but I had it now, and as I got to my feet I picked up the first thing that came to hand. A jar of moisturizer, as it happened. L'Oréal, because I'm worth it. It was on my dressing table – small, round, but good and heavy – and I hurled it at his head. Happily he saw it coming, ducked, and it went flying through the window behind him with a spectacular smash, glass flying everywhere, sailing out to the empty street below.

I wasn't far behind. Not through the window, obviously, but seizing my bag and my car keys from a chair, I ran from the room, slamming the door behind me. But a moment later I was back, hurtling across to face my husband again, to deliver my parting shot.

'Well, you're not trapped now, Ant!' I screamed in his face. 'You're free as a bird. Why don't you sod off to Sheffield?' I was shaking with anger. Positively vibrating with rage. 'Sod off to your ready-made family up there, to your other daughter, the mother of your other child, why don't you? You could slot in just like that!' I snapped my fingers in his face.

He stood there, white and shaken, gazing at me dumbly. Then I turned and left. Across the landing, down the stairs, jumping the last two steps, and into the front hall, just as an astonished Anna, who'd walked back from her piano lesson, was coming into the kitchen via the back door. She unwound a silk scarf from her neck, put her music down on the kitchen table, and gazed at me, astonished.

'What's wrong?'

'Ask your father!' I snarled.

I exited via the front door, slamming it hard behind me.

Outside in the street I stood for a second on the pavement, holding my head. I had to, actually: thought it might come off; felt I might go pop. The houses opposite were swaying alarmingly and I knew I was hyperventilating so I took a few deep gulps of fresh air. The houses jolted back into position and the blood surged to my head, and with it, the rage. Bloody hell. Bloody *hell*. Isabella. Anna *Isabella*. How dare he? Furious, I hastened to my car at the kerb, flung open the door, threw my bag inside, and myself after it. Not a barmaid, I thought as my hand fumbled with the ignition, an undergraduate. A student! My husband, the respected, eminent professor, the man of letters, had an affair with a student. A little voice in my head said he hadn't been so respected and eminent then, or a man of letters, just a fledgeling tutor, only recently with a doctorate under his belt, but still . . .

I wrenched the gear stick into reverse and shot backwards, too fast, into another car. Shit. Sweat breaking out in beads all over, I leaped out to assess the damage. Not much, actually. Well, a dent to mine and a tiny one to his, but only the bumper, and that's what bumpers were for, weren't they? I bent down, licked my finger and tried to rub the scratch off the one behind. Bugger. Bit worse. Best left, Evie. I turned to scurry back to my car, but my way was barred by a dark-haired man, smartly dressed but tie loosened, collar of his unseasonable overcoat turned up. He looked like that Chelsea manager, José whatsisname, and just as furious.

'Is this yours?' He held up a piece of broken china pot between his forefinger and thumb.

'Oh. Yes, where did you—'

'On the back seat of my car. After it smashed through the rear window.'

'No! Oh, how *awful.*' I swung around to scan the cars in the street. 'I'm *so* sorry, which car?'

'That one, behind you. The one you've just reversed into.' He pointed, green eyes blazing, to what I now realized, when I wasn't looking just at the bumper, was really rather a smart locomotive. Dark blue, slightly old-fashioned – perhaps classic was the word I was groping for – and very sleek. Only not so sleek now, with a dented bumper and ... oh heavens: a huge gaping hole in the back window, glass and cream all over the back seat.

'Oh Lord. I – I'm terribly sorry,' I faltered, appalled. 'You see I was having an argument, and I picked up the pot and accidentally, well, I threw it, and—'

'You could have killed someone!' he spluttered. 'Do you realize a *pebble* coming out of that window –' he jerked his thumb up to the gaping hole in our bedroom – 'could have knocked someone for six? This,' he held the piece of china right under my nose, 'could have bloody finished them off!'

His eyes were boring furiously into mine. Quite close. Quite cross.

I swallowed. 'Yes. Yes, I do see. And I'm really very

sorry. It's not like me at all. You see, my husband and I had a row, an argument, and – and stupidly I reached for the first thing that came to hand. Luckily I missed him, because, as you say—'

'I couldn't care less about your steamy bedroom fights or your squalid domestic violence,' he spat. 'What does concern me is my bloody car!'

I drew myself up to my full five foot three. 'We do *not* indulge in domestic violence. My husband and I are civilized professional people. He's a don at the university, if you must know, and—'

'If he was the Archbishop of Canterbury I couldn't be less interested, and if you threw pots of cream at him all night long it would be all the same to me. Just get your insurance details, *right* now, lady, and stop holding up my life.'

'Ooh . . . there is *no* need—' I stopped. Those green eyes were quite intimidating. Rattled, I turned and hastened to my car. I rifled in the glove compartment and found the relevant bits of paper. *Ghastly* man. I quickly wrote it all down on the back of an envelope, marched back and handed it to him.

'There,' I said icily.

As he passed me his, he held on to it for a second longer than was absolutely necessary. I had to glance up. A muscle was going in his cheek.

'You'll be hearing from me,' he snapped.

'Can't wait,' I snapped back, matching him now, glare for glare. I threw a particularly poisonous one over my shoulder before stalking back to my car.

I got in and shut the door with a flourish. As I started

the engine, taking great care not to barge backwards into him again, I realized my wraparound dress had unwrapped itself. I'd been trading insults with him with one black bra cup showing and half a pair of pants with red bows cheekily on display. *Bugger.* I lifted my bottom from the seat to rewrap my dress and my foot slipped off the clutch. The car stalled, lurched forward and into the one in front. *Shit.* I froze, horrified. Oh, thank the Lord, it was Ant's. I peered anxiously over the wheel. Just a scratch. Feeling hot and fumbly now, I rearranged my dress and restarted the car, but as I glanced in the rear-view mirror, Green Eyes was watching me. His expression of exaggerated incredulity, finger at his temple, did nothing to improve my mood. I buzzed down my window and stuck my head out.

'It's *my* car, *actually*, so mind your own business, OK?'

He shook his head in naked disbelief. Mimicking him, I shook mine back, adopting a gormless expression and wishing I was the sort of person who could flick two fingers. Instead, I childishly stuck my tongue out as far as it could go, which made my head wobble. Then I faced front and shot off, kangarooing elegantly out of my space and into the traffic, narrowly missing a car coming up behind me.

Bloody man, I seethed as a horn blared angrily in my wake. *All* I needed. Yes, and you can sod off too. I scowled as my new aggressor swept past, glowering. Bloody men. Bloody male drivers, actually. Raking a harassed hand through my hair, I glanced in the mirror to check the first one was out of sight. Yes. Good. I took a deep, shaky breath, and as I did, he and his poxy car shuffled right down my deck of worry cards and instead, my débâcle with Ant shuffled effortlessly to the top, the trump card flipping over in all its lurid glory.

'Oooh . . .' I shrank down in my seat and exhaled at the wheel. This was all getting far too horrible. *Far* too horrible. He'd felt trapped. Felt he had to marry me. Felt he'd owed it to me – he'd as good as said so – and all the time, all the time he'd been in love with someone else. Someone younger, clever, beautiful . . . I gulped down the bile. Someone, who perhaps he'd have pursued, married even, if it hadn't been for Neville. I filtered in another shaky breath through my teeth.

A few spots of rain splattered the windscreen. I gazed numbly through them into the traffic on the Woodstock Road. No. No, you're wrong, Evie. You're overstating this, overreacting. There's nothing to say he would have even gone out with her, or, if he had, that he wouldn't have come back to you; married you. And anyway, it was all over seventeen *years* ago. Get a grip, woman! Move on. It's history. Except . . . it wasn't. Would never be history, not when there was a child. Living proof. I gripped the wheel. This would never go away, never. They'd always be with me, this . . . this – Isabella – I almost retched – and her daughter, Stacey, and somehow I felt it was my fault. That God was punishing me for forcing Ant's hand, for manipulating him, for letting him know I expected a wedding ring at the end of a decent period of courtship, and, at twenty-six years old, why not? I glanced nervously up at the sky, almost expecting the clouds to part, for God's finger to point, his voice to boom out, 'What goes around comes around, Evie!' No.

No, God wouldn't say that. But it was definitely all my fault.

I was heading, I realized, out of the city and towards the Ring Road, which meant I'd be taking the Daglington road to the lanes. I was instinctively going home, to the farm, which, even after all these years, I knew I still regarded as such. When we were first married I'd say to Ant, shall we go home this weekend? And he'd laugh and say, we *are* home! When we were first married . . . My mind scuttled frantically back. Were we happy? Yes. Very. I knew, in all honesty, that was true. So get *over* this, Evie. It's a blip, that's all. A seventeen year blip, not even one of his making, not even a male mid-life crisis.

On an impulse, I swung the car all the way around the next roundabout and headed back into town. I couldn't go to the farm. Not to Caro. Couldn't tell her this. I imagined her face, horrified, but also . . . slightly censorious? Of me? I quaked. Why should I think that? As if she might know, might indeed be the only one to know, of my culpability? My manipulating ways? I went hot.

And I couldn't go home, either. Ant would be telling Anna. She'd rush upstairs – 'What's wrong?' And he'd meet her on the landing, take her to her room, avoiding ours with its smashed window. He'd sit her down on the side of the bed, take her hand maybe, and explain patiently, truthfully. And she'd be shocked, horrified, jump up, yes, her world would be shattered – a *sister*? Her father had another child? And he'd have to deal with that. Deal with the fallout. My heart ached for her, for her pain, but I also knew, if I was there, I'd make it worse. I'd scream too, point a finger, shout – *your bloody father!*

Turn her against him, line her up with me, and we weren't that sort of family. Oh, I'd fan the flames all right, and in my heart I knew that Ant could work miracles. Make it — if not better — as good as it could be. I had to let him try, at any rate. We owed that to Anna.

So this was where I'd go, I thought suddenly. I swung a sharp right, amidst another blare of horns, at the church by the deli, then down past the row of boutiques into Walton Street. But instead of heading for the villagey bit of Jericho where we lived, I went past the University Press and carried on, turning into one of the side streets. The familiar winding road, with its charming crooked houses and shop fronts painted every colour of the rainbow, soothed me. I felt my bones relax as I swung into a cobbled yard at the back of one particular shop, where the chosen few could ignore the stern warning that anyone other than employees would be clamped, drawn and quartered.

As I got out of the car and made my way wearily around to the front, I passed the fire escape that had hosted many a cigarette; many a laugh in easier days. The sign on the familiar glass door said 'Closed' but I knew better, and as I pushed on through and it jangled reassuringly, I felt I'd come home. A different sort of home.

'Oh Lordy be. What brings you here, flower? When you've been avoiding your old friends previously?'

I forced a smile and shut the door behind me. The lights were off, so the shop was in comparative darkness, but I could just make out the owner of the voice through the open door at the back. He was sitting in his office, long legs propped up on the desk, peering at me over his glasses, a book he'd been reading, by the light of an Anglepoise, in his hand.

'Not avoiding, Malcolm. Just pressures of life, really.'

'Call it what you will.' He swung his legs down and got up to greet me. 'I'm impervious to snubs, as you know. Notoriously thick-skinned.'

I smiled again at this blatant lie. Cinders, his aged golden retriever, thumped her tail in greeting on the floor as I passed, apologizing for not getting up on account of her years, and as her master held out his arms, I stumbled the last few steps into them, managing to knock his glasses off as I squeezed him tight.

'Oops, careful, hon. These are my three ninety-nine specials from Boots.' He disentangled himself and struck a pose, book open in outstretched hand. 'Make me look intellectual, don't you think?' He peered over the tortoiseshell frames at the print. 'Can't see a bloody thing, of course, because I've got eyes like lasers, but they look the part and that's half the— Oh, what's *wrong*, sausage!'

At this point, and in all probability due to the lovely cosy hug he'd just given me, which I needed very badly, I collapsed on Malcolm's bony shoulder, soaking his new Thomas Pink.

'*Well,*' he said emphatically later – ten minutes or so later, in fact – patting my hand as he put the mug of strong, sweet tea he'd made in front of me. 'Well. I can see that it's a *shock*, my sweet, yes, *quite* a revelation. And a real bolt from the blue too. But it's no more than that. And this is the worst it'll get, I guarantee. It won't get any grizzlier or more dramatic than this.'

'You don't think?' I gulped hopefully, installed now in

his leather chair, sniffing into the red spotty hanky he'd given me.

'No,' he consoled, shaking his head as he perched on the edge of his desk beside me, arms folded. 'She won't impinge on your life. Oh, initially, of course, and out of interest – who wouldn't? – but she'll have her own life. School, friends, family – she's sixteen, for God's sake. She's not suddenly going to decamp and live with you, is she?'

'I suppose not,' I said uncertainly.

'You're imagining the worst. Thinking that life as you know it is over. That the whole cosy Ant, Evie, Anna bit . . .'

'Yes!' I wailed.

'. . . is shot to bits, and it's not. And how much better that she's not some grasping tart's offspring, but that of a clever, educated woman? Much more like-minded, much more sane and rational, not some trashy bairn turning up on your doorstep demanding money?'

'I suppose,' I agreed doubtfully. 'Bit more of a threat, though.' This, in a small voice.

'Is that what you're worried about?' Malcolm said kindly.

I nodded mutely, damp eyes trained on lap.

'That just as you would have felt threatened by her mother seventeen years ago, you'd feel threatened by her daughter now?'

I shrugged, eyes still down. Didn't know what I felt. But yes, all that. And more.

'You've got your own smart, pretty daughter, chicken,' he chided gently.

'Yes. I suppose. So . . . it's just me, then, who's not. I'm the odd one out.'

I glanced up quickly, then back into my lap, but with time enough to see his fine, sculpted features, which were still delicate and arresting, but these days fretted with fine lines, looking anxiously at me. He sighed.

'Evie, Ant loves you for what you are. For who you are. You've got to stop living your life wishing you were someone else. *Pretending* you're someone else.'

I sneaked a look into those wise grey eyes. They were monitoring me closely. 'You're right,' I conceded, and I knew he was. I was the one with the problem, the one who felt I wouldn't match up. I felt that Ant would look at his could-have-been family, the mirror image of the one he'd got, and wish he was part of that gang. One of those three musketeers. Malcolm knew me very well.

'He *loves* you, Evie, you know that. You don't doubt that, do you?'

'No.'

'Never have done?'

'No.'

'Well, then.'

I nodded. Well, then.

A silence descended as we sat there together in his little back room. At length, Malcolm shifted off the desk and slipped into the other leather chair opposite me, whilst I sat in Jean's. We still felt it was Jean's, Malcolm and I. Giggled about it. Even though Malcolm had replaced her exploding wicker throne and its squashed, grubby cushions with a smart, antique captain's chair, it still felt a bit wicked. Jean's room: I slid my bottom to the edge of the seat, rested my head on the mahogany back and swivelled around slowly. We'd hardly ever been allowed in here unless it was to unpack books, and certainly never to linger. 'Come on, chop chop, out you go!' she'd shrill in her best Sybil voice, shoeing us out with heavily jewelled hands, reeking of Elizabeth Arden. In those days the walls had been relentlessly magnolia and unadorned, apart from a couple of the *Gruppenführer's* Mabel Lucie Attwell prints. Faded dried flowers had sat in a vase on her desk, together with a twee teddy bear in a jumper, which in true spinsterish style, bore the legend 'Love me'. Naturally the room reeked of cats. Malcolm had painted it a smart navy blue, added a few choice pieces of furniture, and hung huge framed maps on the walls. He loved those antique maps, and in his quieter moments I'd catch him standing before them, eyes narrowed, plotting his course.

'Off on a voyage, Malc?'

'In my beautiful pea-green,' he'd murmur back. 'Just need a pussycat.'

I'd smile at the Ancient Mariner's back. For Malcolm was a frustrated sailor, who'd failed to make it into the navy on account of flat feet, but still dreamed of going to sea. Maps, a sea captain's chair, blue walls and a telescope in one corner were as close as he got to it in here, but it was a calm, soothing cabin; the only vestige of Jean's reign of terror being the old radiator in the corner, which hissed and spluttered, rather fittingly, like a ship's engine. Years ago, on Jean's days off, Malcolm and I would sneak in here and huddle around that radiator, daring each other to tuck into her secret stash of Walnut Whips in her bottom drawer. Malcolm would read out the problem page from her *Tea Break* magazine, mimicking her Sybil voice, and then answering in Basil's voice as the agony aunt, until I thought I'd burst, laughing. Best days of our lives. It was tidy now, which it never had been during Jean's chaotic regime. No unpacked boxes and books littered the floor, for Malcolm was supremely organized, and everything was dispatched *tout de suite* onto the shelves the moment it arrived: no backlog in this cabin. Just a simple cream rug on the polished wooden floorboards, and everything shipshape and tidy.

Malcolm broke the silence: 'You've got the love of a good man, Evie, even if it does come with complications. Hang on to it. Don't doubt it now, just because you can. Because you think you've got just cause. It's a precious thing.'

I swivelled around slowly in my chair to look at him. Gave a tiny nod. I knew he was right. The voice of truth. Knew he was speaking from the heart too, as he gazed up at his map of Ancient Europe. Knew he'd give anything to have Didier back, his partner of four years, who'd been his lover, his soul mate, his everything, but who'd gone back to Montpellier, supposedly for a holiday, nine months ago, and never returned: had seemingly disappeared into thin air, not responding to calls, emails or letters. Malcolm had gone out there to look for him, and when he'd finally tracked down his village in the hills outside Aubais, had been met with the hostile, black eyes of his parents, who, peering round a door revealing a room heavy with crucifixes, had said that Didier was well, but married now. A baby on the way.

'It's not true,' Malcolm had gasped to me, when he'd

returned, grief-stricken and brimming with tears. 'It's *so* not true.'

'Of course it's not,' I'd murmured, holding him tight. I was inclined to agree, knowing Didier as I did. This was surely a big fat lie, but what could we do? Malcolm had gone back to France again and again, and finally found a girl purporting to be Didier's wife, with a very sour face, and no baby. 'Ees gone,' she'd hissed at him, those same black eyes. 'Ees not here.'

Hope had sprung eternal for Malcolm, but then – despair. A trail of boyfriends.

'Any word?' I asked tentatively, now.

'No. Well, a bit, I suppose. More of the same. He's moved on from the matador who ran with the bulls in Aubais, and is now apparently living near Biarritz with a toreador. Gone up in the bull world.'

'Oh. I'm sorry, Malcolm.'

He shrugged. '*Olé* to the lot of them, I say. It happens. Shit happens.' He gazed at his map, then back at me. 'Which is why I say, Evie, hang on to what you've got. Spare Ant your righteous indignation – which of course you have every right to feel, but which he doesn't deserve. He made a mistake. There were consequences. He has to deal with it. Help him. Don't fight him.'

I swallowed. He was right. As he usually bloody well was. And I'd do that, I determined, when I got home. Later. I'd let Ant talk to Anna, and then I'd help too. We'd sit down as a family, as an adult family. Talk about it, about our fears and – yes, I'd express mine. Say I felt threatened, and they'd say, of *course* you do, Mummy, and then we'd hug big hugs, and we'd be like one of those right-on families in daytime TV dramas, *Hollyoaks* or whatever. And there'd be a moral in it. And we'd be stronger for it.

'And maybe,' I blurted out, 'well, maybe Stacey and Isabella could become friends? Maybe we could all help each other?'

'Easy, tiger,' said Malcolm nervously. 'There's a way to go before you're all holding hands and heading off to Center Parcs together. One step at a time, sweet Jesus.'

I nodded, but straightened up in my chair a bit; a regrouping gesture. I felt buoyed up; happier. A bit guilty too. I'd headed for Malcolm's shoulder because he was one of my dearest friends, but a part of me knew I'd sought him out because his life was not great at the moment, so mine wouldn't seem so terrible. I hated myself for that. I knew too that when I stepped back outside, into the real world, I wouldn't be comparing myself to Malcolm and his precarious gay world, but to Caro and Shona, with their perfect nuclear families, their Cornish holidays and their lack of love-children writing emails, and I'd feel threatened all over again. But for now, for the minute, the fear had passed and I was relieved to let it go.

I took a deep breath. Then rather regretted it. I wrinkled my nose in disgust. 'Yuck, is that Cinders?'

'Farting? 'Fraid so. Poor old girl, her digestive system's had it, I'm afraid. Spectacular, isn't it? I'm thinking of bottling them and giving them away free with Piers Morgan. One bad smell deserves another.'

I grinned, looked around properly. 'You've bought a new computer,' I said suddenly, spotting a dark eye with smart chrome surround in the corner. It was all shiny and bright, very different from the tatty old one known as Gloria, which Malcolm swore was fine so long as you kicked her hard enough.

He scratched his head sheepishly. 'Had to, really. Gloria was on her last legs, poor cow. Her hard drive was shot to buggery. And you've got to move with the times, haven't you? Got to keep up with the miracles of modern science.'

I blinked. Malcolm was usually light years behind; a Luddite, like me. I frowned and peered into the main body of the shop, which was almost, but not quite in darkness now, the low summer sun just making it through the pretty bow window and glancing off the books on the top shelves. 'Something's happened out there too,' I said suspiciously. A new carpet, I realized, had been laid: taupe and rather chic, and the limited wall space above and between the shelves was now a rich dark red, like a study, not Malcolm's usual navy blue. It made a nice change.

'You'll be competing with Poo-Face soon. His walls look a bit like that, don't they? How is he, anyway?'

Poo-Face was Malcolm's arch rival: an ex-media type who, a year ago, had bought the toy shop next door and turned it into a bookshop. It had had Malcolm spitting tacks.

'Next door! Right on my frigging doorstep. Direct competition!'

'Calm down, Malcolm, it's not competition. It's different.'

It was, in fact, completely different. I knew because I'd popped in do the recce, Malcolm, hissy-fitishly refusing to do so. The new shop specialized predominately in military history and was a high-falutin establishment, with none of the paperback chart toppers or bodice rippers and thrillers that Malcolm stocked in copious, gaudy numbers as he tried, desperately to compete with the giants roaring at him in the High Street. Instead, large, expensive coffee-table books were tastefully arranged on round mahogany tables: books that, to Malcolm's chagrin, we used to stock here once, upstairs, in Art and Architecture, but could no longer afford to do so. Sexual Relations and Humour were up on the first floor now, Malcolm quipping that you surely needed one to do the other. But this swanky bookshop next door was having a crack at old times. It was run by a man who I'd never met, having only encountered an assistant when I'd popped in, but whom Malcolm had christened Poo-Face, on account of the nasty smell under his nose.

'What?' Malcolm glanced up from thumbing distractedly through a new Frederick Forsyth as I strolled off to look.

'I said, how's Poo-Face?'

'Oh . . . he's not so bad, actually. We're rubbing along quite well.' I turned back to stare at him. He scratched his chin. 'We've . . . well, we've sort of joined forces.'

'What?'

'We've . . . you know. Merged.'

I frowned. 'Merged?'

'Yes. Did you not notice as you came in?'

I glanced back round; went quickly to the front room, where, I suddenly realized, to my left there was a socking great hole. Half a wall missing. An archway had been cut in the dividing wall, which, in my frantic, snivelling state, I'd failed to notice as I'd hurried past. And the new taupe carpet swept right on through into next door: into the red-walled, coffee-tabled sanctuary.

'Oh!' I yelped in alarm. Jumped back into Malcolm's patch. 'Malcolm, I don't believe it!'

'I had to, Evie.' He'd got up to join me now, hands in his pockets as he came through sheepishly. 'Those huge chains with their massive discounts – I simply couldn't compete. It was a case of that, or going bust. We were both sinking, and he'd only been open a year. I was desperate, and he approached me one day, asked me to have lunch.'

'No!'

'He's rather nice, actually. Anyway, he put a proposal to me. Threw me a lifeline, really. But one he needed too. And here we are. My highly commerical shop with a children's section and cards and wrapping paper, and his highly intellectual one with History, Art and Philosophy.'

'And?' I was agog.

'And . . .' he said cautiously, 'if last month's takings are anything to go by, it works. Or is working. I've got my loyal customers and he's got his, but when they've got their new Napoleon biography, they pop in here for something for the wife. A Joanna Trollope, maybe, or something for the mother-in-law, and vice versa. My clients go in there for their dads on Father's Day.' He shrugged. 'So far so good.'

'Crikey.' I was astonished. 'Oh, Malcolm, I'm thrilled.' I was. I know the last time I'd been in, which, I'm ashamed to say was a couple of months ago, he'd been worried sick. It must have been just before he was approached.

'So what's he like?' I asked, gripped. 'I mean – d'you get on? As partners?'

'He's rather attractive, actually.'

'Oh – is he . . . ?'

'No, no, dead hetero. I just meant easy on the eye, which is a blessed relief since I've got to work with him, and you know my unfortunate allergy to unattractive people.' He grinned. 'And he's not nearly as much of an arrogant shit as I thought. There's still a pretty unpleasant smell under his nose, but the more I delve, the more I have reason to believe he has just cause and impediment. Oh, hello . . .' His mobile rang. He drew it out of his jeans pocket and looked at it. 'Talk of the devil. He's supposed to be relieving me tonight – in the nicest possible way. We're supposed to be stock-taking, but I'm allowed out. Got a date.'

'*Have* you? Oh, Malcolm, *good*. I'm so pleased. Anyone nice?'

'D'you know how much like a mother you sound? Hang on.' He was reading a text. Suddenly he threw back his head and laughed.

'Says he'll be here in a mo. Apparently he got held up by some middle-aged tart in Miss Whiplash knickers who threw a jar of sexual lubricant at him she was so desperate. Oh, here he is now.'

I glanced around in horror as the door opened, and pocketing his mobile in his flapping overcoat, in swept Green Eyes.

## 14

I gaped. 'Oh God.'

His face darkened as he registered me. 'Jesus.'

Malcolm raised his eyebrows. 'Shall I invoke the Holy Ghost and complete the trilogy?' He glanced at me, then back at him. 'You two know each other?'

I was already squaring up. 'I'll have you know,' I seethed, 'that my underwear, up until today, has never been anything other than snowy white and my *moisturizing* cream has never been used for anything other than lubricating my face!'

'Then you've got problems,' he drawled, shutting the door behind him. 'A cross-Channel swimmer would be pleased with the level of heavy-duty emollient you sport.'

'Oh!' My jaw dropped. 'How dare you?'

'I dare because I've just scraped it off the back seat of my car. Something you didn't even stop to offer to do!'

'Whoa, whoa!' Malcolm sprang between us, palms up, like a referee between a couple of prizefighters. 'Easy there, Evie. Steady, Ludo.'

'Ludo?' I scoffed. 'Pretentious bloody name. Poo-Face suits you much better.'

'What?'

'Poo-Face. It's what Malc—'

'Ah ha ha!' laughed Malcolm nervously, turning huge

appalled eyes on me. 'Now *clearly* something untoward has gone on here and you two have got off on the wrong foot, but there's no need to—'

'I'll say it's the wrong foot, and the wrong side of two hundred pounds to clean the suede upholstery too, which, incidentally, I'll charge you for.'

'For a bit of cream on the seat? Oh, you stupid, pathetic man with your stupid penis extension. You can't see further than what's between your legs, which clearly, if you need a car like that, isn't big enough!'

'Evie!' Malcolm's eyes were thunderous now. 'She's not been well,' he explained nervously over his shoulder as he seized my arm and tried to hustle me towards the door. 'Family troubles. A bit overwrought.' He found my ear and hissed, 'Evie, he's my partner, for God's sake. Button it!'

'Well, I'm sorry I've ruined your "suede seats",' I made quotation marks in the air and rolled expressive eyes over my shoulder as Malcolm propelled me out. 'Sorry I've made your shagging couch look like it's been used before, like it's actually seen a bit of action!'

'EVIE!' Malcolm roared, pushing me bodily through the door, and out onto the pavement.

'You need help,' was the last thing I heard Poo-Face deliver scathingly at my back, before the door clanged shut behind us.

'For God's sake!' Malcolm hissed, giving me a little shake.

Once outside in the fresh air, I held my head again. It was that old popping-off sensation. 'Oh God.' I shut my eyes. When I opened them, Malcolm had lit a cigarette.

He was watching me closely. 'Sorry,' I muttered. 'Bit strong, I admit. It just all came out.'

'I'll say it did.' He handed the cigarette to me.

'I've given up.'

'It's like riding a bike. Just suck.'

I did. Then coughed dramatically too, but after a few drags, it all came flooding back. Heaven.

'Sorry,' I muttered again, at length. 'So sorry, Malc. I don't know what came over me.' I felt a bit dazed. Light-headed too, with the smoke. I shook my head in an effort to clear it. 'The thing is, I've got all men in the same category at the moment. Can't keep their trousers on. Only want one thing.' I looked at him helplessly. 'It's symptomatic, I suppose, of what's happened. I feel all the points on my moral compass have shifted.'

I handed him back the cigarette. He took a deep drag, right down to his Italian shoes, then blew the smoke out thoughtfully in a thin blue line. 'Go home, poppet. Go home to Ant and Anna. Realign your compass points and make it work, hm? It would be an awful shame not to.'

I nodded, knowing tears threatened again, and knowing that he was right. We hugged each other tight on the pavement. As I gazed numbly over his shoulder, I caught Poo-Face's eye through the window. He hurriedly turned away, busying himself with a pile of books on a table.

As I drove home, I thought about what Malcolm had said. It would be an awful shame to throw it away. To blow it. Don't blow it, Evie, I urged, holding on tight to the wheel: you're very close to the edge right now. I swallowed. I was. Perilously proximate. Knew I was quite

189

capable – as my little explosion at Malcolm's parlour had shown – of losing it. Knew at all costs, I must keep the flame away from the blue touchpaper.

Back at the house, all was quiet. Ominously quiet, I thought, as I shut the front door softly behind me. No screaming and shouting; no teenage daughter throwing the contents of her bedroom down the stairs and herself after it, gathering it all in her arms and slamming out of the front door. But wait: soft music from within. From the drawing room. I slipped off my jacket, dropped it on a chair, and padded down the hall. I pushed open the door.

Ant was sitting by the window in semi-darkness, just a small table lamp burning. His long legs were stretched out in front of him, crossed at the ankles, fingers laced across his chest, as he listened to Mahler's Second Symphony. The saddest. He looked up and gave a wan smile as I came in; his eyes tired. Then he stretched out his hand.

'Hi.' Softly

'Hi.'

I stole across the room, took his hand, and slipped in beside him on the sofa. His fingers curled tightly round mine, then he put his arm around my shoulders. I felt every fibre in my being relax; begin to hum with relief. I felt so safe. I lay my head on his chest.

'How was it?' I whispered into his blue checked shirt.

'Averagely ghastly.'

I could hear his heart beating fast in my ear. I looked up. 'She's bound to be upset, Ant.'

He gave a twisted smile. 'She's more than upset. Her father is the devil incarnate. Either that or Don Juan. Apparently I've ruined her life.' His voice quavered as he said this.

I sat up. Held on tight to his hand. Looked into his kind blue eyes; sad and pained. I knew I had to be strong. 'That's just shock talking, darling. It's a terrible shock for her, of course it is. For all of us. She feels like she's lost her moorings; she feels rocked. But she'll steady up. And when she does, she'll realize it's not so terrible. I have.'

He turned his head to look at me. 'Really?'

'Yes. Ant, I know how she's feeling – as if her life has been a lie up to now; as if, all the time, something's been going on behind her back. She feels betrayed.'

'It's sort of what she said. This girl growing up, furtively, secretively.' He sighed. 'I can understand that. It's how I feel as well.'

'Exactly, and she's bound to be frightened too, because she thinks everything will change, but it won't. Initially she'll have to adjust to this person actually existing –' I couldn't quite say 'Stacey' – 'but her life, our life, will go on the same as ever. Me, you and Anna.'

'Who have you been talking to?'

'Malcolm.'

He smiled. 'Good old Malcolm.' He sighed. 'Let's hope he's right.' He raked a hand through his hair. 'I wish I hadn't told her. Wish I'd kept quiet.'

'You had to tell her.'

'I know.'

'Where is she?'

'In her room, I think. I took her out for a coffee

191

in Starbucks, but she ran out on me. Thought she was going to throw her hot chocolate at me. She came home.'

I caught my breath. Oh God. Poor Ant, desperately following his daughter's tracks through the streets of Oxford. 'But you're sure she's back?'

'Her music's on.'

'Ah.' We were quiet a moment. Then: 'I'll go and see her.'

'Yes. She'll talk to you.' How sad he sounded. Crushed. And usually, it was the other way round. It was Ant she'd talk to, confide in, if I was honest. The two of us could clash over clothes, the state of her room, her giving me lip, but she'd always talk to Ant.

'This is a big shock,' I promised him. 'Give her time. She'll come round.'

'Have you?' His eyes, when they found mine, were vulnerable.

I swallowed. 'I'm getting there.'

I went upstairs and put my ear to her door. Light shone from a crack underneath and the Black Eyed Peas filtered out softly. She never played music at a million decibels, just in the background. I knocked.

'Anna? Darling? Can I come in?'

No answer. I tried the handle. Locked. I called again.

'Anna, sweetheart, let me in.'

There was a rustle within. After a moment, a piece of paper came under the door: 'I don't want to talk about it.'

I went to the drawer in my room and found a pen.

'Not even to me?' I wrote back.

'Especially not to you,' came back the missive.

Oh. Right. I could feel myself bridling involuntarily. Why especially not to me? What the hell did I have to do with it? Feeling anger and resentment, which I'd so painstakingly quelled for the last half-hour or so, resurfacing again, I went off to my bedroom to breathe.

The evening sun was pouring through the French window and the pretty wrought-iron balcony cast an intricate shadow on the cream carpet. I looked out. Below, in the street, a couple of students cycled past, laughing, one nearly careering into the other. 'Oh, Barnaby, you idiot!' Life was going on. Just an ordinary day. Everything will be fine, I told myself, staring out, holding myself tight. It will all be fine.

After a moment, I gave myself a little shake, went through to the bathroom. I turned the bath taps on full and reached for a bottle, shaking in a good dollop of Chanel bath oil, which I'd had for about six months and was waiting for 'an occasion' to be used. Occasions presented themselves less and less these days, I found, but this was as good a time as any, if not quite what I'd had in mind. Oh – and what about these? I took a box from the cupboard under the basin. Candles, a present from Caro last Christmas: one of many boxes of candles in that cupboard, actually. I was bemused that so many of my girl friends gave me them as gifts, but they obviously used them. When? I'd asked once. Oh, in the bath, with all the lights out. Oh. Right. Why? Well, to relax. Ah. It seemed a bit cheesy to me: something Mum might do. But presumably Caro did it too, since she'd given them to me, although I couldn't imagine her having time for anything more than a quick rub-down in the shower with Lifebuoy and a Brillo pad. While the bath ran, I dithered: should I have another crack at Anna? No. Just leave her, Evie. Give her some space. I lit the candles. Golly. Just *lighting* them was soothing. Perhaps there was something in this.

I padded back into the bedroom for the radio and fiddled around for some soft music. I *would* be soothed. The bath was well back from the French window and the evening sun so lovely I left the curtains open. Lit some more candles, and hummed along with James Blunt telling me I was beautiful, then turned him up a bit, so that what with his crooning and the roar of the taps, I didn't hear Anna come in.

'Oh! Darling.' I swung round from lighting candle number twenty. She looked around the flickering room, surprised. Her face was pale; tear-stained.

'What are you doing?'

'Just trying to relax. Get some karma. Like you always tell me.' I came across, cranking up an anxious smile.

'Oh. Right.' She put the loo lid down and sat on it heavily. 'I'm not going to meet her,' she said in a cracked, defiant voice to the carpet.

'You don't have to, darling.' I swooped to hug her, but she quickly turned a rigid shoulder to me. I perched on the edge of the bath.

'There's no reason why I have to. No one can make me.'

'No one's going to make you,' I soothed.

'Then why did he bloody well tell me?' she cried,

looking up. Her eyes were bright, anguished. My heart lurched for her.

'Because you had to know, my sweet. We all had to know.'

'Why?'

'Because – well, it's a fundamental truth, that's why. He couldn't keep it from you.'

She stared at me, her chin wobbling ever so slightly.

'It's gross. The whole thing is just gross. And I mean – what will my friends say? If I suddenly produce this – this *sister*, called *Stacey*, from nowhere? Who talks differently to me, *looks* different to me, all crop tops and piercings.' She was conveniently forgetting she'd wanted her ears done. 'What do I say?' she wailed, which was what I wanted to do: wail. But she was fourteen, and could. 'What will everyone think? It's so embarrassing – oh, this is my father's lovechild. I can't bear it!'

'That won't happen,' I said quickly. 'You don't have to meet her, introduce her to your friends.'

'But if she's coming here to see Dad, it's as if she's saying –' her blue eyes were wide, expressive – 'come on, d'you dare? D'you dare meet me?'

I caught my breath, wishing she wasn't so succinctly putting into words my fears.

'Are *you* going to meet her?' she demanded.

'No!' I yelped.

'Daddy said you might.'

'Did he?' I quaked. 'No. No, definitely not.' I blew with the wind these days. Changed my mind hourly. 'God, what is she to me? Nothing!' I blurted.

'Well, she's your husband's child. But for me it's even

worse – she's a half-sister!' Her eyes were tragic; badly in need of reassurance. 'A blood relative!'

'Who you've never known about up until now, so there's no reason why, just because she chooses this moment to enter our lives, we have to respond.'

'No.' She nodded, liking this. But not entirely convinced. She hunched forward on the loo seat; clasped her hands tight. 'I just feel so jealous,' she whispered, 'even though I've never met her,' she gazed down at the carpet, 'that he's got someone else.'

I swallowed. Couldn't speak.

She looked up. 'It must be awful for you, Mum,' she quavered. 'You were engaged.'

Ah. Right. Warts and all. And I could see she thought this a terrible betrayal. And yet, frankly, if it hadn't been for the circumstances, for Ant feeling pressurized by Neville, that bit wouldn't bother me. Oh, initially, yes, but I rather agreed with Caro; once I'd got over the shock I'd think – well heavens, it was a long time ago and OK, we were engaged but we weren't married and an awful lot of water has flowed in seventeen years, and I'd be in the Brora sale in moments, riffling amongst the cashmere. But in a scrupulous, fourteen-year-old mind, being engaged, or even going out with someone and cheating on them was a terrible treachery. I'd once had to explain to Anna why some family friends were getting divorced, and not wanting to go into the husband's unforgivable serial adultery had said, 'He, um, had a quick fling.' 'Oh right,' she'd said immediately. Case explained. It didn't enter her head that the wife should overlook a quick fling. Her little life was still ruthlessly honest; it revolved around friendship bracelets, promises, trust. She wasn't to know that the vagaries of life and the fallible human condition changed all that later, and that occasionally one had to ... not necessarily forgive and forget, but fudge and forget. Her eyes filled for me, for what she saw as my pain, and I took advantage of it: in that moment, I knew I could reach her. I swooped to hold her and she clung to me as I folded her in my arms, kneeling there by the loo.

'It's fine,' I whispered into her sweet-smelling blonde hair. 'We'll all be fine. It's like being frightened of the bogeyman, Anna. Someone we can't see, looming over us. But she won't be like that at all. She'll be scared, frightened. Imagine this from her point of view. Here we are, this well-off, educated Oxford family, and there she is, an outsider, looking in.'

'Which is where I want her to stay,' she said harshly. 'Looking in. She has no right to come and make demands of us – to intrude!'

It occurred to me that she had every right. I got to my feet and turned to switch off the taps, wearily untying my dress.

'And it's all because he's written a book, I bet! Just because he's well known, she wants to meet him!'

This wasn't my Anna talking. She was upset. And yet I'd felt the same.

'And I don't feel I know Daddy at all now,' she blurted, getting up and turning round to face the street, arms tightly folded. 'Don't feel I know this man who gets students pregnant. I mean, God, it could be one of *my* friends in a couple of years' time. It's just so debauched of him!'

'He was young,' I soothed, hating that she thought of him so. I slipped off my dress.

'Well, youngish. Thirty, *and* he was engaged and—' She turned. 'Bloody hell.'

'What?'

She was staring at me. 'What are you wearing?'

'Oh!' I grabbed a towel. I'd forgotten about the underwear. 'Just something I . . . threw on.'

'Threw *on*?' Her eyes popped in wonder. Then they came up to mine. A light bulb seemed to go on in her head.

'My God, you guys . . .' she whispered.

'What?' I muttered uncomfortably. She looked around. Took in the candles. The soft music. Her eyes came back to me, appalled.

'Are you swingers?'

'What?'

'You and Dad. Are you secret swingers? Is that what this is all about? Do you go to parties and go home with other people's husbands?'

'Anna, don't be ridiculous!'

'WELL THEN, WHAT'S WITH THE UNDER-WEAR?' she roared.

I licked my lips. 'If you must know, I was feeling a little insecure in the light of your father's revelation. Felt like – looking attractive. Young again.' I raised my chin defiantly.

She reached out and yanked my towel away. 'Don't,' she said, recoiling in horror.

'What?' I was covering myself with my hands now,

looking around desperately for another towel. I seized one, but she yanked that away too.

'Anna!'

She looked me up and down, appalled. 'It's sad,' she said finally. 'You look minging. Like a singing telegram.'

'Thank you, darling,' I said stiffly. 'It was supposed to be sexy.'

'On Kate Moss, maybe, but on rippling middle-aged flesh,' she shuddered. 'No way.' She turned the light on to get a better look. 'Where did you get it, Ann Summers?'

'Certainly not. Darling, turn the light off, the curtains are open.'

'No, Mum, you need to look at yourself.' She took my shoulders and swung me round to the full-length mirror. 'You need a reality check.'

'Turn it off!'

I wriggled out of her grip and lunged for the light cord, but she got there first, holding it out of my reach. She was taller than me. I hastened to draw the curtains, and as I reached up to grab them both, hands outstretched in a crucifix position, I saw a man across the street turn before he put his key in his front door. I whipped the curtains together smartly, but not before I'd caught the unmistakable features of Poo-Face, and the astonishment in his eyes as he looked me up and down.

# 15

I spun round flat against the wall. Oh dear God. Did he think I was after him? Yes, of course he did. Here I was in my knickers again; these wretched knickers, semaphoring for him to come hither, like some tart in Amsterdam. I'd have a sign up soon – 'Tasty New Babe Upstairs.' I shut my eyes, gave a little moan, and slid down the wall on my bottom.

Anna, flicking me a last withering look, had flounced out. I listened to her go: heard her stomping downstairs, slamming the kitchen door, making her teenage feelings felt as she was perfectly entitled to. I sat for a moment on the carpet. Glanced down. A rather unattractive sight met my eyes. Knees up, tummy sagging and in a less than coquettish position, I looked, as Anna had so rightly said, gross. 'Arrgh!' I leaped to my feet and in a few swift motions had ripped off the hateful garments and jumped in the bath.

So what? So flaming what? I sank down under the bubbles, holding my nose, immersing myself completely. I came up for air. That unpleasant man could go hang himself for all I cared. In the scheme of things, he couldn't matter less. What *did* matter, right now, was keeping my family together. My precious little family. Being strong when they needed me, keeping them on track. Yes, this might be my chance to shine: to show what I was made of. I wiped the bubbles from my face. What was that Kipling quote? If you can be strong when all around you de da de da ... keep your head when something something ... then you'll be a man, my son. OK, not entirely appropriate, but still. I squared my shoulders in the bath. I could be a woman. More like a tigress, perhaps. What was that other one? About the tiger? Burning bright, in the something of the night. Blimey, I could do this; throw out literary allusions if I felt like it. Perhaps because I *felt* like a tigress in the face of someone threatening my brood. I gazed at my knees sticking out of the bubbles. My brood. They were scared, the pair of them, and neither frightened easily. They were made of sterner stuff than me, but now, I'd be the one looking into the eye of the storm ... another quote? Or just a cliché? But then, clichés often were quotes, Ant said. So yes, looking into the eye of the storm ... or was it a needle? And something about a camel? Anyway, whosever eye it was, I was there, pushing on through it. Absolutely.

The following day, tastefully and maturely dressed in a Country Casuals skirt and blouse I'd once bought in a curious, home-maker moment, I took Anna to school. She had her games kit with her so couldn't cycle. She eyed me warily as she opened her car door to get out.

'Where are you going?'

'Nowhere special, darling.'

'So what's with the Miss Jean Brodie look? You haven't got all that kinky stuff on underneath, have you?'

'Don't be ridiculous, of course not.'

She lunged across and felt my thigh. I flinched.

'Just checking for suspenders. Don't go all weird on me, Mum, I can't cope. Just maintain the generation gap, OK?'

And with that she got out and slammed the door.

I watched her walk up the road, turn in at the school gates: long hair shining, short skirt swinging, bags slung over her shoulder. Usually, as I watched her go, I'd think – lovely. So carefree, no worries, clever, popular, never bullied, never struggling, only now I thought – struggling. Struggling to come to terms with something she shouldn't have to. Shouldn't have to face at such a vulnerable age. I inhaled deeply and lurched off down the road, as another mother managed to slam on her brakes to avoid me, eyes wide with shock. I wondered, as I flashed past mouthing 'Sorry!' if perhaps I'd reached that age when I should take my driving test again. Or was this perfectly normal? Did everyone drive around, a constant blare of horns in their wake? I'd certainly never got the hang of roundabouts. I encountered the first one on the ring road and executed my usual 'pick a lane, any lane, hope for the best' strategy. More horns.

Days passed. Ant was quiet and withdrawn, but loving too. Tired. I sensibly didn't offer any pennies for his thoughts as he sat with a book on his lap in the garden, looking less at the printed page than at the garden wall. I'd potter in the kitchen, half an eye on him through the window, whilst Anna bolshed around tight-lipped, defiant, not speaking to her father. We co-existed, the three of us, albeit rather tensely, but after a few days, less tensely, I thought.

I overheard them talking at breakfast one morning,

admittedly rather stiltedly, about a choral concert in Christ Church Cathedral that evening. I was ironing in the utility room next door, but, ear pressed to the wall, could hear Ant tentatively suggesting it. Then heard Anna, mumble noncommittally, but at least answer him, which she hadn't done for days. I strained to hear more. Burned my tummy. *Ow – shit*! No matter. I set the iron on its base and as it exhaled steam, I did too: a sigh of relief, wondering if I dared hope for some thawing. Because if so – I sloshed some water on my sore stomach at the sink – now was the time – now that the dust had settled a bit – to execute my plan. Now, when the wounds were closing, looking less raw, was the time to act.

To my astonishment they did go to the concert together – an early one, six o'clock – and when they returned, and Anna had gone mutely to her room to do her homework, I cornered my husband, back in the utility room, which, unlike the kitchen, didn't give on to the stairs.

'Ant, I have a plan,' I said quickly, shutting the door behind us.

'Oh?' He went to the drinks fridge and took out a beer.

'Yes, you see, what I thought was, we need to face this head on, don't we?'

He turned.

'It's no good pretending it doesn't exist. That . . . Stacey . . . doesn't exist, so instead of waiting for her to call,' which obviously I was, jumping whenever the telephone rang, 'I've decided we should invite her here, properly. Set a date. None of this, I'll come one day. Let's ask her to tea or something, to meet the three of us.' I beamed. 'I've written to her.'

His eyes widened.

'Oh, no, I haven't sent it,' I said quickly. 'I wouldn't do that, not without consulting you. But don't you think it's a good idea, darling? To – you know – meet this head on,' I'd already said that. I ferreted wildly. 'To . . . confront our demons?'

'I don't think of Stacey as a demon,' he said slowly, 'but in theory, I agree. You're right. I came to the same conclusion. We shouldn't just wait for her to appear, we should invite her. I've emailed her. She's coming tomorrow.'

'Oh!' Tomorrow. And he hadn't even told me. What would I wear? I can't *believe* I'd thought that. Tomorrow.

'You didn't tell me.'

'I was just about to. I only sent it today, on a whim, really. Before I knew it I'd pressed "Send". But she emailed straight back. We're meeting in Browns for lunch.'

'Right,' I breathed.

'Her mother's coming with her.'

'She's *not*!'

'She's only sixteen, Evie. She needs some moral support. I can understand that.'

'Yes,' I croaked, holding on to the washing machine, which was churning like my stomach. Blimey, what *would* I wear? 'But . . . what about Anna?'

'I asked her this evening. She wants to come.'

'*Does* she?'

'Well, grudgingly. But I gave her the choice as we walked to Christ Church, and after the concert, she said yes.'

'You asked her before me?'

'Only because I had the opportunity; it's the first time she's talked to me for days. I was coming back to talk to you.' His words, as usual, rang with the clarity of truth.

'Oh. Right. So . . . five of us.' My head spun. I imagined us all sitting at a round wooden table, fans spinning, palms swaying. 'I'd better book a table.'

He looked surprised. 'Well, four. I don't think . . . well, it wouldn't be appropriate, would it?' His eyes were kind, gentle. It took me a moment.

'You mean . . . for me to come?'

'Well . . .' He struggled. 'Look at it from her point of view. She wants to meet her father, and yes, her sister. She needs her mother there. I don't think—'

'No – no, of course . . . you're right. Doesn't want to meet me. Ha!'

'At this stage, at least,' he went on anxiously. 'Later, sure, if there is a later, but there may not be. I don't know.' He shrugged helplessly. 'This may well be it. But I don't think we should complicate things. Go mob-handed.'

'No, no, quite right.' I was the mob. I was the complication. Surplus to requirements. They were all blood relatives. And I was hyperventilating. The girl needed her mother. Anna needed her father. Two and two make four, not five. I was still holding on to the washing machine as it went into final spin. 'Right,' I said as I vibrated violently with it. I gave a small approximation of a smile, lips blurring, cheeks wobbling. 'Good plan. Good luck, darling.'

He looked at me keenly to see if I meant this or

was being sarcastic. I dug deep. For love. For courage. The washing machine was orgasmic now. I let go. Had to.

'Really,' I gasped. 'I wish you all the luck in the world.'

'You don't mind?' he asked, worried. 'That you won't be there?'

'Noo, not in the slightest. Blessed relief, actually. Oops, too much coffee on a middle-aged bladder. S'cuse me, darling, need the loo.'

And off I slipped, down the corridor, shutting the lavatory door behind me. I didn't throw up, but I did need to sit down quickly. I hunched there on the seat, the heels of my hands pressed to my eye sockets. They didn't want me. I was to be excluded. Just the four of them. Ant, his ex-girlfriend and his two daughters. I took my head out of my hands; exhaled shakily. And let's face it, where would I fit into that little ménage? This was all about making Stacey feel comfortable. What would I bring to the party?

I sat up and stared blankly ahead. Banks of framed photographs faced me, one above the other, by the loo door. Anna at prep school with her reception class, Year One, Year Two, Year Three. Ant had made me stop at that stage, pointing out, quite sensibly, that we'd need to extend the loo to accommodate every single year, so I'd restrained myself, until this year, Year Nine. Then: Anna in the netball team, Anna in the hockey team, Anna in the lacrosse team. Ant at university. Ant in the cricket team. I either wasn't in any teams, or hadn't been to the sort of school that took photos and put them in frames. The latter, I think. Ant in the debating team, Ant as a fledgeling don with his first lecture group. His first lecture group. I frowned. Leaned forward. My heart began to beat fast. His first *lecture* group? I stood up, peering wildly, my eyes scanning the picture. I glanced at the names below. There were lots of them. Lots of tiny names. I'd never read them before – why would I? It took a few moments. But then I found her. Miss I. T. Edgeworth. Fourth name on the second row, so fourth face along . . . oh! That one. The one, in my idler moments, when I'd sat on the loo, mouth open, looking dreamily at all the pictures, I'd pick out. The doe-eyed blonde with the big smile. The beauty. The one I'd thought: that one; I'd like to be that one. Must be fun to be her: pretty, smiley, clever. The one, in my sillier moments, I'd sometimes dreamed of being. Never looked for her name, though. Not that silly. Miss I. T. Edgeworth, Isabella, who'd been in my loo for – ooh, years now. First when we'd lived at Balliol, and now in this slightly swankier Jericho latrine, flanked by smart green and gold striped wallpaper, and whom Ant probably looked at every day of his life and thought . . . what? What did he think?

My heart began to accelerate. He'd known and I hadn't. I felt it a terrible betrayal, somehow, but couldn't explain why. Ant had known she was here, amongst us, and I hadn't. Did he sometimes stroke her face with the tip of his finger? Did he smile affectionately at her, wonder where she was? Or did he – and this sent my heart into overdrive – did he know where she was? Had he known all along?

Suddenly the blood surged to my head. In one deft movement I hoiked the picture off the wall and marched with it back to the kitchen. Ant had emerged from the utility room and was standing at the sink, hands in pockets, beer unopened, gazing out of the window at the backs of the houses that flanked ours, suffused in dying light. I flung the photo down on the kitchen table. Frisbeed it with such force that the glass shimmied in its frame but didn't break. It just stopped short of sliding off the other end.

'Take it to work,' I hissed. 'Put it in your loo there, look at it as you do your trousers up, or pull them down, or whatever you do, but don't keep it here!'

And with that, fists clenched, and for the second time in not very many days, I marched down the corridor and slammed out of the house.

I fled down the steps to the car, knowing he was coming after me, feeling oddly, like a character in *Brookside*. Ours was a quiet, ordered household with rituals and routines – school runs, occasional outings to the theatre, opera, friends for supper – and our door opened and shut quietly to those ends. Never had these steps been tumbled down so dramatically, the door slammed so hard, and even in my despair, I felt I was watching myself from elsewhere: from a sofa – a settee even – in a leisure suit, with a can of Coke and a bag of crisps, observing myself with a slightly bored detached air, as perhaps, behind twitching curtains, our neighbours – in a less bored and more riveted way – were watching too, wondering what was going on, who was having the affair, who'd lost their job. It calmed me down just sufficiently, so that as I got in the car and drove off, too fast, and without my lights – *stupid* Evie, I flicked them on as someone flashed me – I went hot. What was I trying to do, kill myself? Be in *Casualty* as well as *Brookside*? Wheeled into A&E on a stretcher, the crash team poised to resuscitate me? I slowed down. And when my phone rang, instead of diving for it stupidly and reading the text, I pulled over and read it. It was from Ant.

> **I won't go. We won't go. I'll email and say I can't see her. Can't see them. I love U more than anyone in the world Evie. I'm just trying to do the right thing. Struggling to do the right thing. But if it means losing you I can't begin. Please come home. Ant x**

I took a deep breath. Read it again. Then my thumb got to work.

> **Darling. I love U too which is why I'm behaving so badly. I'm scared. But of course you must go, with Anna. And Stacey must have her mother. I WILL get there. I WILL be fine. I just need time. And I need to be alone for a bit. Back soon. LOL Evie xxx**

I sat there, in the dark, head back on the headrest, staring at the stars. All of us are in the gutter but some of us are looking at the stars. Blimey, another one. I'd say Chrissie Hynde, but Ant would laugh and say Oscar Wilde. I took a deep breath. Let it out. Was there something wrong with me? One minute I was offering tea and biscuits to Ant's daughter, the next I was hurling pictures. It was being wrong-footed that sparked me off. Thinking I was in control, and the next minute, knowing I was so patently out of the loop it sent me careering off track. I added a postscript to my text.

**You must tell me what's going on. When you email her, what you are saying, before you do it. It's finding out later and feeling excluded that throws me.**

I stared at it. Then deleted it. Too needy. Too . . . helpless. And yet – why not be needy and helpless? He was my husband, for God's sake, not a boyfriend. But I was going to be strong, remember? Burning bright, like that tiger.

I drove through the city to the other side of town. Down George Street and Broad Street, past the Bodleian and New College, the bells tolling from St Michael's, the mighty spires of Trinity looming over me. Usually I revelled in their majesty, felt proud to be under their spectral gaze, but tonight . . . tonight I hated them. Hated Oxford. Hated the thin, sensible women in their thrift-shop clothes pedalling earnestly to their book clubs; the bearded, scruffy men emerging, blinking like moles in the streetlights, from cello recitals or odd, esoteric talks on existentialism. I hated the brains, the power; felt threatened. Suddenly I wished we lived in Streatham. Or Middlesbrough. Somewhere where I could saunter down the high street, swinging my Topshop handbag, popping into Thorntons for chocolate – somewhere where I belonged. Not here. Not where every other fly poster advertised not Joss Stone, but a Mendelssohn evening, or an opportunity to hear Salman Rushdie speak. They frightened me, these people with their sharp brains and their sharp tongues hidden behind plain, unremarkable, unadorned faces. Tonight, these buildings, the people they harboured, the talent they fostered, the pacts they made, the trysts they kept, the literary festivals they hosted, the privileged societies they belonged to, the visiting clever-dicks they entertained – tonight I felt they were capable of remarkable harm. I felt Oxford and its inhabitants turn on me, their contorted, sneering faces leering aggressively, like some nightmarish Hieronymus Bosch painting.

And yet, and yet . . . I ducked down a tree-lined side street, then another, pulled up outside a familiar little house with a peeling front door. Sat outside a moment. Not this one. Not this inhabitant. The one I'd always rather . . . not distanced myself from, but taken a careful step back from.

Mum was wearing a jogging suit when she came to the door. A lime-green fleecy affair with a pink stripe down the side and matching headband. The tangerine trainers clashed violently.

'Oh! Hello, love.' She was eating a Cadbury's Creme Egg and had some down her chin and her front. She sucked her finger. 'What brings you here?'

'Can't a girl pay an impulse visit on her mother without getting the third degree?'

I regretted it the moment I'd said it. Always the smart remark. Always the confrontation. I could see her back go up as I followed her down the hall. But then she hadn't exactly said, 'Oh, darling, how lovely.'

'Of course she can, but these days it's increasingly rare, that's why I asked.' She stalked into the sitting room. I followed.

'Sorry, Mum,' I said meekly. 'Sometimes my mouth says things my brain has absolutely no idea about. I didn't even mean it. How's things?'

I sat down heavily, glancing around at the familiar pale, minimalist room: cream walls, white Laura Ashley sofas and beige suede cushions: a far cry from the chintzy sofas and curtains at the farm, which, of course, was what she wanted. A dog-eared paperback was spread-eagled on the arm of the sofa. I picked it up.

'Good book?'

'Terrific. Mavis Brian's latest. You should read it, you'd love it.'

It occurred to me that I would. I glanced at the title. *The Miller's Child.* All clogs and shawls and foundlings and smouldering romance. Years ago I'd have sneaked it away, marking her place, and sat for hours in the window seat at the farm devouring it, reading one after the other that Mum passed on to me: sagas, historical romances, lapping them all up. But then, I maintained, my tastes had changed; become more literary. Not like Ant, of course, not Chekhov for pleasure – but certainly Jane Austen instead of Georgette Heyer. *Persuasion,* which I always started, but somehow never finished. It didn't matter of course because they all eventually appeared on the telly so I knew the endings. But it occurred to me I didn't read for pleasure any more. I read to better myself.

'Where's Ant?' Mum crossed the room to her drinks trolley in the corner.

'Oh – at home. Working,' I added quickly to avoid suspicion. 'The house was a bit quiet so I felt like popping out.' I sank my head back on the soft leather cushion.

'Glass of wine?' She picked up a corkscrew and began opening a bottle.

'Actually, can I have the same as you?'

'Baileys? Course, darling. You used to love it.'

'I know.'

I used to have one with her in the evening, when the pair of us had read ourselves silly, full length, a sofa apiece in the sitting room. Then Dad and Tim would join us, coming in shattered from a day in the fields, flicking on the telly. We'd shift up and they'd flop down and we'd watch *Dallas*, *The Generation Game*, anything light, and have eggs and chips on our laps in front of it, or sardines on toast, macaroni cheese, corned beef hash, things I hadn't had for years. And if Mum and Dad weren't rowing, it could be cosy, easy. And then sometimes, particularly if Gran was there, we'd play cards after supper. Hearts, Racing Demon – which always provoked shrieks of laughter. Cribbage, maybe. These days I ate linguine with clams at the table, bought, but didn't read, Zadie Smith, and since Ant only watched documentaries or arty programmes I hardly watched television at all. I don't think Ant knew how to play cards. Oh, bridge. I heaved up a great sigh from the soles of my shoes.

'Penny for them?'

I smiled. 'How funny. I've spent the whole week trying not to throw money at Ant's.'

'I doubt your husband could be so easily bought.' She sank down on the sofa beside me and handed me my drink.

'No, you're probably right.' I gazed at the gathering gloom through the slatted wooden blinds. Then at her.

'Do you like him, Mum?'

'Who?'

'Ant.'

She stared at me wide-eyed. 'What a question! Of course I do. Why d'you ask?'

I flushed under her astonished gaze. Why had I asked? 'I . . . don't know.' Why had I asked? I did my best to answer.

'I suppose . . . well, you're very different.'

She looked surprised, then gave this some thought. 'I suppose we are. But he's true to himself. I like that.'

As Mum was. Which Ant liked. And as I wasn't, it occurred to me, with a horrible rush of adrenalin up my legs.

'He's got another child,' I blurted, and even as I said it, I knew I wanted to tarnish him. To disenchant her. 'By a girl he once taught. A student. She was eighteen and he was thirty. We were engaged.'

She sipped her drink. 'Yes, I know.'

'You know?' I turned to face her, horrified.

'Anna told me.'

My jaw dropped. Eyes popped too, probably. 'When?'

'A few days ago. She dropped by after school on her bike. Told me all about it. We had a long talk.'

'Oh!' I was flabbergasted. And hurt. A long talk. They'd had a long talk. She hadn't had that with me, Anna.

'Why didn't you tell me? Ring me?'

'I figured Anna might not want me to pass it all back ... how she felt. Thought maybe she'd come here to offload.' She sipped her Baileys calmly.

Yes. Yes, she was probably right. And Anna often did come here; cycled round. She liked seeing Mum. Liked playing her Neil Diamond CDs, going on her exercise bike in her bedroom, playing with her china thimble collection. In fact, she sometimes talked to her more than ... well. It was often the way, wasn't it, I told myself stoically. Skipping a generation. I gave my head a tiny shake to regroup.

'How is she?' I had to ask how my own daughter was?

'Not great. Threatened. Jealous. Scared.'

'Makes two of us.'

She sighed. Patted my hand. 'You're bound to be. But, Evelyn, don't make this too big. She's only a child, this Stacey. Imagine if it were Anna.'

'How could it be Anna!'

'Easily. Imagine if he'd married her, not you. Left *you* pregnant. And you'd brought Anna up alone. For sixteen years.'

I gazed at her. Her grey eyes were steady. 'She's done very well. They've both done well. To get this far without contacting you. Without inconveniencing you. She could have made your life very different. But they didn't. They left you alone.'

I went quiet. Put my drink down on the glass coffee table.

'They're having lunch tomorrow, at Browns.'

'I know.'

'Again? *Again* you know?'

'Anna just texted me.' She nodded at her phone on the arm of the sofa. The texting granny. Who'd caught on to technology long before I had. I rubbed my temples hard with my fingertips.

'Browns is a good idea,' she went on. Neutral ground. Neutral territory.'

And I'd suggested tea at home. On my territory, in my smart town house with its challenging art on the walls and its antique furniture giving us – or me – the edge. I swallowed.

'I flounced out,' I muttered. 'I mean, just now. For the second time in days.'

'You've got a lot to flounce about. Where did you flounce the first time?'

'Malcolm's.'

'Ah.' She smiled. 'An excellent choice. Discreet, too. I saw him yesterday. He didn't mention it.'

'Oh?'

'Yes, I popped in to see his ritzy new shop. He offered me a job.'

'Did he?' I boggled.

'Just a couple of mornings a week. Only he's quite busy now he's joined forces with that other chappie. Frightfully attractive – have you met him?'

'Sadly, yes. A little too glowering for my tastes.'

She chuckled. 'Oh, I don't mind a bit of glowering.'

'So what did you say?' I said impatiently. I couldn't help feeling a bit jealous. Mum had been offered a job, in *my* old shop, by *my* friend. But . . . I wouldn't want it, would I? Malcolm knew that. Knew I was too busy. Even so.

'Hm? Oh, I said yes, in theory. The only thing is, it's

Mondays and Fridays, and Mondays I usually do meals on wheels with Felicity.' Her brow puckered anxiously. 'I don't like to let her down. I was wondering, darling . . .' She glanced at me.

'Me?' Do charity work? I was taken aback. But why? Why surprised? Mum did it. Felicity did it. Even Caro, the busiest person in the world, rattled a tin outside Waitrose occasionally for Save the Children. But I'd always been rather snotty about bored, middle-class women salving their consciences by doing Good Works. Why? Because I'd heard Ant say it, that's why. Did I have an original thought in my head?

'Of course,' I muttered.

'Oh, darling, *would* you? Just till I find a replacement. I know you're terribly busy, and I could ask Jill Copeland because she only works at the library three days a—'

'No. No, it's fine, Mum. I'm not terribly busy.'

She looked surprised to hear me say it. I drained my glass. Got up to go. But it was true. I didn't have a job. I had one child at school all day. A husband at work all day. A Portuguese lady who cleaned my house. I sat on no committees. I did no charity work. I did nothing. Who was I?

I walked dumbly to the door. I said goodbye to Mum, but I could tell she was watching me as I went down the path to my car. Who was Evie Hamilton? Ant's wife. Anna's mother. But now, recent events were questioning my exclusive rights to even those claims.

I drove home, staring blankly at the rain on the windscreen. They defined me, Ant and Anna. And now, two other women claimed they defined them too. I couldn't see my way through. Oh. Wipers. I felt panic rising as I watched the blades swish hypnotically in front of me. I wanted to get back quickly to my house. Stake my claim. Wanted to shut the door behind me, bolt and bar it, pull up the drawbridge.

I swung into my road. The rain was torrential now, a huge great summer thundercloud bursting under too much pressure, beating its outraged tattoo on the car roof, a horrible, deafening, threatening noise. I needed to get out. My eyes scanned the road, desperate for a space, increasingly rare these days, even in the enlightened age of residents' permits. Many of the houses were divided into flats, so the road still overflowed. Ours wasn't, of course. Divided. Ours, on four floors, including the basement, was one of the few original houses, I used to think smugly. Smug! That's who I was. Smug Evie Hamilton, who expected the world to come to her. A trophy wife. *Trophy* wife? I blanched as I shot across the road to the opposite side where I'd spotted a space. I lined up to parallel park. God, that suggested Ivana Trump or Victoria Beckham, with beautifully coiffed hair, polished nails, expensive clothes, whereas my roots badly needed touching up, my nails were bitten to the quick and these jeans had been on for three days. I couldn't even get *that* right. Couldn't even be a groomed and manicured credit to my successful husband, I thought with a flush as I swung back into my space. At least, I thought it was mine, but someone, whilst I'd been glancing down at my grubby jeans, had backed in before me, from the opposite direction. So that as I reversed, quite fast, and without really looking, I heard that horrible, familiar crunch of metal on metal.

I slammed on the brakes and stared, aghast, in my rear-view mirror. The headlights of the car behind went out. A door opened, and a foot stepped out onto the sodden, pinging tarmac. I leaned my forehead onto the steering wheel, shut my eyes, and prayed hard.

Oh dear God, no. Oh please, God, no. I'll do meals on wheels from here to eternity. I'll jiggle tins in Waitrose. I'll jiggle my *tits* in Waitrose. Just please, don't let it be him.

# 16

I opened one eye a fraction and saw a pair of jeans and the ends of a flapping overcoat strut my way, towards my open window. His crotch drew level and then he crouched down until his face was proximate with mine. I snapped my eyes shut, kept my head on the steering wheel, and simulated concussion.

'Bloody hell,' I heard in disbelief. 'Bloody hell – you again!'

'Hm? Whaa . . . ?' I opened my eyes blearily, took my head slowly off the wheel, but kept my mouth dopily open. Through half-shut eyes, I gazed around, dazed. 'Where am I?' I whispered.

'In the back of my bloody car again. For the second time in as many weeks!'

I peered at him through what I hoped were semiconscious, but perhaps more drug-crazed-looking, eyes. 'Who are you?' I croaked.

'Oh, don't give me that,' he snapped. 'If that little jolt knocked you senseless you've got bigger problems mentally than I thought!'

Realizing I should have simulated death rather than concussion I sat bolt upright. 'There's nothing wrong with my mental powers,' I retorted. 'It's your bloody car that's the problem. That was *my* space and, what's more, you saw me backing into it!'

'Like hell it was yours. You just barged across from the wrong side of the road, then kept on reversing straight into me!'

'I was committed,' I hissed.

'Doesn't surprise me. Give me the name of the asylum and I'll tell them to take you back.'

'To the space!' I squeaked. 'I was halfway in – you *saw* me. And anyway, how come your car is always outside my house?' I clutched my mouth; stared at him in horror. 'Are you stalking me?'

'Don't be ridiculous, why would I want to do that?'

'You've seen me in my underwear!'

'Which might make me leave town. No, madam, I am not stalking you.'

'Then why are you always in my street?' I hissed.

'Because I *live* in your street,' he hissed back.

'Since when?' I snarled.

'Since two months ago, if you must know,' he snarled back.

We were nose to nose now, snarling and hissing like tomcats, our eyes, centimetres apart. His were flecked with gold; greeny gold. His black hair flopped into them. He looked like a dark lion with that mane of hair. Mum was right. Very masterful.

I jerked away smartly and, without thinking, opened my door, which since he was crouched behind it, sent him flying backwards.

'Shit!' he barked as he sat down in a puddle.

'Sorry,' I muttered, climbing out. 'Sorry . . . here . . .' I attempted to help him up, but he swatted away my hand in horror. 'Oh God – your coat . . .' There was a large wet patch on the back of what was clearly cashmere. It looked as if he'd wet himself.

'Never mind my coat, what about my car!' he roared, staggering to his feet.

'Oh Lord. Oh heavens. I really am terribly sorry.' Blinking through the driving rain we both gazed, aghast, at the crumpled remains of his car. The boot was almost entirely concertinaed in. Even by my standards it was not good. 'That's *dreadful*.' I hastened across. 'I had no idea! I mean – I only *tapped* it. What's it made of?' I touched it curiously. 'Fibre glass?'

As I turned back, his eyes widened. 'Of course, it's *my* fault, isn't it?' He rocked back on his heels and hit his forehead with the heel of his hand. 'My fault, for having a car made of substandard material. It's all becoming crystal clear, forgive me, forgive me. And you, of course, and your Chelsea tractor, made from galvanized steel and with a cowcatcher fastened to the front, have every right to be barging through city centres, mowing down ridiculous fragile cars; innocent people too, no doubt, also made of substandard material – plebs, peasants – yes I *see*, the dawn comes up. Mea culpa. I do apologize.' He put the palms of his hands together and executed an ironic little bow.

'There is *no* need to be like that,' I seethed.

'Isn't there? Isn't there? Righto. My fault again.'

'I'm simply pointing out that I gave it the tiniest of taps. I can only have been doing two miles an hour!'

'Then you don't know your own strength,' he snapped. 'Let alone your own horsepower. Now kindly take your monstrous vehicle away so I can repark what remains of my car!'

'Not until I've photographed the evidence,' I said suddenly. 'You're so sure it's my fault – well, we'll let the insurance company be the judge of that!' Shooting him a triumphant glare I ran across the road, nipped up the steps to my house and let myself in quickly. All was quiet. Trying not to trip over Brenda, who was scrambling up my leg, delighted to see me, I fled down the hall, found the digital camera on the dresser in the kitchen and was about to race out again when – oh, wait: and the chalk from the kitchen blackboard too. Fully equipped, I ran back out, and flashing him another smug look, crouched down and took a few crucial shots, David Bailey style, whilst he stood, arms folded, shaking his head incredulously. Then I bent down and traced around our cars with the chalk, on the very wet tarmac, and therefore with limited, indeed, no visible, results.

'Pathetic, Columbo,' he snapped as I finally got in to drive away, wiping my wet chalky hands on my jeans. 'Truly pathetic. You're insane. Which is no defence, incidentally. Your insurance company will be hearing from me yet again.'

'Bring it on!' I snarled as I roared off.

I had to park flipping miles away, of course. And then walk back, in the rain, sodden.

Feeling utterly miserable, and like a partially wrung-out and slightly soiled dishcloth, I dripped up the front steps to my house. As I'd walked along the street I'd studiously made myself not look at his house across the road, but as I turned to shut the door behind me now, I saw the light go out. I double-locked the front door and turned off the hall light, knowing, as I passed the dark sitting room and went upstairs, that Ant and Anna were in bed.

The bedroom was in darkness, but Ant was still awake.

'Hi,' he whispered.

'Hi.' I chucked my handbag on a chair and began to peel my wet clothes off.

'Problem?'

'Hm?'

'I heard shouting outside.'

'Oh. Crashed the car. My fault.'

'Ah.'

Ah. Just ah. You see? It was indicative of how guilty he was feeling that he didn't hit the roof. Didn't sit up and go, '*What? Again? Bloody hell, Evie!*' May as well go for it. A good day to bury bad news.

'Second time in a fortnight.'

There was a pause.

'Right.'

'Same car, too. I mean, I've hit it twice now.'

I heard him swallow. Then: 'Irritating.'

'Yes, isn't it?' I got into bed.

'But then again, why spread yourself thinly?'

'Well, quite.'

'Keeps the insurance claims simpler.'

'That's the way I looked at it. Night.'

'Night.'

I turned over and lay there, staring at the wall in the dark. His back was to mine and I knew he was wall-staring too. After a while, a tear slowly trickled down my nose, and then another, across my face and in my ear. I gulped. I felt wretched and could bear it no longer.

'Ant,' I gasped, 'thanks for your text.'

He turned over. 'Thanks for yours.'

In another moment we were in each other's arms, clinging on, and I was sobbing. But then, I do sob. Ant knows that. When I was little, Tim used to call me Boo-Hoo. Ant rubbed my back and made comforting noises in my ear. A bit later on, when I'd calmed down, we made love, in a rather desperate fashion. And some time later, I went to sleep.

The following morning dawned bright and sunny; a sunny Saturday, and the one, as we all conveniently tried to forget as we ate boiled eggs in the kitchen, on which Ant and Anna would be meeting the lovechild. Awful, terrible remarks of this nature and worse were rising like poisoned sap within me, like bile in my throat, until I thought my head would rotate and, accompanied by vomit and frogs, I'd snarl in a demonic Hammer House of Horror fashion, 'So what d'you think the bastard will look like, hm? Spawn of Satan.'

Terrible things. I kept shovelling the soldiers down my throat to keep them at bay. Kept a bright smile going and some buzzy conversation, and was glad when the phone rang. I lunged and seized it first.

'Hello?' Please let it be them, cancelling. Saying they'd thought it through and that neither Adulterous Witch nor Spawn of Satan could go through with it.

'Evie, hi, it's Caro. Just to let you know Heccy will be here at ten.'

I frowned. 'Heccy? Who the hell's Heccy?'

'The horse, you goon. Hector. Camilla Gavin's pony.'

'Oh – *Hector*.' I sat down abruptly. Oh hell, I'd forgotten about him. 'Oh God, Caro, I'm awfully sorry. Anna's going out today.'

'Out? Evie, I *told* you he was coming today.'

'Um . . .' I got up and walked through into the hall so the others couldn't hear me. 'Um . . . right . . .' I ducked into the drawing room and shut the door. 'Caro,' I hissed, 'she can't. She's meeting thingy today, with Ant.'

'Thingy?'

'Yes, you know, his . . .'

'Bastard?'

'Yes!'

'Blimey.'

'Exactly!'

'And you're allowing that?'

'What can I do?' I wailed, going to the window, one arm wrapped tightly round my waist. 'He has to meet her at some point, and Anna has to, so they're going to Browns and – oh, I don't know.'

'Browns!' There was a silence as Caro digested this. 'Actually,' she said thoughtfully, after a moment, 'it might be a good idea. When some lardy peroxide tart and her chavvy chain-smoking daughter turn up and hardly know how to hold a knife and fork, Anna will die. She'll never want to see them again. Yes, good plan, actually.'

I massaged my brow with feverish fingertips. I wasn't sure I was up to telling her we'd moved on from Barmaid With Foundling country, and were firmly in Beautiful Undergraduate land.

'She's from the wrong side of Sheffield, right?'

'Yes,' I said doubtfully. Was she?

'Then she'll probably bring about six along. Children, I mean. Like Vicky Pollard. Six children from seven different fathers. Claim they're all Ant's — you mark my words. Ant and Anna will be out of there like scalded cats. Anyway, you'd better come. Camilla will want to see at least some representation from your family, or she'll wonder where her horse is going to.'

As I put the phone down it occurred to me that, firstly, I was pretty sure Vicky Pollard was from London, and secondly, I wasn't sure a horse who needed to know who Our People were, was entirely what this family needed right now. But Caro was a very persuasive woman and I dutifully trotted upstairs to change out of my dressing gown, and into jeans and a T-shirt appropriate for the farm.

I wasn't the only one changing. I tried very hard not to notice, but couldn't help spotting Ant had his corn-flower-blue Oxford button-down shirt on, the one that matched his eyes, and that Anna changed three times. She finally settled for studied casualness in skinny white jeans, a pale blue peasanty smock clinched with a big belt, and lots of ethnic scarves and jewellery. She looked gorgeous. I told her so as I went out, pleased to be leaving before them. Held her tight as I said goodbye.

'Good luck,' I whispered.

'Thanks, Mum,' she gulped gratefully in my ear. 'What are you going to do today?' she asked anxiously. 'Will you be OK?'

'Course I will.'

'Where are you going?'

'To meet Hector. You know, your horse.'

'Oh!' A shadow of surprise passed across her pale blue eyes as she registered: remembering, perhaps, a sweet, faraway time when ponies had been at the forefront of her mind. A gentler age. Her brow puckered. 'Will it matter I'm not there?'

'Course not! I'm just going to pop him in a stable and thank the owner.'

'Oh. OK. Take Brenda, or she'll be all on her own.'

'I will,' I promised, bending to scoop up the dog, taking her lead from the hall table.

'Bye, darling!' I called back to Ant in the kitchen, and without waiting for his response, but knowing he was coming towards me down the hall to say goodbye, went down the steps and quickly walked away. Didn't want him to spot the lump in my throat. Knowing they were standing together in the doorway, watching me go, and wanting to appear jaunty and casual, I swung my bag. Quite difficult with Brenda under one arm. Two minutes later I walked jauntily back past the house, still swinging my bag and clutching Brenda, because of course, my car, after last night's little débâcle, was in the opposite direction. They watched me go.

Caro was waiting in the yard as I drew up to the farm, wearing her very best 'meet the pony's mother' kit: lovat-green Puffa, black jodhpurs and fashionably soiled Dubarry boots. She frowned as I parked and got out; slapped a whip impatiently on her boot.

'Come on, quick,' she muttered. 'She's here.' Her eyes were roving straight ahead, up the lane. I scuttled to her side, leaving Brenda yapping and circling hysterically in the car. Sure enough, a ruddy great lorry, all hissing air brakes and hundreds of huge rumbling tyres, trundled down the lane and turned into the yard. I watched as Caro's frown for me turned into a beam of pleasure for Camilla, looking regal, perched on high at the wheel. I wondered if I could even smell fresh paint on the stable doors.

'Camilla!' Caro called in the hearty voice she reserved for her hearty friends. 'You made it!'

'Only jarst. Bloody tyre wars flat. Had to bloody change it!'

A formidable-looking blonde with a weather-beaten face, also in tight jodhpurs and a Puffa, jumped athletically from the cab. She slammed the door on two obedient fox terriers. They didn't move a muscle and sat bolt upright, staring straight ahead to attention, unlike Brenda, who'd stopped circling and was now eating the car seats. I imagined Camilla changing the wheel herself: hoiking this enormous great lorry single-handedly up onto her shoulder. Yes, probably.

'Camilla, this is my sister-in-law, Evie. Camilla Gavin.'

'Hi!' She strode across and flashed me a smile. Nearly broke my fingers as she shook my hand.

'You're the mummy, ya?'

'That's it.'

'And where's the gel?' Camilla looked around brightly, in that slightly vacant way overbred people have, as if expecting Anna to appear from behind a stable door.

'Oh, she's —' Caro and I made frantic eye contact.

'Meeting someone,' I said quickly.

'A friend.'

'Of her father's,' I finished.

Camilla frowned. Looked piqued.

'Eau. I rather wanted to see her orn him. See how she sits.'

She walked around to the back of her lorry and began flicking catches and bolts back. She reached up, and with a deft heave-ho tug on a rope, had the ramp down before you could say Jack Robinson.

'Oh, she sits beautifully,' I assured her, hurrying round to assist. 'Got a lovely little . . .'

'Seat,' put in Caro, helpfully.

'And hands?'

'Yes, she's got hands.' Heavens. What a question!

'Are they light?' Camilla turned to me impatiently.

'Oh, yes! Terribly light. Hardly weigh a thing!' Had I missed that in the Penelope Leach book of mothering? Who weighed their child's hands?

'Only Heccy's very sensitive.' She eyed me gravely.

Aren't we all? I thought as she fixed me with a gimlet eye. I couldn't think of anything to say, so I just brayed chummily. 'Heu heu!' She swept on, ignoring me.

'J'a hunt?'

This, delivered like a pistol shot. I glanced at Caro. She nodded, eyes huge.

'Oh . . . yes!'

'Who j'a hunt with?'

'Oh, er . . . you know. The usual ones. The local, um, hunters. And gatherers. At least – Anna does,' I said quickly, which she hadn't. Ever.

'Bicester?'

Bicester. Blimey. Wasn't that a town?

'Yes, quite a lot in Bicester.'

She gave me an odd look but, happily, disappeared into the depths of her lorry. Moments later she reappeared, leading an immaculate, but disconcertingly purple horse: purple coat, purple leggings, purple ribbons in his tail. I could just about see, under the purple head collar, its head, which was dazzlingly beautiful, with huge eyes and a dished forehead. He tossed it disdainfully as he came down the ramp, all pointy toes and tossing mane, like something out of a Disney cartoon.

I drooled quickly. 'Ooh . . . isn't he lovely! He's blond!'

'Palomino. Welsh crorss.'

'He doesn't look cross. Or Welsh. He looks lovely!'

She had a disconcerting clipped way of talking as if she was far too busy or posh to begin or end a sentence. In fact her machine-gun delivery was almost as hard to follow as Mr Docherty's brogue. Perhaps speaking in tongues was a prerequisite for horsy people.

'J'a ride yourself?' She tied the pony to a bit of binder twine on the side of the lorry and was busy whipping off rugs, pulling ribbons from his tail, quick and dexterous, but eyeing me beadily the while.

'Um . . .' I twiddled my hair, sensing a route, equestrianally speaking, to her heart, but also sensing she might find me out in seconds when she'd hoiked me into the saddle, which she was even now, fixing expertly to his back. Sensibly I plumped for: 'A bit. I mean – I used to. As a child.' I rubbed the base of my spine. Winced. 'Got a bit of a bad back.'

'Ah.'

She smiled wryly as she flicked up the saddle flap and

clinched the girth, and I realized it would take more than a bad back to keep good old Camilla out of the saddle. Probably born in it. I imagined her mother out hunting, hugely pregnant, slipping little Camilla out onto the pommel, slapping her on the breast as she soared over the next hedge. I was rather fascinated by her face. You could put a whole tub of Clarins on that and it would suck it in like a sponge – *shloop!*

She'd popped the bridle on now and, rather impressively, the pony was standing to attention without being tied up. As petrified as the dogs, I imagined. She turned to face me, legs astride, hands on hips.

'Want me to run through your wardrobe?'

I gaped. Visions of her powering, in slow motion and in jodhpurs, through the rails of my extensive fitted wardrobe, sprang confusingly to mind.

'Not . . . unless you . . .' I waved my hand vaguely, playing for time.

'Think I will. Hang on. Just take these orf. Should have done it first, of course, but wanted to show you how they work.'

She turned and removed Hector's purple legs, which, I realized, stood up by themselves and were made of polystyrene.

'Oh my God – *thigh* boots!' I squealed.

'Travel boots.' She shot me an icy look as she peeled off the last one. 'Velcro, see?'

'Ah, yes. Right.'

I remembered Tim telling there was no end to the money these horsy women would spend on their mounts, and that the next time he diversified it wouldn't be bloody pick-your-own, it would be selling this stupid bloody stuff to these stupid bloody women in a barn. She'd disappeared into her vast lorry now, only to reappear with a wheelbarrow, piled high with blankets. She set it down with a thump.

'Right.' She proceeded to toss the blankets on the ground, one at a time. 'Stable rug, turn-out rug, summer sheet, fly sheet, sweet itch rug, all-weather turn-out rug, sweat rug and thermal. Got it?'

I gaped. 'Blimey. He's got more clothes than me!'

She treated this with the contempt it deserved, gazing at me steadily, hands on hips. I realized she was still waiting for an answer.

'Oh! Got it.' I chewed the inside of my cheek. This horse wore thermal underwear? I couldn't look at Caro, who was whispering, 'Sooper,' unctuously, every so often. I felt about fourteen.

'And this is his hood.'

He had a hood? A horse with a hoody?

'What, for when he goes mugging?' I spluttered, which was quite amusing, I thought, but her eyes were like flints.

'For when it gets a bit chill. Goes orn like this, see?' She snapped it onto his neck like nobody's business. 'Take it orf when it's milder.' She unsnapped it.

'Righto,' I agreed meekly.

'Now.' She reached into the wheelbarrow again and her voice boomed out like a loud-hailer as she threw more garments on the ground. 'Jumping boots, over-reach boots, crorss-country boots, exercise boots, competition boots, brushing boots, more travel boots, support boots . . .' and so it went on. On and on, until I was beginning to long for Molly. Dear, scruffy, wild-eyed, caravan-pulling Molly, who wouldn't have worn a stitch in her life, would have spent her entire career naked. And not, now I came to eye him nervously, this rather imperious Hector, who was looking down his very refined nose at me, flaring his nostrils. I wondered if he could sense I was a fraud.

'Now.'

In a trice she'd bundled it all back in the barrow again and was legs astride, hands on hips, facing me, her athletic stance reminding me of a keep-fit instructor from the fifties. 'Personal hygiene.'

I guiltily clamped my arms to my sides. I was a bit warm. It had been a sweaty morning, one way and another.

'Orbviously you pick his feet out every day, and you brush him down, ya?'

'Ya.'

'Then you clean his eyes and his hoo-ha with a damp sponge, but you must also clean his sheath.'

I stared at her. I had a vague understanding of what that word meant, but I hoped I was wrong.

'Sheath?'

'Because it gets a bit crusty, hm?'

Oh dear God.

'So like this, with a wet wipe . . .' She produced a packet from her Puffa pocket, flicked out a wipe, bent under his tummy and . . . I couldn't watch; pretended I was rubbing my nose with my fingers, but also couldn't help peering through with morbid fascination as she took hold of his . . . *thingy* . . . which was *whopping* . . . pulled it right down, then pushed back . . . oh, gross. Even Caro was finding it hard to keep a yuck-a-roony face at bay, and her 'soopers' were fainter now, as good old Camilla, good old dauntless Camilla, swabbed it down. Poor *chap*. Did he want that done to him? I looked at his quietly bulging eyes. So what if it was crusty? So what? I felt like whispering in his blond old aristocratic ear, which had a touch of the Michael Heseltines about it, that fear not, never would I be interfering with him *in that way*.

'And eyes before hoo-ha, orbviously,' she said, lifting up his tail and peering in intrusively. 'Don't want any muck on the sponge. Don't want him getting an eye infection.'

'No,' I agreed faintly, making Michael Heseltine another silent promise. Not only wouldn't I touch his sheath, but never would I touch his hoo-ha, either.

'Want to hop on?' She swung about, legs planted, beaming broadly.

'N-no,' I cringed. 'No, I'm fine, honestly.'

'I'll do the honours then.' In one fluid movement she'd seized the reins, put her foot in the stirrup, and sprung up into the saddle.

'Manege?' She looked enquiringly at me. I gaped.

'Evie,' I croaked. Had she forgotten my name?

She looked impatient.

'Yes, yes, in the manege, sooper,' twittered Caro.

In a trice they were off: Hector and Camilla, trotting away towards the sand school, Caro trotting behind. After only a moment's hesitation, I too was scampering in their wake.

Camilla trotted efficiently around the sand-menage in

big circles, then smaller circles, then sweeping figures of eight. Even to my untutored eye I could see this pony was cool. All archy neck and high knees and pointy toes. She came to a halt in the middle of the school.

'I'll just pop a cavaletti,' she called.

Pop what? I tried to see if she was delving in her Puffa pocket for drugs. But no, she appeared to be trotting towards a jump, which Hector hopped over effortlessly. She came trotting back.

'OK?'

'Sooper,' I whinnied, tossing my head.

'Right.' She vaulted off smartly. She was taking the tack off now, busily putting a head collar on. Everything this woman did was at breakneck speed.

'Caro, where are you putting him?' she barked.

My sister-in-law jumped to attention. 'Oh, I thought in the front paddock. With Pepper, Phoebe's pony.'

'Ragwort?'

'No, not a bit.'

Camilla threw the end of the head collar rope at me, and they marched off together to inspect the paddock. Clearly Hector wasn't going anywhere Camilla hadn't thoroughly vetted first. Which left us alone, Hector and I. We eyed each other warily as I very much held the very end of the rope.

'Good boy,' I whispered. I could have sworn his lip curled contemptuously back.

The paddock evidently got the seal of approval and, moments later, they were back. Camilla relieved me of Hector, leading him away to be set free in his new home, but not before she'd put some sort of fly sheet on him.

Caro and I followed and leaned on the gate to watch, as Pepper, Phoebe's pony, trotted up inquisitively. The two horses circled each other warily, heads and tails held high, snorting excitedly.

'Gets fed twice a day,' came a voice from behind us. We swung around to see Camilla's departing back, heading on back to the yard. No sylvan scene-gazing for her. Caro and I scuttled after her. 'Meadow mix, chaff, and I find a little sugar beet goes a long way if he's tucked up. Obviously he comes in at night.'

In? Tucked up? Visions of Hector beside me in bed in a purple hoody, hoofs neatly crossed over the duvet, sprang alarmingly to mind.

'What?' I gaped stupidly as we followed.

'Of course,' Caro said quickly, eyeing me, then jerking her head meaningfully towards the stables. Happily the moment was lost on Camilla, who'd marched to the cab of her lorry to ferret in the glove compartment. Her fox terriers were still sitting ramrod straight to attention. Were they drugged? No. Bloody terrified, no doubt. Weren't we all?

'Drew up a little agreement.' She was striding back to me now, a piece of paper in her hand. 'Makes everything march simpler. One year's loan to you, all shoeing and vet's bills your shout. He's due a tetanus next week, incidentally. Eau, and not to be ridden by anyone other than your daughter. OK?' She handed me the paper and a pen. I leaned it on my knee and signed dumbly, feeling the same weighty responsibility I imagine King John did when he signed the Magna Carta.

'Get him in at eightish. Quick rub dine and rug him up

well, and then put him ite again at seven o'clock in the morning, sharp.'

Seven? Seven in the morning? Was she mad? I hadn't even opened my eyes. Hadn't got my lippy on. I handed her back the pen and paper in a trance. In a trice she crossed the yard and was vaulting back into her cab. She slammed the door on us, energetically winding down her pre-war window.

'Eau, and when you catch him . . .' She started the engine; was revving it up like nobody's business, pumping hard on the gas and yelling at me out of the window as she manhandled the gear stick. Despite possessing a voice that would galvanize the Coldstream Guards, the hiss of air brakes and the roar of an HGV engine ensured that whatever she said was lost in the wind. She performed an efficient three-point turn in the yard, no mean feat when you weigh ten tons, and prepared to head off. But I was keen to hear, to be fully informed.

'What?' I yelled, running alongside her, cupping my ear as she shunted into first and rumbled through the gateway. She glared down at the urchin running beside her.

'JARST NUTS!' she bellowed crossly at me. Then she vroom-vroomed out of the gate, in a shower of mud and stones.

'Just nuts to *you*, dear,' I muttered, as Caro and I stood and watched her go, roaring off up the lane, needing to get on.

'Pony nuts,' said Caro faintly. 'In a bucket. When you catch him.'

'Oh,' I nodded, equally faintly, back. 'Right.'

## 17

'Rude woman.'

'Oh, yes,' Caro agreed wearily. She turned and went to fetch a wheelbarrow, came back and began piling the blankets into it. 'She can afford to be, I'm afraid,' she called over her shoulder. 'It's a measure of the respect she commands in circles round here.'

'Well, not in *my* circle. And as if I'm going to fanny and fart-arse around a horse like that – worse than having a husband!'

'Oh, much.' She glanced round, surprised I didn't know.

'An invalid husband, at that. Feed him twice a day, change his clothes . . . At least I don't have to clean Ant's cock. I am *not* doing that.'

'She'll check!' Caro squealed, dropping a rug in horror. 'I swear, she's going to pop round, Evie. Do spot checks, pick up his feet, look in his ears—'

'Let her. She'll find a dirty but happy horse. And seven o'clock in the morning – dream on.' I went to let Brenda out of the car.

'Oh.' Caro stopped her blanket tossing, straightened up and turned to face me, hands on hips. 'Oh, I get it. I know exactly what's going to happen here. *I'm* going to have to do it, aren't I? I *knew* this would happen. You'll still be getting your beauty sleep in town and I'll be the one getting the horse in!'

'No, no, Caro, of course not,' I soothed, instantly contrite. 'You are *absolutely* not going to do that. Here, let me put those away.' I scuttled across and took the barrow handles from her, but it was piled high and promptly toppled over, spilling its load. 'Oh Christ.' I began slinging the rugs back in. They weighed a ton. 'I intend to do everything,' I informed her. 'I just rather object to her giving me a schedule, that's all. I mean, what's wrong with nine o'clock in the morning? Hector might like a lie-in, for heaven's sake. He's a horse of a certain age, after all.'

'Well, the later you leave it, the more poo you have to muck out, you realize that? Added to which— Oh, hello. Look who's here.'

Jack, Henry and Phoebe were shuffling warily out of the barn that housed the ping-pong table, hands in pockets, glancing about shiftily.

'Has she gone?' whispered Phoebe.

'Yes, well done, you've missed her.' Her mother bent to help me with the rugs.

'God, that was close,' shuddered Jack. 'We were literally in the middle of a rally and we heard her voice. Phoebs got under the table. You might have warned us, Mum.'

'I deliberately *didn't* warn you because I was *hoping* one of you might hop on that pony of hers.'

'What, with her watching? No way.'

'I wondered where you lot were.' I gave Jack's shoulders an affectionate squeeze. 'Thanks for the moral support, guys.'

'You didn't need it, you were awesome,' he assured me.

'I loved it when you said thigh boots,' giggled Phoebe.

'Well, why on earth would a horse want those?'

'And you should see what her kids wear,' put in Henry. 'They've hardly got shoes at all!'

'All right, Henry, that'll do,' muttered Caro.

'You said so the other day, Mum, on the phone to Lottie. Said she hardly slows the car down when she drops them off for sleepovers, just tosses them out and drives on.'

'She is a bit slapdash with them,' she admitted to me. 'Never a toothbrush or clean underwear, just what they stand up in. But then I find the opposite equally irritating: children who come from ultra-hygienic homes with no pets, and who arrive with kidskin slippers and a disposable loo seat cover.'

'There is that,' I agreed.

'Where's Anna?' asked Phoebe at my elbow.

'Oh, she's . . . meeting someone in town.'

'Oh.' She nodded. I could tell she was disappointed. 'Is she excited about Hector?'

'Oh, very! I'm sure she'll be here as soon as she can. After school, next week. To ride him.'

But not today, to meet him; her new pony, I could tell she was thinking. No, no doubt her older, cooler cousin had bigger fish to fry: probably meeting girlfriends in Starbucks, shopping for earrings in Claire's. If only.

'Mum, there's a woman waving at you.'

We followed Jack's narrowed gaze to a silver BMW, parked just outside the gate, tucked into the verge in the narrow lane, engine purring, looking rather temporary. A fat woman in a tight lilac blouse with very black hair arranged elaborately on top of her head, was waving a bit of paper out of the passenger window, a furious look on her over-powdered face.

'Oh my God,' muttered Caro. 'Mrs Goldberg.'

'Who?'

'The mother of the bride last week. The strictly kosher wedding from hell, when the loos overflowed, the caterers let us down and Tim and I ended up doing the food ourselves.'

'I hulled six hundred strawberries,' put in Henry, grimly. 'I counted them.'

'I'm not paying this!' she screeched, venturing forth from her car while her husband sat, staring stonily ahead at the wheel. She was picking her way towards us in a tight white skirt and lilac heels. 'Not any of it! My Michelle had to spend a penny in the bushes when she was caught short – in her wedding dress!'

'Your Michelle was so pissed she couldn't find her way up to the house where the rest of the guests were using the house loos I'd so graciously provided, when your wedding party thought it would be oh so funny to block the Portaloos with party poppers. And she was sick in my birdbath.'

'And the food was a disgrace.' She'd reached us now and was trembling with rage, fat and shrill, shaking the bill in Caro's face, her cheeks pink under the powder. 'An absolute disgrace!'

'Because you insisted on booking your own caterers, who didn't turn up, so my husband and I did the very best we could *under the circumstances.*'

'The canapés were still frozen!' she shrieked. 'Had ice

on them! Aunt Nina broke her front teeth and Cousin Shylock choked and had to have the Heimlich manoeuvre from my brother Raymond!'

'Yes, well, Phoebe didn't realize I'd only just taken the vol-au-vents out of the freezer. She passed them round before I could microwave them – *since* none of your waitresses turned up. I told you, Mrs Goldberg, we did our best.'

'You roasted a pig!' she squealed, fists clenched, looking rather like one herself. 'Served it to my guests!'

'Yes, I'm sorry. That was thoughtless. But we were only given two hours' notice and we were under pressure. We roasted a lamb too.'

'A pig! At my daughter's wedding!'

'Because you didn't provide any food! And it was one of my *own* pigs, actually, a precious Tamworth I'd raised myself, and had slaughtered that week, and was saving for the family, and which actually, the non-Jewish contingent wolfed down with alacrity. There was none left, you know.'

'A pig . . .' she muttered faintly, fluttering her lilac eyelashes, swooning and looking as if she might pass out. Suddenly she snapped to, realizing there was a lot of mud about. She shoved the bill in Caro's hand. 'Well, I'm not paying it,' she said savagely. 'You can sing for it. Take me to court for all I care. I'm not paying a penny!'

And with that she turned on her lilac heel and stalked off.

'Good God. What a nerve,' I gaped.

'Oh, yes,' said Caro wearily, watching her go. 'Unbelievable nerve. And unbelievably common too.'

'Yes, she looked it.'

'Well, that too, but no, I meant not unusual. That sort of behaviour. And you should see them before the wedding, when they come to look at the venue. All cooing and gushing over the setting and the ducks, couldn't be nicer. Then they go a bit steely when they're organizing the flowers and the food, trying to shave money off, and you think, aye aye, and then the moment something goes wrong they turn ugly. Really ugly. And it's always our fault. Two weeks ago we had a sit-down wedding lunch for a couple of midgets with supposedly a hundred guests, and a hundred and twenty-five showed up. I was expected to find twenty-five chairs from nowhere, *and* stretch the food like loaves and fishes. Luckily a lot of the guests were midgets too, so I bundled them two to a chair, and of course their appetites weren't enormous, but what do you do?'

'Well, quite,' I said faintly.

'I think that was our worst one yet.'

'No, the worst one was when someone died on your bed,' Henry reminded her.

'No!' I gasped in horror.

'An aged uncle,' said Caro. 'Another story.'

'Dad didn't know he was there, right,' Henry's eyes were huge, 'and got into bed with him—'

'Al*right*, Henry!' She fixed him with a look.

'Good heavens,' I said somewhat inadequately. 'Well, I certainly won't be adding to your workload, Caro. You've clearly got a lot on your plate. Rest assured I will be up here at eight o'clock tonight to put Hector out, and back at seven in the morning to get him in again.'

She sighed and picked up the barrow handles. 'Oh, don't worry. I'm here. I can do it this evening.'

'And I always muck Pepper out and feed her, so I could feed Hector, too,' said Phoebe eagerly, knowing her cousin would be pleased.

My heart warmed to both of them. 'You're sweet, both of you. But I'll definitely be here in the morning. If I have a crisis I might call on you, but I'm going to jolly well do my best. Sort this pony lark out.'

Yes, I would, I thought as I drove home. They had their work cut out, that family – my family, I thought with a lurch – and I hadn't always realized it. Hadn't realized how other people struggled to keep body and soul together and how lucky I was to be cruising. Well, not cruising now, obviously: pretty much in the eye of the storm. But this morning had at least taken my mind off the storm; off what was happening in town. I glanced at my watch. Yes, right now. One o'clock. My stomach tipped. And with it, that familiar sicky feeling that soared up my throat like a high-speed elevator, so that by the time I got back to my house I realized I shouldn't have come home. Should have stayed longer at the farm, taken Caro up on her offer of lunch. Shouldn't have come back here to wait, to stew, to listen for their key in the door, hear their hushed voices in the hallway. I should have gone . . . well, where? Not into town – I might see them. And they might see me, think: what's she doing – spying? And I couldn't go back to the farm, not now.

Well, they wouldn't be long, I reasoned. I'd turn on the television. Or read. No, turn the telly on.

Upstairs in the bedroom, I flicked on the one we never

used – Ant couldn't bear it; 'the dreaded lantern', he called it – so an illicit pleasure. I'd find a soap opera, like I used to years ago, something frivolous to take my mind off things. Oh, and eat chocolate.

The television was on only ten minutes, though, and I found I couldn't even eat chocolate on account of my sicky tummy. Instead I sat hunched and watchful at my dressing table, which had a view of the street, so I'd see them coming. I sat there and waited. I looked at the framed photograph of Ant and me on our wedding day; at the one of Anna in her christening robe: the familiar perfume bottles and brushes, the pottery house Anna had made in Year Two. The cross-stitched mat from Year Three. I sat, and I waited.

I was still sitting there, when, an hour later, at half-past two, my hands clenched and sweaty on my lap, I saw them coming down the street. They were laughing and joking. Anna was swinging her tapestry bag, and Ant was grinning. My heart plummeted. Oh dear God. The key went in the door and I heard their voices in the hall. Not hushed; not quietly relieved that that little ordeal was over, but bubbly, buoyant. I went to the top of the stairs, feeling my way. My legs full of pins and needles from having sat in one position for so long, I was a frail, shadowy figure, like something out of a Hitchcock film: the slightly unhinged woman at the top of the stairs.

'How did it go?' I managed.

They broke off their chatter and glanced up.

'Oh, hi, Mum.' Anna unwound a beaded scarf from her neck. 'Actually it was fine. They were great.'

My heart, which, as you know, had already plummeted,

slipped through my shoes and tumbled down the stairs. On the landing table beside me was a vase. I nearly seized it and hurled it after my heart.

'Good. Well, that's good.' I executed a tight smile. 'Relieved it's over, I expect?'

'Oh, no,' she smiled up at me, eyes shining, 'it was cool.'

Ant was watching me anxiously as I slowly descended, hand on the rail in case I fell, knowing he had to temper our daughter's enthusiasm.

'It went much better than we expected,' he explained.

'Stacey – Anastasia – is really sweet and really good fun and soo pretty, Mum. Really tall, with this long blonde hair – she was spotted by Storm Models in the mall in Sheffield – and she's really clever too. She's here because she's got an interview at Trinity, and she's only sixteen. I was like – omigod, a year early!'

I couldn't speak.

'And Bella – that's her mum – God, she's *soo* nice, just your type. Really sweet, you'll really like her, and she's a writer. You know those historical romance books Granny likes? Bella Edgeworth – that's her!'

I stared as if I didn't recognize her. Bella Edgeworth? Yes. Yes, I'd vaguely heard of her. Anna was clattering through to the kitchen now, tossing her bag on a chair, running the tap at full pelt so it splashed everywhere, which I hated, reaching for a glass in the cupboard above. I followed dumbly. Ant was slowly taking his jacket off behind me. Anna filled the glass and glugged her drink down noisily.

'Aahh . . . that's better. God, I'm *so* thirsty. I was so

nervous I had a whole glass of wine!' She wiped her mouth with the back of her hand and turned to me. 'She used to work in a bank, Bella, and she started writing one day, under the desk and got the sack. She was really upset 'cos she had no money, and a baby, of course, but actually she said she was quite relieved too, because she hated Stacey being in day care, and so at first she was like – bloody hell! – but then she was like – right, damn it, and she wrote this book. Finished it in six months, sent it off and it was published – and she was like, oh my God! Isn't that an amazing story? Just like J. K. Rowling – well, the single mum bit.'

'Amazing.'

'And now she's written four more,' she refilled her glass, 'and they've all been published – abroad too – and Stacey wants to write as well. She's going to read English, which Dad's so pleased about, aren't you, Dad? He went all pink when she told us. At his old college too. How cool is that!'

'And you didn't feel –' my voice was strained, unnatural. I didn't recognize it. I was aware of Ant in the doorway – 'a tiny bit jealous? A bit . . . I don't know, resentful?' I gave a cracked laugh. 'This – this strange *person*, sort of – invading your territory?'

'D'you know what I felt, Mum?' She put down her glass. Her eyes were huge, candid. 'I felt – how amazing. I've got a sister. I honestly, *honestly* didn't feel a twinge of jealousy, and I *so* thought I would. Thought I'd want to kill her and like – you know – strangle her, right there at the table, with my bare hands.'

I nodded encouragingly. Yes. Or with string.

'But it was so weird. I didn't.' Her brow puckered in an effort to explain. To understand. 'Maybe . . . maybe if she hadn't been so nice . . . and so worried about how I'd feel. If she'd been pushy, or cocky, but she wasn't. She was more like, worried, nervous. Kept saying – you must be so shocked, must hate me, but I just couldn't. She was trembling, wasn't she, Dad? But not at the end. At the end we were all laughing.'

Laughing. And I was finding it hard to breathe.

'I felt . . . d'you know, I felt almost guilty? That here she was, Stacey, sixteen, with no father, and I'd had Dad, my dad – *our* dad – had his love all those years, and she hadn't.' Her guileless eyes filled with tears as she looked behind me to Ant. Despite myself, mine did too. Could have been for Stacey, could have been for Anna, could have been for me. Hard to tell.

'And I also thought – there we'd been, sisters. I'd had a *sister*, Mum, and I'd not had the pleasure of it. Always been an only child.'

'You said you didn't mind that. Always said you liked being an only, all the attention, the love—'

'I know, 'cos that's what I was. But today I was like – God, all those wasted years.'

Wasted! My heart curled into a tight little ball in my chest in defence. Tucked itself in. I clenched my teeth tightly.

She took another gulp of water, gazed over my head, thoughtful, her eyes shocked. 'And I really didn't think I'd feel like that. But I honestly feel . . . I've found her.' She brought those astonished blue eyes back to me. 'Found a sort of . . . missing link.' She gave her head a bewildered little shake. 'I can't explain it, Mum. Maybe it's because she looks so like Dad. Maybe that makes it easier.'

Easier! Don't faint. Don't faint.

'And it's odd, because if you'd told me that before, that she looked so like him, I'd have said that would have made it worse. But *we* look alike too. We look like sisters!' Her face was alight, on fire. 'Don't we, Dad?'

Ant had hung his jacket on the back of a chair. He looked up slowly. 'Yes. You do look alike. Anna, you've got a clarinet lesson later. D'you want to have a go at that Schubert?'

'No, it's OK. I know it pretty well.'

'Anna, go and do some practice! Your father and I want to talk!' I yelled, fists clenched.

She looked at me astonished. We didn't say things like that. Ever. 'Your father and I want to talk.' We were a modern, emancipated family. We all talked together. But I was back at the farm. I was Mum. No, I was Dad. Both of them.

There was a silence. Anna glared at me. 'I thought you'd be pleased! You knew this was going to be hard for me – I thought you'd be pleased I liked her!' Her face buckled as she pushed past Ant and ran out. I made to follow her down the hall.

'Anna!'

Ant caught my arm. 'Let her go. You'll make it worse.'

I'd make it worse. Me? What had I ever done? This mess was *not* of my making.

I came back into the room; gripped the work surface

in front of me, then changed my mind, and turned to face my husband, folding my arms in front of me, needing them there.

'So,' I whispered, raising my chin, 'it all went swimmingly.' I didn't want to be this person. This hard, sarcastic person. Didn't recognize her. Felt I'd been forced into her shoes.

'No, but it went better than I expected. Anna's only young, Evie. Everything's either brilliant or awful in her book. And her emotions are bound to be heightened because she's so nervous. She's high, at the moment, but she'll come down. I hope not with a thud, but she'll realize that the situation is still complicated. It can't be sorted out in a few hours as easily as she's suggesting.'

I nodded. He was right. The voice of reason, as ever, echoing in my kitchen. Anna was high. On adrenalin, nerves, a glass of wine and now she wanted everything to be all right. Children do. Eternal optimists. Ever hopeful.

'But it is more complicated?'

'Of course it is. But essentially . . .' he spread his hands, palms up, in a familiar gesture, 'well, essentially, they're nice people. Who thus far haven't wanted to invade our lives. And who feel . . . very nervous . . . about doing it now. But the fact is, Stacey has an interview at Trinity, and it looks very much as if she'll get a place. How could she be in the same town as her father and not say anything? You must see that. Added to which, she's sixteen now. The time is right.'

I nodded. Yes, I could see that. Could see everything. I pulled a chair out and sat down shakily.

'Was she . . . is she, very like you?'

'Enough not to bother with DNA.' He sat opposite me, watching me carefully.

'And . . . nice?'

'Yes. You'd like her. You'd like them both.'

I knew what was coming. 'You want me to meet them.'

'Well, that's what you originally wanted, Evie. You wanted to have them here, for tea.'

Yes, before I knew how nice they were, I wanted to say. How beautiful, how apologetic, how tremulous, how everything they should be. When they were outsiders, that's when I wanted them. Now I was the outsider. No, of course I wasn't, but that's what it felt like.

'Or, we could just leave it at that, if you like. They certainly aren't asking for more. For any integration. Stacey just wanted to meet me, set eyes on me.'

'Of course she did.' In spite of my jealousy and fear I knew this to be true. Ant was encouraged.

'And now – well, now, I don't feel *I* can just leave it. Walk away.' He looked at me pleadingly. Took my hand across the table. 'Do you see that?'

'Yes,' I whispered. Yes, of course I saw that. And how I loved him for it. How odd it would be if he didn't feel that. What sort of a man would that make him? But still. I was fighting myself. I looked at him.

'How did it feel? Seeing Stacey?'

He caught his breath. 'Indescribable, Evie. Imagine how you'd feel meeting . . . your child . . . after all these years, knowing she'd grown up without you.' He struggled for composure. 'I felt shame. Terrible shame. But they

252

were quick to dispel that. Bella was at pains to point out that I couldn't have known, she hadn't told me. Because . . . well, obviously . . .'

I nodded. Because he was engaged to marry me. But still, she could have done. Other women might. Other, less educated, more money-grabbing women.

'And love,' he said suddenly, astonished. 'Which completely took me by surprise. After all, she's a stranger – Stacey. But I sat there thinking, how odd, I feel . . .'

I got up quickly. '*Love?*'

'Not love,' he said quickly. He ran a despairing hand through his hair. 'Forgive me, Evie, all my emotions are heightened too, but – a definite pull, something strong.'

I nodded, staring at the wall above his head. The big question. Pull it out, Evie. Pull it out.

'And how did it feel seeing . . . you know,' I glanced to get his reaction, 'Bella?'

Something flickered in his eyes. I caught it just as he tried to mask it. It killed me.

He sighed. 'Very odd. She's changed a bit. But not much. Peculiar.'

'No, not what did she look like. How did you feel inside?'

He looked at me squarely. 'OK. Fair question. I felt . . . something leap. My heart perhaps, my nerves jangling, but it was a nostalgic pull. Mixing memory with desire – yes, to do with memory. With the past. Not the here and now.'

He was always going to be honest. I knew, if I asked, I had to accept the consequences. He would be scrupulously honest. As I folded my arms protectively tight he struggled to get it all out. 'And of course the fact remains she is very beautiful, and she's—'

'OK!' I said breathlessly, holding up my hand. I shut my eyes. 'Enough. I know I asked, but . . .' I froze a smile. Shook my head. 'You might have to lie to me a bit, Ant.' I opened my eyes. 'To spare my feelings. Not sure how much truth I can take.'

He smiled, got up and took my hand. 'There is no more. That's it. She's very attractive, but she's someone from my past, when I was young. When I was a bit insecure, a bit directionless. She is what she was then: a final fling.'

I wasn't sure that was true. Ant didn't do 'fling', and how come he was directionless when he was getting married to me, but then I had asked him to dissemble.

'You didn't think — I wish I'd married you, wish I'd stayed with you and Stacey all these years?' I blurted out in a rush, shocking myself.

He looked horrified. 'Of course not. How could you think such a thing?'

I shrugged miserably. There was no end to the things I could think. How tormented I could be.

'Although, of course,' I saw him plucking up the courage to be honest again and flinched; almost put my arm over my eyes, 'the fact remains we have an unbreakable tie. We have a child together.'

I gulped. 'Yes.'

Damn. Should have put that arm up.

On Sunday we took Anna over to the farm where she spent the day falling in love with Hector. The following morning, however, it was my turn, so as promised I drove down the lanes, swung around the familiar last bend with its high hedge, and swept through the gate into the farmyard. I turned off the engine. All was quiet; all was still. The hens had been let out and were pecking in the dirt. The cockerel, pleased with himself for having serviced most of them at least twice, stretched his neck and shook out his feathers, having had a celebratory dust bath in a long-abandoned flowerbed. A faint mist was lifting, rolling up like a fleecy grey blanket over the vale, but still shrouding the hills beyond, where our cows, having spotted Tim's white pick-up rolling towards them with their hay, lowed in Pavlovian response. I was early, as instructed, and as I got out of the car, I stood for a moment, breathing deeply, savouring, despite everything, what had always been a special time of day; when my father – now Tim, of course – had been hard at it for hours, but the rest of the village slept or slowly stirred.

It was a beautiful hazy morning. Soon it would be my favourite time of year. Not Ant's, because he said everything died, but for all his wisdom of the Romantic Pastoral tradition, he'd grown up in town. He didn't know autumn wasn't about fading beauty, but a last strong push: the elderberries clinging in luxuriant clusters in the hedgerows, the blackberries with second wind, plump and swollen by the rain, and when the mist lifted, that fabulous light no Hollywood movie could recreate would cast long, shifting shadows conjuring up all the shadows of my childhood. By then the apples would be dropping off the trees faster than Caro could pick them; pears and plums, gathered so eagerly a month ago, squashed underfoot by children's wellies. Summer would be long gone and all the bustle and organization that went with it. I didn't mourn it. I loved the limbo of autumn, the wondering when to get the logs in and light the fires, the sparkling spiders webs glistening with dew stretching from one blade of grass to the next in the early mornings, the soft mists and mellow fruitfulness. Who'd said that?

At the sound of my car door shutting, Megan, the old sheepdog, spayed and fat now, came lumbering up. As I stroked her bony head, I made out Tim's pick-up, coming, sure enough, back through the mist in the distance, from the few cows he kept as a nod to auld lang syne: rather like Caro's pigs, I thought, as I passed Harriet in her stable, curled up in a bed of straw, snout in trotters. I smiled. They'd be surprised to see me so early. But then, I hadn't been able to sleep anyway; had lain awake half the night, so I might just as well be here.

Sounds of activity were coming from a stable further along the row of loose boxes. I put my head over a door in time to see Phoebe putting the finishing touches to Pepper's immaculate bed.

'Morning, Phoebs.'

'Oh, hi.' She turned from where she'd been patting down some clean sawdust with a pitchfork. 'You're here!'

'I am indeed.' I grinned. Oh, ye of little faith.

'I put Hector out for you with Pepper 'cos he'd have got all stressy on his own. I was just going to start on your stable.'

'You will not! Look, I'm all wellied up and ready.' I raised an immaculate pink boot with two hands above the door for her to see.

She blinked. 'Cool. Well, I've filled a hay net for you, but I might go in, if you're OK. I've still got some homework to finish. You're next door, by the way. You know where the muck heap is, don't you?'

'Of course. Don't forget I lived here, Phoebe!' And flashing her a bright smile I opened the adjacent stable and went in.

A moment later her face appeared over the door. She grinned. 'Right.'

'What?'

'Nothing. It's just I've never seen anyone go in a stable with a handbag before. Mum will be pleased you're here. I'll go and tell her.'

And off she went, bounding away to tell Caro. I thought what a sweet girl she was as I popped my Chloé bag outside the door – or maybe in the car, bit grubby there – and how I didn't know her well enough. Caro was right. I came back across the yard from the car. We should get the children together more. All five of them, now. I seized a pitchfork and steadied myself on it. Took a moment. Yes, how would the cousins take to Stacey?

With alacrity, I should imagine. I could just see Jack's eyes lighting up, Phoebe's jaw dropping with admiration as this prospective Storm model sashayed into their yard. Well, good. That was good, Evie, wasn't it? Excellent. Taking the fork firmly in both hands, I marched off to muck out.

My, what a lot of muck. I looked around the stable in dismay. An awful lot of dung one way and another, and all sort of spread around the place. Not in neat piles. It was as if the wretched horse had tap-danced in it. Oh, well. I set to work, wrinkling my nose in disgust as I balanced one load of ordure after another on the end of a wobbly pitchfork – jolly heavy stuff – and plopped it in the wheelbarrow. Yuck. Urgh ... I tried not to retch. Lift, wobble, urgh, plop. Lift, wobble, urgh, plop.

I began to get used to it. My arms were aching, but I'd stopped retching and I gazed around, panting. My barrow was full, but the stable still didn't look anything like Phoebe's. I popped next door. Nothing like. Hers was neat and tidy, a flat bed of sawdust banked up slightly around the walls and finishing in a neat line about three foot from the door, revealing a strip of clean concrete. Right. I beetled back, banked up the sawdust around the walls and swept a clear strip of concrete between the bed and the door. There. I stood back. But no, because – there were still lumps of doo-dah everywhere. Small lumps that – I seized my pitchfork – fell through these wide prongs. I hastened next door. Did Phoebe's stable have ... ? I rooted around in her sawdust with my fork, feeling treacherous. No, no little lumps. I patted her sawdust down. So how . . . ? Ah. I hastened to the tack room: found a smaller fork with narrower prongs. Hurried back. No. The little bastards still dropped through. Were they Hector's speciality and not Pepper's? And was it a one-off? Had he had a nervous evacuation on entering a new pad? Should I just ignore them, hope he wouldn't notice when he turned in tonight?

I could just imagine his refined nose wrinkling in disgust; saw him whipping a mobile from the pocket of his purple bed jacket: 'Camilla darling, this place is a disgrace. I simply can't stay.'

I threw down my fork and hurried up to the house, skirting round the back to the kitchen window, where . . . I couldn't quite believe what met my eyes. It was like something out of a TV commercial. Three children in school uniform, hair neatly plaited or parted, sat at a scrubbed farmhouse table, Terry Wogan warbling merrily, whilst Caro, strapped into a Cath Kidston pinny, fried bacon and eggs at the Aga. How unlike my own chaotic, much smaller, household, where Ant and Anna foraged for themselves in a cupboard, found cereal if they were lucky, tested it tentatively with their teeth to see if it was stale, whilst I, when they'd gone, nipped back to bed to read secret copies of *Hello!* and eat chocolate. I was a terrible mother. Terrible.

I banged on the window. Caro turned.

'Oh, well done, Evie!' she shouted. 'Phoebe said you were here. I couldn't quite believe it!'

God. They *really* thought I wouldn't. Jack leaned across the table to swing the window wide.

'Well, I'm not making much headway, I'm afraid. Lots of really annoying little ponky poos keep slipping through my fork.'

'What?' She cupped her ear and lunged to turn the radio down.

'*Tiny bits of shit!*' I yelled, as a rather glamorous blonde turned from where she'd had her back to me in the shadows by the Aga. She gazed in wonder.

'Oh, this is . . . Alice,' breathed Caro, going pink. 'One of my brides. Getting married in the autumn. Phoebe, go and speak to your aunt.'

I must make a tremendous spectacle: sawdust in hair, red of face, shouting obscenities through the window. Perhaps they'd pass me off as the mad aunt. Pass me off? I *was* the mad aunt. On a rogue impulse, as the young woman gave me a dazed nod, I rolled my eyes up into my head in an insane manner and gave a half-baked smile. She looked startled and turned away. Happily Caro missed it, but Phoebe giggled as I bent to whisper urgently in her ear. She listened, then whispered urgently back; saw my eyes widen as she divulged her advice.

'But you don't have to,' she said quickly. 'Lots of people don't. I'm just fussy.'

I gazed at her in wonder. 'Me too,' I whispered. I hastened off.

Back at the stables I located said bucket in said tack room and found said Marigolds at the bottom covered in . . . ugh. Face averted I slipped them on, and then arms outstretched, ran to the stable. I could do this. I could. Crouched in my Armani jeans, hands still miles away, eyes half shut, I picked one up . . . dropped it in the wheelbarrow . . . picked one up . . . dropped it in. Just grass, I told myself, nostrils clenched, breathing through my mouth. Herbivores. They just eat hay and grass.

Twenty minutes later, barrow now brimming, I stood and gazed around. Immaculate. In fact it was so flipping immaculate and I was so exhausted I was tempted to lie down on it myself. But it wasn't over yet. Phoebe had kindly filled a hay net for me, which I strung up for Hector's tea – I very much felt he was a Hector, not a Heccy – then I filled a bucket of water and lumbered back across the yard with it. As I set it down with a triumphant thump in the corner of his stable, half of it sloshed down one of my pink boots.

You'll get there, I told myself later as I sped back down the lanes, one leg completely sodden. It's all a matter of practice. You're just not used to it. And you a farmer's daughter, a little voice in my head said. What had I been doing with my life whilst my sister-in-law held breakfast meetings – which I now realized that little tête-à-tête had been, both women finding a window of opportunity before they started work, proper work. What had I been doing? Reading trashy mags and eating lime creams, that's what.

But I was focused now, very focused. And I knew where I was going next. To Malcolm's. To his shop, to raid his shelves. To get the lowdown on Bella Edgeworth, to ferret amongst his paperbacks and get the full story. I sped towards town, crossed the river – the amount of driving I did you'd think I'd be quite good at it – skirted round the centre and headed down St Giles. The larger bookshops wouldn't be open yet, but one of the ways

Malcolm stole a march on the bigger stores was by tempting customers in with an early-morning coffee and a possible purchase on their way to work. I swung a left down Clarendon Street. He'd be there.

I parked in the little cobbled yard at the back. Good: just Malcolm's car. Changing my wellies for a pair of old flip-flops on the back seat, I got out and hurried round to the front. Quietly opening the shop door, I glanced through the archway to my left . . . but no. No one there. No sign of Poo-Face. In fact, the whole shop was empty and still in semidarkness, save for Malcolm, who was behind the counter at his computer, glasses perched on nose. Cinders was lying at his feet. He peered over his specs as I came in. Beamed.

'Darling! You're up bright and early. What a treat.'

'Malcolm.' I shut the door and hastened towards him urgently. 'Malcolm, have you heard of Bella Edgeworth?'

'Yes, of course I have.' He took his glasses off. 'She writes those lovely Victorian romance books. All crinolines and petticoats. Why?'

'Lovely? You think they're lovely? I thought they were more sort of . . . throwaway and trashy.'

'Well, they're not highbrow or literary, if that's what you mean. But they're certainly very charming. And very accessible.'

Oh God. Like her probably. 'Sexy?'

'No-o,' he said slowly. 'Not really. I mean, a hint, but it's always dot dot dot and shut the bedroom door. No throbbing members, if that's what you mean. I've got some here. Why?' He got up and went to the shelves to peruse.

'Because she's the sodding ex-girlfriend, Malc. The one with the child!'

'Oh!' He turned in astonishment, stared at me. Alarmingly, his eyes began to shine. 'Oh, how *thrilling*. Oh, Evie, d'you think she'd do an event for us? A reading? She's awfully popular.'

'Malcolm!'

'No, no, sorry. Silly me,' he said quickly. He snatched a couple of books from the shelves and hurried back with them. 'But you must admit, quite exciting. And so much better than a Doreen, don't you think?'

'From whose point of view?'

'Well—'

'You mean, if one's fiancé is going to shag another woman and have a lovechild, much better that she's beautiful and famous?'

Malcolm shifted his weight onto one leg and scratched his chin thoughtfully. 'Ye-s. Yes, I think that's exactly what I mean,' he declared defiantly, deliberately ignoring my sarcasm. 'The daughter's bound to be a chip off the old block – great genes, especially with Ant as the father. How much better than traipsing a couple of dogs round the Bodleian?'

'Oh, yes, marvellous. Perhaps they should have some more? I could give guided tours to any number of tall, blonde brain boxes. Recreate the Aryan race!'

'Now don't be like that, petal. As I said the other day— Oh!' He broke off as he flipped open the back cover of one of the books. A young woman of quite astonishing beauty was revealed. Her hair was long and blonde, her eyes doe-shaped and limpid, her cheekbones high, her

263

lips full; her bosom too, what one could tantalizingly see of it in the bottom left-hand corner. It had clearly taken Malcolm's breath away, and he was of the other persuasion. Mine too. We stared at it together.

'Right, that's it,' I whispered, when I could tear my eyes away. 'I'm off to Magdalen Bridge. I'll be the one on the riverbed with stones in my wellingtons.'

'It's probably a good picture,' he soothed, snapping the book shut. 'Vaseline on the lens, lots of retouching.' He was looking inside the other one now. 'Oh God . . .'

'Let me see!' I lunged.

'No, no.' He held it up high, out of my reach.

'Even better?' I breathed.

'Well . . .'

I jumped and snatched it from him. Flipped it open.

'AARGHH!' I dropped it. Then I collapsed into his chair and brought my forehead down dramatically onto the counter.

Malcolm bustled away into his back room. A few minutes later he was back with his usual remedy: hot and strong. I raised my head weakly from the counter as he put the mug beside me.

'Two sugars?' I whimpered.

'Three. One for the nerves.' He patted my back. 'Now listen, flower. I know you're in a bad way, but would you do me a humongous favour?' He clasped his hands, knees bent as he lowered himself down to my line of vision.

'Anything,' I murmured bleakly as I picked up the spoon and stirred my beverage miserably.

'I'm supposed to be taking Cinders to a doggy training class in five minutes, and your ma is supposed to be relieving me here, only she's a bit late. You wouldn't hold the fort for *moi*, would you? Till she comes? Would you, would you?' He fluttered his lashes at me.

'Mum? Oh. Oh, yes, she said.' I shrugged resignedly. 'Sure. Why not?' I rested my head on his counter again. 'I have no life. Nowhere to go. I am a zero.' I gazed down at my thighs. 'If only I were a size zero too, like Bella Edgeworth. Go.' I waved him away. 'Just go. Be gone. Don't crawl.'

'Thanks, hon.' He straightened up. 'We're running over The Three Commandments again today. D'you want to hear them?'

'Three what?'

'Commandments. At doggy training, I told you, with Cinders. Shall I tell you what they are?'

I raised my head wearily. 'Why do I know you're going to tell me anyway?'

'First you say – "Sit!" Then you pat your dog and say, "*Good* sit." Then you say, "Down! *Good* down." Then, my favourite,' his face twitched with suppressed mirth, '"Come! *Good* come."' He giggled. 'Isn't that killing?'

'Killing,' I muttered. Annoyingly, though, I could feel my mouth twitch.

'I just dissolve. No one else does, though. Dalmatian's owner looked very snooty, but I did catch American Cocker's eye last week. He gave me a very knowing smile, which I thought was encouraging, *n'est-ce pas?*'

I shrugged. '*Peut-être.*' I sipped my tea weakly, wondering if I should read her biography on the back. Might it go something like:

Bella Edgeworth was a student at Oxford. She has written four novels and lives with her daughter in Sheffield. Although single, she has a long-term boyfriend with whom she is deeply in love, and plans to marry in the spring.

Yes. Maybe. My eyes roved towards the books.

'And don't torture yourself with those books, hm? As I said, a little bit of Vaseline goes a long way. I should know.' He gave me an arch look and went to pick them up, but I slapped my hand down on the pile.

'Leave them,' I said savagely. 'Torture is what I want right now. When in pain, only more pain will do. Don't take my hair shirt away from me.' I raised anguished, possibly over-melodramatic eyes.

He shrugged. 'Whatever,' he said peevishly. 'But don't slit your wrists in my shop, hon. It wouldn't be good for business.'

And with that, he was away, slipping into his crushed linen jacket, whistling for Cinders, who was instantly at his heels, whisking out of the door and down the street. I sank back in my chair and watched them go. Cinders, it occurred to me vaguely, was not only pushing twelve, but also the most obedient dog in Christendom. Puppy-training classes? Old dog, new tricks? I smelled a rat. Suspected the tricks were all Malcolm's.

I slumped right back in his chair, head lolling, eyes shut. After a moment, I reached out a hand and drew one of the books towards me, the one Malcolm hadn't wanted me to see. I opened the back cover gingerly, peered at the photo again. A second view confirmed my fears. Worse. Much worse. Older than in the previous picture, but more sophisticated. More elegant. Less pout, more poise. Less bosom, more *bon point*. Eyes wild, I read the biography.

Bella Edgeworth was born and brought up in the north of England. She was a student at Oxford University, and now lives near Sheffield with her daughter. She won the Herald Book of the Year for historical romance in 2006.

I read on feverishly:

Critical Acclaim for Bella Edgeworth
'Brilliant! Witty and compelling' *Scotsman*
'I loved this. A sharp, sexy romp' *Daily Mail*
'A wise, funny book, beautifully written' *Northern Star*
'What a find! Who is Bella Edgeworth? I want to have her babies!' Mark Cox, *Daily Express*

I gaped in horror. 'Join the fucking queue!' I shrieked, dropping the book like a hot coal. I sprang from my seat and shrank back from it, gazing at it as it lay there on the floor.

'*Arghhhh!*' I roared, as, fists clenched, I ran and jumped on it. Childish. I did a little stamping on it, like a Russian Cossack. Totally immature. Then I kicked it, as hard as I could, to the back of the shop, and my bare toe in its flip-flop caught the edge of the counter. *Painful.* I screamed out in agony as the book spun into the doorway of Malcolm's back room. '*Shitshitshit!*' Clutching my foot, and hopping across to the chair, I collapsed into it. And then, predictably, and for the third time recently – I didn't earn my childhood nickname for nothing and my toe *really* hurt – I burst into tears.

It was quite a noisy outburst, with a fair amount of shuddering and vivid dramatic accompaniment, but I got relatively quickly to the catchy breath, hiccupy stage that heralded an end in sight. All cried out, perhaps. I cradled my toe in my lap, whimpering softly. Was it broken? I wiggled it gingerly. No. Don't think so. I was almost disappointed. I did a bit more shuddering, coughed a bit more . . . then froze, mid-gulp. Coughed? I wasn't coughing. A deep throat-clearing noise came again.

'Who's there?' I sat bolt upright.

Out of the shadows, halfway down the shop, and from behind the archway, came a tall dark figure. He was frowning at his shoes, hands in pockets.

'Oh. You!'

'I, um, didn't know whether to . . .' He began gruffly.

'How long have you been there?'

'Well . . . a while, I suppose.' He looked up, defensively. 'I came in through the back. My office has a door to the yard. You and Malcolm were talking, and it seemed inappropriate to announce myself. I didn't like to—'

'You were listening!'

'Well, not intentionally,' he spluttered. 'I can assure you I've got better things to do, but these walls are very thin and there didn't seem to be a convenient moment when I could declare my presence.' He looked at me defiantly then his eyes slid away. 'And it appeared to be . . . quite a personal conversation. But then, when you were . . . you know.' His brow puckered. He looked uncomfortable. 'Just now. I couldn't just sit there and listen, so . . .'

'No,' I said quickly. He really did look uncomfortable. Awkward, even. 'No, I understand.' I gulped and rummaged around in my bag for a tissue. Pulled out something of a more intimate nature. Shit. I dropped it and used my sleeve instead. 'Well, then,' I forced a bright smile. 'There you have it. If you were paying attention, which I'm sure you were, you'll know that the mad woman who parades in kinky underwear at her bedroom window, sucking bed-knobs and throwing lubricant at cars before reversing into them, is married to a man who's ex-girlfriend is not only beautiful and famous, but has recently pitched up with his lovechild. No excuse for such terrible histrionics in a bookshop, I agree, but perhaps at least it goes some way to explaining it.' I flashed him another thin smile. Used my sleeve again to wipe my nose. Saw snot. Attractive.

He shrugged and moved cautiously my way, head still bent, hands in pockets. 'It . . . fills in a few gaps.'

I nodded bravely. Gave a last mighty sniff. Waved a dismissive hand at the book on the floor. 'That's her,' I said bitterly.

He stooped. Picked it up. 'Bella Edgeworth. So I heard.' He looked inside the back cover.

'If you whistle, or say "tasty", I will go outside and torch what remains of your car,' I snarled.

His mouth twitched. 'Well, it's a hire car – mine's at the garage being fixed – so help yourself.' He put the book down. Looked at me. 'You all right?' His determinedly brisk tone betrayed kindness. Not good for me.

I felt my chin wobble. I nodded wordlessly, my face full of snot and tears. Hands in pockets, he came slowly to the counter where I was sitting.

'I, um, met her, actually. At a literary festival. In Cheltenham, last year.'

I glanced up. 'Is she a whore?' I gasped hopefully. 'Does she sleep around?'

He threw back his head and barked out a laugh. 'No, I don't think so. Not that I noticed. But then, maybe I wouldn't.'

'Why not? She's gorgeous, isn't she? And single. Are you married? Not that that appears to matter,' I added bitterly, aware I was flying now, my sails full, anchor adrift, all moorings gone, despair emboldening me.

He smiled. 'I'm not married. I was.'

'Divorced?'

'Widowed.'

'Oh.'

The wind changed, the boom came over with a mighty smack of canvas, and my boat tacked and rocked.

'Oh,' I said again as I rootled around for something better. That put my petty problems into perspective, didn't it? At least all the people I was angsting about were alive.

'I'm so sorry. Really.'

'Thank you.'

A silence ensued. He was standing in front of the counter, and I was behind it. His head was bent and he still had his hands in his pockets. His averted gaze gave me the advantage. His legs were long and slim. Good legs, actually. I ran my eyes up them.

'Here, why don't you . . . ?' I swung the other chair behind the counter around to face him.

'Oh. Thanks.' He came and sat beside me. Another silence.

'D'you mind me asking . . . I mean, how did she . . . ?'

'She was killed by sniper fire in Uzbekistan.'

'Good God. A soldier?' A rather butch woman running around in khaki trousers and brandishing a Kalashnikov sprang to mind.

'No, a photographer. War photographer. For a newspaper. *Le Figaro*. She was French.'

'Gosh. How brave. You mean . . . in a flak jacket?' Now she was whippet thin with high cheekbones and long flowing hair. Or was that Bella Edgeworth? I shook my head confused. 'Like Kate Adie? Dodging bullets?'

'Or not, as the case may be. But actually, that was me. I mean, I was Kate Adie, the reporter. But she did have a flak jacket, for all the good it did her. Anyway, that's how we met.'

'Oh my God, how romantic. So how come—'

'I'm running a bookshop?' He shrugged. 'I don't know. I carried on reporting for a year or so after Estelle died, but then I didn't really have the stomach for it. Or the guts, maybe. Thought if I saw another teenage Iraqi boy shot as he threw a stone, or another truckload of young British soldiers ambushed and blown up by grenades, I'd jump on a grenade myself. I think you have a certain shelf life as a foreign reporter, if you're going to be any good, and I'd come to the end of mine. I'd done fifteen years. Estelle was dead. Time to move on. Leave it to the young and the unembittered. Running a bookshop had always appealed.'

'Very different,' I ventured.

He shrugged. 'I like books.'

'Me too. It's what I used to do. I mean, work here. With Malcolm. Years ago.'

He looked surprised. 'I didn't know that.'

'No reason why you should.' I regarded him, sitting beside me, long legs stretched out in front of him, crossed at the ankle. He seemed intent on his shoes. Funny, I'd always thought him arrogant. Maybe shy. It was very quiet.

'Don't you miss . . . being abroad? In Afghani . . . Paki . . .'

'Sorry?'

'The stan place. One of the stans.' What, like one of the shires, Evie?'

'Uzbekistan?'

'That's the one.' I flushed.

'You mean, do I miss the action?'

'I believe I do.'

'Sometimes. But it's her I miss. Estelle. And it wouldn't be the same. Wasn't the same, reporting without her. Not seeing her face in the pack of photographers as they rolled into town.'

I gulped. He had a way of telling it like it was. Painting a picture. Reporting, I suppose. Telling the truth. Which was what he did. Or had done. I imagined him, camped out in the top floor of some deserted building, scanning the dusty streets of a Middle Eastern town as more trucks arrived in a convoy, looking out for the one she'd be in, with her French crew. Making sure she'd made it.

'Had you been married long?'

'Five years.'

'Children?'

'No. The lifestyle wasn't conducive to children. Wasn't fair. We wanted them, though. Estelle was twelve years younger than me, so we had a bit of time. But when she died . . . well, she was pregnant.'

'Oh! Did you know?'

'No. She was only just. Maybe she hadn't known herself.' A muscle went in his face.

'Oh God, I'm so —'

'So you see,' he swept on, 'our lives would have changed anyway. That's the way I looked at it. We wouldn't have been reporting from Baghdad together, it's not as if we'd have gone on like that. My life — our lives — with responsibilities, children, would have changed anyway. It seemed like the right thing to do. To adopt a different lifestyle. Settle down a bit. Buy a house. Get a steady job. And obviously to get a penis extension.'

My hand flew to my mouth. 'I'm so sorry!'

'Don't be. It amused me.'

'So stupid.'

He shrugged. 'You weren't to know. And maybe you were right. Maybe I was an older man in a cool car cruising for chicks. It certainly made me think.'

Older. Was he older? Not than me, surely. Just Estelle.

'Well, under the circumstances,' I blustered, 'who can blame you if you were? You must be lonely.'

'No, no,' he got to his feet suddenly and I realized I'd gone too far. 'No, I'm very busy. Life's . . . very full.' He walked to the shelves and realigned some books unnecessarily. 'Lots of friends, lots of plans.' His profile was to me now. A strong jaw. Strong nose, slightly hooked with faintly hooded eyes like Charles Dance's. But dark. Better. I could see him in Baghdad, head down, running across sniper-watched streets, his film crew behind him: no guns, of course, so vulnerable; his beautiful French wife, camera around her neck, racing along beside him, or just behind him. Was that how it happened, I wondered. Was he running ahead of her, heard her cry out, turned to see her crumple, fatally wounded in the dirt? Or had he not been there? Had he got a call, raced to the teeming, overstretched hospital, pushed through the banks of wailing, shrouded women, to see her being rushed in on a stretcher, or in someone's arms, bleeding, head lolling back. I wondered if I could decently, or even indecently, steer the conversation . . . No, of course not. Well then, maybe I could steer it back to how life was for him now, how he'd coped, moved on, but his stony profile didn't invite enquiry. I opened and shut my mouth a few times, uncharacteristically stumped for an opening gambit, and then, just as I thought I'd found one, admittedly along the rather gauche lines of how come you're living in my street, the door flew open.

On a gust of wind and eau-de-something-strong, my mother burst into the shop, jogging. She was in her pink catsuit, jogging as she turned and shut the door, jogging up to the counter, gasping for breath.

'Evie! What are you doing here?' She jogged on the spot in front of me.

'Waiting for you. Malcolm had to pop out, so I said I'd hang on, but you were supposed to be here ten minutes ago.' My voice, I knew, had become unattractively sharp. But then I was ridiculously disappointed to see her for some reason. 'But don't worry,' I rushed on in a much chummier, gentler tone. 'It couldn't matter less. I wasn't doing anything and, anyway, you're here now.' Hopefully he'd see me as a nice girl now. I glanced across to the shelves, but he'd gone: melted around the archway into his half of the shop.

'I know, I'm sorry,' she puffed, still jogging, 'but I decided to run, and it's further than I thought. But, darling, you're supposed to be with Felicity. Why haven't you got the lights on?' She lunged for the switch. Illuminated the shop.

'Mum, could you please stop jogging? It's making me feel ill.'

'Sorry, wanted to do my full hour.' She glanced at her watch. Surreptitiously jogged a few more steps.

'Felicity?' I frowned.

'Yes. Remember you said you'd do meals on wheels for me? She'll be waiting for you at the Civic Centre. Sixty-four liver and bacons gently congealing.'

I stared at her. 'Bugger!'

I scrambled to my feet, shoved them in my flip-flops, and grabbed my handbag. I made for the door. 'God, how stupid! Sorry, Mum. *So* sorry!'

'Don't worry, you'll make it. Am I here on my own?'

'In this bit, yes, but Malcolm will be back in a minute.'

'No Ludo? Incidentally, I can't think why you dislike him so much, I think he's charming.'

I turned at the door and made crazy eyes at her, pointing my finger into his half.

He was at the back, behind his desk, reading in the light of his Anglepoise. I caught his eye. He looked a bit shocked. I fled.

## 19

'Felicity! I'm so sorry!' I yelled out of my car window as I pulled up in the Civic Centre car park.

She was already loading what looked like dozens of polystyrene boxes from a stainless-steel trolley into the back of her old green Subaru. She glanced up in relief.

'Oh, Evie. Thank heavens.'

'I'm so late!' I wailed.

'Don't worry, I'm just pleased you're here. I had a nasty feeling you'd forgotten, and of course I should have rung you last night, but your mum assured me there was no—'

'No, *no* need, and you abso*lutely* shouldn't have rung. My fault entirely, it just went clean out of my head. Now. What can I do?' I got out, slammed my door and hurried across to her.

'Well, there are about ten more of these boxes on another trolley in the kitchen.' She jerked her head back towards the town hall, a crumbling crenulated stone affair behind us. 'But if we go together, we can carry them, and then we won't have to wheel the trolley out and back. We'll be out of here in a jiffy.'

Together we swung her empty trolley round and hurried it through the back door, through another set of swing doors, and down a corridor to the kitchen. In a vast, operating theatre-style, stainless-steel emporium, we found the remaining boxes. I took half, piled up high

in my arms, and we headed back down the corridor, turning to push open the swing doors with our bottoms.
I wrinkled my nose in disgust.

'Yuck. School food.'

'Takes you back, doesn't it? And, of course, all these
old dears expect it right on the dot of twelve, just like in
kindergarten.'

'Back to their childhood. So what have they got today?'
We hurried to the car.

'Oh, all sorts. Nothing as simple as one meal for all.
They all have something different,' she said, as we loaded
them into her open boot.

'Good heavens, why?'

'Different dietary requirements. Some are no pork,
some are no fowl or no fish, some have to be puréed –
no teeth – and some, no beans or onions,' she raised her
eyebrows, 'for obvious reasons.'

'Oh. Right.'

'And the coloured dot in the corner of the box tells
you what's what. Here's your crib sheet.' She shoved
a piece of paper in my hand.

'Crikey. I'd no idea it was so complicated. And you do
this every week?'

'Every week. But always two of us. One drives, one
delivers. Makes it quicker. I'd better drive this week since
it's my car, so you pop in with the meals, OK?'

She was already in the driving seat, strapping herself
in. My God, she was efficient. I'd forgotten how efficient.
Thank heavens I hadn't let her down. I would have done
if Mum hadn't reminded me. I beetled round the other
side and strapped myself in beside her. She was still

talking nineteen to the dozen, looking immaculate in a pale blue twinset, pearl earrings and a soft suede skirt, her honey-blonde hair beautifully highlighted and swept off her face.

'They're all elderly, obviously,' she was saying, glancing in the rear-view mirror and reversing out smartly – note to self: use rear-view mirror more – 'and they're always the same. The complainers always complain, the sunny ones are always sunny, some haven't seen anyone all day – or all week, even – so you might have to linger a moment, OK?'

'Yes, fine,' I mumbled. I felt humbled. I did nothing. Nothing. No committees, no charity work. Ah, yes, back to you, Evie. As usual.

'And then of course there's Caro's cakes, which they love.' She jerked her head towards the back seat.

'Cakes?'

'Yes, well, the puddings are *so* filthy, usually prunes and congealed custard, or spotted dick with the consistency of brick, so Caro made cakes for us one week, which went down brilliantly. They wolfed them down, so now she does it every week. I've just picked them up.'

Lordy. It would take me years to catch up. Years. I shrank down in my seat feeling about six inches high. But I would do it, I would. I'd become a better person.

'Only last week they were a bit hairy.'

'What were?'

'The cakes. That ancient sheepdog of Caro's – Megan – is moulting like billyo, and your mum and I had to brush them off a bit.' She grinned. 'Not that the old dears would probably notice, or care.'

'No, I suppose not.'

'And I'm not even sure if some of them eat anything, but they're pleased to see someone, at any rate.'

'Yes. I bet they are.'

She frowned at my tone; glanced across. 'What's up?'

I shrugged. 'Oh, just thinking how good you all are. And you're all so busy. You and Caro, anyway.'

She gave me a look. 'I'm not good, Evie.' She turned away, narrowing her eyes into the traffic, which was heavy as usual. 'But I suppose I'm busy. But you know what they say: ask a busy person . . .' She paused. 'Your mum's busy too, you know. You left her off your list.'

I smiled. 'I know. Her jogging, her reiki. But yours is proper stuff. Giving lectures, holding seminars, that sort of thing.'

'Well, each to their own. Don't decry what your mum does, Evie. She's a better person than I'll ever be.'

I struggled with this, as I always did when Felicity praised Mum from the rooftops. She knew what I was thinking. She smiled.

'The thing is, Evie, you tend to confuse being clever with being nice. It's often not so. The nicest people are often the least intellectual.'

'The least intelligent.'

'No, the least academic.' She looked at me. 'You've no idea how poisonous clever people can be. Your mother's the complete antithesis of that. That's why I like her so much. She doesn't have a mean bone in her body.'

I nodded. Yes, that much was true.

'And don't feel guilty about your own lack of Good Works either.' She swung the car around a mini roundabout and headed off down a suburban street. 'You have your own problems at the moment.'

'She told you?'

'She did.'

'And?' I sat up.

'And what do I think?'

'Yes.'

We'd pulled up outside a row of tiny bungalows that seemed to stretch on for miles, into infinity. She sighed and turned the engine off. After a moment, she said, 'I think that if I'd had one child, I'd be the happiest woman alive. If it turned out I had two, like Ant, I'd be delirious.'

I gazed at her. I'd never thought of it like that.

'And if you were me?'

'I'd look at it as one and a half. Which is still better than one.'

I swallowed. It occurred to me that Felicity, like Stacey, was an outsider who had integrated into our family. She'd adopted us. As we'd adopted her. And what a success that had been. What a runaway success. My heart began to purr down a runway, to pick up speed, then soar. All the lights went on. I felt alive suddenly, electric: plug me in and I'd light up every bungalow in this street. Yes, look what Felicity had done for our family. She'd made us. Completed us. Complimented us. She, a 'step', had so wonderfully extended us.

'You're right!' I said, eyes shining as she got out of the car. I sat there for a moment or two in dazed wonder. Then I hurried round to join her at the boot. She handed me two polystyrene boxes. 'You're right, Felicity, and I'd never looked at it like that. Never thought of her as an asset!'

'Well, one step at a time. You've yet to meet her, but you're getting the idea. Now. This one for Mrs Carmichael at number six – no fowl – and this one for Mr Parkinson, see the blue spot, no red meat, next door. He's quite a distinguished old boy. Just to give you a flavour, when he filled out his original order form, under "Any Special Dietary Requirements", he put, "Red meat and good claret."'

I grinned. 'Good for him! So what's he getting?'

'Lentil stew and rice pudding.'

'Oh.'

'He's got gout.'

'Ah.'

As I beetled up the path to his door, I wondered briefly if he'd prefer to be gouty and take his pain relief in the form of a very fine Fonseca '66, or to be pain free and sucking lentils. Mine was not to reason why, though, and anyway, I was miles away. My heart was still up there, at three thousand feet, soaring through the stratosphere, cutting a dash through the clouds. Trust Felicity. Trust Felicity to turn on all the lights. She was right. She was *always* right. And don't tell me that had nothing to do with being clever.

'You're late. Seven and a half minutes.' A snowy-haired man, almost bent double with arthritis, opened the bevelled glass door with a shaking hand.

'Yes, I'm sorry about that.'

'What?' He cupped his ear.

'Sorry about that! Shall I put your lunch in the kitchen for you?'

'Always take it in and put it down,' Felicity had said,

adding, 'Never let them take it from you. They drop it. I've never handed a meal over to anyone over seventy-five and not been scraping it off the carpet two minutes later.'

I slipped past him. 'In here?'

He grumbled as I whisked through to the kitchen – mistake, tiny galley, no table – so I slipped back into the sitting room whilst he was still shutting the front door. I put the box down on the ring-stained coffee table. The smell of old people, stale pyjamas and unaired bed linen pervaded. The television was on, but the sound off, as if there was only so much reality, or perhaps reality TV, he could take. I watched as he slowly shuffled in: his cardigan stained, trousers baggy, old eyes tired. I bet he'd been in the war, brave, strong and upright. Now cross and alone. Sad. A shrinking life. A shrunken life.

Next door, the same smell, but a wary, toothless old woman – puréed – and then next door to that … I hastened back to the car as Felicity kerb-crawled along … a nice old couple who chortled with delight when I told them it was lamb stew today. Well, she did. He was prostrate on the sofa, a vacant smile on his face, but she shuffled over to him to relay the good news, bent right down beside him and they clasped hands, their eyes wide with delight, as if they'd both won tickets to Acapulco.

'It's our favourite,' the sweet old dear confided, turning back to me, taking my hand too. Now we were all holding hands. Hers felt like a few silver teaspoons, wrapped in thin velvet. 'Lamb stew's our favourite!'

'Oh, *good*,' I beamed trying to match her skippy enthusiasm and smiling at her husband, who smiled weakly back, raising a quivering, triumphant hand, eyes pale and watery, unable to do more, it seemed.

'Is he all right?' I whispered.

'Oh, yes. Just having a lie-down.'

When would it become her favourite stew, and not theirs, I wondered with a lump in my throat as I let myself out and walked back to the car. Not long, surely. If only couples like that could go on for ever together. Die together. I'd like that for me and Ant, I decided, as I stood for a moment on the pavement in the hazy sunshine, the mist taking its time to clear. You did hear of that, didn't you? The husband going on a Monday, the wife on the Friday, the latter losing the will to live. Yes, we would be one of those couples, holding liver-spotted hands and drifting up to heaven together. Well, hopefully heaven. My heart seemed to be on fire. Was it Felicity's wise words, or was it charity work? Either way, I liked it.

'All right?' shouted Felicity through the car window.

I came to; ran towards her. 'Yes, fine. I'm getting the hang of this. You don't have to get out. What's next?'

'No fowl, number ten. No lumps, number sixteen,' she barked.

'Right.' I beetled to the boot; set off with my booty.

Two minutes later I was back. 'OK. Go again!' I yelled, having delivered the last two at racing speed. I adopted a 'Ta-dah!' pose on the pavement, dusting off my hands as she consulted her list. Too quick for her, you see.

'Two no fish – yellow dot – number twenty-two. A couple of ageing lessies. Watch your back. Quite an eye-opener. They fight like cat and dog and the butch one's convinced we're after her girlfriend, who's a toothless eighty-five. Don't forget the cakes. They adore them.'

No fish, yellow dots, cakes. Right. I could do this. I mean, more. Each week. Take another day. Maybe Sally Powell, down the road, would do it with me? She did almost as little as I did. Not quite. I'd tell her about the lovely feel-good glow. She'd love it, I thought as I raced up the path, a halo over my head.

'You're late.'

Predictable. 'I know, I'm sorry. In here?'

A decidedly masculine old woman with trousers up to her armpits was determinedly blocking my path. Cropped hair and a cravat. Very Noel Coward. Certainly not the distaff side. The place stank of gin and cats.

'Shall I . . . ?' I managed to sidle past her, turning left into the sitting room as she looked over her shoulder at me suspiciously.

'You're new.'

'Yes, my mother couldn't make it today, so I've come instead. Hello there!' This to a tiny, white-haired old lady, wrapped in a pink shawl and propped in a chair like a doll. Despite being eighty-five I could see she once would have been a doll. Good bones. Her rhuemy blue eyes lit up when she saw me.

'Hello, dear.'

Noel Coward instantly hastened in to stand between us, hands on considerable hips.

'Cakes?' Toothless siren peered around her boyfriend's legs.

'Yes, cakes in here.' I put a paper bag on the coffee table in front of her. 'And your lunch is— Oh . . .'

Her shaky, bony old hands had already reached out

and torn open the paper bag. She was cramming a whole fairy cake in her mouth, spitting crumbs, beaming happily. Right.

'She likes her cake first,' her partner explained gruffly.

'Oh. Yes, well, why not? Except – oh Lord.' I lunged forward as I spotted one of Megan's long white dog hairs disappearing into her mouth. Would she choke, croak on the floor in front of me? I plucked at it before it disappeared, but her upper lip lifted too, as if I'd caught a fish. I tugged harder. Her lip came up again.

'Oh!' I let go suddenly.

'What are you doing!' barked Noel Coward.

Heavens. It was attached. I stared at the downy old upper lip, still taking its time to crumple back into place.

'Nothing. Sorry. So sorry.'

Pink Shawl looked startled, but not unduly displeased. She smiled flirtatiously, coquettishly stroking her upper lip. Suddenly she began to warble in a reedy little voice: 'If You Were the Only Girl in the World . . .'

Noel Coward's eyes hardened to bullets. I turned and ran, fleeing through the happily still open front door, and down the path.

'All right?' said Felicity as I flung myself in the passenger seat beside her.

'Yes, fine,' I breathed.

'Only she can be a bit antsy, the butch one,' she said, as she shifted into first. 'She threw a vase at your mother once, when she thought she was being over-felicitous with the one in the shawl, who, incidentally, claims to have danced with the Tiller Girls. If she starts singing "If You Were the Only Girl in the World" you're in trouble.

I glanced back over my shoulder to see butch partner in the doorway, calmly loading an air rifle. She took
aim.

'Drive on!' I squeaked.

As she did, a shot rang out. Felicity looked at me in
horror; put her foot down.

'I, um, think you might have to smooth some troubled
waters next week, Felicity,' I said, hanging on to my seat.
'I've upset her.'

'Don't worry, it's easily done. And she'll have forgotten
in a week's time. None of them remembers anything
beyond tomorrow. Now,' she pulled up further down the
road, 'Mrs Mitchell has a stiff drink on the dot of twelve
every day, and since we're late,' she consulted her watch,
'she'll be away with the fairies by now. Chopped liver,
red dot. And Mrs Mason next door is black dot.'

I ran to the boot and hurried up the path, delivering
to an old dear who was clearly flying – and why not, I
thought, as she opened the front door with a flourish and
swept me a curtsy. I hurried past her to the kitchen, put
the box down, but as I made to leave, she stopped me by
way of sticking an arm in my path, a glass of what was
patently neat gin in her hand.

'Definition of a teetotaller?' she demanded.

I plumped for one of two. 'Someone who knows their
day isn't going to get any better?'

She threw back her head and cackled in delight, letting
me pass: cheering me on my way as she knocked back
the rest of the tumbler prior to settling down to her liver
and bacon. Good on yer, girl.

Next door, a frail, wraithlike figure with a vacant

expression opened the door in a diaphanous nightie. She stared at me and my purple box in wonder.

'Oh dear,' she whispered. 'I keep forgetting if I've had lunch or not.'

'I know the feeling,' I muttered, hurrying past her to put it on her table, then very quickly, out.

'That poor old soul,' I said to Felicity as I got back in the car. 'Should she be on her own?' I glanced back over my shoulder as I put my seat belt on.

'What d'you suggest, a home?'

'Well . . .'

'She'd hate it. No, the trick is, not to get involved. Just deliver them their nice hot meal and know you've made some sort of difference to their day. Now. Two to go. Mr Bernstein – no pork, pink spot – and Mrs Partridge, purple spot, everything puréed.'

'Right.' I tumbled out again as we stopped. Ran round to the boot. Two boxes left. One black spot, one green. Not pink and purple. I frowned. Shouted through the car to the front. 'Sure it's pink and purple?'

'Positive.'

I opened the green box. Sniffed. Pork. Oh Lord. Opened the black one. It was very far from puréed. In fact, a fully dentured person would have trouble with the lumps in that.

'Er . . . Felicity, I think I may have boobed.'

'Oh God,' she groaned. 'What did you give Mrs Mason?'

'Well . . . purple. Isn't that no beans, no onions?'

'No! Black is no beans – and Mr Clarke at number sixteen?'

'Oh God – yellow. Oh, Felicity, I think I've got them muddled!'

'Quick, get in.'

I ran round, jumped back in, and before I'd even shut the door, Felicity was executing an immaculate three-point turn in the road. We roared off back to number sixteen. Dangerously close to the ageing lesbians, as far as I was concerned. I glanced nervously down the road to their bungalow. The front door was shut but I was convinced Noel Coward was at a bedroom window on one knee, taking up a sniper position. Felicity got out with me and we ran up the path as one; leaned on the doorbell.

As Mr Clarke came to the door, napkin tucked in under his chin, knife and fork in hand, Felicity slipped past him.

'Hello, Mr Clarke, have you eaten it yet?'

I moved to join her as she spun around the sitting room.

'What?' He cupped his ear.

'HAVE YOU EATEN LUNCH?'

'Not yet, just about to. Looks delicious.'

He shuffled past us through an archway to a tiny dining room and sat down in front of a full plate. Felicity lunged and whipped it away.

'It's not. But this is.' She gave me a nod and I quickly replaced the fish with the pork. Together we raced out. As I shut the front door I just caught a glimpse of his startled face, his mouth slowly opening and shutting. Then he shrugged and tucked in.

Felicity was already a few doors down, ringing the doorbell. I took a short cut across the tiny front gardens, leaping over a few rose beds and chain-link fences to join her.

'This could be disastrous,' she muttered, leaning hard on the doorbell again. 'Mrs Mason has the sort of flatulence that could propel a small moped. You've just given her puréed beans, onions and prunes.'

'Oh shit.'

'You bet. No plumbing in the civilized world could accommodate what she might evacuate.'

Finally, after three more mighty rings, she came to the door beaming vacantly in her diaphanous nightie, a few telltale stains down the front.

'Hello, Mrs Mason, have you had your lunch?' breathed Felicity urgently.

'Yes, delicious,' she beamed. 'And prunes for pudding. Lovely!'

'Good, good,' purred Felicity nervously. 'Well, jolly good, Mrs Mason. Just checking you enjoyed it.'

'It made a nice change, thank you, dears.' She went very red in the face suddenly. Her flimsy nightie floated up at the back. *Vrrrrp!* She looked astonished. And not a little delighted.

'Mrs Mason,' Felicity was rooting around in her handbag, 'take a couple of these pills with a glass of water, hm?' She punched out a couple of tablets from some silver foil.

'What are they dear. Sweeties?' She gazed at them in wonder. A spectacular smell was unfolding.

'Yes. Sort of. But take them right now, hm?'

'Oh, I *will*. Thank you, dear!' And her face began to

turn pink again, her nightie wafting up, as she shut the front door.

'Don't be surprised if that bungalow takes off of its own accord before the Imodium kicks in,' warned Felicity as we got back in the car. 'We'll probably bump into it on the other side of Oxford.'

'Oh Lord, I'm so sorry. How stupid of me!'

'Don't worry, these things happen.'

'But what about the last one,' I wailed. 'Mrs Purée? Mrs Mason's eaten all her prunes!'

'We'll go to McDonald's and get her a strawberry milkshake and some ice cream. She'll love it. Oh, and a few chips to suck. Perfect.'

'Right,' I agreed faintly.

When we'd delivered the fish to its rightful owner we did just that, and Mrs Purée did indeed seem to love it, greeting her more than usually decorative polystyrene box enthusiastically.

'Ooh, look at that lovely clown's face on the top. A Happy Meal, it says.' She opened it. 'Oh, look, a robot!'

'Yes, for your . . . grandson,' purred Felicity.

'Marvellous, I'll keep it for him. Thank you, my dears.'

One satisfied customer at least. Albeit with quite a lot of sugar and additives inside her.

'I'm so sorry, Felicity,' I muttered as we drove home. God, I couldn't even get that right.

'Oh don't worry, it's easily done,' she smiled. 'Your ma's got them muddled up once or twice too.'

Yes, I bet she had. Like mother, like daughter. Hopeless. And actually I was exhausted. Needed a little lie-down.

Forty winks, as Mum would say. Felicity was consulting her watch.

'Perfect. Well, we may have been erratic, but we were quick. I'm in bags of time.'

'For?' I turned my head wearily towards her on the head rest.

'I'm delivering a lecture on the microbiotic principles of dormant white blood cells at Keble in ten minutes.'

Of course you are. I faced front again. Shook my head in wonder. She dropped me back at the Civic Centre beside my car. I got out, then stuck my head back in.

'I think you're marvellous, Felicity. Absolutely marvellous.'

'Oh, no.' She gave a faint smile, shifting into first. 'I can assure you, Evie, I'm not.'

And off she went.

Later, much later, on the other side of Oxford, a typically quiet evening unfolded at number 22 Walton Terrace. I was sorting through a pile of odd socks at the bottom of the laundry basket in front of the tiny television in the sitting room, the sound turned down low. Anna was in the far corner on her computer, Ant was in his study. After a bit, he came through to join me, Mozart's Clarinet Concerto wafting out after him through his open study door. I instinctively reached for the remote and hit the television mute button. He took his glasses off; sat on the footstool in front of me, coming between me and *Corrie*.

'I've just had an email from Stacey.'

'Oh?' I glanced up from my basket.

'She's asked us all up to Sheffield, after the summer holidays. At half-term.'

I stared at him. 'Ah.'

'Not for all of half-term, just a couple of days.'

'To stay with them? In their house?'

'Yes.' His eyes were steady. Kind. My heart began to pound. I was aware of Anna, her back rigid, as she listened in the corner on her computer, hand frozen on the mouse.

'All of us? Or just you and Anna?'

'All of us. What should I say?'

I took a deep breath. Let it out slowly. 'Say yes. Yes, we'd love to come.'

He smiled, leaned forward and kissed me.

'Thank you, darling.'

My heart was leaping in my throat now, like a salmon, and it had nothing to do with Ken and Deirdre Barlow sharing a tender moment in a quiet corner of the Rovers Return. Ant went back to his study.

Later that evening, as I was drawing my bath, Anna came to find me.

'Thank you, Mum.' She put her arms round me from behind and squeezed me tight. A lump rose in my throat as I turned the taps off. I couldn't answer her. As I turned to face her, she stepped back and looked at me.

'I know this is really hard for you, must be really hard for you, and I know I was a bit over-the-top the other day, but I just want you to know, what you're doing here is seriously awesome.'

I took her in my arms. She rested her head on mine. 'Thanks, darling. Respect?'

'Oh God, yes. Respect.'

# 20

The Hamilton family were driving north. The early hours of the morning had been stormy, thunder and lightning erupting over our heads as we awoke. Now, mid-morning, the heavy rain had eased but the wind hadn't. It seemed the whole dirty sky was shifting fast as we drove with it, the last spots of rain drumming with soft fingers on the roof of the car. Ant and Anna were in the front since Anna was always car sick, and I was in the back reading old copies of *OK!* and sucking Werther's Originals, neither of which Anna could do without retching. So there we had it: the two grown-ups in the front listening to Brahms and chatting about – I glanced up from Liz Hurley's wedding, my finger marking my place as I strained to hear – oh, bird-watching, their latest shared passion; more starlings, fewer finches in the north, apparently, with Mum in the back, reading comics and eating sweets.

We'd been lulled by the summer holidays, then distracted by the new term, then, as half-term approached, it had taken a frantic few days to get us to this ostensibly cosy, familiar point. Not withstanding the nervous flutterings of my heart, there had also been Hector our new dependant, to deal with. I'd first prevailed upon Malcolm to horse-sit, pretending that, since he was doggy, he might also be horsy. There'd been an astonished silence on the other end of the telephone.

'How long have you known me, Evie?'

'Er . . . twenty-two years.'

'And in that time, have you ever, ever seen me with a horse?'

'Um . . . no. I suppose not.'

'Have you ever heard me mention a horse? Affectionately or otherwise?'

'You told me Toby Brewer was hung like one.'

'Don't be fresh. Comparative allusions aside, do the phrases "tacking up" and "trotting on" seem synonymous with one Malcolm Pritchard?'

'Not entirely. But the horsy world's very gay, you know. Lots of leather? Tight jodhpurs? Might be right up your alley?'

'You leave my alley out of it. Do you see me wielding a pitchfork, perchance? A dirty barrow?'

I sighed. 'It was a long shot, Malcolm.'

'Longer than you'll ever know, sweets. Surely your horsy sister-in-law is the obvious port of call?'

'Which is exactly why I don't want to ring her.'

'Needs must, petal. Steel yourself.'

I put the phone down. No. Out of the question. I sank back into my chair in despair and gazed bleakly at the kitchen wall. Years ago, of course I'd have rung Mario, Dad's farm worker. Dear, wizened old Mario, with his round walnut face and his eyes that all but disappeared when he smiled. Dad had liked the colour of them, he'd said, and his wife, Maroulla's, when they'd come to the farm one day looking for work. What, black? Tim and I had asked in surprise, and Dad had laughed. Originally from a poor village in Andalusia, they'd come across to work at the Triumph factory, planning to stay for five years and take the money back to Spain. Instead, they'd lasted one at Triumph, missed working on the land, come to the farm and stayed for ever. Mario had died just ten days after my father, and Maroulla had moved out of the cottage to live with her daughter. Whenever I thought of Maroulla now I felt a sort of non-specific guilt. No, specific guilt actually, because I knew she'd recently moved to a nursing home and I hadn't been to see her. I told myself I was wary of bumping into her children, who, despite having grown up with us, viewed us with suspicion – the rich, posh folk – but there was an element of idleness too. I sighed. But, yes, Mario would have looked after Hector like a shot. 'Of course, Eviee – ees no problem!' I could hear him saying in his severely broken English. 'I look after thees horse for you. You go!'

Instead I shut my eyes tight and punched out another number. Malcolm was right. Needs must. Caro was silent for a long moment when I'd finally gabbled and stammered my way through.

'Well, I think you're very brave to go and see them. Where are you staying?'

'With them.'

'God, won't that be awkward?'

'Well, I'm not exactly relishing it, but I promised. Can't go back on my word, can I?'

I seemed to remember Caro saying something very

similar about how she, A Good Mother, would never break a promise. Might as well earn a few brownie points in lieu of horseflesh.

'Well, good for you,' she said grudgingly. 'Yes, I'll do Hector for you. Or you could even ask Phoebe and pay her. Children will do anything for money.'

'Will they?'

'Of course, didn't you know that?'

It occurred to me that Anna did hardly anything for money, since we gave it to her anyway. Well, she was an only, and we had plenty, but that wasn't entirely the point, was it? She wasn't learning the value of it.

'Is she there?'

'Hang on, I'll get her.'

Phoebe came on, breathless. 'Hi, Evie!'

'Hi, Phoebs. Darling, I wondered, would you be an angel and look after Hector for a few days? Only we're going away at half-term.'

'I know. Mummy just told me. Does that mean Anna won't be doing Pony Club with us?'

'Oh, some of it she will, just not at the beginning. But we'll be back on Tuesday, don't you worry.'

'Oh. OK. Most of it's over by then.'

As I secured a deal with her and put the phone down, it occurred to me she was bitterly disappointed. During the summer, Anna had practically lived at the farm, and these last few weeks after school had spent most after-noons there too, riding Hector, who, true to Camilla's word, always behaved beautifully and hadn't put a hoof wrong. The two cousins had trotted around the fields together on their ponies, Anna, nervous but getting there,

Phoebe, encouraging her, revelling in teaching her cousin new tricks, and then together they'd mucked out, preferring to do it together in the light autumn evenings, the clocks not yet gone back, radio blaring, laughing and joking. I'd wondered how long it would last, but thus far, Hector had been a huge success. It occurred to me that Phoebe had been looking forward to this holiday, to see even more of Anna, show her off to her friends, and possibly show off a little herself too. But as I said, we'd be back.

Right now, we were nearly there. In Sheffield. I sat up and looked around. I'd rather imagined it would be more built-up: rows and rows of little terraced houses snaking up hills as we approached, perhaps with a few disused pits and crumbling mills. More Lowry country and less, well, less beautiful countryside, which, as we cruised through it now, looked more green and pleasant than dark and satanic. As one lush field gave way to another, punctuated by a few dreamy-looking sheep and enclosed by neat dry-stone walls, I frowned.

'Are we nearly there?' I really was the nine-year-old in the back. And actually I needed the loo too.

'Very. The next village.'

I blinked. 'But I thought they lived in Sheffield.'

'No, close by. Their village is eight miles outside.'

'Oh. You said Sheffield!'

'Only as a point of reference. A bit like Tim and Caro living in Oxford.'

'Down here, Daddy.' Anna was navigating from her vantage point in the front, a printed out email in her hand. 'And then left at the postbox, apparently . . .' Ant swung the car obediently, 'and then down the hill into the village . . .'

I gazed in wonder. By now the rain had dried up, the blustering wind had spent, and a bright blue sky had been offered by way of apology. Down the bottom of the hill, in a fold, an adorable little village came into view. A huddle of grey slate roofs grouped around a skinny church spire; loose, crooked walls ran around gardens under chestnut trees, their leaves golden against the blue October haze. A river warbled and rushed through the middle of the village, fleeing west down the valley. Beyond, the toppling steepness of the hills rose up as a backdrop, painted with a smudgy green brush, and just a daub of purple heather.

As we followed the sinuous course of the lane to its conclusion in the valley, it came to rest amidst a string of grey cottages. We purred through. There was a sudden darkening of ancient yew trees, which clustered around the church in the centre, all but hiding its steeple.

'Just the other side of the church, Daddy, the very next house. Here, with the five-bar gate.'

Five-bar gate? My head snapped around.

Set back slightly from the lane was a detached, but compact, grey stone house. It was twin gabled and symmetrical, and of that more attractive ilk of gothic architecture once reserved for the clergymen of the Church of England: indeed the twinkling stained-glass gaze of the small grey church beside it testified as much. As if more proof were needed, the discreet wooden sign on the gate bore the legend 'The Old Rectory'. It opened automatically, sensing our car bonnet, and as we crawled across the crunchy gravel under the roomy shade of a splendid old beech tree, the sun, with a flash of cussed brilliance, picked out the mellow stone façade of the house, complete with pretty wooden porch painted a tasteful grey-green, one I recognized from the Farrow and Ball colour chart, crawling with late and fading roses.

As if this paralysing sight weren't enough, the front door opened and there, on the door step, before I'd had a moment to compose myself, were mother and daughter, although it took me a moment to decide which was which. Both were tall and slim, with long blonde hair, and wearing jeans, T-shirts and big anxious smiles. I suddenly felt incredibly overdressed in my meet-the-mother-of-my-husband's-love-child kit of long floral skirt, little nipped-in tweed jacket and suede boots. And she was gorgeous. *Gorgeous.* For some reason it was the mother my eyes flew to first, with those fabulous cheekbones I recognized from the photograph: full mouth, flawless pale complexion and teeny tiny figure. Beneath her thick blonde fringe I caught a glimpse of amazing blue-green eyes. I gulped. Your average nightmare.

Ant and Anna were already out of the car as I was gawping through the back window taking all this in, embracing, kissing, exclaiming. As I hurriedly got out to join them, my heel got caught in the hem of my floral skirt, which meant I fell out of the car, and in an effort to save myself, cannoned headlong into the mother, Isabella, arms outstretched, as if intent on embracing her.

She steadied me in astonishment as my nose squashed hers. Ant lunged to catch my arm.

'All right, old thing?' he laughed.

Old thing. He never called me that. But beside this enchanting creature it was decidedly apposite.

'Yes!' I gasped. Shit, my *ankle*.

'Evie, this is Bella. Bella, my wife, Evie.'

Flushing with shame and annoyance and, actually, *pain*, I flashed a manic smile. 'Hi!'

'We're so glad you've come,' Bella said eagerly, meeting my eyes. 'You've no idea what this means to us.'

It was a simple little speech, but heartfelt; unrehearsed, unlike so many of mine, and consequently disarming.

'It's . . . lovely to be here,' I managed.

'And this is Stacey.'

I turned, properly, to the daughter. Wide nervous blue eyes gazed at me, like a frightened deer, the colour of Ant's, the shape of her mother's. Her blonde hair was swept back off a high forehead, her bottom lip almost quivered as she plucked nervously at the bottom of her T-shirt with long sensitive fingers. She was so obviously Ant's child it took my breath away.

'Hi,' she whispered, averting her eyes to the gravel.

'Hello, Stacey.' I smiled and held out my hand, which she took eagerly.

A young springer spaniel came wiggling out of the door between their legs, barking uncertainly. Anna exclaimed in delight and bent to pat him, and as Stacey eagerly introduced her pet, her mother ushered us inside, me, gushing nervously about the proportions of the wide hall, its ancient flagstones, the paintings on the walls, Bella, thanking me for my compliments as I secretly marvelled at the two girls, drifting to each other's side at the foot of the stairs, smiling shyly, the puppy having bounded off. Sisters, I thought with a lump in my throat as I saw them exchange hushed enquiries, cheeks flushed, admiring each other's bracelets, and I realized Bella was watching them too, eyes bright. I glanced at Ant, but his eyes were full of such an extraordinary light, such pride and astonishment, I had to look away.

We followed Bella through to the kitchen: a square sunny room painted duck-egg blue with a terracotta floor and a smart black Rayburn. French windows were flung open onto a sunny terrace and garden. I prattled away nervously, admiring everything, which wasn't difficult – even a bantam hen that had wandered in, and which Bella shooed out, clapping her hands at it: tiny hands, I noticed, with translucent skin. Ant was quiet, as was his wont, unforthcoming, and I wondered who was making who feel comfortable here; who was carrying the show, as usual.

'Have you been here long?' I asked, limping finally to the wider extremities of my opening gambits, and also, rather gratefully, to a chair she'd pulled out for me at the table. I sat and rested my ankle.

'Not really, we – oh, *coffee!*' she yelped suddenly, rushing to a rather too ferociously bubbling percolator on the side. I gazed at her blue-jeaned bottom as she ministered to it. It reminded me of someone's . . . oh, yes, Kate Moss's. She poured the fresh coffee.

'Two years, not long.' She turned to flash me a smile. 'We're still settling in, really, and it's quite a change from what we're used to. But we love it here.'

'You were in the city before?'

'Well, in the suburbs. Long Haden, d'you know it?'

'Um, no.'

'But – well, when we could afford a bit more, I thought, why not?'

She brought a tray of coffee to the table with a plate of cakes, clearly home-made, arranged on a plate, as if any of us could eat a thing.

'We'd always wanted to live in the country, and we drove out here one Saturday afternoon, didn't we, Stace?' She glanced across at her daughter but she was deep in whispered conversation with Anna at the other end of the kitchen. 'Saw this place, and thought, let's have a look. It needed quite a bit of work – still does – and it's probably too big for the two of us, but we fell in love with it.'

She flushed and I flushed and then Ant did too.

Falling in love. Brought up, inadvertently, and really quite early on in the proceedings. I saw Ant watching her as she busied herself with cups and plates, and tried to interpret his look. Found it was one I wasn't familiar with. Or had I just not seen it for a while?

'Well, I can quite see why,' I rushed on approvingly, knowing, with an aching heart that I liked this girl, with her quick nervous manner, her obvious efforts to please me, and her blushing highly strung daughter; knew they were entirely my type: the sort of people who, had I met them first, I'd come rushing home to enthuse to Ant about. 'Oh, you'll love them, Ant, they're a stunning mother-and-daughter act, clever, pretty, sensitive,' as one does when one is secure in love, in a relationship, knowing they would pose no threat. And this was often the way in our marriage. I was the open gregarious one, the one who made the friends. I'd come home from a school coffee morning or lunch party and say, 'She's divine, Ant, and he'll be heaven too, I'm sure. Let's have them over for dinner.' And I'd invite this new couple, and invariably Ant would like them, but from a distance, cautiously; gradually getting to know them in a quieter, less headstrong way. Yes, I always paved the way, did the groundwork. But this time, Ant had done the groundwork. He knew this girl so much better than I did. She was his friend, his ex-lover and I felt the disadvantage keenly.

Suddenly I was determined to rise above it. Something in my character longed to be able to say to him tonight, as we got into bed, 'Well, she's lovely, Ant, quite splendid. And did you know she's going to start Open University next year? Yes, and the watercolours in the hall are by a friend of hers in Leeds . . .' to be the one informed, the informer, the chatty, gossipy one in control, whilst he smiled indulgently and sank back into his familiar role of slightly disinterested husband, in his propped-up pillows, reading Brecht, as I bustled around the room slapping cream on my cheeks, brushing my hair. But I would never be able to tell him about this girl, I realized with a jolt. It brought me up short. Except . . . he hadn't seen her, Bella, for over sixteen years, had he? She would have changed, and I'd be able to tell him how; fill in the gaps, help him understand her and her daughter more. I realized I very much wanted to do that; to assist, not to hinder relations, which surprised me enormously. Pleased me, too.

'Your garden's beautiful,' I was saying, cradling my coffee and getting up to admire it, trying to ignore my ankle, which was making me wince.

The terrace gave onto a tidy enclosure of about half an acre, the foreground of which was crisscrossed with low hedges of well-educated box, which ran in tandem with gravel paths. It was an agreeable arrangement I recognized from glossy magazines, and which I had a nasty feeling bore the deeply romantic title 'knot garden', something, in a half-formed way, as soon as I set eyes on it, I knew I'd always wanted. Why, I'd even got round to tearing out the relevant pages in *House and Garden*, but never to planting it. Had she grown it all from seed? Perhaps I could hate her after all?

'Oh, it's one of the reasons I bought it,' she enthused, coming to join me and stroll amongst it. 'Sadly I haven't the faintest idea how to maintain it. It needs a lot of TLC and I don't know the first thing about gardening.' No. Couldn't hate her. 'But I'm learning. I bought my first book the other day – Alan Titchmarsh no less – thought, now this is positively grown-up!' I smiled. She was, after all, still young, and boy, had I done the maths. Eighteen plus nine months plus seventeen – thirty-six. With the face and figure of a twenty-six-year-old.

Ant was talking to the girls on the terrace as Bella and I strolled out onto the lawn; damp and shiny and strewn with curling yellow leaves. A cherry tree planted centrally enjoyed sole occupancy, its skinny grey branches scantily clad now, just a few yellowing survivors of summer clinging resolutely to their posts. They fluttered valiantly in the breeze, their comrades littering the sodden lawn below. Around the trunk was a circular wooden seat, which I admired.

'Except I hadn't realized my tree was so fat, and look,

it doesn't meet!' Bella wailed, showing me round the back, where a six-inch gap prevailed.

'Looks like the zip of my jeans on a bad day,' I commented. 'You need someone to knock a piece of wood in there for you,' I advised, and as I said it, I knew I meant a man, a husband, an Ant, which of course she'd been without all these years. As it had struck Anna that Stacey had been without a father, so it struck me that Bella had been without a husband. That I'd got in first. And she'd been pregnant first. I had a sudden vision of her carrying Stacey, nine months pregnant in a Laura Ashley maternity dress. Then with a pram around the streets of Sheffield.

'I . . . want to thank you so much for what you've done today.' She looked at me, eyes huge in a pale face. 'You have no idea how much it means to Stacey. To both of us. And a lot of women wouldn't have done it. Wouldn't have come. I think you've been tremendous.'

My eyes filled with tears and I wanted to tell her I hadn't been tremendous. That up to now I'd been filled with jealous loathing, had stamped on her face in a bookshop, had never wanted to meet her, hoping all summer to be able to cancel this visit, and until recently had had every intention of carrying on in the same hate-filled vein, but now, now that I'd met them both, I knew it was impossible. That I could quite see why Ant had fallen in love with her. That I was mortified he'd ended up with me. That the comparison was odious. I tried to steady my breathing. Her fingers were twisting nervously in the hem of her T-shirt, like her daughter's.

'It hasn't been easy,' I admitted. 'I have to tell you,

Bella, when I first heard about you and Stacey I wanted you both burned at the stake.'

'I can understand that,' she said quickly. 'I'd feel just the same.'

'So . . . did you feel the same? When you heard he'd married me? And you were left holding the baby?' ·

She narrowed her eyes at the untamed hills beyond, the sedgy wilderness interspersed with dense clumps of bracken, still darkly green and untouched by autumn, as if groping there for the truth.

'No,' she said slowly, 'I didn't hate you, because I knew your claim to Ant was more valid than mine. I was the interloper, the cuckoo in the nest. You'd been the girlfriend. The fact that I got pregnant was immaterial. And immature and stupid. But . . . I resented you the cosy family life. Which I didn't have. I had a bit of a struggle.' She sat down on the rickety seat.

I sat beside her. 'What happened?'

'I came home when I knew I was pregnant. Left Oxford. It just seemed like the obvious thing to do. I was terrified.'

'Of your parents?'

'No no, my dad was brilliant. Shocked, but brilliant. My mum died when I was little, so he'd brought me up. He works at the Vodaphone factory down at Sutherton's. You know, by the port?'

'I . . . don't.'

'He'd already brought up one little girl alone, and suddenly here he was with another. But he just took it in his stride. Rose to the occasion and gave me all the support I needed. We lived with him for six years, Stacey and me.

I mean, it was my home, anyway. I was only eighteen when it happened.'

'He must have been very disappointed about Oxford.' A factory worker. His only daughter. Beautiful and bright as a button too. Ticket to ride.

She smiled. 'You'd think so, wouldn't you? Me, an only child, getting out of our tiny council house to the dreaming spires, and then made pregnant by a don. Most fathers would bustle down south rolling up their sleeves brandishing a meat cleaver, but he's a remarkable man, my dad. He was completely with me when I decided not to have an abortion. He couldn't bear the thought, either. Told me, when all's said and done, a human life is more important and more magnificent than any degree, or any lucrative career it might have fixed me up with. And he has to be right, doesn't he?'

I followed her gaze to her daughter, Anastasia, talking with Anna and Ant on the terrace, blushing every time Ant addressed her, eyes firmly on the York stone: older than Anna but not as confident, desperately shy. Not the Storm model type I'd envisaged at all.

'Yes. He has to be right.'

'And he's a great believer in what goes around comes around.' She flattened her vowels to mimic a broader accent. 'Things 'ave an 'abit of comin' right in the end, pet,' she smiled.

'And he's right, they have,' I said slowly. 'Your books . . .'

She shrugged. 'Came about because I didn't want to work in a bank and put Stacey in childcare, exactly. And they've paid for all this. And I love doing it.'

'He must be very proud.'

She smiled. 'Brimming. You'll meet him tonight. He's coming for supper.' She looked at me anxiously as if to check this was all right.

I smiled. 'I'd like to meet him.'

I wanted to ask, if apart from her father, there'd been any other man in her life. There must have been, she was so lovely. I was wondering how to couch it, without sounding crass, but the others were strolling over to join us: Anna, aglow I could see, chattering away; Stacey, face still trained to the ground but smiling broadly; Ant . . . oh, Ant. Like a tall, pale daffodil, head bowed, but looking as if his heart would burst, his bright eyes glancing up and finding mine, anxious suddenly, saying – is this OK? Are we going to be all right? Are *you* all right, darling? And that wretched lump rose up in my throat again as I flashed him a quick nod and a smile. Yes, I'm fine. We're fine. It's going to be all right.

The atmosphere at supper that night put paid to the notion that you can't force jollity. Force is perhaps putting it too strongly as no one was attempting to drag it kicking and screaming, and jollity suggests dizzy heights of levity, which weren't necessarily reached, but we did our best to ensure the evening was a success and pretty much pulled it off.

We ate in the kitchen. There was in fact a tiny, dark red dining room at the front of the house, but Bella deemed it too formal, and claimed people's expectations of the food were always higher. She confided to me as she bent to take a casserole out of the oven, peering in with an anxious look I recognized, although mine usually bordered on the fearful, that actually, she'd never used it: always used the kitchen when she entertained, which was rare anyway. As I laid the table for her, I trembled on the verge of asking who exactly she entertained when she did, albeit rarely, but before I could decently, or even indecently, pose the question, her father walked in.

He was a great bear of a man, who, when he'd squeezed through the doorway, seemed to fill the small kitchen, his sandy hair skimming the oak beams as he ducked. He was brick red in the face and perspiring as he kissed his daughter and granddaughter, his arms full of flowers as he exploded out of a hairy tweed jacket several sizes too small for him. Although I saw immediately where the height and blondness came from, I detected little else: the fine features must be from the mother. Ant had followed the girls into the room and Bella's colour too was high as she turned to make the introductions: I could see she was wondering how to do this. Her fingers were in the hem of her T-shirt.

'Hi, I'm Evie,' I stepped forward smiling and proffering my hand. 'And this is my daughter, Anna, and my husband, Ant.'

Bella shot me a grateful look and muttered, 'My Dad, Ted.'

The two men's eyes met and they shook hands, but it was brisk and brief. I realized, with a start, how hard that must be for Ted: to shake the hand of the man who'd got his teenage daughter pregnant, the teacher man who'd been employed to instruct his child in the language of the poets, of rhyming couplets and iambic pentameters, not the language of love. Despite Bella's protestations to the contrary, he must have hated him. And no one ever hated Ant. Always said how kind and wise he was, what a gentle man – he was often described thus. I saw the colour shoot to Ant's cheeks too, in this moment of . . . well, shame. Again, not something he was familiar with, because he was rarely the guilty party. I was the one who ran furtively up the stairs with yet another Nicole Farhi bag to be hustled under the bed. I was the one who drove, red-faced and sweaty-palmed, out of Tesco's car park knowing I'd reversed into yet another car, then roared back ten minutes later to leave a note on the bonnet with my number, only to find the car had gone.

Oh, my life was one long perpetual guilt trip, but not Ant's. I felt very protective of him suddenly.

'What lovely flowers!' I said, breaking the moment and seizing a jug from the middle of the table. 'Shall I put them in water for you, Bella?'

'They're for you, luv,' Ted said gruffly, handing them to me. 'I know you're stayin', like, so I thought you could put them in your room.'

'Oh. Thank you.' I was taken aback.

'No, thank you. It's a rare and fine thing you've done for us here today.' His pale blue eyes under sandy brows swam a bit. I took the flowers, touched; aware of quite a few eyes on me. Aware that he was deliberately making a moment of it, and although I was embarrassed, I was grateful too.

'Well, they're my absolute favourite. I adore lilies.' I buried my nose in them, suddenly at a loss.

'Drink, Dad?' Bella reached up to pull a bottle of wine from a high rack above the fridge.

'Please, luv. Here, I'll do that.' He got the bottle for her as Ant, who'd also gone to help, looked awkward. 'But I might take a beer off you first just to take the edge off it.' He loosened his tie. 'Phew, bit hot in here, isn't it?' He glanced at Ant in an open-necked shirt and, in a trice, whipped off what I felt was an uncharacteristic jacket and tie. He rolled up his sleeves and I saw Anna's eyes pop at the tattoos.

'It's the Rayburn,' Bella told him, and I realized how faint her accent was compared to that of her father, who was a northcountryman right unto his syntax. 'Throws out a lot of heat.'

He undid his top button. 'Aye, in return for a lot of brass. All that expensive iron just to cook a stew. Four grand, that were!' He turned to me in astonishment. 'Reclaimed, an' all!'

'I know,' I agreed. 'We've got one too, I'm afraid.'

'Why?' He looked genuinely baffled. 'You could buy a car for four grand, but a bleedin' cooker . . .'

'Here, Dad.' Bella handed him a drink, obviously keen to head him off the subject of money, which, alas, was a stimulating topic in this part of the world.

Stacey was more animated now, clearly enamoured of her grandfather and showing him Anna's bracelets from Accessorize, then her own jangling assortment on her wrist. 'The same, Granddad, d'you see? We bought them separately and chose exactly the same. How weird is that?'

As he knocked back half his beer in one thirsty gulp, his huge stomach straining the buttons of his shirt, he exclaimed with her. 'Aye, luv, look at that, you have! And right tacky they are too.'

'Granddad!' She swatted him with the back of her hand as he roared with laughter.

'Well, lime green and pink, I ask you. What rotten taste you've both got!' He looked from one girl to the other, teasing them with his eyes, but they were keen too, those eyes, as he took in my daughter, this half-sister of Stacey's. I wondered what he'd see. No, knew what he'd see. The astonishing similarities: the big smile, the high cheekbones and then, as Anna spoke, the educated Oxford accent, unlike his granddaughter's local one, the poise, the confidence an expensive education could buy as she explained; 'Tat is the new style. It's very avant-garde to be kitsch.'

'Is it, by 'eck!' he marvelled, but you could tell he was impressed. His gaze roved to Ant: more brains and more blond hair, the missing link, who was pulling the cork from the bottle, and I saw Ted sip his beer more thoughtfully now, take a moment to digest the provenance, the gene pool that defined his granddaughter.

The evening slipped on. For slip, read well oiled, for Bella forgot to put the vegetables on, which prolonged the cocktail hour, and also people were nervous, so by the time supper was finally on the table, I for one was flying. The table was a long thin slab of oak, and to prevent us being miles apart, Bella had seated three down each side, with Ted and I opposite one another, then the girls, then Ant and Bella. It was the obvious placement: I could hardly sit with Ant, nor Bella with her father, but as the girls chattered to each other across the table, eventually three conversations developed. And I got on famously with Towering Ted, who looked like Gulliver in his tiny chair, most of him spilling over the side. His voice boomed out as he talked, mostly about his daughter, and how all his colleagues at work bought her books, and how he was constantly getting them thrust under his nose to get her to sign.

'"Hey, Ted. Get your lass to sign this for our Sandra, would you? She loves 'em, can't put 'em down. And me mam!"'

I smiled. 'You must be very proud.'

His eyes filled as he seized his wine glass. 'You'll never know, lass.' His lower lip gave way to an involuntary quiver. 'Never know.'

And then he knocked back another glass of wine, his

face quite purple, and my eyes filled too – why? – as I also knocked back another one, for moral support, for sympathy, for courage.

The girls, who'd managed craftily to recharge their glasses whilst we weren't watching, shrieked and laughed at each other across the table, clearly quite tight, whilst Ant and Bella fell into a quieter conversation at the end. I strained to hear as I pretended to listen to Ted, who was telling me now how a book group near him, down his road in fact, had picked one of Bella's books and then '– would you believe it – a couple of months later, on account of enjoyin' it so much, picked another!' As I nodded and smiled, marvelling and exclaiming, I felt a hand reach in and squeeze my heart. What were they talking about? I heard Stacey's name. Yes, of course. Their daughter. Their *daughter*. The bizarreness of it hit me. I lunged for my glass. God, this was surreal. What was I doing here? No wonder Ted had given me flowers, no wonder Caro had – for once – been lost in admiration for me. Was I mad? Completely insane? Or a fool? I felt myself wobble, thought, at any moment, I might just get up and announce, 'Sorry, I can't do this,' and run out. I steadied myself as Ted rattled on. No. This was right. The right way forward. The only way forward. And I was up to it.

But I needed some help. I seized the wine bottle and topped Ted up – rude not to join him – so that by the time Ant and I climbed the stairs to bed in the pretty pink spare room, me carrying the vase of lilies precariously, I was plastered.

'Aren't they lovely, Ant? My flowers?' I demanded in

a overly loud voice. I crossed the room, sloshing water on the carpet and setting them unsteadily on the chest of drawers, right beside a vase of roses already put there by Bella. I blinked in surprise. 'Blimey. Looks like a bloody florist's in here. Either that or a funeral parlour!'

For some reason that struck me as terribly funny. I fumbled around the room sniggering, 'Funeral parlour . . .' foolishly to myself, knocking into furniture and leaving a trail of clothes in my wake. Ant was calmly brushing his teeth in the ensuite bathroom in his boxer shorts. I stopped in the doorway to watch him, swayed as I frowned at his back view. Not pissed, I decided. No. Really quite sober. Still. You never know. I sashayed up behind him, clasped him round his waist from behind. Then I rocked him gently and sang a little Rod Stewart in his ear. 'Tonight's the night . . . s'gonna be all right . . .'

He laughed, disentangled himself and turned round to hold my arms.

'D'you think?'

'What?' I tried to focus on his face. 'Tonight's the night? Or, s'gonna be all right?'

He grinned. 'I certainly agree with the latter. Not sure about the former.'

It took me a moment to remember which was which. I pouted. Pulled out the elastic on his shorts and pinged them back. 'Spoilsport.'

'Not sure these walls are up to it.'

'*We could be quiet!*' I hissed drunkenly in his face. 'And anyway,' I swayed, 'those Victorians knew a thing or two about building. Knew how to soundproof the unlacing of their . . . whatsit. Strait laces. Look at bloody Brunel!

Look at all those bloody viaducts!' I waved my hand at the window as if there were a few outside, then went in for a snog, shutting my eyes. A mistake.

'Shit,' I gasped, rocking back abruptly on my heels. 'Head spin.' I clutched the offending article. 'Nurofen, Ant. Fast.'

He turned to rummage in the bathroom cupboard which, being spare, was also bare.

'In my bag,' I groaned, still holding my head and staggering back to the bedroom to sit on the edge of the bed.

He found some. As I glugged gratefully on the glass of water he put to my lips, gulping down the pills, I allowed myself to be laid back on the pillows. Tucked in.

'Sleep,' he said firmly as he straightened up. He swam before my line of vision.

'You think?' I murmured doubtfully. 'Rather than sex?' 'Definitely.'

I shut my eyes, gave it some thought. 'OK.' And then just before I blacked out, I whispered hoarsely, 'I've done well though, Ant . . . haven't I? Been good?'

He kissed my lips. 'You've been very good.'


The next morning I awoke in terrible, terrible pain. My head was in a much worse state than it had been the night before, and my mouth hung open on its hinges, refusing to close, severe drought having set in. I felt really extraordinarily ill. After a few minutes I managed gingerly to open my eyes. I peered at the light streaming through the thin curtains, then shut them again. Oh God. I groaned, turned over and opened them again to peer at the clock. Ten o'clock. Ten o'clock! Oh Lord, quite late. After a bit,

I sat up slowly. Ant's side of the bed was empty, the covers thrown back. Were they all downstairs having breakfast? Waiting for me to appear?

I staggered to the loo, found some more Nurofen in my bag, guzzled them down. Then I got dressed, tidying up last night's clothes as I went. I had to crouch straight backed to retrieve everything, rather than bending over, to avoid head rush.

I sat down and peered in the mirror at the dressing table. Shocked myself. My face looked as if it had been punched, and my usually wavy hair was plastered to my head in a centre parting, like an ageing hippy. All I needed was a guitar. I brushed it and tried to fluff it up, but in vain. I gave up, got to my feet, and toddled out to the landing clutching the furniture. The thought of breakfast made me feel ill, but happily I couldn't smell anything. Perhaps not a fry-up? Perhaps more a cereal household, like mine? And perhaps I could force a Weetabix down, for form's sake. I gulped. Clutched my mouth. Perhaps not.

As I went to go downstairs, I glanced back and realized I hadn't drawn my bedroom curtains, which looked a bit slutty. I waddled back in and swept them aside, and that's when I saw them. At the bottom of the garden, sitting on the circular seat around the cherry tree. Bella and Ant. And why not, I thought as my hand nevertheless went straight to my mouth. I instinctively ducked back behind the curtain. Why not sit and chat – I peered round cautiously – catch up on all those years, discuss Stacey . . . Oxbridge interviews . . . whatever . . . So why was my heart beating so fast? So furiously?

I watched, fascinated, from behind the curtain. Their heads were close together and both were leaning forwards intently, hands clasped on knees, almost as if in prayer. Certainly deep in conversation. But I couldn't really see who was doing all the . . . I glanced behind me to our open suitcase: Ant's bird book and binoculars were stuffed in the side pocket. I lunged, seized the binos. Then I kneeled down under the windowsill and tried to focus. I'd never used these things before . . . oh, I see . . . twiddle the knobs . . . and . . . golly, amazing. It was as if the pair of them were right in front of me, huge, and beautifully focused. Ant's head was cocked as he listened intently to what Bella was saying. She seemed to be struggling to explain something, definitely a monologue, her lips moving rapidly, tongue swishing over them occasionally. Ant gazed at her intently, nodded occasionally and then he spoke . . . and then she said something back – how I wished these things had a microphone – and then they both looked at each other without speaking for a moment. As they gazed at each other, a lock of hair fell forward into her eyes. Gently, and in an unbearably sweet gesture, Ant reached out and tucked it back behind her ear.

'Eh up, twitcher!'

I swung around in horror. Bella's father's bulk was filling the open doorway.

'Oh!' A *curtain* twitcher. I scrambled to my feet. Dropped the binos. 'Oh, no, I was – I was watching the birds!'

'Aye, like I say, a twitcher. A girl after my own heart. I come here sometimes to do just that. Got my own binos in here.' He patted the black overnight bag he was carrying and crossed the room in one giant stride. 'What 'ave you seen then, luv?' He peered keenly out of the window. 'A red kite? You get a few of them in these parts, whirling round those tree tops yonder.'

'Yes,' I croaked at length. 'Yes, there was one . . . yonder . . . but it flew away.'

'Where?' He picked up the binoculars from the floor and raised them eagerly to his eyes. I pointed up high in the sky, in the top right-hand corner, well away from the cherry tree. Into the heavens. But he was lowering them even now, to where the action was. He gazed for a long moment. Lowered them and looked grave.

'Tit,' he muttered.

*Tit?* I cringed. What, me? Or her?

'Some kind of tit. Probably greater crested. You get a lot of them in these parts, but I dare say not so much down South. You can see its yellow underparts, look.'

He handed the binoculars back to me. 'In the cherry tree, just behind your Ant. See?' I was grateful for the possessive article before my husband's name, and of his guiding hand, but mine were a bit sweaty, and all I got out of the binoculars was wobbling blur and fuzz.

'Yes, I see it now,' I breathed. 'Very pretty. Lovely.'

'Aye, and tha's what we need to keep focused on, eh?' he said gently. 'The lovely birds.' His eyes were kind as they held mine a moment; then they drifted away out of the window. 'But you keep your eyes peeled for the red kite, luv. That's a rare treat, that is.'

'I certainly will,' I whispered.

'They've only just been reintroduced you know, back into the wild.'

'Have they really?'

'Aye, but you'll know that!'

'Of course! How silly, I forgot.'

'Aye, in fact if I remember rightly, they released more down your way than they did up here. You're in the Chilterns, aren't you? Down there in Oxfordshire?'

'I believe we are.'

He looked at me in astonishment. 'Well, that's where they all are, you great ninny!' He gave me an affectionate nudge, which knocked me halfway across the room, nearly dislocating my elbow. 'Call yerself a twitcher!'

I gave a high, hyena-like laugh. 'Heee! Yes, hopeless!' I steadied myself on the chest of drawers.

'Well, anyway, luv,' he straightened up, almost to attention, head grazing the ceiling, 'I'm away. Just popped up to say goodbye to you. Thought you might be up by now.'

'Yes, I . . . overslept a bit. But I'm very glad you did. Goodbye, Ted.' I went to peck his cheek but he'd already enveloped me in a huge bear hug and I found myself pressed hard against his chest, arms clamped to my sides.

'Goodbye, luv,' he said gruffly. 'I'm that made up to have met you all. Really I am. All of you.' I couldn't breath. My eyes bulged into his shirt.

'You too!' I managed when he'd finally released me.

And then he was gone – out of the room and down the stairs, no doubt to say goodbye to the others. I watched as he reappeared below, through the French windows into the garden; saw Ant and Bella stand up to say goodbye as he approached, bag in hand. And he saw nothing peculiar, Terrific Ted, as he'd become in my mind, in the two of them sitting under the tree together, and she didn't get up with a start. I watched as Ant shook his hand, and then Bella hugged him as he took his leave. How I envied him. I clutched the windowsill. I wanted to go too, wanted, with all my heart, to be a hundred miles from here. The look Ant had given Bella as he'd tucked her hair back had pierced my heart. It spoke volumes. Because I knew Ant. Knew he wasn't given to little gestures like that. This man, Terrific, Tactile Ted, who squeezed me at a moment's notice, who'd gently chided me back there for reading too much into the situation, was wrong. He was clearly a demonstrative huggy man but not my Ant.

On an impulse I darted to the bathroom, threw my toothbrush and face creams into my handbag and went downstairs. Ant and Bella were strolling up the garden with Ted, towards the side of the house, making for his car at the front. They saw me and stopped. Waved.

'Hiya!' called Bella.

'Hi!' I called back.

'Did you sleep well?'

I tripped across the lawn to join them. 'Really well, thank you.'

She shaded her eyes with her hand against the sun. 'Only the girls wanted to wake you, bring you a cup of tea, but I told them you'd rather have a lie-in. I know I would!'

'Yes! Quite right.'

She was looking particularly lovely, I noticed, in a white pin-tucked peasanty top, a tiered denim skirt and floppy suede boots. What teeny tiny legs she had poking out of them.

'Um, where are the girls?'

'Oh, they went into town after breakfast, caught the bus. Stacey wanted to show Anna around, have a hot chocolate, mooch round Topshop. I hope you don't mind?' She looked anxious, suddenly.

'Oh, no, not at all. It's just . . .'

'Is everything all right, darling?' Ant looked concerned. Much as one would about a maiden aunt, I felt.

'Well, not entirely. I've just had a call from Caro,' I lied.

'Oh?'

'I'm afraid someone's ill.'

'Oh Lord, who?'

It couldn't be one of the cousins. I never, ever used a child, not now. Not after using Anna once, claiming she was sick and we couldn't go to dinner with Ant's terrifying faculty head and his fearsome, moustachioed wife, and then the very next day – the *very* next day – she'd been *so* sick, with a raging temperature and a thumping headache, which I was convinced was meningitis and God's finger pointing, and I'd rushed her to the doctor's, heart in mouth, Anna's chin welded to her chest where I made her keep it for days on end . . . no, not a child.

'It's – Hector.'

'Hector?' Bella frowned.

'Oh, thank God. The horse,' Ant explained.

'Yes, but he's really bad,' I urged. 'Been terribly sick all night, and Caro's so worried.'

'Can horses be sick?' wondered Ant, aloud.

There was a reflective moment as we all tried to remember if we'd seen horses quietly vomiting at the side of the road. Dogs, perhaps, but not . . .

'Nay, luv, you mean colic!' said Terrific Ted, galloping heroically to my rescue.

'That's it! Very bad colic. He might die. *Is* dying. I must go, Ant.'

Ant scratched his head. 'Really? I mean – is there actually anything you can do? Surely Caro's the best person. Or the vet . . .'

'Oh, they've called the vet, he's been there all night, but I'm responsible for him, you see.'

'He's not actually our horse,' Ant explained. 'We've borrowed him.'

'Oh, well, surely the owner—' Bella began.

'She'll be livid,' I gasped, quaking at the very idea of Camilla discovering Hector's colic, fictitious or otherwise: beginning to believe my own lie. I went quite prickly with fear. 'She's besotted with him, you see. She'll kill me. Ant, I must go,' I trembled.

'She's a grand woman, your wife,' announced Ted suddenly in a broken voice. His arm went round my shoulders. He squeezed, gently breaking them. 'A grand woman. She's all heart.' Oh Lord, he was misting up again. 'All heart. And if it was a tiny kitten, maybe even a mouse, you'd go, wouldn't you, luv?' He regarded me keenly, this living embodiment of Francis of Assisi.

I didn't know what to say. 'Yes,' I croaked into his swimming blue eyes.

'See?' He turned to the others triumphantly.

'We'll all go,' Ant said decisively. 'I'm not having you go back on your own, Evie. I'll ring Anna.' He whipped his mobile out. 'Tell her to come back.'

'No!' I stayed his hand as I saw Bella's face fall. Ted's too. 'No, she'll be so disappointed, everyone will. Stay, Ant. I'll get the train. And don't tell Anna Hector's so ill, just say – he's caught a cold, or something. But honestly, darling, I really can't dump this on Caro.'

Ted was gazing at me dreamily now, loving me. Ant looked uncertain, but I could tell he was halfway there.

'There are trains to London from Sheffield, surely?' I turned to Bella, who was looking distressed, her fingers in her peasant blouse. That fidgeting might, eventually, drive me mad, I decided.

'There are, but then on into Oxford . . . ?'

'Oh, that's easy, I've done that loads of times. Straight from Paddington. Padders to Oxford – simple. Where's the bus stop?' I glanced around, as if half-expecting a friendly bus stop on a pole to bend over the hedge and wave cheerily at me. 'I'll do the same as the girls.'

'No, no—' began Bella,

'I'll drop you, luv,' said Ted, gruffly. 'I live in town. I'll give you a lift.'

'Oh, perfect.' I beamed. 'Thank you so much. And thank *you*,' I turned to Bella, on a roll now, powering on through, home and dry, practically back in Walton Terrace. 'You've been so marvellous,' I gushed. 'With all your hospitality and everything.'

'No, no, *you've* been marvellous—'

'We're all marvellous!' I trilled as I kissed her goodbye, and then kissed my husband, in perpetual motion, all smiles. 'And give my love to Stacey and Anna,' I warbled, making for Ted's car around the front of the house, forcing him to follow. 'Bye, darling!' I sang to Ant, giving him a jaunty backward wave. 'Bring my things with yours. I've got all I need.'

'Evie,' he caught up with me, jogging anxiously at my side as I strode off. 'Are you sure? Sure you don't want me to come with you?'

'Perfectly.' I patted his cheek as I got in the car, something I'd *never* done. 'You stay till Tuesday as planned, and I'll go and sort old Hector out. Give him a good – I don't know – rub down.' I shut the door.

'OK,' he was saying doubtfully as Ted started the car. I buzzed down the window to smile broadly. 'If you're sure . . .'

'Of course I am. Really. Toodle-pip, my darling – have fun!'

And off we purred, Terrific Ted and I, with Bella and Ant standing together on the crunchy gravel drive, waving us off uncertainly. The bright morning light streamed through the canopy of frilly yellow beech leaves above them, casting a delicate pattern over their blond heads. When they were out of sight and I could legitimately wave no more, I turned and rested my head on Ted's sheepskin head rest. Shut my eyes.

'Oh God, what a nightmare,' I whispered. 'What a complete and utter nightmare.'

Happily Ted was too busy leaning out of the window calling his own goodbyes to catch my heartfelt aside.

'Good.' He smiled, facing front and shifting in his seat, a regrouping gesture. He pulled his seat belt across his ample stomach and snapped it in with a decisive click. 'That went well. She'll be pleased, our Bella. She's been that nervous.'

'I bet.'

'And as I say, it's all down to you. You made it work.' He reached across and squeezed my hand, giving it a little shake.

'Nonsense,' I murmured absently as we drove on up the lane, following its snaking course to the top of the hill. I felt quite weak with relief. Felt I'd sneaked into this wooden horse of Ted's, this chariot, at the very last minute and escaped. My head lolled sideways on the rest and blinked out of the window. It was a heavenly morning, touched with frost, gilded with sun, and now that we were out of the shelter of the valley, the landscape spread about us frigid and ghostly white, the sky above as blue as the Costa Brava's.

'She's a lovely girl, your Bella,' I said at length as I dimly admired the dull sheen on a glistening pond.

'Aye, she is that.'

'Gorgeous-looking, too.'

He swallowed. Reached for his hanky. 'Aye.'

O Lord, here we go.

'I'll bet she has masses of men chasing after her, doesn't she?'

He smiled. Tucked his hanky back in his pocket. 'She's not like that, luv.'

'No, no, I'm not suggesting she is. But surely, well, a lovely girl like that, all on her own, would attract men even if she's not interested!'

'Oh, aye, she's had her fair share of admirers, if that's what you mean.' It was very much what I meant.

'And any,' I persisted nosily, 'that she's tempted by? You know, gone out with?'

'Aye, she's had a boyfriend these last three years. Mike Hathaway, a local solicitor.'

'Oh.' I perked up no end. 'A solicitor. That's good, isn't it?'

'Aye, he's done well, Mike. Pulled himself up the greasy pole. Didn't come from much, neither – his dad was a butcher. Hathaway's, in Alshot.'

'Gracious, good for him.' I liked the sound of Mike. 'Good-looking?'

'The girls like him.'

'So why wasn't he . . . ? I mean, we could have met him, surely?'

'They split up six months back. He buggered off.'

'Oh. Shame. Did you like him?'

He shrugged. 'I did, but I don't now. Like to punch his lights out.'

Right. Things were obviously done slightly differently in Yorkshire.

'Yes, of course you would. But maybe he'll be back? Maybe it's just a blip? I mean, three years is a long time – you don't just walk away from that sort of investment.'

He turned to me. 'He ran, luv. And no, he won't be coming back.'

'Would she have him back?' I went on doggedly. 'I mean, hypothetically speaking?'

'Not now she wouldn't.' He glanced in his mirror as he indicated off onto the spur of a dual carriageway, turning the radio on, and perhaps indicating too that this little interview was at a close. We drove for a bit in silence, Classic FM gently easing our path.

'He's a grand chap, your Ant,' Ted remarked as *Clair de lune* tinkled up to its closing chord.

'Yes, he is.' I licked my lips, dug deep for courage, or neck, even. 'Although I don't suppose you thought that seventeen years ago.'

He shrugged. 'He was young. He made a mistake. We've all done that, haven't we? And he's more than made up for it now. He could have run too, couldn't he? But he didn't.'

'No, you're right.'

'And don't forget, he didn't know back then, did he? Didn't know about Stacey. Who knows what might have been?'

My throat constricted. What Totally Truthful but verging on the Tactless Ted was indirectly saying here, whether he realized it or not, was that Ant might have stood by Bella and Stacey. Might? Would, I thought with a jolt of horror. Honourable Ant? Yes, like a shot. So

329

where would that have left me? High up on the stale bun shelf, that's where.

We drove on in silence, both lost in thought. When we'd left the bypass and negotiated a sprawling, but strangely captivating city with a startling juxtaposition of old and new architecture, which had even my distracted eyes swivelling around, we pulled up at the station.

'Thank you, Ted.' I leaned across and kissed his cheek.

'My pleasure, luv. Now don't forget to keep him upright. Don't let 'im lie down, or his gut will twist.'

I stared at him a long moment. 'Oh! Hector.'

'Tha's it. Me dad told me that, with colic. He knew about ponies.'

'Did he?' How extraordinary. Oh, wait: 'Pit ponies?'

'Nay, luv,' he laughed. 'He rode a lot as a youngster. Hunted mostly. Me grandfather farmed.'

'Really? So did mine.'

As I got out, he leaned across the seat to smile up at me under the door. 'You see? What a lot we've got in common!'

Yes. Although not too much more, I hoped, as I waved him goodbye. Didn't want any more skeletons clambering out of the Edgeworth/Hamilton closet: any more charming brothers and sisters with high cheekbones and winning smiles looking up at me under Shy Di lashes whispering, 'Hi, I'm Ant's progeny.'

With the sort of luck that is never habitually on my side, a train bound for the south was waiting, expressly it seemed for me to secure a ticket and race breathlessly aboard. Then, by some small miracle, and with the sort of ruthless efficiency one usually only associates with a German, or perhaps Swiss, rail transport system, a connecting train was patiently biding its time at Gosport to deliver me to Paddington, where another spookily convenient train whisked me to Oxford in record time. It gave me, in effect, only a scant four hours to reflect on why I had left Yorkshire in such a tearing hurry, and then to come to the startling, but alarming conclusion that, as usual, I'd not only acted impulsively and foolishly, but also imprudently. As I got off the train and it pulled out of the station, I had to stop a moment on the platform, put a hand to my brow; wonder what the bloody hell I was doing. Standing on Oxford station like a middle-aged waif, clutching a handbag containing a toothbrush and two jars of L'Oréal Revitalift for mature skin, one Day and one Night? Why not a hastily scrunched-up pair of pants too, Evie? Why not go the whole knee-jerk hog? And what had I really been afraid of back there in the Peak District? The sparking of Ant's latent emotions for Bella, or the sparking of all sorts of unattractive emotions in me, all sorts of jealous rants and possessive outbursts I'd have bitterly regretted later? I let out a low sigh. The latter, I suspected. With a bit of the former thrown in just for good measure.

But I was here now. Could hardly go back, could I? Could hardly turn round and get the four fifty-two, which, I discovered, as I whipped the timetable from my bag and scanned it feverishly, would take me back via Gosport to Sheffield, then a taxi from the station to burst back into the kitchen saying – 'Ta-dah! I'm back! Hm . . . ? Oh, yes, *much* better thanks. Made a miraculous recovery. Anything I can do for supper?'

No. Of course I couldn't. I put the timetable away. I'd made my bed and I jolly well had to lie on it. I walked slowly out of the station. But by the same token, I couldn't go home either. I stopped abruptly on the forecourt outside. Felt a bit wobbly. Because now that I was here, I knew I didn't want to be alone. Didn't want to get a taxi to my own home, to open up an empty house, walk from room to room, arms tightly folded, imagining the rest of my family in that idyllic rectory in Yorkshire, bonding seamlessly in the knot garden – so *stupid* to leave – whilst I laid the first fire of the autumn and wondered, fretfully, what time on Tuesday they'd be home, my family: wondered, now that I'd lit the blue touchpaper and stood well back – a hundred and fifty miles back, in fact – just how long that fuse would take to gently smoulder and reach my husband's heart?

My hand shot up in the air impulsively and two minutes later, I was in the back of a taxi bound for the river. Not to weigh my pockets with stones as I'd once darkly hinted to Malcolm, but to avail myself of his company, which, right now, I decided, I badly needed. I knew he wasn't working today, wasn't in the shop, and as I paid the driver on Hythe Bridge and hurried down the steps and under it to the canal, I was confident I'd catch him at home.

I hastened along the dusty towpath by the side of the meadow behind Worcester College, the sun, doggedly bright for the time of year, but low in the sky, glancing through the seed heads in the long grass and glinting on the water and the brightly painted longboats slumbering peacefully at its edge. A few occupants had been drawn out of their boats by the unseasonable weather and were sitting by the towpath in deck chairs, chatting and smoking. I looked for Malcolm but couldn't see him, although . . . I craned my neck around the next boat . . . yes. I could see Cinders, lying on her side, asleep in a sunny spot, beside Malcolm's very idiosyncratic barge: navy blue with red and yellow tulips painted in bold sprays. Quite the prettiest, I always thought, and as close as Malcolm got to life on the ocean waves. Cinders slowly got to her feet to greet me and wag her tail. I stroked her silky head. Her being here was a good sign but by no means conclusive. She'd lie by her boat unattended, waiting for her master to come home, come hell or high tide.

As I crouched down and knocked on the window, a freshly washed blond head and an eager smile popped out of the trap door.

'Oh.' His face dropped. 'It's you.'

'Oh, thanks.'

'Sorry, petal.' He clambered out on deck and came to greet me. 'It's just I was expecting someone else.' He shaded his eyes when he'd kissed me and peered anxiously down the towpath.

'A date?'

He sighed. 'I thought so. He should have been here an hour ago, though.' He glanced ruefully at his watch. 'And anyway, I've promised to relieve Ludo in the shop at five, so he's too late,' he said petulantly. 'Ah, well, it was only going to be Earl Grey and perhaps a strategically placed Wagon Wheel if things went according to plan. Can I interest you?'

'Please. Although I might pass on the Wagon Wheel.'

'I wasn't offering,' he said tartly. 'It'll be Garibaldis all the way for you.'

He went to reverse back down the ladder; stopped to peer up at me halfway down. 'You look a bit peaky.'

'So would you if you'd just sat on a train for four hours.'

'Where from?'

'Yorkshire.'

'Ah.' It dawned. 'The wicked witch of the North. Well, come on down, as Jeremy Beadle used to say. We may as well be miserable together. How was she?'

I followed him down the steep wooden ladder, ducking low to achieve the main cabin: a long tube of yellow with green checked curtains at the tiny windows, and at the far end, benches upholstered in the same check around a little table, laid, I saw now, with a heavily embroidered cloth, plates of cakes and biscuits, and a gleaming Minton tea service.

'She's hardly wicked. In fact quite the opposite.' I slid in and sat down heavily. 'She's Snow White. Sweet, beautiful, kind, successful – oh, Malcolm, how can he not fall in love with her again?'

'You've left him there?' he said, horrified, slipping in beside me.

'I had to!' I wailed. 'I certainly couldn't stay – although I bloody wish I had now – but at the time, oh, I so, *so* couldn't.' My voice dropped dramatically. 'I made a feeble excuse and fled.'

He blinked. 'Interesting decision.'

'I panicked!' I pleaded. 'Thought, I've got to get out of here, can't do it. I nearly did a runner at supper the night before. It's just so weird, Malcolm, you've no idea!'

He shrugged. 'Well, yes, I can imagine. And you've put in a token appearance, which, if they lived closer, is perhaps all you'd have done anyway. You've got to leave them to it to some extent. See how it plays out.'

'You think?' I said eagerly.

'No, I'm just trying to say the right thing. It's what friends do. Earl Grey or builders'?'

'Builders',' I said miserably. 'Good and strong.'

'You'll have it as it comes,' he said primly. I could tell he was in a bad mood too. 'But I don't doubt Ant for one moment.' He eyed me as he poured. 'I just think you've made it harder for him, that's all. Taken away his natural support system. Sugar?'

'No. Actually, yes.'

He didn't doubt Ant. No one ever did. Ant could do no wrong. Ant would never be sitting under a cherry tree tenderly brushing hair out of another woman's eyes, oh, no. I mean, how familiar was that? Or perhaps it wasn't? Impulsively I unleashed a lock of hair from behind my ear and let it fall over my face.

'Milk?'

'Please.'

He glanced up. Didn't notice. I flicked it forward more so it flopped over one eye.

'You haven't admired my tea set. It was my granny's.'

'It's lovely.' As he handed me the cup and saucer I held on to it a moment so he had to look at me.

'She bought it in nineteen twenty-nine – imagine!'

He was talking to my one visible eye for crying out loud: the one that wasn't curtained with hair. In desperation

I plucked a socking great clump from the top of my head and flopped it forward, right over my face.

'Bought it piece by piece in the Army and Navy Stores. Isn't that sweet?'

'Divine,' I agreed through a blur of henna.

'Evie, why are you doing that?'

'What?'

'Why is your hair all over your face?'

'Is it? I hadn't noticed.'

'Yes, you need to sort of . . .'

'What?' I waited. Held my breath.

'Well,' he waved a vague hand in my direction, 'you know. Push it back.'

'Go on then.'

'What?'

'Push it.'

'Me? Why?'

'Because I'm holding my saucer.'

'Well, put it down.'

'Malcolm.' I clenched my teeth. 'Push my hair back!'

He stared. 'Oh, for heaven's sake.' He reached forward and brushed it clumsily off my nose. 'There.'

'Was that so difficult? *Why are you wiping your hand?*'

'I'm not!'

He was, though. On his trousers.

'You are!'

'Well, it just looks a bit – you know . . .' He pulled a face.

'I washed it yesterday!'

'Right, sorry. Blimey, chill, Evie, will you? What's with you?'

He shrank back from me, making a you've-gone-really-weird face. I glared back, then abruptly my shoulders sagged as I caved in. 'You're right.' I nodded miserably, eyeballing the heavy embroidery on the cloth. 'It is a very familiar gesture, isn't it?'

'What is?'

'Brushing hair out of someone's eyes. It's what Ant did to Bella. I watched from the bedroom window.'

'Oh!' His face flashed with recognition. 'Oh, no, not at *all*. It's just – well, you know how fastidious I am, always washing my hands. I've practically got that disease house-wives get, can't stop reaching for the Fairy Liquid. I'll have no skin left soon. Ooh, look, my godson gave me this heavenly badge, he found it in Woolies.'

I knew he was trying to distract me. 'What?' I said peevishly as he pulled a badge from his pocket and pinned it on his shirt. '"My name is nuff and I am a fairy",' I read listlessly.

'Fairy-nuff,' he sniggered. 'Fair enough. Fair-y— oh!' He froze, mid-sentence, eyes wide.

'What?'

'*Shhh!*' He hissed, holding up an index finger. He listened, ears pricked like a rabbit. 'Did you hear something?'

'No, I—'

'*Shhh!* What was that?'

The boat suddenly gave a terrific lurch. I clutched my tea.

'Helloo?' a voice called. 'Anyone at home?'

Malcolm's face lit up like a torch. 'It's him!' he breathed. He got to his feet, radiant suddenly, smoothing down his hair. 'Evie, you must go!'

'Oh, thanks very much.' But I was already draining my cup.

'No!' He grabbed it from me. 'Now!'

'All right, all right,' I grumbled, as Malcolm bundled me towards the door.

He flung the trapdoor wide and scampered up the ladder with me following in his wake. As I emerged in the sunlight, it was to see pristine brown Docksides on the deck in front of me, then pale cream chinos that seemed to go on for ever, then a navy-blue jumper, topped by the face of the most beautiful black man I'd ever seen.

'My, but this is pretty,' he was saying admiringly, glancing around the boat. 'Very *Swallows and Amazons*. Sorry I'm late, I had a bit of a crisis.'

'No, no, not at *all*.' Malcolm was beaming and squirming delightedly, simultaneously jerking his head for me to go.

'Sooty had a difficult stool,' he informed us.

'Oh, poor luv!' cooed Malcolm.

'Sooty?' I asked.

'My dog,' he explained, and I followed his gaze to where a little black spaniel puppy was leaping delightedly around a prone and indifferent Cinders, goading her with shrill yelps and trying to raise more than an indulgent wag of her old tail.

'Oh!'

'Quite fun calling her in the park. I'm afraid I couldn't resist it.' He flashed me a wicked grin. 'Clarence Tempest.' He held out his hand, his eyes all but disappearing as they crinkled up at the edges. Was he really gay? What a shame.

'Evie Hamilton,' I murmured, basking in his dazzling good looks.

'And she was just leaving,' purred Malcolm, hustling me away; practically pushing me overboard.

'Oh, don't go on my account,' smiled Clarence.

'She's not, she was going anyway,' Malcolm assured him with a pussycat smile, ushering him down the steps to his lair and making wild 'go *away*' faces over his shoulder at me. I grinned and stepped gingerly off the boat; made my way down the towpath towards the bridge. Two minutes later, Malcolm was panting beside me, holding my arm.

'Evie, do me a favour,' he gasped. 'Stand in for me at the shop for an hour? I promised Ludo I'd be there.'

'Oh God, I'm not sure I'm up to Ludo in my present state.'

'You don't have to be up to him, you just have to take over from him. He wants to go to his sister's party and I promised – please, hon!' He clasped his hands in prayer and made pathetic Uriah Heep eyes at me, fluttering his lids.

'Oh, all right. Although I'll probably be hopeless. I haven't worked in years.'

'You don't have to work, no one comes in. It's late-night shopping but they're all too busy buying three for two in Waterstone's. Thanks, luvvy. What d'you think, by the way?' He couldn't resist adding, eyes shining.

I grinned. 'He's gorgeous, Malcolm.'

'Isn't he just? He's on sabbatical from King's in London, doing an exchange at Corpus Christi. Teaches law. Imagine, beautiful *and* clever! Aren't I lucky!'

'You certainly are. Although you might lose the badge.'
I pointed to his shirt.

'Shit!' His hand flew to cover it. 'What must he think?'

'Probably what he already knew. Have fun.'

He hastened away, unpinning himself. Yes, beautiful and clever, I thought as I watched him scurry off. And there was I thinking one was enough. Couldn't even compete with her in that department. Bella, I mean. I turned and trailed my heart back along the towpath, then bounced it up the steps behind me to the top of the bridge.

I needed to take a very deep breath before I pushed open the jangling green door with discreet gold lettering in Percy Street. My last meeting with Ludovic Montague, as I now knew him to be, had been of a fairly highly charged nature. Intimate, even. Let's face it, I'd made a complete fool of myself, and he'd shown himself to be a man of substance. A widower, with a beautiful dead wife – well, of course she was dead if he was a widower – and an action-packed past. And for some reason, what he thought of me mattered, I realized with a start as I turned the brass handle. So now I would be brisk and efficient, not tear-stained and needy. As I shut the door behind me I caught sight of my reflection in the glass: someone a bit like me but older, fatter, gazed back. Too late to reach for the lippy, I was in.

'Well, hello.' He looked up from behind the counter where he'd been at the computer as I turned.

I smiled. 'I've come to relieve you. Malcolm asked me to step in. He's entertaining.'

'Ah.' He took his glasses off. 'Would that by any chance be Clarence from puppy-training group?'

'It would.'

'And has he come clean about Cinders yet? Or is the poor girl still lying through her teeth about her age?'

'Is that what he's doing? Passing her off as a puppy?'

'Hasn't he told you? He saw this doggy group parading round in circles through the window of the church hall in Cardigan Street – or, more particularly, saw Clarence – and after weeks of lusting and steaming up the window, minced in with Cinders declaring she was nine months old. "But she looks so much older!" said the Barbara Woodhouse lookalike who was running the show. "Yes, she's very mature," purred Malcolm, joining the circle.'

'I can just see him,' I giggled, relieved we were exchanging light-hearted banter, 'prancing around after Clarence, poor old bemused Cinders at his heels following all the other dogs. Lots of bottom sniffing.'

'That'll be the canines?' He raised his eyebrows.

'Of course!'

He grinned and we looked each other in the eye for the first time. I was at the counter now.

'You look better,' he commented shortly.

I wasn't. But I wasn't going there. 'I am,' I lied. 'Much.'

'Good. These things have a way of sorting themselves out.'

'They certainly do.'

It occurred to me there was quite a lot to sort out in a few days, but I was grateful for the gloss.

'We've just been up there.' I pointed somewhere, vaguely.

'Where?'

'Up North.'

'Oh. Right.' He looked confused.

'It's where they live. Bella Edgeworth and her daughter. Who's lovely, actually. They both are. And we all got on terrifically well, so that's marvellous, isn't it?'

'Marvellous,' he echoed faintly.

Damn. Why had I embarked on this? I hadn't needed to.

'So.' I joined him behind the counter, put my bag down and straightened a pile of books efficiently. 'Just another hour or so, is it? Till we shut?'

He wasn't deflected so easily. 'So, what – you made a flying visit?'

'What? Oh, yes. Well I did, but Ant and Anna are still there. Lots of things to discuss, naturally.'

'Naturally.'

'And obviously he needs to – you know – get to know Stacey.'

'Stacey?'

'The daughter.'

'Ah.'

'And she him . . .'

'Her father?'

'Exactly.'

'And I felt a bit . . .' I tried to gather myself, 'well, superfluous, really!'

I stuck the exclamation mark on the end for courage, but the sentence rocked me none the less. Superfluous. Ludo didn't say anything, but he wasn't making any move to leave, either. Stayed motionless on his stool beside me. Arms folded. Watchful.

'Well, no, not superfluous,' I went on as he watched

me dig my hole. 'But obviously the sisters, Stacey and Anna, wanted to get to know each other. Bond.'

'And your husband and Bella Edgeworth?' he asked gently.

'Needed to talk,' I managed. 'About their daughter. Daughters,' I added. God, how many sodding daughters did they have? Had I said sodding out loud? I wasn't sure. A silence ensued. It hung there, waiting to be filled.

'I trust him implicitly,' I said, apropos of absolutely nothing.

He gave me a steady look. 'Good.'

'Even though,' I couldn't quite believe I was doing this, 'even though I'm sure he likes her very much.'

'She's a likeable woman.'

'Of course. You've met her. Yes, she is. It would be hard not to like her, wouldn't it?' I appealed to him. 'I mean – *I* liked her.'

'It would be hard,' he agreed. We didn't seem to be getting anywhere.

'And it would be odd too,' I blundered on, flying kamikaze now, 'not to be attracted to anyone else at all, other than one's spouse, during the entire course of one's marriage.' Who was one, the Queen?

'It would,' he agreed, ever watchful.

'Were you ever?' I fumbled on, keen to dodge the spotlight. But what a *question*, Evie. She was dead!

'No.' Shortly.

'No, of course not,' I said quickly. 'I think I meant now. Yes, I'm sure I did. Now you're not married.' Worse?

'You mean, have I been attracted to anyone since Estelle died?'

'Yes,' I cringed.

'Only once.'

'Oh.' Something of a result. 'What happened?'

'Nothing. Nothing's happened. I mean – not yet.'

'Yet? It's happening now?'

He shrugged. 'Nothing's happening.'

'She doesn't know?'

He didn't answer. As we looked at one another, a lock of hair worked itself free from behind my ear. He reached forward and gently pushed it back off my face.

## 23

A silence spread out around us. I recovered first.

'Right.' I got up with a start. Brushed an imaginary spec of dust from my jeans. 'You must . . . go to your party.'

'I must.'

'At your sister's.'

'That's it.'

I licked my lips and turned to straighten more piles of very straight books on the counter. Then I slunk out from behind it to what I felt was the relative safety of the shelves, humming wildly as I realigned the shiny black spines of the Penguin Classics, my hands fluttering.

'Is it a big party?' I asked brightly, foolishly, for something to say, face averted.

'It's a bit of a late engagement party,' his voice came evenly from behind me. 'My sister's getting married at the end of the week. It's a drinks thing.'

'I see.'

I didn't really. I was miles away. Had he meant me? Or was I imagining things? I turned, quite boldly, and his eyes snagged briefly on mine. I quickly turned back to the books. Madame Bovary, Anna Karenina – hardly the role models I needed right now, adulterous little minxes. My hands scuttled nervously along to *More Dick*. Heavens. Oh – *Moby*. Right.

'Have you got secrets and lies?' asked a voice in my ear.

'Certainly not!' I spluttered. I turned to find a middle-aged woman in a pac-a-mac with thin lips and a tight grey perm, frowning at me. She looked disconcerted.

'I think we have, actually.' Ludo swept by me to the Young Adult section. 'It's by Ian Atkinson, isn't it?'

'Quite possibly. It's for my grandson.' The woman flicked me a contemptuous look and bustled away to line up with the professional bookseller.

A few minutes later, her purchase made, she hurried from the shop, squeaky in her plastic. Which left just Ludo and me. He glanced at his watch.

'There's only fifteen minutes till closing time. We may as well shut up shop, it's so quiet.' It was as if nothing had happened. Nothing had been said. No eye contact made.

'Oh, no, I'll stay. I promised Malcolm.'

'Except you haven't got keys, and even if I give them to you, you've still got to get them back to Malcolm or me, which is a hassle. No, we can close early today. It's not as if people are hammering on the door to get in.'

There didn't seem to be any answer to that. Wordlessly, I gathered my bag and scarf, and waited as he locked the till, then turned out the lights, plunging us into semi-darkness. I followed him outside.

'How did you get here?' He glanced briskly up at me as he bent to lock the door.

'I walked. From Malcolm's. I came down by train, you see.'

'I'll give you a lift home.'

'No, no, I can walk.'

'Don't be silly, I live opposite you.'

'But you're going to a party.'

'That's where it is. I live with my sister at the moment.'

'Oh.'

There didn't seem to be any answer to that either, so I followed him mutely to a blue hire car, with 'Ratners Hill Garage' painted in large gold letters down the side.

'Why do they write on cars like that?' I said jovially, my mind whirring as I got in the passenger seat. Keep it light, keep it light.

'Oh, I don't know. I'm rather in favour of it.' He got behind the wheel. 'I think every thrusting executive with a company car should have the name of the firm they're accepting the tax-free perk written on it. See how cool they look in a BMW with "Durex" down one side.'

I giggled. This was better. Safer. But I couldn't think of anything to follow it up with. We drove through the backstreets of Jericho, still bustling with late-night shoppers and commuters on their way home: heads down, collars up against a brisk wind that had picked up and was rustling the plane trees above, bullying them to lose their leaves, which spiralled to the ground. As we approached my road, his road, I glanced at him.

'How come you live here? You haven't always lived here?' Implicit in that remark was – I'd have noticed you before. I think I would.

'No, I was renting a flat in Summertown before, but my sister's going to live in Scotland when she's married – Angus, her boyfriend, has a pile there – so I'm taking

347

over her flat. It seemed sensible to move in now. I'd have had to fork out another year's rent in Summertown. But you're right, I've only been here a few months.'

We drew up outside my house. I looked up. It was dark and shuttered. Cold and uninviting. Across the street the lights shone from where he was going. Through an upstairs window a party could be seen silhouetted and in full swing, walls practically vibrating. On the front steps below, a couple were ringing the doorbell even now.

'Come and have a drink.'

'Oh, no, I couldn't possibly.'

'Come on, it'll do you good. Do *me* good.'

'D'you think? I mean . . .'

He turned in his seat, his arm resting on the back. Smiled. 'In light of what I've said? Look, Evie, I realize I've shown my hand, but I'm not going to jump on you. I'm not fifteen.'

I smiled into my lap. Nodded. 'No. I know. I'm sorry.'

'You asked me if I'd been attracted to anyone since Estelle died. Not if I was wasting away in a garret writing love-sick poems. Carving hearts on trees. Succumbing to thunderbolts.'

That put me in my place. 'Quite.'

'No cause for alarm. I believe it's what's called an idle crush.' He grinned.

An idle crush. Well, I'd had a few of those in my time, who hadn't? I remembered a certain floppy-haired Italian boy behind the cheese counter at Waitrose; Ant and I had eaten a lot of Dolcelatte for a while. Oh – and a heavenly Latin teacher at Anna's school who I'd fondly imagined declining a few verbs with – but nothing more.

For idle read harmless. I felt relieved. Flattered. But also ... no, not disappointed. What did I need with thunderbolts?

I took a deep breath. 'I'd love a drink.'

As we got out and walked across the road, I glanced doubtfully down at my jeans and pink jumper.

'I'm not exactly dressed for an engagement party, though. More a rural weekend in Yorkshire.'

He looked me up and down. 'I think you look terrific.'

It was a casual, throwaway remark, but it didn't do to toss remarks like that at vulnerable, insecure women. It verily made my knees knock, at the same time as making me feel about ten foot tall. My heart was going like a kettledrum anyway, so a knee trembling, heart thumping giantess loped along beside him. We went up the few steps to the front door, which the last couple, seeing us approach, had left open in a friendly fashion. Another couple, I realized they imagined, as they smiled back at us. We followed the sound of merrymaking up two flights of cream-carpeted stairs.

The party was indeed at full tilt. Plenty of bright young things were packed in like so much human lasagne, knocking back champagne, shrieking and braying at each other in a high-ceilinged room with an enormous chandelier hanging pendulously in the middle. Amy Winehouse was doing her best over the noise but it was nip and tuck. God, I hoped Ludo's sister was younger, I thought, looking around nervously as we plunged into the scrimmage, otherwise I'd just arrived with a toy boy.

'They look about nineteen,' I shouted over the din, accepting a glass of champagne from a passing waiter who was squeezing his way round with a tray above his head, having a precarious time of it.

'Twenty five-ish,' he shouted back. 'Alice was an afterthought. Ten years after my little brother Ed. Ah, here she is – Alice, this is Evie. Evie – Alice.'

'The bride.' I smiled as an attractive blonde with very pink cheeks swayed towards us in a pissed fashion in a plunging black dress. She looked vaguely familiar. 'Congratulations!' I shouted.

'Oh, we've met!' she squeaked. She reached out and clutched my hand. 'Don't you remember?' She staggered a bit. Steadied herself on a friend's shoulder. 'Oops.'

'We have?'

'Yes – you were having trouble with your poos!' she yelled.

I flushed. It was true, I did suffer spasmodically from constipation. Had news of it reached this side of the street? Had flags been hung out, or even noses pinched, when movement was finally achieved?

'Really?' I gasped, several shades brighter than my jumper.

'Little annoying ones you had to pick up in your hands.'

No. I was pretty sure I'd never . . . 'Oh!' It dawned. 'Hector's!'

She shrugged, eyes like road maps.

'The horse,' I hurried to reassure Ludo, whose eyebrows were gently raised. 'I was mucking him out, and your sister was in the kitchen and – oh, you're getting married at the farm!'

'That's it.' She beamed happily. 'Caroline Milligan's

place. It's so fabulous – well, you *know*. You keep your horse there.' She waved her champagne glass at me and some spilled down my jumper.

'Yes, I used to live there, actually. It was my home.'

'Really?' Her bloodshot eyes widened. 'Gosh, how could you bear to leave it, it's *idyllic*. Angus and I just love it.'

'Well, it was my childhood home.'

'What?'

'My childhood home!' I yelled. 'It's my brother's now, he farms it. He's married to Caro, she's my sister-in-law.'

This was too much for Alice at this time of night, with the amount she'd shifted. She tried gamely to make sense of it. 'Caro is married . . .' she yelled, 'to a farmer?'

'That's it,' I shouted back, feeling weary. 'My brother, Tim.'

'Is he a farmer too?'

I remembered why I hated these stand-up-and-shout parties. 'Yes, he is.'

'Oh. And you're married to him?'

'No, Caro is.'

'So you're both married to farmers?'

I began to lose the will to live. Ludo's sleeve had been plucked and he'd half turned away to listen politely, head down, to what a tall redhead in a green halter-neck dress had to say in his ear. A very beautiful tall redhead.

'Can I just say,' Alice had found my ear too and was hissing into it in a slurred fashion, 'how thrilled we all are. Mummy and Daddy. Ed and me.' She rocked back on her heels, chin disappearing into her neck, missive delivered.

'Thrilled?'

'Yes, since Ludo's met you – he's a different person. You've no idea!' She flung her arms wide, champagne flying again. 'Oops – sorry!' This to a drenched back.

'Oh, no,' I shouted above the din. 'You've got this wrong. I'm married!'

'Yes, I know, and he knows there's no chance, knows you're happily married, it's just – well, he never thought, after Estelle, he was capable of feeling anything, ever again. Thought he'd sort of fossilized. The fact that he can, even if it's not to be, is just a miracle.' She swayed and spilled champagne on my bosom again. I looked like I was lactating. 'Angus and I are going to be like that.' A faraway look came into her eye. 'Really, really happy.' Then she frowned, concentrating, realizing she'd lost her thread. 'It's been ages, you see, since Estelle died – over three years. The fact that he can *feel*, even if it's *you*, and even if you're *married*, is just fantastic!' Bug-eyed at the magnitude of this, she lurched, suddenly, to grab a passing waiter, refilling her glass when he wasn't quick enough on the draw with the bottle himself. Ludo was well out of hearing range now and I wanted to get to the bottom of this.

'Are you sure you've not exaggerating?' I shouted. 'I've met him about three times. I smashed up his car. Twice!'

She nodded. Lurched backwards. Someone steadied her elbow with an indulgent smile. 'That's right,' she yelled. 'He met Estelle when she reversed into him in Sainsbury's in the Cromwell Road. That's what's so spooky. *And* she was engaged to someone else. He'd married her within three weeks!'

I stared at her. Felt my Shetland wool jumper tighten around my throat. Felt it knit itself a few more rows. She shrugged helplessly, throwing up her arms for dramatic emphasis. More champagne flew through the air. 'That's Ludo for you! Take it from me, he's got you firmly in his sights. This is no idle crush! Oh, s'cuse me. *Clemmie!*' she shrieked as a girl in a tiny white dress and a bottled tan fell through the door, clutching a bottle. 'Where've you *been*?' They laughed hysterically and fell on each other's necks. I hastily downed my drink. Shit. I must go. Three weeks. I must go now. Three *weeks*.

I began to thread my way towards the door, around Alice and the girl in white, towards freedom. I glanced over my shoulder. Ludo's back was still to me, talking to the redhead: tall, broad, but diminishing. I'd just slip away. He wouldn't notice for ages, and I could say—

'Evie!' I jumped out of my skin. Felicity had my arm. She followed my gaze.

'Rather gorgeous, I agree,' she yelled. 'Half these young girls are lusting after him.'

That hadn't escaped my notice. As we'd walked in, quite a lot of eyes had darted our way: hair had been flicked back, and skirts hitched up or down, depending on the state of the legs.

'Felicity. What are you doing here?'

'You mean at my age?' She laughed. 'I used to teach Alice, and she rather sweetly invited me. But I won't be staying.' She made a face. 'Not my scene.'

'Oh – biology.'

'Rather a bright little thing when she could get up for lectures. Quite a party girl too.' We watched her swaying

353

in her friend's arms, the pair of them singing loudly together now.

'But not a patch on her brother, apparently,' she yelled in my ear. 'I mean, brains-wise. Not my department, though, a historian.' She nodded in Ludo's direction. 'Bit of a legend by all accounts.'

Christ. Another bloody brilliant Oxford scholar. A legend. Why did I always pick them? Pick? No. I hadn't picked. Not remotely. I must go.

'Ed, the brother, is very clever too, but this one's much sexier.' She pointed out the younger brother over by the window. Prematurely bald with a shiny forehead. Short.

Yes, much sexier. Help.

'Felicity, I must go. Shield me, would you? I'm going to squeeze out.'

She blinked. 'Sounds dramatic. But listen, Evie, before you go, have you seen Maroulla?' Her eyes were anxious suddenly, and she had my arm again.

I went hot. 'No, but I keep meaning to. Damn, I keep forgetting. I will go, Felicity. Definitely, next week.' I glanced over my shoulder as I edged away. Ludo was still talking.

'No, no,' her hands were fluttery, 'I'm not saying you should. I mean – well, the thing is, Evie, she's so gaga now, I went the other day. And it'll just upset you.' She looked agitated.

'Is she? Oh God, how awful, *poor* Maroulla.' I stopped still. She'd been like a second mother to us when we were little: cooking endless plates of spaghetti with fresh tomatoes, showing us how to use garlic and basil, chucking away in disgust the fish fingers Mum had asked her to cook. The thought of her gaga in a home somewhere was ghastly.

'I will go,' I determined, edging door-wards again and whipping my phone out. 'I'll put the address in here. It's Parsons Road way, isn't it?'

'Yes, but, Evie, I wouldn't, because—'

'Bugger, who's this?' My phone tinkled suddenly in my hand with a text, making me jump. 'Oh – Caro.'

Felicity and I exchanged fearful glances as we often did at the mention of Caro's name. I read it out loud.

> **In Carluccio's with Tim when Camilla rang. Wants to see Hector NOW. And you told Phoebe he could sleep rough. Thanks a bunch. On my way. Caro.**

'Who's Camilla?' Felicity yelled.

'Oh!' I gazed at the text in horror. Then I hastily punched in Caro's number. She answered immediately. 'Caro? I'm here!'

'What?' There was background noise at her venue too.

'Back in Oxford,' I shrieked, sticking my finger in my ear and making determinedly for the door, and then the landing outside.

'I thought you were in Yorkshire?'

'I was, I'm back. It's a long story. What's the problem?' I kept my finger in my ear and turned my face into a huge stack of coats and pashminas hanging in the hall.

'The problem – hang on, I'll just go outside . . .' There was a pause and some rustling. Then she was back in my ear. 'The problem is bloody Camilla Gavin. She's just rung to say she's on her way back from the sales in Newmarket, and she's passing our gate and wants to see Hector and give him a carrot. At this time of night!'

'Oh.'

'Which, as you know, will be tricky, since Hector hasn't slept in his bed for days, which means she'll go to his stable and find it empty!'

I shut my eyes. Oh, blinking heck. And stride around the yard demanding my guts for garters. Or reins, perhaps. She didn't seem the garter type. And then she'd look around some more and see Hector sleeping in the paddock with his lady friends, which was what he loved most, with a nice cosy rug on, which, when Anna and Phoebe's enthusiasm for mucking out after school had waned, had seemed the obvious solution.

'Right,' I quaked. 'I'll go over. Unless, of course, the children . . . ?'

'Phoebe's at a sleepover and the boys are on a school trip. And I'm in Carluccio's because it's my bloody birthday and the first time I've been out in eight weeks. We'd just sat down to the sun-blushed tomatoes.'

Her birthday. Oh God, I'd forgotten.

'Happy birthday,' I said weakly, massaging my forehead with my fingertips. 'Of course I'll go, Caro.'

'Well, I'd get down there fast, if I were you. She's just leaving Newmarket now, and she drives like a whirling dervish. Oh – and don't forget, Pepper's in season so Hector's pretty sexed up at the moment. He might be a bit bolshy about coming in.'

'Not a problem,' I croaked. 'Don't you worry, Caro. You, um, tuck in. Enjoy your meal.'

I pressed the over-and-out button. When I glanced up, Felicity had been nabbed by a prematurely aged young man with a high, academic forehead, a type quite prevalent in this city. She was making wild 'help-me' eyes at me over his shoulder. Ludo, on the other hand, was at my elbow.

'Problem?'

I gazed up into his dark eyes. The greeny-yellow flecks in them were glinting.

'What's your experience with sexed-up horses?' I whispered.

He returned my gaze steadily. 'Extensive.'

'You're lying.'

'Of course. But how else am I going to keep a grip on your company tonight?'

I took a deep breath, dithered momentarily, then: 'Come on,' I said grimly. 'We're leaving.'

# 24

'Where exactly are we going?' Ludo asked, not unreasonably, following at a more leisurely pace as I hurried down the stairs. I tumbled out of the open front door and across the street to my car. 'Why not take mine?' he called after me, as I fumbled for my car keys. Again not unreasonable; we'd just got out of his.

Because I want to feel in some sort of control, was the answer, but I substituted it pathetically with, 'Because I know the way. To my brother's place,' I added, in answer to his first question as he got in beside me. 'The farm, where your sister's getting married. It's where this wretched horse is.' I turned the ignition, and because I'd left the car in gear, we kangarooed elegantly down the road.

He clutched the dashboard in mock terror. 'The horse with the unnaturally small faeces? Christ, steady.' He braced himself against the door as I found second and picked up speed, wheels screaming as I took the corner.

'The very same.' The car righted itself. 'And the voracious sexual appetite that keeps him out in the field with the ladies, and not in the stable where he belongs, and where the woman who owns him thinks he is right now, and is hot-footing it to come and check.'

'Now? In the middle of the night?'

'Oh, Ludo, you have no idea.' I passed a harassed hand through my hair as we sped towards the ring road. '*No* idea. These horsy women are unbelievable. Particularly this one, Camilla.'

'Not . . . *the* Camilla?'

'Oh, no, not that one. Much more terrifying.'

'Good Lord.'

'That one would be fine. I could imagine having a giggle and a fag with her. This one . . . well, you'll see.'

There was a silence as he sensibly let me negotiate a roundabout in peace, his white-knuckled grip on the upholstery the only giveaway.

'Have you actually imagined a giggle and a fag?' he asked lightly as we embraced the A40.

I flushed in the darkness. Not stupid, was he? I glanced at his profile, his twitching mouth.

'What – you mean have I fantasized about knowing her when she was ordinary old Mrs Parker-Bowles, and now she's married to Sir, and on account of our long girly friendship, I'm forever at Highgrove toasting muffins by the fire with the pair of them?' Well, if that didn't put him off nothing would. And put him off I surely needed to do.

He grinned. 'Not the sexiest fantasy I've ever heard.'

'I'm not a sexy person.'

'I'm not sure you can be the judge of that.'

'Oh, for God's sake . . .'

I wondered if I should go further. Mention that I didn't call him Sir any more, and that we were planning a holiday together, the four of us: a riding safari in Botswana –

Charles being very taken with Ant in a Laurens van der Post sort of way. Perhaps not. I wanted to put him off, not think I was mentally unstable.

'Do you always drive as if you're about to throw up over the dashboard?'

I gritted my teeth and sat back. No, it didn't work for me. I assumed my edge-of-the-seat position again, wheel to chest.

'We're here,' I announced some minutes later, as, having belted at record speed down the lanes, I swung the car round the stone gate post, only just grazing it this time.

We came to a halt in the stony drive: gravel, as I've mentioned, would be pitching it too high. The coach light was on above the front door, illuminating the Virginia creeper and little wooden porch with white window seats either side. A friendly row of wellingtons sat beneath. Caro had left the sitting-room light on too, which shone through a gap in the red curtains.

'Pretty,' said Ludo admiringly, as we got out.

I smiled the smile of one who knows. 'Yes, but tumbling down round their ears. Come on, the yard's over here.'

He followed as I marched off round the side of the house.

'So, presumably you grew up with horses?' he said, looking about as I flicked on the yard light. Felix, Henry's pony, who was deemed too delicate to stay out under any circumstances, had his head over the door, ears pricked with interest.

'No, it was only ever Dad's thing,' I said, disappearing

into the tack room and emerging with a head collar. 'Tim and I never really got involved. I was much happier with a book.'

'Ah,' he smiled.

'Mills and Boon,' I said tartly, before he got too excited. Before he had me curled up with *Don Quixote*. 'Or even trashy mags. *Tit-bits*, that kind of thing.' I flashed him a triumphant look, wishing I had some gum to chew. 'Right. Now you hold this . . .' I handed him a bucket with pony nuts in it, 'and when we're in the field, rattle it loudly to make a noise. When he comes across I'll try and nab him.'

'Got it, sir.'

I ignored him. It occurred to me he'd become remarkably skittish since his earlier revelation, not quite the brooding, dour chap of yesteryear. Really come out of his shell. Perhaps he felt he had nothing to lose? Or was this him turning on the charm? If it was, I had to admit, it was rather attractive. And it was forcing me into a shrewish, exasperated role I knew wasn't attractive at all. But then, that was the point, wasn't it, Evie? I shut the feed-room door.

'Had much success with this method in the past?' he asked as I locked it behind me.

'Not a lot, but it's dark, so we might surprise him.'

'Right. But essentially,' he glanced in the bucket, 'we're counting on his physical appetite, triumphing over his sexual one?'

'Yes, I suppose,' I said impatiently. 'Whatever.' Whatever. When had I ever said that? But quite good. I should have dropped the T for more chavvy effect.

'Come on,' I set off. 'Less theorizing, more action.'

'Mind if I take a couple more of these?' He turned to grab a pair of head collars hanging over a stable door.

'Wha'ever.'

I strode off, pleased with myself, towards the paddock. I let us in through the iron barred gate, then sent it sailing back to click shut with a clank, behind us.

'Now. They're usually down by the river in a huddle. Jiggle your nuts.'

Ludo's face in the moonlight lit up. 'How I wish you were ordering me to do that under different circumstances,' he breathed.

I swallowed. Felt the blood in my cheeks. 'Just ... shake them,' I muttered. 'Hector!' I called, striding out down the hill. 'Hec-torrr!' Quite hard to call out and not feel ridiculous. My voice warbled operatically.

'Aren't you just alerting him to our presence?' whispered Ludo, beside me. 'I thought an element of surprise was part of our plan?'

Bloody man. I didn't answer him, but he had a point. Hector was probably even now nudging his mares, saying – eh up, girls, the old bag's here. Bolt when I give the word.

We advanced river-wards, like a drummer boy and his army of one, I thought, as our battle cry rang out in the still, starry night. Ludo was deliberately jiggling much too loudly, I decided; enjoying himself rather too much, an annoying smile on his face. I wasn't convinced he was taking this seriously.

Sure enough, as we marched down the grassy slope,

we saw Hector standing under the willows with his two grey mares lying at his feet in an idyllic, pastoral scene, like a Stubbs painting.

'How cosy is that,' muttered Ludo. 'Three in a bed.'

'You can see why he likes it.'

'But hasn't he had the snip? He can't be a stallion.'

'No, a gelding.' We inched forwards. 'But Caro reckons he might be a rig.'

'What's that?'

'A stallion who's had the op but it hasn't quite worked. He's lost most of his tackle, but some of it might have got left behind. So he still gets the urge.' I was quite glad it was dark.

'Blimey. Poor bastard.'

'Now. You rattle, and I'll go round the back.'

'Hang on.' He stayed my arm. 'Can I just try something?'

'What?'

'You'll see. Wait there.'

I folded my arms. Whatever it was, it wouldn't work. Recently, possibly because he wasn't coming in at night and being handled much, Hector had turned rather feral. Had taken to tossing his handsome head at me, rolling his eyes and with a flick of his heels, trotting away in the equal and opposite direction. Gone was the impeccably mannered, biddable Hector, a vision in purple with immaculately groomed mane and oiled hoofs, and in his place, a thuggish, intimidating Hector, with a very muddy hoody. He'd be in a mall soon, sipping Red Bull straight from the can.

I watched as Ludo put his bucket down and stole across

to the pliant, sleepy mares, one Jack's, one Phoebe's. Within seconds he'd slipped the ropes round their necks and got a head collar on each. They got to their feet, bewildered. Hector, sensing their captive state, instantly tossed his head and trotted away, metaphorical fag in mouth. Ludo ignored him and led the mares to me. I took their halter ropes, somewhat taken aback.

'You've done that before.'

'Alice had a pony. I have put the odd head collar on, but other than that, it's common sense. Or sexual psychology. Never chase a man. Ignore him, and he'll come running. You'll see.'

He challenged me with his eyes. I turned away abruptly and walked off, taking the mares with me.

Annoyingly, Hector, who'd initially bolshed off towards the river, had turned, and was even now following us to the gate, albeit at a wary distance.

'Shall I have a go at getting him now?' I asked, realizing I'd lost control in so many ways.

'No, let him suffer. Wait till he's desperate. Don't tell me you've never kept a man at a distance, Evie? Made him wait?'

I clenched my teeth. I certainly wasn't going to tell him I'd always done the chasing. We'd reached the gate and Ludo went ahead to swing it open for me. I led the mares through, one on either side.

'Now?' I glanced back. An uncharacteristically anxious Hector was hovering.

'No, take them up to the yard. We'll teach him a lesson.'

Feeling like a pliant old grey mare myself, I dutifully led them away into the night. When we got to the stables

I waited on the hard standing with them, three heads drooping submissively together. A few moments later, Hector's smooth clip-clop clip-clop came at a smart trot, up the cinder path. He appeared out of the darkness looking pretty worried, I must say, not his usual arrogant self at all. The ponies all whinnied to each other in relief, and Ludo popped Hector in a stable, bolting the door firmly. Then he jerked his head at me and the mares. Clearly I'd morphed into the sort of woman who understands the jerk of a man's head, because I instantly turned and led the bemused mares back to their field. As I slipped off their halters and let them go, I watched them saunter off down the valley without even a backward glance: not looking overly disappointed at having a quiet night in in front of the river, away from Himself and his demanding ways. Not looking too deprived.

Back in the yard, Ludo was propped up against a stable door, hands in pockets, one knee bent, looking impossibly handsome and pleased with himself.

'Are we done here?'

'Not quite. But you can wait in the car, if you like. I won't be long.'

I disappeared into the tack room to get a bucket of water and a sponge. Please go.

'Why, what happens now?'

I was inside Hector's stable now, bolting it firmly behind me. I wondered if I could do this in the dark, with just the diffused light from the yard. There was a stable light, but I certainly didn't want to turn it on.

'Oh, I've just got to change his rug,' I muttered, whipping off the muddy one and seizing the little purple

365

number from a hay rack. I slipped it on him. 'Amongst other things . . .' I was buckling him up underneath.

'What other things?'

'Um . . . give him a wash.'

'A wash? Here – look, there's a light.'

He flicked it on, just as I'd crouched down with my bucket and sponge and teased out Hector's . . .

There was a highly charged silence as I determinedly finished what I'd set out to do. After a while I couldn't bear it.

'Please wait in the car,' I whispered.

'You're kidding,' he drawled breathlessly. 'I wouldn't miss this for the world. Do you do this to all the boys?'

'It's Camilla,' I hissed, red-faced. 'She insists. She'll check.'

'I've changed my mind about Camilla,' he said after another long pause as he watched me. 'I love her. I want to have her babies.'

'Oh, no, you don't.' I straightened up and threw the sponge in the bucket. 'Camilla's husband won't get this sort of treatment, I'd put money on it. Camilla's husband probably gets missionary position sex only on his birthday.'

'And what sort of sex, hypothetically speaking, d'you think he'd be missing out on?'

I regarded him lolling, arms folded over the stable door, eyes dancing.

'Shut up, Ludo, and pass me that hoof pick.'

'I love it when you talk horse,' he moaned as I pointed to the pick, hanging on a hook by the door.

'Just belt up and – oh. Shit!' I stood stock-still in the middle of the stable. Listened.

'What?'

'She's here!' The unmistakable sound of thundering tyres and hissing air brakes filled the night, as the lorry surely rumbled through the front gate. A cab door slammed, echoing in the quiet night, making the dogs inside the house bark. I recognized Brenda, sleeping over whilst we were supposedly in Yorkshire, yapping shrilly; Megan's throaty old woof.

'Quick, turn off the light.'

Ludo flicked it off, and in an instant I was out of there, the stable door shut and bolted behind me. I looked around wildly, quivering with indecision. Too late, her heavy footsteps, like a man's – like a giant's, actually – came earthshakingly towards us. Fi-fi-fo-fum . . . I longed for a handy beanstalk and glanced, terrified, at Ludo. There was only one way into the yard, and she was coming through it. We were trapped.

'In here,' he muttered.

Quick as a flash, he'd bundled me into the adjoining stable, which happened to be Felix's. Felix eyed us in astonishment, but he was a mild-mannered little pony, and a very greedy one, and once he'd given us the cursory once-over, he carried on pulling at his hay net, munching hard. Ludo and I scuttled to a far corner of his stable and crouched down, Ludo's arm clamped pseudo-protectively around my shoulders, but I knew better. I glared at him and tried to shake him off, but he clamped himself even harder, frowning at me to be quiet, a finger to his lips, enjoying himself hugely, not remotely scared. Not like me. But then he had no idea of the ramifications. No idea of the magnitude of Camilla's wrath, nor my sister-in-law's, nor Anna's grief when her beloved pony was taken away.

I shut my eyes, bent my head and began to pray hard, hands clasped. There was the sound of a bolt shooting back on the adjacent door: Hector's box. Then the stable light went on, and then ... I was going to say the unmistakable tones of Camilla Gavin rang out into the night, but although it was undoubtedly her voice that came, one could be forgiven for mistaking her. Instead of her usual clipped, posh bark, came the breathy, treacly tones some people reserve for small babies, some for their lovers, and some, for animals.

'Oh, Heccy Heccy, wath he a lubberly, lubberly boy then? Wath he? Kissy kissy, Hec. Brrr ... brr ... !'

Sounds of a horse being open-mouth-snogged ensued. Or something horribly similar. I couldn't look at Ludo. Knew it was vitally important to keep staring straight ahead at Felix's broad brown backside and think about, um, Gordon Brown's position on, er, global warming.

'Wath he Mumma's precious? And hath he been looked after like Mumma's precious boy should?'

Thank God Hector couldn't talk. Ludo was squeezing my shoulder, trying to catch my eye and, foolishly, I glanced, just once, at his delighted incredulous face. Memories of Tim in church threatened. I bit the inside of my cheek and thought hard about Gordon Brown's wife, Sarah. Rather stern, I imagined. No fast food for her children. No Big Mac cartons in front of the telly.

'Hath she been picking out your feet, then? Hm?' Pause while she checked.

'No, Mumma,' came a high-pitched, tremulous lisp. 'She hathn't.'

Oh dear God, he *could* talk. It was too much for Ludo. He snorted.

A horrible hush ensued. It hung there in the night air, suspended. I shut my eyes tight, held and clenched everything.

'Who's there?' The unmistakable tones of the real Camilla Gavin rang out from next door. 'Who's there?' she barked again, fearlessly. Oh, no, no fear, not like me. I was the fourth-former hiding in the loos, and she was the headmistress, out of Hector's box in a trice, bolting it shut. Working her way along the line of stables, happily away from us, in the opposite direction, we heard her kick in the doors, one by one. Not a headmistress now, but a cop looking for villains, like something out of *The Sweeney*. She wasn't even armed, I thought in awe. There could be anyone in there. But then again, who'd tangle with her?

'Come on – come out! Bloody gypos – out!'

She marched back our way, towards the only box she'd yet to kick in, Felix's. I moaned low. My fate was sealed. As she opened the door and expertly pushed the pony back, simultaneously flicking on the light, Ludo seized my face in his and kissed me very hard on the lips.

'Good *God*,' she spluttered.

I pushed Ludo away and sprang to my feet.

'What on *earth* are you doing?' Her incredulous eyes darted from me to Ludo, then back to me. She knew exactly what we were doing.

'Well, excuse me, Mrs Horse-lady,' Ludo drawled, straightening up. 'This is Evie's family home. One might just as well ask what *you're* doing here, interfering with horses in the middle of the night. But since you ask, I came to check out the lighting for my sister's wedding here. Found Evie checking old Hector's rug – she's that fussy about his layers. The fact that I backed her into a stable and stole a kiss is really none of your business.'

'Good gracious,' she gaped, momentarily stunned. 'Evie, are you all right?'

'Yes,' I whispered pathetically, hanging my head. It wasn't hard.

'What's the matter, Milly?' Ludo teased. 'No one ever backed you up into a stable before? Except old Heccy, perhaps?'

'How dare you!'

He sauntered past her, hands in his pockets, out into the yard. She stared after him, her mouth hanging open. Ludo turned to flash her a grin, then strolled off whistling, around the corner towards the gate, and out into the night. When he'd gone, she turned to me, aghast.

'What a *dreadful* man!'

'Dreadful.'

'Is he a gypsy?'

'Quite possibly. Some sort of vagrant.'

'A very well-spoken one. Perhaps a drug addict? From the Varsity?'

'Perhaps.'

'*Are* you all right?'

'Yes. Thanks to you.'

'You should have slapped his face!'

'I . . . was about to.'

'Wish I'd slapped it for you!'

'I wish you had too.'

We stared at each other. I had a nasty feeling she wasn't entirely convinced. Could go either way.

'Would you like me to put another rug on Hector?' I asked unctuously. 'I was worried he might be cold.'

'No. No, I've felt behind his ears, he's fine.' It was the right move, though.

'Good, well, if you're sure . . . I'll be off then.' I slid past her nervously in the stable. Out of the door.

'Sure you're all right to drive?' she said gruffly. 'Want a lift?'

'No, no, I'm fine, the car's just here. Thanks, though!' I fled towards it, feet flying.

'Good for you for checking on old Hector!' she called after me.

'Not a problem!' I trilled back, throwing myself into the front seat. I glanced in the rear-view mirror. She was coming after me. Oh God.

'Sure you're OK?'

'Absolutely!'

I turned the ignition and performed an immaculate three-point turn in the drive. Then I roared out of it, wheels spinning in the mud, hopefully not splattering her too disastrously.

A few hundred yards down the dark lane, under the lee of a tall elderberry hedge, and a smattering of stars, Ludo was sauntering along, hands in pockets. Swaggering, almost. I slowed down beside him, leaned across and threw open the passenger door as I stopped.

'Get in,' I muttered.

He hopped in, grinning. 'I thought that went rather well.'

'Did you.'

'Thought I got us out of a tight spot rather adroitly.'

'Really. Except that when she's given it some thought and finds out who you really are, she'll realize we've duped her, and then it'll be all round the village in moments. Evie Hamilton, found snogging in a stable with a man half her age.'

'Being assaulted in a stable,' he corrected me, 'by a man surely only a few years younger than herself. How old are you, anyway?'

'None of your business.' I suppressed a smile and drove on fast towards town.

That shut him up. The driving, I mean. Occasionally I heard him utter a profanity under his breath as we took a corner, but then, most people did.

When I drew up outside Ludo's house, the lights were still blazing on the second floor, windows flung open to the night. The party was in full swing, music even louder. The noise drifted down the street, echoing in the still air. I turned to look at him. His eyes were shut.

'Dare I look?'

'Idiot. We're here.'

'Thank the Lord.' He opened his eyes, gazing around in mock wonderment. 'You're quite a motorist.'

'You're quite a liar.'

'Hm?'

'Back there. In the stable.'

'Oh.' He shrugged. 'Goes with the territory. I'm a journalist. I make up stories.'

'Not that sort of journalist. Hardly gutter press.'

He laughed. 'No. True. That, indeed, was a lie.'

The mirth in his eyes slowly subsided as he looked at me. Watched me, rather. Fondly. Consideringly. All the frivolity of the last couple of hours seemed to slip out of the car and down the street. It was as if a convenient cloak of disguise had been plucked away and tossed aside to reveal something altogether more dangerous.

'Fun, though, wasn't it?' he said lightly.

I wasn't deceived by his tone but his steady gaze was very affecting. 'Yes.' I agreed softly. 'It was.' I sat, motionless, in the warm focus of his regard. The silence hung around us.

'Night, Evie.'

'Night.'

He leaned across to kiss my cheek, but instead, his head dipped, and his lips brushed my neck. It was the gentlest of touches but the most electrifying.

As the blood surged under my skin, I knew, in that instant, I desperately wanted him to kiss me properly. The thought shocked me. I was startled by my complicity.

'Ludo—'

'Shh.' He put his finger on my lips and I saw in his eyes he'd read both emotions. The desire, and then the shock.

'Don't panic,' he told me quietly. 'But don't go away.' And then he got out of the car and was gone.

## 25

The following morning, Caro was on the phone before I'd even opened my eyes.

'Are you all right?'

'Yes, why?' I turned my head on the pillow and blinked at the clock, trying to focus.

'Camilla said you'd been assaulted. In a stable!'

I propped myself up on one elbow. Switched the phone over to the other hand. 'Caro, it's a long story and it's only half-past seven.'

'And I've been up for an hour and I'm armed with a coffee. Tell.'

I sighed, but knew better than to argue. When I'd finished there was a long silence.

'So he did kiss you?'

'Yes, but purely in the line of duty.'

'On the lips?'

'Yes, OK, on the lips, but—'

'Tongues?'

'Certainly not!'

'Just asking. Was it nice?'

'Caro!'

'It was!' she breathed ecstatically.

'Goodbye!' I snapped, putting the phone down.

I swung my legs out of bed, sat hunched on the edge for a moment, then heaved myself up and padded heavily to the loo, reaching in to turn on the shower en route. *Was it nice?* What a question! I pulled my oversized T-shirt over my head, got in the shower cubicle and shut the glass door behind me, turning my face up to the jet of hot water. I opened my mouth to let some in. *Was it nice.* I washed my hair vigorously, then, steaming and dripping, got out, found a towel and wrapped it around me. Walking slowly to the long mirror and, towelling my head at the same time, I gazed critically at my reflection. My slicked-back dark hair, usually a riot of bouncy curls, was already crinkling back into shape, framing my face, with its still creamy complexion, rather too full lips. Kissable lips, Ant used to say. I stared. Yes, OK, it was nice. Very nice. Especially the one I hadn't told her about. I towelled myself dry and got dressed.

As I drew back the curtains in the bedroom, my eyes darted across to the other side of the street. Closed curtains at number 52. Still asleep. Alice and her fiancé certainly, and probably for quite some time, but what of her brother? Had he gone back and partied with the best of them, smooched around the dance floor with the redhead in the green halter-neck dress? Or had he gone straight to bed, lain there in the dark, heart pounding, as I had.

I turned quickly from the window. As I bent to pick up my brush on the dressing table I caught my reflection in the mirror. Tipsy-looking almost; cheeks flushed, eyes over-bright, as if I'd been at the bottle.

Giving myself a little inward shake and reminding myself of certain friends of ours involved in unseemly midlife crises, I went downstairs to make a cup of tea.

The house was very still, very quiet. Unnaturally quiet: no Brenda, of course. Usually she'd be scrambling up my legs for her breakfast. I went to the calendar on the side of the fridge: flipped over the page. Tuesday the twenty-third. Ant was going on a book tour in the West Country on . . . the twenty-sixth. Oh. So pretty much the moment he got back, I realized. He'd unpack his suitcase only to re-pack it. I wouldn't see him. Not properly, anyway. I certainly wouldn't be able to talk to him prop-erly. Hear about Bella and Stacey. As much as he'd tell me, anyway. As much as he'd tell me? We'd always told each other everything. But then, I wouldn't tell him about last night, would I? Make a funny story out of it? Make him laugh. I inhaled sharply. I didn't want secrets. Didn't want guilt. I hadn't done anything. And yet, it seemed, I had. We both had. Ant and I. Because what other tender gestures had he been guilty of in Yorkshire? Apart from the one under the cherry tree? My heart pumped. None. Absolutely none, you're imagining things, imagining the worst. The kitchen clock ticked quietly on the wall be-hind me. Because I had nothing else to do. Wasn't busy. Because I live in this smart town house – clean because Maria had come yesterday, gardened because we had a gardener – so I stood, in my immaculate house, with its hushed old-lady feel, imagining the worst, but also, my mind flew suddenly to Ludo's dark head bending to kiss my neck last night, also, the best.

A few minutes later found me on the other side of the kitchen picking up the phone, punching out a number. Felicity's answer machine was on. I waited for the tone.

'Oh, hi, Felicity, it's Evie here!' My voice had taken

on an unnatural glittery tone. 'I was just wondering, if Mum can't make it, I could easily do meals on wheels with you next week. Or, um, any other charity work you do. OK – bye.'

I stared at the phone. On an impulse, I rang Mum. Her machine was on, too and her breathy voice informed me: 'I'm sorry I'm not here, but if you're ringing about reiki, and would like to make an appointment, please leave a message after the beep.'

I put the receiver down. Where was Mum at eight o'clock in the morning? Jogging round the park, probably. In training for that moonlit breast walk or whatever her latest challenge was. I walked to the windows and gazed out, picking at a spot that was brewing on my chin. A familiar, panicky feeling, one I'd had quite a lot lately, threatened. I turned and went briskly to the laundry room, lifted the wicker basket onto the ironing board, and began sorting the socks at the bottom. But I'd only paired up one or two, before I found myself back in the kitchen, at the French windows, staring out at the leaf-strewn lawn. The phone rang behind me, making me jump. I turned and snatched it up, like a drowning man a life belt.

'Hello?'

'Hi, it's me.'

'Ant!'

I sat down abruptly on a kitchen stool, flooding with relief. I'd been on my own too long, in an empty house. That was all. Well, one night. 'Darling, how are you?'

'I'm OK.' He sounded guarded. My chest tightened.

'Good,' I said lightly. 'And Anna?'

'She's fine.'

I licked my lips. This wasn't right. Didn't sound right.

'So, when are you coming home?'

'Well, there's been a bit of a hitch. The publishers have just rung to say that the rep who was taking me on the book tour in Devon is ill. He's put his back out, apparently. Can't drive.'

'Oh, well, never mind. Another time perhaps?'

'But they've managed to cobble something together with the rep up here, in the North, and he's going to take me to Harrogate, Leeds and Ripon instead.'

'Near where you are now?'

'Exactly.'

'But . . . what about publicity, that sort of thing? Will anyone know you're coming?'

'Oh, they've managed to do a few flyers, and they've just about caught the deadline on the local paper, apparently. They've clearly known about this for a few days and have jacked it up, knowing, of course that I'd be available.'

'Right.'

'So I'll stay here, if that's all right?'

'With Bella?'

'Yes, it makes sense.'

Was he telling me or asking me?

'Of course. And Anna?'

'Well, Anna says she's got some Pony Club rallies—'

'She has,' I said quickly.

'So I'm going to put her on a train.'

'Oh!'

'She's quite old enough, Evie. You protect her far too much.'

Right. It was all coming out, wasn't it? I was an overprotective mother.

'So if I put her on the nine fifteen, she'll change at Ripon, get to Paddington, and be on the twelve o'clock to Oxford, but I'll get her to ring you en route, OK?'

'Yes, OK.'

Silence.

'Ant, is . . . everything really all right?' I asked tentatively.

'It's fine.'

My mouth felt sticky. No saliva. 'Why don't I come too? We could stay in Harrogate. It's such a pretty town, apparently, and I've never seen it. We could find an old coaching inn or something, make a break of it.'

He laughed. 'It's half-term, Evie. What about Anna?'

I swallowed. 'Yes. No. Silly of me. OK, I'll meet the twelve o'clock. Tell her not to talk to anyone.'

'I will.'

We said goodbye and I put the phone down. Gazed at the wall. A damp patch we'd been meaning to sort out for ages stared back at me. A huge lump had lodged itself in my throat. I was cold, I realized. I got up and went to the understairs cupboard to flick the thermostat on. Heating an entire house for one person to sit in the basement with a cup of coffee was absurd, but Anna would be home soon. I looked at my watch. In . . . four hours. I stood, for a moment, in the hall. Then I took a duster from the cupboard and a can of Pledge. Upstairs, in the dining room, I began polishing the furniture that Maria had already polished. But she didn't quite buff it up the way I liked. We didn't use this room enough, I decided, straightening up and gazing around. It was a lovely room. I'd have a dinner party soon, I determined. Been meaning to have one for some time, kept putting it off. I'd get Lottie and her husband round, the Devlins perhaps. I polished away. The longcase clock in the corner ticked on.

Anna got off the train at two minutes past one and walked towards the barrier carrying a Cath Kidston overnight bag and looking deliberately nonchalant. Like she alighted from trains from York every day of her life having changed at Paddington. Like this was nothing new.

'How was it?' I slipped round the barrier to greet her and give her a hug.

'Fine,' she said with studied boredom Her hair needed washing. 'I was in bags of time at Paddington, so I had a hot chocolate in Pret a Manger.'

I smiled and took her bag as we walked along. Now that would hit the spot. Having a hot chocolate in London, alone, at fourteen. Would have hit my spot too, at that age. I'd probably have imagined a romantic encounter as I sat there with my *Jackie* magazine.

'Bye, Anna.'

'Bye.' She flushed as she nodded to a tall, sandy-haired boy who'd handed in his ticket at the same time as us, and was strolling off across the concourse to the taxi rank, shoulders hunched.

'Who was that?'

'Rory,' she said, unable to keep a little smile from her lips but keeping her eyes firmly on the ground. 'I met him in Pret a Manger.'

Blimey. Not fantasizing like me, actually *having* a romantic encounter. My family were streets ahead of me. In so many ways.

'Is he a student?'

'What?'

'Rory. Is he a student?' He looked about eighteen. But then Anna was tall for her age.

'Dunno.'

'At the university?'

She shrugged.

'Where does he live? We could have given him a lift.'

She rolled her eyes at me as we went out to the car. 'Mum . . .'

I opened the doors and she got in. Perhaps she was right. Perhaps it was none of my business who she met in coffee bars. I waited as she got in beside me. Odd how, in such a short space of time, she looked different. Thinner. Taller.

'Next time, don't bother to pick me up. I'll get a taxi.'

'Right.' I wasn't sure there was going be a next time. I went to put the key in the ignition. Dropped it. 'My God – you've had your ears pierced!'

'I know.' She twisted a tiny gold stud in her ear. Guilt mingled with brazenness flooded her face.

'But—'

'Dad said I could. Chill, Mum, I'm fourteen. And I'm the last one in my class.' Her eyes challenged me. 'I had this done as well.'

She pulled up her T-shirt and a tiny gold stud winked at me from her tummy button.

'Anna!'

She met my eyes, defiant. Suddenly I knew what she

was doing. I fumbled for the keys on the floor. Started the engine.

'I suppose Stacey's liberally pierced, is she?' I said, trying to keep my voice steady.

'Well she's seventeen, so why not? But as it happens, no.' There was real aggression in her voice. Her face looked pinched. Older.

'Where did you have it done?'

'Claire's. And no, it won't go septic. I've put surgical spirit on it.'

'Excellent news.'

Breathe, Evie. Breathe. It's hardly a tattoo. Nothing permanent. She was texting on her mobile now. Rory? Stacey? Either way, she wasn't paying attention to me. I fought for composure.

'So how was it, oop North?' I said with studied lightness.

She shrugged. 'You were there.'

'Yes, but yesterday.'

Another shrug. She put her phone back in her bag and stared out of the window.

'Did you have fun with Stacey?'

'Yeah, it was good.'

'Did you go out at all? Meet her friends?'

'No.' She turned incredulous, you're-such-a-loser eyes on me.

'So what did you get up to last night? What did you do?'

'Stuff.'

'Watch telly?'

'A bit.'

'Did you all have supper together?'

'Who?'

Blood from stones. Teeth from hens. 'You and Daddy, with Bella and Stacey.'

She swallowed. Stared out of the window. Didn't answer.

'Anna?'

She turned back. Her eyes were bright. 'Look, Mum, you're going to have to ask Dad about this. I promised, OK?'

I nearly crashed the car. 'Promised what?'

Silence.

'Promised *what*, Anna?'

What I could see of her fingers, which protruded from fingerless gloves and overlong cardigan sleeves, were plucking frantically at the strap of her bag. I stopped the car. Right there on the Banbury Road. The back end swung round in surprise.

'PROMISED WHAT?' I shrieked in her face. I'd truly lost it.

'I can't tell you, OK?' she shrieked back. 'I can't!'

And with that she burst into tears, got out, slammed the door and began to run. Jesus. I got out and ran after her.

'Anna!' I caught up with her and seized her arm. Swung her round to face me. Gripping both her shoulders, I shook her hard. It's no excuse, but I was very frightened. She wrenched herself free, face streaming with tears.

'Ask Dad, OK?' she yelled in my face, her own, red and contorted. Ugly.

'Anna, this is ridiculous,' I breathed. People were

watching. A man walking his dog on the opposite side of the road had stopped to stare somewhat censoriously. 'Please tell me.'

Tears were filling my eyes now, and she saw it. Saw my anger was over. 'I can't,' she said miserably, eyes still streaming. 'Don't make me. You'll find out. I can't.'

Every fibre in my being turned to ice. It was as if something dangerous had slipped to join us on the pavement. We stood staring at each other on the Banbury Road as the traffic flashed passed. Suddenly she looked about ten. As if she'd fallen off her bike. Found her hamster dead in its cage. I held out my arms and she walked into them. We held each other close. I listened to the sound of her heart pounding, as, no doubt she listened to mine. Then we walked back to the car together, got in, and drove home.

Later that afternoon, she found me sitting at the kitchen table in the fading light, a cold cup of tea in front of me, the violet light of a long autumn evening beginning to threaten. My mobile flickered feebly in my hand. I'd thrown it at the wall when an anonymous voice had informed me for the tenth time Ant's mobile was switched off.

Anna stood in the doorway. 'I've just spoken to Phoebe. You know this Pony Club thing is a three-day event?'

'Is it? I didn't.'

'She says why don't I stay there. At the farm. It's happening in next door's fields.'

I looked at her. She felt like a stranger. 'Do you want to?'

She shrugged. 'It would be easier.'

She did. Wanted to get away.

'OK. I'll drop you over there.'

'Tonight?'

'If you like.'

Even though it didn't start till tomorrow. I saw relief flood her face, which she tried, amateurishly, to mask. Then she disappeared to get ready. I heard her footsteps bounding quickly up the stairs, taking them two at a time.

I didn't go in at the farm. Brenda was in the yard with Megan, and came wagging towards us, jumping straight on the back seat when I opened the door. I just dropped Anna off, with her overnight bag and her jodhpurs and hat, and some chocolates for Caro, telling Anna to let her know I'd got the dog. Normally I'd always pop in, have a chat, a cup of coffee, thank her, but I knew Caro would take one look at my face, drag me to the sitting room, shut the door on the children, and then the floodgates would open. I kissed Anna goodbye, turned the car around in the yard, and was just driving away when I saw Tim, limping towards me with an empty barrow, a cigarette hanging from his mouth. I buzzed down the window.

'Hiya. Whacha doing?'

'Looking busy,' he said, deadpan, without removing the fag.

I grinned. 'How's the hip?'

'So-so.' He leaned in at my window; threw the butt on the gravel and ground it out with his boot.

'Doesn't look great.'

'Always looks worse than it is. You don't look so great yourself.'

'I'm tired.'

'Aren't we all.'

'I've just dropped off Anna.'

'I saw. Phoebe will be pleased. You coming in?' He jerked his head.

I shook mine, not trusting myself to speak. My lovely, kind, caring brother. Just what I didn't need right now.

'I'm in a bit of a rush. Give Caro my love.'

'Will do.'

He was looking at me closely but, being a man, didn't push it. As I drove away, though, I glanced in the rear-view mirror and saw him standing in the gateway, watching me.

Ten minutes later found me parking at Worcester College, in a private car park where they talked a big clamping story, but where the *cognoscenti* knew it was an empty threat. I walked, head bent defensively against the wind tunnel, around the side of the building and then down a dark alleyway. Under normal circumstances I didn't take this short cut in the dark, but in my present state of mind I felt a friendly cosh from a shadowy figure in black might well be a blessed relief. The alleyway led to the playing fields, which in turn led to the longer grass of the meadows that ran down to the canal. A couple of students were slowly making their way back to the college towards me, and in spite of myself I marvelled that they could walk, snog and grope all at the same time. I joined the towpath halfway along, achieving the canal at its longest stretch. It was dark, but Malcolm's boat was always lit up like a Christmas tree, making it easy to find amongst the other barges, which lay like so many sleeping crocodiles at the water's edge. As I approached, I saw Cinders and Sooty rolling around together in the grass. I stopped. What might I be interrupting? I hesitated.

'Well, hello.' Malcolm's voice, not discernibly displeased, hailed me.

I hastened on, encouraged, and saw the pair of them, sitting in wicker chairs on deck, wrapped in overcoats, scarves and blankets, like a couple of old dears on a P&O Cruise, a bottle of wine on the table between them.

'Clamber aboard, m'hearty.'

'You're sure? I'm not interrupting?'

'Certainly not,' said Clarence, standing up to offer me a hand. 'In fact you're just the girl I need. I'm trying to piece together the jigsaw that is Malcolm's life, and all I'm getting at the moment is sky. I feel you might be a crucial corner.'

Malcolm beamed, thrilled that Clarence was bothering to piece him together, and I sat down relieved in a spare wicker chair. The water lay still and inky around us, and as the stars above twinkled down from the velvet heavens, I thought, as I did occasionally, that although most of the time I couldn't imagine how Malcolm lived like this, some of the time I could. There was a very special freedom to it. To be able to untie a few ropes and be gone. Float away. And to have your very own waterside view without paying fancy prices for it either, although, as Clarence confided to me as Malcolm got up to pour me a glass of Chablis, 'If you're wondering what we're doing out here in the middle of October, I get horribly seasick down below.'

'Do you?' I took my drink. 'But it's hardly moving.'

'Yes, but then I get seasick on my granny's swing seat in her back garden.'

I giggled.

'I kid you not. Malcolm's cabin makes me feel like I'm being tossed around on the high seas.'

'That might be a problem, then?' I ventured, accepting the crocheted shawl Malcolm threw at me and wrapping it round my shoulders. I sank back, sipping my wine gratefully.

'Nothing we can't handle. And Sooty loves it. She's never had such freedom.'

We glanced across to where Sooty was chasing Cinders in mad, frantic circles in the grass. 'Look at Cinders go!' I marvelled.

'I know,' agreed Malcolm. 'New lease of life. It's the puppy she never had.'

As two pairs of eyes gazed gooily at their dogs, I realized a little seasickness was not going to be insurmountable.

'So what brings you here, sugar?' asked Malcolm breezily, passing the Hula Hoops, knowing full well it had to be a major catastrophe, but begging me, with his eyes, not to rain on his romantic, starlit parade. Which I wouldn't. And I wouldn't linger, either. I cut to the chase.

'I need a job, Malcolm.'

'A job!'

'Yes, I've decided I don't do enough. And I think and imagine far too much, when what I actually need is occupation. But the thing is, all I've ever done is sell books. So I was wondering . . . well, I wondered if you needed anyone in the shop. Any more help. I wouldn't want much money,' I rushed on, 'hardly any at all. Nothing, if you can't afford it. But I badly need to work.'

My voice was in danger of quavering and I sensibly sank into my wine, wondering what on earth Clarence must think of this little outburst, but beyond caring really.

'I wondered when you'd get bored with your gilded cage,' said Malcolm lightly.

I glanced up. 'You think that's what it is?'

He shrugged. 'I think you lead an enviable, cushioned existence. Which would be enough for many women. But you're brighter than the average monkey, Evie. And you can't just be the supporting act.'

I swallowed. 'Even though it's what I've always been. What I've always wanted to be.'

'People start out one way, and by the time life's finished with them, they end up another. They change. You've changed, Evie. You've grown up.'

I wasn't quite sure what he meant by that. I could feel Clarence watching me.

'And it's not just me,' I said, instinctively dodging the spotlight. 'Ant and Anna would be pleased too, I'm sure. Would like me to do something.'

Malcolm frowned. 'You're doing it for them?'

I knew he was trying to corner me. I ducked and weaved some more. 'Of course not. I'm just saying . . . well, obviously I'm doing it for me. For self-esteem, and – oh, give us a sodding job, Malcolm. Or do I have to

389

get a stand in the market? Flog second-hand paperbacks?'

He smiled. 'I'll give you a job. Now that the shop's so much bigger we could do with the extra help, and you're a good bookseller, Evie. Good with people.'

I glowed. 'Thank you.'

'But this isn't to be some dilettante stance you adopt to piss off Ant, and which you chuck in after a couple of months when your family life is back on track, OK?'

I gulped. Talk about getting to the crux of the matter. 'Absolutely not.' I meant it.

'You have to be committed. And I don't want you saying you'll do five days, and then cutting it down to three.'

'No, I won't.'

'Or not putting in the hours. Gone are the days of half-day closing on a Wednesday. These days we work one late night, and Sundays too. It's tough out there.'

'Fine by me.'

I could see Clarence watching this little exchange with interest. Seeing another side to his foppish new friend: a presumably not unattractive, forceful side.

'So when can I start?'

'As soon as you like. Tomorrow if you want. Half-term's a busy time. Your mum does Tuesday afternoons now, and Sundays and Mondays are quiet, but Wednesday to Saturday would be good.'

'Perfect,' I said firmly.

'And you don't have to do every Saturday,' he said kindly. 'We tend to rotate them, Ludo and me.'

I nodded. 'Um, Malcolm, that's the only tricky bit, actually.'

'What?'

'Ludo.'

'I thought he'd forgiven you for trashing his car?'

'He has. The problem is, Malcolm . . .' I took a deep breath, 'Well, the problem is, he fancies me.'

Not the word I meant to use at all. Teenage. Smutty. Malcolm frowned. 'Ludo?'

'Yes.'

He stared at me. Suddenly he threw his head back and roared with laughter. 'Don't be ridiculous, Evie!'

'I swear to God, Malc, he does.'

Malcolm gave another incredulous bellow of laughter, right up to the stars this time. 'Evie!' His head came back, eyes huge and delighted. 'How can you *tell* such lies?' He turned to a bemused Clarence. 'Ludo's hot,' he explained.

'Oh, thanks!' I spluttered.

'No, but he is hon, isn't he?' He pleaded, eyes brimming with ill-disguised mirth. 'He's young and he's fit and—'

'Sounds just like Evie,' smiled Clarence loyally.

'Oh, no, he's *much* fitter than Evie!'

'Malcolm! He's not even that much *younger* than me, *actually*, and thanks *so* much for the vote of confidence.'

'Petal, he must be,' squealed Malcolm. 'Must be half your age! He looks like something out of the SAS,' he explained to Clarence.

'I must meet this man,' purred Clarence, which made Malcolm do a swift double take.

'Anyway,' I went on doggedly, albeit through clenched teeth, 'it would be better, certainly in the short term, if I did my shifts with you, rather than him.'

'What, in case he ravishes you in Fantasy Fiction?' he

snorted. 'Backs you up against *Lady Chatterley's Lover*?' This went down best with Malcolm himself. It struck him as unbearably funny. Clarence and I waited patiently as he rocked about, clutching himself. He composed himself briefly, pausing to wipe his eyes. 'Oh God,' he moaned, 'marvellous. Absolutely priceless. Yes, sure, whatever you want, Evie. Ludo's mostly there at the beginning of the week, anyway. Just as long you don't go completely delusional on me. I wouldn't want you fretting that *I* fancy you, or something.' This set him off again.

'No danger of that, Malcolm,' I said. He'd got to the coughing and spluttering stage now. 'And thanks for the drink.' I stood up.

'You're going?' Clarence got up too as I drained my glass. We both studiously ignored Malcolm, bundled in his rugs, sniggering weakly.

'I am. I shall leave you in peace. I wouldn't want Malcolm to have a hernia. But thanks, Malc.' I prodded my incapacitated friend with my toe. 'You're a star.' He raised a weak hand in recognition.

'My pleasure, hon. You've made my evening.'

I smiled. Then I disembarked with a little help from the lovely Clarence and, refusing his offer of walking me to my car, made my way across the meadow, back towards Worcester College.

## 26

If I were to put my motives for going back to work under a mental microscope, I'd probably conclude that I'd wanted to impose some control on my life: that it seemed to be spiralling away from me; that this was a stab at self-preservation. I certainly felt dangerously stretched, like pizza dough that's been spun around too much, and I wanted to ball myself up again, be me. But I wanted that ball to be unlike the old me: not soft and vulnerable, but hard and knowing. I had a feeling work would help. Who was it said it was the only dignity? Malcolm's theory – that I also wanted to prove something to Ant, that this was a knee-jerk reaction, which, quite rightly, he didn't want me jerking out of equally sharpish – also rang true, and it's as well he alerted me to it. I've always had to beware of myself: to be on the lookout for subversive behaviour. But whatever my motives, what I hadn't bargained on, particularly in my current frame of mind, was enjoying it. Remarkably, though, those first couple of days in Malcolm's shop were the happiest I'd had for some time. Why? Because they were mine? Who knows. Because, even if my motives were unclear, the end result, the satisfaction, wasn't? Not sure. All I know is I dived in and woke up to marvel. Days like these were rare, and I clung to them.

Initially, of course, I was distracted by the sheer

mechanics of the task, by the enormity of being employed again. I was ridiculously nervous, thinking I couldn't begin to remember how to do this; couldn't begin to get to grips with the new computer system, or the credit card machines, that everything had changed too much and got horribly technical. But within moments of Malcolm showing me, explaining how to look for a book a customer wanted, how to check stock and availability, how to order if we hadn't got it, I was away. The rest was like coming home. As I unpacked the latest glossy autumn hardbacks, putting the Booker Prize shortlist contenders on a separate table at the front as Malcolm instructed, taking time to arrange them in an eye-catching, decorative way, I remembered why I'd done it for so long; why, when friends said, 'But isn't it just like being a shop assistant?' I'd smile, knowing it wasn't. Particularly in a small shop like this, where people came for help and advice, and often with only the scantest shreds of information.

'It's red,' one faintly harassed woman said, as she glanced back at her car outside on a yellow line, fairly vibrating with children.

'Red,' repeated Malcolm, patiently.

'And quite big.' She demonstrated with her hands. Next she'd be making curtain-sweeping gestures and we'd deduce it was also a play.

'Big and red,' said Malcolm, as she turned to shake her head furiously at the wild animals in the Discovery. 'What's it about?' he prompted gently.

She turned back distractedly. 'I meant to get it last week, it's my husband's birthday tomorrow.'

This didn't move us forward.

'D'you know what it's about?' he enquired again.

'Battles. Wars.' She cast about wildly for inspiration, as if at any minute she'd mime that too, fling herself to the floor with an imaginary machine gun. Malcolm steered her through to Ludo's side.

'Military history? A new one?'

'Yes!'

Getting warmer.

'Been reviewed?'

'Yes. He read about it at the weekend, said he'd like it.'

'What paper does your husband read?'

'The *Telegraph*.'

'At the weekend too?'

'Oh. No, the *Sunday Times*.'

'*The History of the Crusades* by Victoria Clark?'

Malcolm plucked a large red book from a pile on a round mahogany table.

'Oh! That's it. Oh, you *are* clever.'

She glowed, paid, and left the shop at racing speed, waving her keys furiously at her brood. I too looked admiring. 'Nice work.'

He shrugged.

Then came some browsers – students, mostly – then more women and children, which was right up my alley as Anna had read a lot of the books they were after, and I was able to guide and enthuse accordingly. Then an elderly woman, in a long brown coat, who smelled of spearmints. She plucked a Catherine Cookson from the shelves, gazed at it avidly and shuffled to the counter.

'I've found one I haven't read!' she declared, taking her

purse out of her bag and counting out the money in small change. Malcolm picked it up.

'Joan, you've read this.'

'No, I haven't.'

'Yes, you have.'

'I've never read one with a windmill on the front.'

'Ah, but they've repackaged them. Changed the covers. This one,' he reached under the counter, 'is this one.' He produced another book.

She stared, dismayed. 'I've read that.'

'I know. Sorry, pet.'

'Oh.' She put her coins away downcast. 'Oh, well.' She turned to go. I nipped round the counter, went after her.

'Um, Joan, have you tried Lyn Andrews?'

'Who?' She regarded me suspiciously.

'Lyn Andrews. She writes lovely period romances, very Catherine Cookson.' She took the book I'd plucked from a shelf behind me.

'Well, I don't know . . .'

'Try it,' I urged. 'I love them.'

She dithered.

'Try it, and if you don't like it, I'll give you your money back.'

Behind me I heard Malcolm moan low and drop his head like a stone on the counter. He banged it up and down, Basil Fawlty-style, which took me right back. I suppressed a giggle.

'All right,' she said, brightening. 'I'll take it.'

'Hon!' Malcolm wailed, jerking upright when she'd left the shop. 'I'm not running a charity.'

'Trust me. She'll be back.'

'Indeed she will,' he muttered darkly.

Sure enough she was. The next day. 'Read it in a day!' she declared. 'In the bath too.' We cringed. Too much information. 'Has she written any more?'

'Yes, loads.' I hastened to the shelves, flicking Malcolm a triumphant look.

Some were harder to please. One tall, haughty-looking woman with a cut-glass accent and a nose a great deal of breeding had gone into, wanted a light romance for her niece. I offered her the bestselling chick-lit title.

'Has it got any sex in it?' she demanded, swooping from a great height to eye me fiercely.

'None at all,' I assured her.

'Well, that's no good, is it?' she snapped and left the shop.

I turned helplessly to Malcolm.

'Never fall for the niece ruse, hon,' he murmured, stroking Alan Hollinghurst reverently before popping him back on the shelf. 'It's as old as the hills. Point her in the Anonymous direction, next time. She wants to get horny by teatime.'

The shop had changed since my day. For the better. It was a friendlier place than I recalled in Jean's reign. Most people knew Malcolm by name, some asked for Ludo, who happily wasn't there, some came to buy, some to browse, and some, it seemed, just to lean on the counter, chat and stroke Cinders. One or two curled up on the sofas upstairs for hours, read books they didn't buy, and even spilled coffee on them, brewed for them by Malcolm in his kitchen, complete with a chocolate digestive.

'Don't you mind that they don't buy?'

'Oh, I charge them for the coffee.'

'No, the books.'

He shrugged. 'They're students – no money. Not really. They make the place look busy and tell other people about it, who do buy. I had a visiting American professor in here the other day who'd heard about us from his students. Spent nearly a hundred pounds. Anyway, they're nice kids.'

I watched him go carefully back upstairs balancing a tray of Nescafé. He was a sweetie, Malcolm. But sweeties didn't make money. I tackled him on it.

'Oh, there's no money in it. Not really. I mean, I make a bit, obviously, but probably less than Jean made. Specially now that the supermarkets do discounts. But it's a nicer place to be, isn't it? And isn't that what life's about? Having a nice time?'

He had a point. And with only a houseboat and a dog to run, what did Malcolm need with money? I sensed, though, that he was distracted, these days: his eyes were permanently on the door, looking for Clarence to come in, which he did, every lunchtime, on a gust of fresh air and a big smile, sporting heavenly Ralph Lauren shirts and cashmere jackets, which had Malcolm and I drooling and fingering the cloth, and often a bunch of flowers too for the counter, before whisking Malc off to Bertorelli or somewhere equally smart.

'How come Clarence is so rich?' I asked one day as we waited for him. 'He's a college lecturer, isn't he?'

'He inherited it.'

'From who?'

'His family, who else? He's a trustafarian. No irony intended. Close your mouth, Evie, it's not becoming.'

I shut it. 'What did they do?'

'I've no idea. I've yet to be so crass as to ask. Here he is. Can you see my spot?' He raised his chin anxiously as a sleek convertible Mercedes drew up outside.

'Hardly. Just keep your chin resting pertly in your hand all lunchtime. You'll be fine.'

And off he went, frisky with excitement, hopping into the open-top car with a toss of his blond head, and leaving me in charge of a shop and two dogs for a couple of hours, which I loved.

I wandered around, trying not to think too much, passing the time with customers, helping where I could – my embarrassingly thorough knowledge of light romantic fiction helping enormously – doing my best in Ludo's bit, where, I found, most people were experts anyway and knew what they were looking for, and surprisingly, managing not to dwell too much on my own problems. Managing not to go there. Up north.

After Anna's little outburst on the Banbury Road, I knew, of course, that something reasonably monumental had happened. And initially, I'd rung, of course I had, nearly broken my phone in the process. Something had stopped me calling The Old Rectory – pride, maybe – but the very next morning, on my first day at work, I'd tried again, hoping to get Ant on his mobile, when I knew he'd be in the car with the rep, and not with Bella. His answer machine was on. I left a message. No reply. I sent a text.

'I know you can't talk, but Anna was very upset when

I picked her up yesterday. What's going on? LOL E x.'
Quite measured, I thought.

I got an equally measured one back. 'I'm sorry she was
upset. Can I please tell you when I get back? LOL A x.'

I read it again. I was making coffee in Malcolm's back
room at the time, Malcolm having just popped out to get
the croissants. As the kettle came to a rolling boil I felt
my blood rise with it. My thumb got to work.

'No. Tell me now. If you think I'm going to sit here
and stew while you . . .'

What, Evie? While he what? I stopped. Stared into
space. Slowly erased the message. Scrubbed out my rant.
Some quiet wisdom, something very un-Evie Hamilton
stole over my soul. Something in my daughter's face
in the Banbury Road, which I couldn't quite put my
finger on.

Feeling curiously light-headed, I put the phone back in
my pocket and walked into the main body of the shop.
It was empty, happily. I went to the shelves, still feeling
a bit . . . peculiar. Anna's face. Frightened. Contorted.
Angry. I leaned my forehead on the spines. Breathed in
. . . out . . . in . . . out . . . inhaling and exhaling the smell
of new books, the paper, finding some small comfort in
it, as I always had done. I shut my eyes. Tried to think.
To find a sliver of light. Something Ant had to tell me
face to face. Something to make Anna rush out and have
every orifice pierced. To make her turn on me, accusingly,
in the car, almost as if she hated me. And then want to
get away from me. I stood up straight. Felt frightened. I
went upstairs and plumped the sofas where the students
sat. Came back down with the books they'd been reading

and replaced them in the shelves. Frightened? Why? What had I ever done? This mess was all of Ant's making, this child of his. I was an innocent, a pawn! I'd ring again. Of course I would. No, I couldn't frigging well wait. No way. I reached for my phone, began to punch away – stopped. It was almost as if an invisible hand was staying mine, saying . . . no.

There was, of course, the very certain knowledge that Ant wouldn't tell me anyway if I rang. I knew that. And that only a fraction of him would come to the phone. The last time we'd spoken, when he'd informed me he was staying on, I'd got about a tenth of him. This time I'd get even less. He'd be polite yet firm. Whilst I got shrill and desperate. Cried, perhaps. I looked at the text. He'd asked if I could please wait. Asked politely. And implicit in that, I realized in a sudden rush of blood to the head, was Trust Me. My heart stopped rattling around in its cage and lay down quietly for two seconds. And Ant was an honourable man. I mustn't lose sight of that. Mustn't doubt him. I went about my work, opening a new delivery that had just come in from a supplier, with something approaching calm. With a dawning sense that something bigger than the personal happiness and well-being of Evie Hamilton was going on here.

Some customers came in. Two women, early forties, wanting to start a book club. Did I have any ideas? Obviously as the weeks went by they'd ask for suggestions from the rest of the group, choose the titles that way, but what would be a good book to start with, did I think? Not too heavy, said one, glancing nervously at her companion, and not too – you know – frivolous, countered the other. Something middle groundish, they agreed, to get the ball rolling, to get together and have a chat over, maybe a bite to eat. Remarkably I managed to lose myself in their enviable dilemma, watching as their brows furrowed and they argued this way and that, discussing the relative merits of John le Carré or Martin Amis. Oh, to be starting a book club. Oh, to be choosing my first book and for that to be keeping me awake at night. They left with eight copies of *Atonement*.

The next day, I got another text. 'I've booked Carluccio's for Friday night. LOL Ant x.'

Carluccio's. Where we always went for major chats. The biggies. Which school for Anna? Should she board? As an only child, wouldn't she enjoy the companionship of others? Or would I miss her too much? Where to holiday? Should we ski, because once you start, there's no stopping, they want to do it every year.

I texted back: 'Fine.'

That night, as I lay in bed, in that slightly delusional state halfway between sleep and wake, I conjured up what seemed an entirely plausible scenario. One that had Bella and her father blackmailing Ant. Yes, that was it. Caro had been right all along. They were after his money. And once I'd gone, it had all turned ugly. Bella had hissed bitterly that Ant had ruined her life by getting her up the duff, Ted had pinned him to a chair to make him listen, Stacey had slumped in another, glaring at him, chewing gum. Ted had slapped him across the face, or maybe even pistol-whipped him, yelling, 'Bastard!' I vowed sleepily to myself that I'd go and rescue him tomorrow. Drive up first thing and spirit him away. Bring him home, which I had a vague, fuddled idea was at the farm, in the kitchen, where, as Ant came in, face swollen from pistol-whipping, I was the child standing on a stool by the Aga, helping Mum – or was it Maroulla? – make cakes. Clearly I'd slipped my moorings and drifted into sleep.

I was woken some hours later by the sound of a sash window sliding up. Still in the folds of a disappearing dream I groped groggily for the clock in the dark. Ten past two. I lay there listening. No. Nothing. Must have been the wind. The veils of sleep swathed me once more and I began to doze off, when another noise jerked me into consciousness. A creaking noise from below, in the kitchen. I sat bolt upright. Soft footsteps were stealing around down there. I jumped out of bed and threw on my dressing gown. I'd often wondered how I'd react to a break-in. Lying doggo and simulating sleep whilst the masked intruder went through my jewellery box, then realizing there was nothing of value, decided to rape me instead, whereupon I'd simulate death, which would surely put him off, I'd once laughed to Ant. It was a surprise, therefore, to find myself on my feet, clutching the lapels of my dressing gown at my neck, my heart pounding.

It occurred to me that I'd forgotten to lock the kitchen window. I listened, terrified in the dark. Faint, deliberately cautious footsteps crept towards the foot of the stairs. I prickled with fear; felt the hairs on the back of my neck literally rise. Panic button. I knew we had one, or even two, one downstairs in the study, the other – under the bed. I dived underneath. But it was pretty crowded. Over the years I'd stashed a lot of rubbish behind the valance, and the panic button, up by the wall, had mountains of detritus in front of it: old duvets, shoe boxes, plastic crates of Lego. I couldn't get to it, I realized in horror. Couldn't reach it.

The footsteps kept coming up the staircase, creeping . . . then stopping. Creeping . . . then stopping. Sick with fear, I realized I had two options. To stay hidden under the bed and hope he didn't find me, or scramble out now, break the window, and scream into the street. Break glass, Ant had said. People always came running, always phoned the police.

The door softly opened. Too late: he was in the room. There was a pause as he assessed the situation, and then his footsteps stole on. I put my fist in my mouth to stop myself screaming. I heard him first at the chest of drawers, scooping up the loose change Ant kept in a saucer. Then drawers opened softly, but didn't shut. Next I heard him at my dressing table, rustling in my jewellery box. Despite my terror I wondered how old he was. Was he on drugs? With a knife? I bit my fist, willing my body not to shake, to rustle and give me away. He came towards the bed. I could sense him standing there above me, breathing. I stared, wide-eyed into the darkness, nerves as taut as violin strings, ready to wriggle out backwards, spring up and keep the bed between us. Then, improbably, awfully, the mattress above me sagged heavily as the springs gave way. My eyes bulged in the darkness. He'd got in my bed. This was beyond my stunned intelligence. A tramp? A vagrant? I lay there, rigid with horror. Then he cleared his throat. I slowly took my fist out of my mouth.

'Ant?' I said, mostly under my breath.

'Yes?' came back a cautious response from above.

It still took me a moment. I scrambled out of there on my tummy like a crab, stumbled to my feet and darted to the light switch by the door. As I illuminated the room and swung about, we stared at one another in astonishment.

'Where did you spring from?' he gaped, sitting bolt upright in bed in his old Balliol T-shirt, clutching the duvet, looking about twelve.

'Under the bed!' I gasped.

'Why?'

'Because I thought you were a bloody burglar, that's why! What are you doing here, Ant?'

'I live here!'

'Yes, but you were coming back tomorrow.' Fear had sucked the air from my lungs and I sounded like I'd inhaled a helium balloon. 'I was about to break a window, couldn't reach the panic button – what were you doing in my jewellery box?'

'I wasn't in your jewellery box, I was putting my watch down.'

'Opening drawers, scooping up money—'

'Putting my clothes away, putting *down* money – for God's sake, Evie!'

I stared at him in disbelief. 'How did you get in?'

'Through the door.'

'But the window. I heard it—'

'You left it open. I shut it.'

'Why didn't you ring?'

'Because it's the middle of the night. I didn't want to wake you.'

'But you must have known I wasn't in bed!'

'Only when I got in!'

'Didn't you think it was a bit odd?'

'Yes, but I assumed you were at the farm or something. I wasn't going to go looking for you. I've just driven a hundred and fifty miles, for heaven's sake!'

We stared at each other, temporarily mute. I came to first.

'Oh, Ant . . .' I flew to him. Threw my arms around his neck and he held me close. I could hear his heart doing gymnastics like mine. 'I was so scared,' I breathed in his ear. '*So* scared.'

'I'm sorry, I'm sorry, I'm sorry,' he whispered back. 'You scared the living daylights out of me too, as a matter of fact.'

We held on tight like that for a minute. Eventually I drew back; sat opposite him on the bed, still gripping his hands. My heart rate was coming down a bit.

'Why are you here?'

'Because when I got your terse little text, I suddenly realized what you might be thinking. I knew I had to come back. It hadn't occurred to me until then.' I looked at him. My text. What had I said? Fine. Yes, a bit terse, but then I'd felt terse. He took my shoulders. Gave me a lopsided, intent look.

'What's this about, Ant?' I managed, as something familiar tightened inside me.

'It's about Bella. But it's not what you're thinking.' He shook my shoulders gently, a little reproof. Those eyes were kind. Full. But I still couldn't read them.

'What is it then?' I whispered.

I saw him weigh the possible routes in. He took a breath to steady himself. 'She's ill.'

'Ill?'

'Yes. Very ill.'

His eyes were sad too, I realized. Full of emotion. Some distant wave of consciousness, some swell of comprehension was gradually building out at sea, gathering momentum, slowly approaching.

'Define very ill.'

'It's terminal. She's got cancer. She's dying.'

He watched me absorb it: watched the wave break over me and throw me onto the beach. Like so many tiny pebbles I skittered wildly up the shore in its wake.

# 27

I let go of his hands as if they were molten. Felt one of mine go up to cover my mouth. I hadn't been expecting that. I stared at him. 'Shit, Ant.'

We gazed at each other, our eyes silently communing. I shook my head slowly in disbelief as the enormity of what he'd said continued to filter into my consciousness; as I thoroughly absorbed it. My eyes filled quickly. I raised them to the ceiling, then brought them back level with Ant's. Shook my head again, dumbfounded, my fingers still pressed to my mouth.

'She *can't* be,' I heard myself say eventually, in the smallest voice.

'She is,' he said, a sad little smile bringing down the corners of his mouth. He took my hand, waiting for me to catch up.

'How long?' I whispered.

'How long has she had it?'

'No, how long until . . .'

He made a helpless gesture. Spread his hands. 'I don't know, exactly. No one does, yet.'

'That beautiful girl?' I narrowed my eyes at him incredulously, as if perhaps he'd got it wrong, hadn't entirely been telling the truth.

'Yes,' he agreed.

'But . . . isn't there something they can do? Surely these days – chemotherapy, radiotherapy—'

'It's spread too quickly. Far too quickly. And it wasn't caught in time. Wasn't picked up.'

'From where? Where did it start?'

'Oh . . . women's . . . you know.'

'Breast?'

'No, I think . . .' His eyes slithered past mine awkwardly.

'Cervical?'

He nodded. Obviously couldn't say it. It struck me there were a lot of words Ant couldn't say; this literature professor, this dealer in the English language. Cervical. The silent killer, they called it. The one you didn't know about till it was too late. Non-negotiable. The one that grew where babies were supposed to, but where instead, a hobgoblin had set up his stall, rubbing his hands with glee. Size of a grapefruit, women would whisper later, huddled in supermarkets, sucking their teeth. 'When they took it from that poor girl's body . . .'

'She doesn't look ill,' I said stubbornly, fighting her corner.

'She's very thin.'

Yes. Yes, she was thin. I remembered those tiny legs protruding from her denim skirt and disappearing into floppy boots. Remembered being taken aback.

'And very pale,' he added.

'Yes,' I conceded numbly, recalling her face as she turned it up to me when we'd walked together in her knot garden, in the evening light. Pale. Anxious. A very slight tinge to the whites of her eyes too. I remembered feeling ruddy and hulking, beside her. Beside what I imagined to be her ethereal beauty. I just didn't know how ethereal. How rude my own health was. I quickly got off the bed, wrapping my dressing gown around me tightly. And I remembered Ted's face too, when I'd commented in the car on how lovely she was. How the tears had welled up again, his face creased with grief. Of course. Tearful Ted. No wonder. His daughter. His *grand*daughter.

'Stacey!' I breathed, swinging back to Ant.

'I know.'

'Oh my God – does she know?' I asked stupidly.

'Of course. From day one.'

Yes. Of course she knew. I came quickly back to the bed. Sat down, curling my legs tightly under me. What had that been like? How had that little scenario played out? Telling your only child. It didn't bear thinking about.

Questions were muscling through the wall of shock now, in no particular order. 'When did she tell you?'

'Bella? The second day we were there. You were still asleep upstairs, I think. Or getting dressed. She told me in the garden.'

I stared at him. 'Under the cherry tree?'

'Yes.'

'On that little round seat?'

'Yes.'

'You pushed her hair back.'

'Did I?' He looked startled. Then bewildered. 'Maybe. I don't remember. Perhaps I felt I had to . . . you know, do something.'

I squinted at my husband. 'She tells you she's dying and you push her hair back?'

'Well, I—'

'Oh, Ant.'

'What?'

'Ant!'

'What? What should I have—'

'You should have taken her in your arms!' I roared. 'Held her close, held her tight, my *God*, Ant!' I gazed at him. What kind of uptight emotionally repressed academic was he?

He shrugged helplessly. 'I didn't know what to do, what to say. I needed you then, Evie. You'd have known what to do.' He looked at me beseechingly. 'She'd have sobbed on your shoulder, told you everything, but I couldn't.'

I shot my fingers through my hair as I stared at him.

'You came to meet me in the garden together, all smiley.'

'Because she was smiley,' he said desperately. 'I just took my cue from her.'

'You should have stopped me going home, taken me to one side – told me!'

'I know, I know, but—'

'Oh Lord,' I breathed. I remembered them waving me off, her diminutive figure beside his. So brave. And Ant, smiling, waving too, playing a part. What part? What planet was he on? But actually – oh, what did it matter: the girl was dying. What did it matter how emotionally strait-jacketed my husband was? What did it matter he probably suggested popping the kettle on? I scratched my head energetically. Stood up again, needing to distance myself.

I heard him sigh behind me. He knew me very well. I turned. He looked wretched. I swallowed my irritation and went to sit beside him, took his hand.

'Is that why they asked us up there?'

'Yes. Mostly.'

'So does Anna know?'

'Yes. I told her.'

'Which is why she's so upset?'

'She was terribly shaken.'

'But why with me? Why is she angry with me?'

He took a deep breath. 'Because . . . one thing I did do, when Bella and I talked later, with the girls, which I shouldn't have done without consulting you, and the reason I needed to talk to you face to face, and didn't want Anna saying anything first . . .' This was all coming out in a bit of a rush. He stopped, hesitating.

I frowned. 'Is?'

'Is I promised to look after Stacey.'

'Well of course.'

'No,' he swallowed. Didn't meet my gaze. Kept his firmly on the duvet. 'Not just keep an eye. Really look after her. For ever. With us.'

I stared.

'To live here with us. To bring her up – what's left of her upbringing – here, in Oxford. I'm her father, Evie. And I haven't been much of a father so far. She needs me. Bella asked me. And I said yes.'

My heart thudded. Which is all it took. A heart beat. I'm ashamed it took that long.

'Yes, of course.'

'Yes?'

'Yes,' I repeated.

He looked at me. I glimpsed fear vanishing from his eyes. Then they filled up. 'Oh, Evie.'

He pinched the bridge of his nose with his thumb and forefinger, his eyes screwed tight. I'd never seen him cry. Not even after Neville. It only lasted a moment. He unbuckled his face and let out a breathy sigh.

'What did you think I'd say?'

'I didn't know. I'm really appalled to say, I didn't know. But I should have known. But . . .' he struggled, 'she's mine, after all, not yours. And Anna's too, of course, and we thought—'

'Anna thought I'd say no, too?'

I remembered her face in the car: challenging, defensive, gold earrings glistening aggressively.

'She came back from town that day with Stacey and you'd gone, so she assumed you'd flounced off home, couldn't hack it. You told me not to tell her about Hector so—'

'Oh, Ant, use your judgement! I didn't know the girl was dying!'

'Well, quite. Perhaps I should have,' he licked his lips nervously, 'perhaps I should have said. But then later, when she found out about Bella – well, she assumed you'd say . . . well, it's a big ask.'

I was shocked. They both thought I'd say no. That I wouldn't welcome Stacey into our family. Wouldn't bring up someone else's child. And actually, if he'd asked me in the beginning, when he'd first got the letter, yes, I might well have said forget it. A big ask. Was it? I supposed it was. But it didn't feel like it now. What – that shy, sweet, seventeen-year-old girl? With no mother? Oh, no. She had to come here. Did they think I was a witch?

'Evie,' he took my hands, reading me, 'what you fail to realize is that an awful lot of women, regardless of how nice Stacey is, would not want their husband's child in the house, let alone living with them.'

I gave this some thought. Put like that . . .

'And what *you* don't realize,' I said slowly, 'in the spirit of full disclosure, is what I thought was going on. That in my darkest moments, I thought I'd lost you. Give a child a home? Oh, Ant, there's no comparison.'

We sat facing each other on the bed. After a moment, I lay my head on his shoulder. He drew me in close. We sat there huddled in silence. Eventually I sat back.

'I know you don't know exactly, but . . . weeks? Months?'

'Months. Maybe weeks. She doesn't want to suffer, or make Stacey suffer too long. She's in and out of the hospice. She'd like it all to be over by Christmas.'

My eyes widened. 'Like Ali MacGraw.'

'What?'

'In *Love Story*.' A lump rose in my throat. 'When Ryan O'Neal goes to the hospital, she say she wants the troops home by Christmas.'

'Oh.' He looked blank, his knowledge of romantic movies less encyclopaedic than mine.

'Ryan O'Neal gets on the bed, to hold her.' My eyes swam as I remembered, even though it was the only scene I wasn't terribly comfortable with: all those tubes, blood bags . . . 'And the father – the father's waiting in the corridor, trying not to cry. Oh – Ted!'

'I know.' Ant nodded, swallowing. 'Ted's not good. Not good at all. Stacey's being unbelievable, but Ted—'

'But surely Stacey might have gone there?'

'Well, of course, he was the obvious choice. And he would have had her like a shot. Wanted to have her. But he could see . . . well, we all talked about it—'

'Did you?'

'Oh, yes, round the kitchen table the next day. Ted came back. Bella rang him to say she'd told us. So Ted, Bella, Stacey, Anna and I discussed it.'

Blimey. Anna. What a very grown-up conversation. No wonder she looked older.

'And Bella was very firm. Ted's a tremendous grandfather, always will be, but she wanted a proper family for Stacey. A young family, and when Stacey got the interview at Oxford—'

I inhaled sharply. 'It was a no-brainer.'

'Exactly. They knew I was here. So that's when they wrote. Bella said they agonized for ages, thinking it wasn't fair on me, on you, knowing we had another child, knowing it was like dropping a bomb, that it was going to cause chaos, maybe even break up a family, that we might say bugger off, but knowing too, at the end of the day . . .'

'She had to do the best for her child.'

'Quite.'

'Nothing else in the world matters.'

'No.'

'She did the right thing.'

'I'm so glad you think so, Evie.' He couldn't mask his

relief. His hand closed over mine and he squeezed it, summoning up something else. 'And I'm so, so glad I'm married to you.'

I couldn't help but smile. That was huge, coming from Ant. We sat there on the bed together, exchanging sad little smiles: a much emotionally travelled, middle-aged, married couple, holding hands. At length, I exhaled the deepest sigh. It seemed to unfold from the pit of my stomach. I stood up, tightening my dressing gown cord around me. Then I found my slippers and went to the door.

'Where are you going?'

'To ring Bella.'

'It's the middle of the night.'

'She'll still be awake. And she'll be waiting for me to call.'

## 28

The following morning I drove to watch Anna in the final day of her pony competition. You couldn't have scripted the day. It was one of those hazy golden ones with just a faint breeze, which the calendar swore blind was late October, but the soft blue sky and diffused sunshine could lull one to believe might just as well be August. As I turned into Ed Pallister's farm, just down the lane from ours, and joined the line of parked cars abandoned by other Pony Club mothers in his front yard, it occurred to me that Bella Edgeworth wouldn't wake up to too many more mornings like these. Something Margaret Thatcher said the morning after the Brighton bombings about not being meant to see a similar day sprang to mind. I locked the car and made my way, head down and thoughtful, towards a farflung field, full of circling ponies in the distance, reaching in my bag for my sunglasses in defence of the low sunshine and much else.

We'd talked at length last night, Bella and I. And when I'd finally come back up the stairs to bed, my knees cramped from sitting on the stairs in one position for so long, I'd repeated it all pretty much verbatim to Ant. I was tired – wrung out too – but he needed to be brought up to speed while it was still fresh in my head. I told him about the medication she'd been offered at vast expense, but which the NHS didn't pay for and which would only prolong her life for a couple of months in any case, and how she'd rather leave the money to Stacey. About the white mice treatment she'd plumped for instead.

'White mice?' Ant propped himself up on one elbow as I kicked away my slippers and shrugged my dressing gown off.

'It's early days research stuff. The sort of thing Bella says they give to white mice.' I gave him a wry smile as I got into bed. 'She's volunteered to give it a go, since it's too late for conventional medicine. It makes her pretty sick, though.'

'Oh.' His eyes widened slightly at me. 'I didn't know that.'

'Didn't you ask what she was on?'

'Well . . .'

'What about Ted?' I plumped my pillow, trying to hide my impatience. 'Didn't you talk to Ted about it?'

'I tried but he got so upset. He's very emotional, Ted,' my husband informed me gravely, as if perhaps I didn't know. 'Blew his nose a lot.'

I smiled. 'I'll talk to him. He'll have to come and stay often, certainly at the beginning, so that Stacey's got an ally, a friend. Bella agreed. Long weekends, that sort of thing. I thought he might even come on holiday with us.' I turned to switch the bedside light off.

'Right.' I heard Ant say faintly.

We carried on talking quietly in the dark, or I did. He listened. Familiar roles. I told him about Stacey's reservations about contacting us in the first place, how it had been her mother's idea and how, initially, Stacey had resisted. How she'd said she'd like to live with her granddad, stay up north with her friends, cling to what she knew, maybe not even go to Oxford at all, or any university come to that; how, under the circumstances, it all seemed stupid and irrelevant. They'd argued. Stacey had talked of getting a job, doing a secretarial course. Bella had had to push.

'She's scared,' I'd said to her mother on the phone. 'Terrified of being without you.'

'Of course she is, but the thing is, Evie, Dad would just give in to her. He's a complete softie, he'd let her have her way, say – whatever makes you happy, luv – and that would be such a waste. And I'm running out of time here. I'm having to edge her on all the time, persuade her.' A note of panic had crept into her voice.

'But her reservations are understandable. We're strangers, effectively.'

'Of course you are, and she loves her granddad very much, and doesn't want to leave him alone with his grief either, and I understand *all* of that, and there's an element of me that says – oh, let her be, Bella. Let her have a year off at least, she's so young after all. She could apply next year, or even the year after, but an even bigger bit of me knows she wouldn't.'

'What, wouldn't reapply?'

'Not without me there to push her, no. If she spent a year up here, she'd spend another. Start a job and sink without trace. She'd still be in Russell & Bromley in three years' time with her friend Jordan. She's clever, but she's not brave. Not remotely.'

'Like Ant,' I said suddenly.

'Oh?' She snagged on that bit of information like it was barbed wire.

'Yes. I mean . . . well. It just sounded a bit familiar. Go on.'

'I just need to know she's on track before I die,' she said with an air of desperation but not a hint of martyrdom. 'Is that so selfish of me?'

It occurred to me to wonder how anyone could think this remarkable woman selfish. 'Not at all,' I said slowly, 'and you're the best judge. You know her better than anyone. Presumably you're equally certain once she starts her degree she'd enjoy that too?'

'Oh, she'd love it, that's entirely my point. She'd never look back. She'd be away.' I was dimly aware of history not being allowed to repeat itself, either, courtesy of a quiet determination; a very steely core.

'OK, so now that she's met us, how does she feel? About coming?'

'Much happier. As long as she knows *you're* all happy, that's her biggest angst. She keeps saying – but, Mum, why would they want me? They might say they do, but why would they really? She doesn't want to impose.'

'She won't be imposing. Ant would love to have her. Anna would love to have her. I'd love to have her,' I said, with a truthfulness that surprised me. 'But she does need to be handled very carefully, I can see that. It all has to be done softly-softly.'

'Otherwise she'll feel bamboozled, I know. I'm so worried she'll get the next train back and I won't be there to stop her.'

'I'll stop her.'

I heard her swallow. 'Oh, Evie . . .' she managed.

'And anyway, she won't do that,' I rushed on, saving us both. 'As long as everything's done sensitively, with patience —'

'*Endless* patience, which is a lot to put on you, a lot of pressure. She's going to be desperately grief-stricken, she's got no idea. It really has just been the two of us all these years, and it's going to hit her like a truck.' Her speech was coming rapidly now, as if she really were running out of time. 'I know she hasn't properly got her head round that. It'll be awful for her, and pretty grim for you too, picking up the pieces, walking on eggshells when she's down, depressed, which she can be, occasionally, even at the best of times, let alone when —'

'No, it won't be grim,' I interrupted firmly. 'It'll be fine.'

I'd heard her wobble over the last few minutes as I sensed she hadn't wobbled very publicly before. By adopting a position of strength, assuming the role of pillar, I'd allowed her to lean. I'd offered her that brief luxury, invited her to be weak for a moment. And I understood all too clearly that most of the time she was being strong for Stacey, and for Ted, holding it all together for them, greasing the way so they could glide on without her; resolutely persuading them this was the best course of action, when, in reality, she had doubts. Of course she did. Real reservations about uprooting her child at such a cataclysmic time. She knew it would be hard.

And as I informed Ant now, in bed, of the reality of what it would really be like, which Bella hadn't burdened him with either, he blinked rapidly.

'It's not going to be easy,' he said, and I saw a hint of misgiving flit across his eyes.

'No, it's not. But it's not going to be impossible either. Trust me, Ant. It'll be fine.'

Which is what I'd said to Bella. Trust me. Odd, wasn't it, I thought as I turned over on my side and bunched up my pillow, endeavouring to find a cool spot on it, how I had no fear about this. No fear at all. Ask me to take an exam, or indeed put pen to paper about anything – even thank-you letters were a trial – and I'd come out in a muck sweat, but help an emotionally insecure teenager who's recently lost her mother? Integrate her into our family on a permanent basis? Cope with her grief, the fallout when Bella had gone? I'm not saying it would be a walk in the park but I'd roll up my sleeves without trepidation. And I needed a challenge. Except . . . my eyes widened slowly to the wall in the dark . . . I already had one. Shit. I sat up suddenly.

'I've got a job,' I announced to no one in particular, but presumably my husband beside me.

Ant sat up too. Sighed. 'Macbeth does surely murder sleep tonight. We may as well give in gracefully. What d'you mean?'

I told him about the shop.

'Right.'

'D'you mind?'

'Of course I don't mind. I'm delighted. But it's slightly come out of left field, hasn't it?'

'Isn't that where everything's coming from at the moment?'

We sat a moment in silence. Then: 'Did you enjoy it? I mean, the few days you've done there?'

'I absolutely loved it.' The passion in my response surprised even me.

'Well, good,' he said shortly. Although I could tell he was faintly hurt. 'Why didn't you tell me?'

'I was . . . going to surprise you.'

Not quite true. It was my insurance policy. Something to do with Bella Edgeworth. Which of course, I didn't need now. But I did love it. Loved being useful. Except now that Stacey was coming I'd be useful in my more familiar, maternal way: my supportive role. The one I still felt was instinctive, biological. I hesitated.

'Don't even think about it,' he said, lying down again. 'If you love it, do it. You'll need a distraction. Something for you. Don't even think about chucking it, Evie.'

I lay down quietly impressed. Quite forceful, for Ant.

I went on through the fields following the post-and-rail fence that bordered our farm, past the cottage Maroulla and Mario had once had, now occupied by Tim's farm worker, Phil, and his girlfriend, Carly. Glancing in I saw that the sentimental print of a gypsy girl with a tear in her eye that had once hung over the fireplace and I'd thought the height of sophistication, had been replaced with a mirror. I remembered plates of pasta in front of that fire – in front of the telly too, if Maroulla was in a good mood.

Carefully skirting piles of manure I achieved the gate to the main horse arena. It had a bossy notice on it: 'Shut firmly behind you.' I did as I was told. Vast horseboxes and lorries, which, by virtue of their cargo, were allowed to progress here whilst lesser pilgrims like me had to stop short in the yard, were parked in neat lines just proud of the collecting ring, which was cordoned off with white tape. Every so often a harassed mother in wellingtons would run past in that middle-aged, shuffle bottom way, shouting, 'Kick *on*, Clarissa!' or 'Shorten your *reins*!' as a tearful, red-faced child on a pony yelled back, 'I'm trying!' Lots of fat little girls on thin ponies, and lots of thin little girls on fat ponies. Apparently Norman Thelwell's house had backed on to just such a field, and he'd stood at his garden fence with his sketchpad and pencil, and smiled at his good fortune.

Despite the numbers, and the frenetic activity, almost the first person I saw was Anna. She'd tied Hector to a fence post where he was munching a hay net, and was sitting cross-legged on the grass beside him, iPod in her ears, texting away on her phone. She looked up as I approached. Her face, which a moment ago had been a blank, teenage canvas, suddenly became watchful, apprehensive. I gave her a broad smile. Then a little nod.

I watched relief flood her face. She got up with just the merest tinge of uncertainty, pulled her earplugs out and came towards me tentatively, eyes searching my face.

'Really? Have you talked to Daddy? Have you – did you—'

'Yes, yes and yes. What a lot of doubting Thomases I've got. Did you really think I wouldn't?'

She flew the last few steps into my arms. I gathered her to me. Her eyes were damp when she pulled back.

'Well, you might have said no, why shouldn't you?' she demanded, brushing her eyes roughly with her sleeve. 'She's not yours, after all.'

'No, but she's yours. And Daddy's. And that's good enough for me.'

We laughed and she hugged me again.

'You and Bob Geldof,' she said suddenly, drawing back.

'What?'

'Bob Geldof took on Tiger Lily after Mike Hutchence and then Paula Yates died. She wasn't his, but she was Peaches and the other sisters'.'

I blinked. 'Right.' I wasn't quite as *au fait* with the pages of *OK!* as my daughter these days. I had a vague idea what she was talking about, though.

'And she's lovely, Mum, isn't she? Really sweet. You'll love her when you get to know her properly.'

I smiled. 'She is, and I will. I know I will.'

We linked arms and walked back towards Hector.

'But, Mum . . .' she hesitated. Stopped suddenly. 'She's not like my other friends.'

'What d'you mean?'

'Well, she's not – you know – like Chloe and Poppy. Not . . .' she struggled to explain; looked worried, as Ant had looked worried last night. About reality dawning. Not posh, was what she meant. Not Oxford High. Not flicky-haired and clued up and rally rally nice. So much the better. But in their initial rush of enthusiasm, in their desire to make it work, my family had forgotten these minor details – grief, different social background, lack of confidence, etc. – and were handing them to me now, no

– *dropping* them at my feet, hoping I'd pick them up, as I'd picked up behind them all my life: scooping toys into the toy box, dirty socks into the linen basket, wet towels from the bathroom floor to rails.

'Of course she's not like them, and that's very refreshing. And after all, the majority of students at Oxford don't actually come from a twenty-mile radius of here, or from public schools. And although she's coming to live with us, that's where she's going. To the university. She'll be in the majority there.'

'I suppose,' she said in some surprise, and I saw it cross her mind that if she, Anna, ever went there, she'd be in the minority.

'We'll make it work, Anna, you'll see. Everything's going to be fine,' I assured her, as women have assured children for years, and then, even if it killed them, made sure it was. We sat down on the ground together. As Anna pulled at the grass, she told me how we were going to redecorate the spare room for her – no – she sat up straight, eyes bright – she and Stacey would redecorate it together, paint it lilac, or apple green. I sat and listened and smiled.

'Number one five two!' sang out the nasal loudspeaker. 'Number one five two to the collecting ring now, please.'

'Ohmygod – that's me!' She leaped up.

'Go – *go*. Does that mean you're on?' I got to my feet as she fled to untie Hector.

'No, next but one. Quick, Mummy, my hat.' I ran around picking things up. See? Scooping. A hat, a whip, her jacket – handing it all to her as she pulled her stirrups down and did up her girth.

'Are you enjoying it?' I asked as she turned round so I could tie her number on her back for her. 'Hold still.'

'It's OK, but there's so much standing around and *so* many bossy women telling me I'm not getting my tail bandaging right or my plaits straight. And hardly any boys do it, either.'

'Right. Where are your cousins, then?'

'Oh, Jack and Henry don't do this. They only hunt. Phoebe's around somewhere, but she's giving up Pony Club next year too. Did you know you don't have to be a member to go to the balls? I thought you did.' She leaped into the saddle. 'See you!' she called as she trotted away.

'See you,' I echoed faintly.

'Oh, by the way,' she called, turning back. 'My ears have gone septic!'

Excellent news. I made a mental note to get some witch hazel on the way home. To scoopeth some more.

I followed at a slower pace, and by the time I'd got to the ring, the last competitor had finished and Anna was cantering in. She set Hector at a fence of coloured poles, which he cleared easily, then another, and another, but then I think she missed one and had to go back and do it again, and then the last one she knocked flying. She cantered out, laughing.

'Whoops!' she yelled as she flew past me.

'Well done, darling!'

'Seven faults, for competitor number one five two,' the loudspeaker informed us. 'Seven faults.'

'Abysmal!' came an even louder voice to my left.

I turned to see Camilla, her face an arresting shade of pre-coronary purple, striding towards me, fists clenched. A small boy was trailing in her wake. 'Seven faults! She didn't line him up at *all*.'

'Oh, Anna won't mind,' I assured her. 'She's dead relaxed about that sort of thing.'

'I mind!' Camilla exploded. 'That's my pony, and half of Orxfordshire are watching!'

I looked around. An awful lot of women with horse blankets round their shoulders by way of pashminas, and who looked as if they'd been standing in a wind tunnel half their lives, were, it has to be said, looking our way and talking behind their hands.

'Yes, but it's only a bit of fun,' I said nervously. 'I mean, it doesn't matter. Better luck next time and all that.'

'Better luck ... ? That pony has been doing clear rounds all its life! Jumps out of his skin in the right hands, and now look at him. Ruined! *And* I think there's more to what went on at your sister-in-law's yard the other night than meets the eye.' I quaked nervously under her gimlet gaze. 'I don't think you've been bringing that pony in at all!' Oh, *that*. 'His ears are filthy!'

'So are your son's.'

'What?' she gasped.

'Just a hunch. And no, you're right, he hasn't been coming in. He's been frolicking in the fields, footloose and fancy-free.'

'Oh! Just like you with that – that man!' Ah. Spoke too soon. 'Gypsy my foot. He's got that bookshop in Jericho, *and* I've seen him again today, hanging around, up to no good. Well, that's it, Hector's coming home. You're not to be trusted.' With men, or horses? I wondered. 'I shall be collecting him forthwith.'

'You do that. And if Anna still wants a pony, which I'm not entirely sure she will, I'll buy her one, and we'll treat it with care, but like an animal. Your son needs a hanky, by the way.'

She glanced at the small boy beside her, thin and cold-looking, his nose streaming, who no doubt spent all his half-terms and holidays thus, trailing round after his mother and sisters.

'And if that tack isn't cleaned to within an inch of its life I'll want to know why,' she ranted on, ignoring me, and her son. 'That breast plate is brand new. It's Dobson and Farrell!'

I leaned towards her. Put my nose close to hers. 'You can stick your Dobson and Farrell breastplate where the sun don't shine, Camilla. You don't frighten me.'

And with that I sauntered off, sticking my hands in my pockets, wishing I could whistle. Me and Bob Geldof, eh? I'm sure his language would have been much more colourful. I must brush up on my abuse.

'Evie.'

I stopped; realized in a flash what she'd meant about seeing that man again, which had momentarily thrown me. For here he was, saying my name, strolling towards me in jeans and a white T-shirt, looking so devastatingly handsome it fairly took my breath away; looking actually, just like the boy in the Levis ad. Boy. Yes, indeed. I was fairly sure I could resist him, but I kept my eyes firmly on the horse manure, just to be on the safe side.

'Ludo.'

We kissed: a public, social exchange of pecks, one on each side. I stepped back smartly. 'What the devil are you doing here?'

'Stalking you. I knew your daughter would be here with her pony and I imagined you'd be watching, so I thought I'd lurk behind the horseboxes and spy on you. D'you find that creepy?'

I laughed. 'I would if I believed it.'

He grinned. 'I'm checking out the noise level for this afternoon's shindig.' He jerked his head across the hedge to where Caro's pink and white stripy marquee was flapping in the breeze in the distance.

'Oh! Is it today?'

'Three o'clock. I was just casting a weather eye over the booze supply when I saw – heard, more like – this malarkey going on over the hedge. I'm not convinced loud-hailers and strident women yelling at their children is quite the ambience Alice had in mind, but I gather it finishes at three.'

'Who told you that?'

'Some very forceful women in the secretaries' tent, one of whom I recognized from our encounter the other night, but all of whom could quite easily have led the Charge of the Light Brigade. I don't know what they do to the enemy, but by God . . .' He shuddered.

I giggled. 'Camilla and cronies. She said you were here.'

'She clearly couldn't *quite* place me until it was too late. Kept peering at me, head cocked, eyes narrowed, rather as she peers down the barrel of her shotgun, I imagine.'

I laughed. Then a silence prevailed. We both regarded the ground with interest.

'Anyway,' he went on briskly, his head coming up. 'You're stalking me. You're working in my shop.'

I flushed. 'It's the only place I *can* work, Ludo. But I know, I'm sorry. I'm working towards the end of the week, though.'

'While I'm at the beginning, Malcolm said. So in fact, you're avoiding me.'

'No,' I said carefully, my toe scuffing the grass, 'I just thought . . .'

'Relax, Mrs Hamilton. I'm teasing you.'

I glanced up. Grinned. We smiled at one another, standing there in the hazy October sunshine.

'You look different,' he observed, at length.

'I am different,' I said in surprise. Then I remembered why. I sighed. Ploughed on. 'Ant came back last night. Bella Edgeworth is dying, Ludo.'

He blanched in astonishment. Then he squinted, head jutting forward incredulously. 'What?'

'I know.' I gave him another moment.

'Shit.' He ran a hand through his hair. Ruffled the back of his head in a dazed fashion. 'Of what?'

'Cancer.'

'Oh.' He blinked. 'Right.'

'And she wants us to bring up her daughter.'

'Christ alive.'

I shrugged. 'She's Ant's daughter, too.'

'Yes, of course she is.'

'And she's seventeen. Hardly a child.'

'Right. Blimey. Still – heavy.'

'Doesn't get much weightier.'

'And you said?'

'I said yes. We all said yes.'

A shadow crossed his face. 'Right.' He gave me a slightly rueful, lopsided smile. 'Which gives me a no.'

It was my turn to blanch. Had he really . . . ?

'No, no,' he went on quickly, seeing my face, 'I don't mean that. You're quite right. I always knew it was a no. I shouldn't have said that.'

I didn't know what to say. He smiled, a proper smile this time. Took my hand.

'I have a theory about you.'

'Oh?'

'Actually, it's more about me. Some men find women who pick badly, attractive. I've decided I'm the opposite.'

Pick badly. I didn't understand. Waited for him.

'I find myself inconveniently drawn to women who pick well. Who love their husbands. Who are in a happy place. It's what I lost, you see.' He looked at me searchingly, willing me to understand. I did. In an instant.

'Yes, I do see.'

'I'm quite aware that I could bag a single young girl, like the ones at Alice's party, but I want . . . someone who knows how to make a commitment.'

'Not much of a commitment if I go off with you.'

He laughed shortly. 'No. Not much of a commitment. But then, at one point, you thought you were losing him. And I'd lost my wife.'

I shook my head sadly. 'It's too neat, Ludo. Promise me you won't go looking for young widows?' I caught the tail end of a guilty look. 'Oh God, don't tell me there's a website . . .'

'No!' He laughed. 'Well, not that I know of.'

'Because, it's not a good idea, I swear. Just wait. The right, gorgeous . . .' I glanced up, searched the sky for words, '*joyous* – young girl, will come along, unattached and unencumbered, and will make you happy again. You'll see.'

He remained unconvinced. 'It wasn't just the attachment kick.' He frowned angrily at the ground and I braced myself for something heavy. His eyes came up full of mischief. 'I also really fancy you.'

I laughed. Blushed a bit too. 'Right.'

'As I said in my note.'

'What note?'

'With the flowers.'

'What flowers?'

'You didn't get the flowers?'

I shrugged, at a loss.

'I only sent them for a laugh. I was a bit pissed, actually; thought I'd try a different tack. A rather cheesy, obvious one. And only because I knew your husband wasn't at home.'

It dawned on us collectively.

'Oh shit.' He whipped out his phone. 'Don't worry, I'll call them. They said they wouldn't deliver till this afternoon, anyway.'

I waited anxiously as he walked round in small circles, talking on his mobile. After a moment he snapped it shut. 'They hadn't gone. They're still in the delivery van and they're ringing the driver to say hold fire.'

'Oh, thank God.'

He smiled at my relief. 'Why, what would he have done, punched me?'

'No, of course not. Ant's a gentle man. But he's quite . . .'

'Possessive?'

'I suppose.' It surprised me to say it.

'I don't blame him.'

Still we didn't seem to have moved: a solitary couple facing each other in this teeming milieu of horses and children. He held out his arms and I walked into them.

'Bye, Evie.'

'I'll see you in the shop,' I muttered into his neck.

'I know. But you know what I mean.'

'I do. Bye, Ludo.'

We squeezed each other and then, after a long moment, I pulled back. Eyes averted, I walked away. With a bit of a lump in my throat. As I went, I saw Anna tying up Hector again, watching me with her mouth open. It occurred to me to go and explain, and then it occurred to me not to. I put my sunglasses back on, thrust my hands in my pockets, and walked on to the car.

## 29

I walked across the fields feeling slightly choked; slightly sad for the loss of something I'd never even had. But I felt implausibly calm too, as if things were finally slotting into place. Clunk, clunk, clunk. I was squaring away, as my dad would have said, and even though I was pretty sure I'd never be able to square Ludo away entirely – was pretty sure my heart would always falter when he walked into a room and then rattle on at an unsettling pace – well, hey, that wasn't too terrible, was it? Wasn't too shameful? And if, too, I really had been the anti-freeze his atrophied heart had needed after Estelle, the catalyst for kicking on again, then I was glad. And proud. And very flattered. It was not an unpleasant feeling. One that would stay with me a while. For many years, I'd hazard. What was that Yeats poem Ant liked? When you are old and grey and full of sleep ... dream of the soft look your eyes had once ... de dum de dum. Something like that. And something about the love of a good woman, too. Or was that another poem? I smiled. A secret smile, down at my shoes. But as my path took me, for the second time that day, past the little brick and flint cottage with the pointed Hansel and Gretel roof, and my eyes leaked through the leaded windows, not to the dun-coloured walls of my childhood, but to a much brighter, more modern room, a gilt-framed mirror where once the sentimental print had hung, my smile faded and I became less pleased with myself. Less proud.

I got into my car and sat there a moment. Don't kid yourself, Evie. Or, if you must, then at least attempt to match up. To be that good woman. Square away some more. Clean up completely. I started the car, turned it round in the yard and, leaving a cloud of dust hanging suspended behind me, headed off down the lanes and back towards Oxford, in the direction of the Banbury Road, and ultimately, Summertown.

Summertown was as breezy and bustling as ever, its wide pavements ensuring it lived up to its name, as, on a pleasant day like today, the cafés and bars spilled onto them. Most of the roads leading off the main drag were leafy and affluent, but not the one I was looking for. I took the one I had a hunch about and cruised down: past the Launderette, the fish-and-chip shop, the 7-Eleven, but after some shabby Edwardian houses broke out in a rash around the corner, the road finally committed suicide at a dead end. Damn. I turned round, sped back to the main road and tried another. Ah. This looked more promising. Another chip shop, another row of dismal houses, one or two sprayed with Arabic graffiti, and then, right at the end, a double-fronted cream house with peeling green windows, which also claimed to be St Michael's Hospice.

I parked, walked through the front garden, such as it was – a tangle of weeds and plastic dustbins – and rang the bell. After a moment light footsteps came down the hall and a tired, fragile-looking woman in a white house-coat opened the door. I explained who I'd come to see and she stood back wordlessly to let me in. She asked me to sign the visitors' book, then led me down a corridor, pointed to a door, and disappeared.

It was unbearably hot and the soles of my shoes clung to the plastic tiles underfoot. The cloying smell of unaired beds and institutional food left to moulder in stainless steel was oppressive. I breathed through my mouth and pushed on through the swing doors the woman had indicated. Six beds, three down each side, were occupied by wraithlike women, mostly catheterized, and all in various catatonic states: one or two were asleep, but the ones who were awake gazed straight ahead with dead eyes, their heads not moving as I came in.

Maroulla was in the bed at the far end on the left, eyes shut, mouth open. Her once-brown face was faded and peppered with pigmentation spots, her eye sockets hollow. I stood a moment at the end of her bed before moving to sit on the grey plastic chair beside her. A tiny trickle of saliva dribbled from the corner of her crimped mouth. I gazed at this once energetic, noisy woman, who'd chased Tim and me around the garden with a stick, threatening to beat us if we didn't come in for tea – 'You come! You come now!' – whilst Tim and I escaped and crouched giggling in the tree house.

'Maroulla.' I lifted her limp hand off the bedclothes: a clutch of twigs wrapped in translucent brown paper. Her eyelids flickered, her mouth juddered, and she slowly turned her head on her pillow. All of which took some time. Then her once dark, but now yellowing eyes focused on my face. As recognition dawned, a weak smile materialized.

'Evie?'

'I'm sorry I haven't been before.' I really was. She gazed at me, her eyes not wavering from my face. 'I should have done. I don't know why I haven't.'

'You busy,' she said, giving my hand the faintest squeeze. I was so relieved to hear her voice. Faint, but not too diminished. 'As it should be. Family . . . Anna . . . how is my Anna?'

'She's well, thank you. And lovely. Riding her pony. Maybe I'll bring her to see you?' As I said it, I knew it was a bad idea.

She smiled faintly. 'No. Let her not see me so, hm?'

She was right. Anna would be frightened. Fourteen-year-olds were not great at old people dying. We regarded one another fondly.

'And Ant?' she asked.

'Ant's fine.'

'Good.'

Her eyelids were closing. I watched as the lids slowly came down like parchment shutters. I sat there, holding her hand, wondering whether to prattle on as people said you should, so they could hear your voice, or just to sit quietly as she slept. Her hair was so thin I could see her scalp. I licked my lips.

'Yes, Ant's very busy. He's writing, of course, and—'

'He no blame himself, no?' Her eyes had flickered opened again as she interrupted me.

For a moment I couldn't think what she was talking about, then realized she'd gone back in time. Way back to Neville Carter, the boy Maroulla had found in the river and never forgotten. In some small, non-specific way, I still thought about it every day. I knew Ant did, and no doubt Maroulla, too. It had taken all of this tiny, but once wiry woman's strength to drag that body from the river, weighed down as he was by sodden clothes, choked with reeds, water pouring off him, and on her own death bed, I imagined it would be a rather potent image.

'You theenk is why he marry you.' She looked directly at me. I was aware of a brightness behind through those deceptively cloudy eyes.

'You knew that?'

She waited, not inclined to waste words.

I sighed. 'I did, Maroulla. But I was young, then. Insecure. I don't think so now.'

'Good.' She smiled. 'He no panic buy.'

Panic buy. Maroulla's English, dodgy at the best of times, was sometimes unnervingly spot on. When we were young we took full advantage of her limited vocabulary, knowing she couldn't always find the words to reprimand us, but occasionally it worked in her favour. Once she'd yelled up to the top of the hay barn where we were hiding, 'You tread me like dog dirt!' We'd slunk down the ladder shame-faced, pretty sure she meant treat, not tread, but either way it wasn't good.

'How are you, Maroulla?'

'I die.'

'Well. Not yet.'

'Soon. And good job too. Time to see Mario.'

I smiled. 'You reckon he's waiting for you?'

'Of course.' She gave a ghost of a smile. 'He be cross I so late.'

I grinned. Yes, he probably would. If Maroulla was

fiery, Mario was more so. I had the feeling she was rather looking forward to it.

'And your father too.'

'Dad?' I was surprised. 'Yes, I suppose.'

'No suppose, he good man. He be there.'

Quite a party she was anticipating, at the virtuous venue. And she had no doubt she was going there – why should she? All Maroulla had ever done was serve others: her husband, her children, Spencer and Tracy (I kid you not), our family – how could she not get to heaven?

'He good master.'

'Maroulla . . .' I hated it when she was the forelock-tugging tenant and we the autocratic landlords.

'And he make good sex love too.'

'Dad?' My eyes popped. Good Lord. Feudal rights?

'No. Mario.'

'Oh!' That master.

'And I know what he say when I see him.' She tapped my arm with a bony finger, wide awake now. 'He say – you keep it safe?'

'Hm?' I was thinking about Mario being her master and her lover.

'Because I take photos.'

'What photos?'

'In village shop.'

She'd lost me. 'The photocopier in the village shop?' I hazarded.

'Yes, ten pence each. Right rip-off.'

'Oh. Of what, Maroulla?'

'Of thees. Mario say keep it safe, but when I die, who knows? I can't keep it safe no more, can I? So

440

I geev one to Tim, yesterday. And Felicity when she come.'

'Tim's been here?'

She was sitting up now, or attempting to; pushing herself up her pillows, opening the drawer by her bed, rummaging with fluttering hands.

'Of course. He come one time every week.'

'Does he?' I was appalled. 'Oh, Maroulla, how awful. I knew Felicity came, but I didn't know . . . I don't know why . . .'

'You busy. I know. I bring up family. I work. I know.'

Well, she knew about running two households, scrubbing two kitchen floors and making endless meals. She didn't know about paying a cleaner and putting a little business the local restaurant's way.

She was lighting upon a brown A4 envelope now, her eyes eager, opening it with a shaking hand. She pulled out a piece of paper and gave it to me. 'There. You read.'

'What is it?'

'I no know, I no read.' No, of course she couldn't. Not English, anyway. 'But he make us watch, and sign it. And when I ask Mario, he say very important paper, but he no read either. So I clean office every day, and your father, he so very untidy, and many things get lost in there, and always he rage and shout he can't find things and I worry. So one day I open drawer and find paper, and I take to rip-off shop to copy.'

I gazed at her a long moment. Then down at the paper. An A4 sheet bearing a photograph of a piece of notepaper, clearly torn from a pad; the ring binding visible down one side. In my father's scrawling hand, I read:

*This country is a complete and utter disgrace. More crap from*
*Defra, more unwarranted restrictions on my land, more*
*outrageous demands from Brussels and piss-poor market prices.*
*Christ Almighty. Felicity, my darling, I have no option but to*
*leave the whole bloody shooting match to Tim. Farm, land, money*
*– everything. Poor bugger. He'll have a hard enough time of it as*
*it is with this government, and you always said you'd be happy*
*going back to your flat in college. You have your work, and Evie*
*has Ant to provide, so I don't feel bad about the division of*
*spoils. I'm sorry, my love, but I can't in all conscience saddle him*
*with the bricks and mortar and not the wherewithal to run the*
*wretched place. It will break him, as it's surely breaking me.*
  *Your loving husband, Victor Milligan, 27 February 1999*
  *Mario Rodriguez, 27 February 1999*
  *Maroulla Rodriguez, 27 February 1999*

I read it again. Looked up slowly. 'He asked you to witness this?'

'Yes, see there.' She tapped her signature impatiently. 'In his office. I weed the garden. He call to me through the French windows. No, Meester Milligan, I say, muddy shoes. But he say bloody well come now, Maroulla, impatient. Mario, he there, by Meester Milligan's desk, making cross face at me to hurry.'

'So where's the original?' I breathed.

'*Qué?*'

'The first one he wrote, from the notepad.'

'Back in his drawer, I tell you.'

'You put it back in his desk?'

'Yes, his desk. In special folder.'

But we'd gone through his desk when he died, Felicity

and I. We'd done it together: taken that whole, chaotic room apart; stacked all the papers in cardboard boxes, all the bills, files, tax forms, receipts that had exploded from drawers, that had been piled up on the floor – a backbreaking task. There'd been nothing. He'd died intestate, nothing at all.

'Ees good?' She looked at me, anxious.

I exhaled. 'Ees bad,' under my breath.

'*Qué?*' She looked stricken.

'No, no, it's good, Maroulla. Yes, I'm sure. And Tim's seen this?'

'Yesterday, when he come.'

'And what did he say?'

'He lose blood.'

'What?'

'In his face. Whiteness.'

'Oh. Right.' I swallowed.

She frowned, worried. 'I do wrong?'

'No, no, you did right, Maroulla.' I forced a smile. Took her hand. 'As ever. You did right.' But I was worried, very worried. I thought of Felicity's pretty Regency town house. Felt sick. Or did I? After all, Tim hadn't rung me, hadn't had the phone lines buzzing in high dudgeon. Perhaps it was nothing. Just a photocopied scrap of paper after all, of no worth or relevance: something Maroulla and Mario had thought fearfully important, because it had made them feel important.

I made myself talk some more: ask after Tracy, husband still unemployed, oh dear, but Spencer working in Currys now, at management level, good, good. Then she looked tired. I kissed her papery cheek as, simultaneously, her eyes closed. I slipped away. Through the double door, down the corridor, out.

Just a scrap of photocopied paper, I thought as I shut the green front door behind me. I stood on the step a moment. But . . . couldn't you write a will on anything? Back of an envelope? An elephant's bottom? As long as you had it witnessed? I stared at the houses opposite: dusty laurel hedges surrounded them. Wait: of course. February 27. Six months before he died. The end of a long hard winter, never a good time in farming. He'd had a bad day. He'd written it in a fit of pique, but later, after Maroulla had copied it and put it back, he'd taken it from his drawer and destroyed it. That was it. That was why we hadn't found it. I imagined him standing facing the fire, the one he always had going in his office in winter, legs astride, tall, very broad, red hair faded, screwing the piece of paper in a ball and tossing it in the embers. 'Flog the bloody place,' I'd heard him say to Tim, on more than one occasion. 'When I'm under the sod, bloody flog it. It'll be a millstone round your neck.' And Tim would smile, say nothing, knowing . . . what? That he didn't mean it? Or he did mean it?

I drove home, unsettled. Something Felicity had said at Alice's party, about how I shouldn't see Maroulla, how she was gaga, reared up at me. But she wasn't really, was she? Just old. Glancing in the rear-view mirror I saw my lips were pursed, my eyes fretted with worry lines. I gave myself a dismissive little shake. Inhaled deeply. No. Forget it, Evie. It's nothing. Tim hasn't reacted, so it's clearly nothing.

On the way back, though, I saw a sign to Holywell, and on a whim, I took it. My tyres screamed in outrage as I cornered left with a spectacular lack of caution, and an angry horn blared after me. I went hot. Christ. I could have caused an accident. I'd end up where Dad was soon, where I was going: Holywell. No room in village churchyards any more, not even if your family had farmed next door for four generations, not even if your house was called Church Farm, not even if all your ancestors were buried there. So Dad was here, on the outskirts of town, beyond the bypass, in a not particularly rural, not particularly lovely spot, behind this long, dry-stone wall, in this vast old cemetery with its dismal dark yew trees and its never-ending lines of graves.

I parked easily at the entrance, perhaps the only place in Oxford one could these days, and went through the towering iron gates. They knew how to impose, those Victorians: knew how to say Remember Where Ye Enter. Rows and rows of graves ran away from me down a grassy slope, with a tarmac path dividing them neatly through the middle. I followed it right down to the end. He was in the second to last row if I remembered rightly, ten from the left, thirty to the right. I'd been back once or twice since the funeral. OK, once. On the first anniversary of his death. I'd meant to come more, but somehow hadn't got round to it.

I found the grave and stood gazing down. A slight breeze had picked up, ruffling the grassy mound. Felicity had chosen the headstone: grey slate, solid and simple, with black lettering. Nothing fancy, she'd said. And indeed it was very fitting. 'Victor Milligan,' it read, '1934–1999. A loving father and husband.' Father first, husband second, she'd insisted: because she'd come along later.

Suddenly I felt ashamed. What was I doing here? Why was I standing, like a melodramatic heroine from a gothic novel, with the wind in my hair, at the foot of my father's grave? What was I waiting for? Vibes? For a voice beyond the grave? An extremely well-tended grave, at that, with fuchsias shivering in a vase, atop a nicely mown mound: fuchsias, which could only have been put there by Felicity, who came regularly to change the flowers and the water – the vase, sometimes, when it was stolen – and yet, here I was, for only the second time since his funeral, and all that had brought me here . . . was money. I caught my breath. Swallowed. Then I turned on my heel and walked away: back up the tarmac path, arms folded, head bent, and out through the wrought-iron gates.

Caro rang me on my way home, breaking into my thoughts, making me jump.

'I've got a police car up my backside so I've got to be quick.'

'Well, I'm driving too. What is it?'

'A lorry has shed its load on the A40 and I am completely and utterly stuck in stationary traffic. In about twenty minutes I've got a wedding reception in the garden and I'm not going to make it.'

'Oh Christ. Alice Montague.'

'Exactly, and I can't get hold of Tim. Can you get there for me, please, Evie?' She sounded desperate.

'And do what?'

'Not a great deal, just organize the children to park the cars – the boys know where – and then sort of stand around looking charming. They don't actually want you there but they really *really* mind if you're not, if you know what I mean.'

'OK,' I said doubtfully.

'You're a star, because I have absolutely no idea when I'm going to get back, and I've got Leonard with me and he's a bore,' she hissed.

Leonard. I had an idea he was an elderly uncle. I hoped his hearing wasn't too acute. 'Where is he?'

'In the back. Thanks, Evie, bye.'

She rang off quickly before I could change my mind.

Right. I clicked my phone shut and tossed it on the seat beside me. Well, yes, I could do that. Stand around like Lady Bountiful, be a sort of mistress of ceremonies. I hadn't entirely planned on seeing Ludo quite so soon after saying goodbye, I thought with a sudden qualm, but then, as Caro said, it was a background presence she needed: I probably wouldn't even set eyes on him. And I certainly owed Caro. Hadn't thanked her yet for having Anna for most of half-term. And she'd sounded all right, hadn't she? Caro? Not in any way pissed off or livid about anything Tim had told her? Or shown her? No. So forget it, Evie. Another little inward shake.

And a wedding would take my mind off things, I decided. Be just what I needed. But what I really must do, I determined, glancing down at my jeans, was change. I was very much the Pony Club mother at the moment and I needed to be the lady of the manor. I'd seen Caro do it once or twice, lipstick smile in place, hands clasped, floral frock: 'Yes, *aren't* the roses lovely, but then it's been a very good year . . .' I wasn't sure I could run to the

447

floral number, but I might give my linen trousers an airing, with a white top and a long chiffon scarf . . . ideal.

I parked creatively outside the house and nipped up the steps. Everyone double-parked these days, and I'd only be a minute. The door was double-locked so Ant wasn't at home. Must have gone into college. I was pretty sure he didn't have a lecture today, but then, as he occasionally drily observed, it was all very well for writers who were just writers, but when one was juggling a day job as well . . . I wondered if he'd chuck it in one day – college. Just write. Couldn't quite imagine it somehow.

As I went in and shut the front door behind me, a heavenly smell wafted up the passage way. Mmm . . . jasmine. Or was it sweet peas? I pursued it to its source, down the hall, to the kitchen, which was where I realized it was neither of those, but roses. Two dozen at least, bright red, sitting plumb in the middle of the kitchen table in one of those sort of colostomy bags full of water. I stared. Slowly put my bag and car keys on the table. My heart began to quicken as my eyes snagged on a white card, waving at me in a jaunty fashion, on the end of a long green plastic stick. No envelope. I released it from its clasp. In a small, round – presumably the florist's hand – I read:

*Dear Evie,*
    *Can't stop thinking about you in your Miss Whiplash underwear. Isn't it time it had another outing?*
    *Love and heavy breathing, Ludo.* xx

## 30

I dropped the card as if it were white hot. Oh hell. Oh, blinking blithering hell, they'd made it. Despite Ludo's best efforts, the message hadn't got through and the roses had persisted. They'd scrambled over the wire, dodged the florist's searchlights and made it to 22 Walton Terrace with a little help from a lethargic delivery boy who hadn't picked up a message on his mobile. Ant must have taken delivery of them, bemused – 'Are you sure?' 'Yeah, Mrs Evie Hamilton. Sign here' – then walked them down the hall to the kitchen, read the card – no envelope – and been taken aback. No. Downright shocked.

I went hot. Pulse racing, I scrambled in my bag with fluttering fingers for my mobile. His phone was switched off. I left a breathless, thoughtless message about needing to speak to him urgently, to, um, explain, erm, the underwear thingy, which was just a silly joke, a message that even to my ears resonated with guilt, and then rang his office. Mary, the secretary he shared with various other dons in the English Department, said she hadn't seen him, but that didn't mean he wasn't about somewhere. Try his mobile? Thanks, Mary.

I stared out at the back garden, dry-mouthed, mobile clutched to my heart. I imagined him in the quad, walking through the cloisters, hands in his pockets, head bent, saddened, appalled: I pictured him being hailed by students, colleagues who wondered why he didn't acknowledge them, why he walked on by. I had to find him. I seized a piece of paper from the kitchen pad and wrote in large capitals: 'THIS IS NOT WHAT YOU THINK! I CAN EXPLAIN!' – and left it on the flowers.

Then I hurried down the hallway, out of the front door, and down the steps to the car. I vacillated on the bottom step. Hang on. Where was I going? To Balliol? Where Mary said he may or may not be? And what would I do when I got there – race through the hallowed portals, charge around like a lunatic, my frantic footsteps echoing in the hushed cloisters, poke my head into crowded lecture theatres, barge in on a tutorial where he was one to one with a shy young student? No. Of course not. Ant wasn't unhinged, wasn't about to hurl himself into the Thames, and I'd look ridiculous. And guilty. I must wait. Explain later. And meanwhile, exhaust all other possibilities. Because if, say, he wasn't in college, where might he be? Was there anyone he'd confide in? I racked my brains. Not Anna, obviously. Mum? Quite possibly, actually. I sat down abruptly on the bottom step and rang her. In an effort to make my voice light and carefree, I sounded shrill and hysterical.

'No, darling, I haven't seen him. Has something happened?'

'No, no, nothing, everything's fine.' I massaged my temples with my fingertips. 'It's just – if he does ring or call by, would you tell him I'm at the farm? Caro asked me to step in for her at a wedding.'

'I will, but I'm going there myself soon. Are you OK?'

'I'm fine.' I hesitated. How would it sound aired in the open, I wondered. 'It's just ... Ludo sent me some flowers as a joke, and I'm worried Ant might get the wrong idea.'

'Ludo? Oh, I doubt it, Evie. He's much too young for you. Ant will know that.' She laughed.

Loyal, my mum. But on another level, encouraging. I tried the shop. Ant might look for me there. Clarence answered.

'Malcolm's at Alice's wedding. Ludo invited him and sweetly asked me to the reception too. I'm just shutting up here for him before going across. D'you want me to give him a message?'

'No, don't worry, I'm going there myself in a minute. I'm looking for Ant, actually. He hasn't popped in, has he?' I said casually.

'Not that I know of. But if you're going, why don't we go together?'

Good plan. Safety in numbers. I leaped back up the steps and into the house to change, and ten minutes later, was driving through Jericho to collect Clarence. Bafflingly, all the clothes I'd been planning to wear had shrunk in my wardrobe, so after struggling out of the linen trousers and yelling 'You Bastards' at them, I'd thrown on a kaftan, a look I knew was fashionable again, but perhaps not the way I'd interpreted it: over beige culottes and with a pink straw hat. I slid by the shop just as Clarence was locking the door.

He looked quite delicious in his morning coat and was kind enough to give my attire only the briefest of glances. In fact he was so smiley and chatty I relaxed, and as we drove along, on the wings of an impulse, I ran the roses up the flagpole again. And the sexy note. And then of course I had to *explain* the sexy note, which involved explaining the scantily clad siren at the window. I cringed behind the wheel as I awaited his response. The first stone. He laughed.

'Well, I haven't met your husband, but from what Malcolm tells me he's a rational, intelligent man. He'll surely wait to hear your side of things? Before he jumps to any conclusions?'

'Yes,' I breathed happily, my head appearing out of my shoulders like a tortoise's. 'Yes, he will.'

'Anyway, it was clearly only a joke.'

I flinched. Odd how everyone thought that; how risible the notion was.

I felt soothed, though, and my bones unclenched as he chatted away sociably. Clarence was a honey, I decided, a real honey. Perhaps he'd help me meet and greet? Park cars, press the flesh, whatever it was we had to do, and hopefully Caro would arrive soon and then I could escape and find Ant, and he'd see the funny side, as everyone predicted, and we could have a glass of something, and all would be well? Manically checking my mobile every few seconds for messages, and with half an ear on what Clarence was saying about how much he'd enjoyed Oxford and how sad he was his sabbatical was coming to an end, we finally arrived at the farm, having been forced to take the scenic route on account of the traffic.

The congregation was already drifting out of the church, following the bride and groom. It was a rare and lovely sight. Under a bright blue sky and a canopy of spreading, golden chestnut trees, Alice, beautiful in ivory silk, white roses scattered in her long blonde hair, on the arm of her new husband, was leading the procession down the narrow lane, *Far From the Madding Crowd*-style – always Caro's vision – through the field gate at the bottom, and into the meadow, where the marquee flapped gently in the breeze against a vista of green hills and gently swaying russet trees.

We waited for everyone to pass by, a happy, smiling throng. I spotted Felicity in the crowd, in a pale blue suit and hat, talking to Malcolm. She looked lovely. *Was* lovely, I decided, unclenching some more, banishing impure thoughts. As the last of the guests strolled by, I swung the car into the yard. I got out and, with Clarence following more sedately, hastened around to the back of the house where I found Jack sitting on the back doorstep, talking to a very pretty young waitress.

'Oh, hi, Evie.'

They both stood up guiltily. The waitress melted away, taking Jack's cigarette with her.

'Jack, I'm supposed to be helping. Did you manage to park the cars OK?'

'They park themselves in the churchyard. Mum gets stressy but it always goes like clockwork. She rang and said you were coming but there's no need, honestly. No offence.'

'No offence taken. This is Clarence, by the way.'

'Hi, Clarence.'

They shook hands.

'So, waitresses circulating with drinks and all that sort of thing?' I swung round, taking a few tottering steps down the lawn in my heels and shading my eyes against the sun towards the marquee. I spotted Ludo, looking devastatingly handsome in the receiving line, because – yes, that's right, their father was dead, so he'd given Alice away – beside a distinguished-looking grey-haired woman with good bones, who must be their mother. I watched, fascinated for a moment as they smiled and shook hands with everyone.

'Yeah, the waitresses have got trays of champagne and some orange juice for the drivers.'

'Well done. Canapés?'

'Not yet. Mum usually let's them have a drink first. Canapés in half an hour.'

'Right. Well, it looks like you've got it all under control, Jack.' I smiled back at him. 'D'you get paid for this?'

'Dream on. Mum's far too tight. And, actually, it's just as well she's not here, she wouldn't like that.'

He jerked his head across the hedge to the lane, where, having waited for the procession to pass, the last of the horseboxes were sneaking out and rumbling away in convoy, dripping straw and poo in their wake.

'Anna must be about somewhere, then,' I said, as we watched them go.

'She was, but she and Phoebe went to a friend's house in the village.'

'Oh, right. I don't suppose Ant's here, is he?' I asked nonchalantly.

He shrugged. 'Dunno. Dad might know. He's inside.'

'Is he? I thought he wasn't here?'

'Yeah, he's around somewhere. See you.' He loped off, weary with interrogation, towards the marquee.

Actually, Ant could be with Tim, it occurred to me. Perhaps they were ensconced in the study? Deep in chat? About me? The black sheep? A family pow-wow? My chest tightened and I went to go in, then remembered Clarence. But he'd already spotted Malcolm, who was coming up the garden to meet him, looking rather radiant in his morning coat, blond hair freshly washed. It wasn't lost on Clarence and I saw their eyes shine at each other as they shared a moment. I'd just got my foot in the back door when I saw Caro's car draw up in the yard. She leaped out almost before the car had stopped.

'Everything OK?' she called anxiously, bustling across.

'Perfect. The cars are parked, and everyone got from the church to marquee without incident.'

'No wretched horseboxes dropping poo in the lane from next door?'

'No,' I lied, 'and now everyone's drinking champagne.'

'Waitresses circulating?' Her eyes narrowed with professional alertness down the lawn.

'Yup, and Jack and I held off on the canapés for a bit, just while they have a drink.'

'Excellent.' Her face relaxed and swam with relief. 'Honestly, Evie, it's like a military operation. By the time Phoebe gets married I'll be doing it in my sleep. But thank you, it all slightly needs overseeing. Mother of the bride happy?'

'I came out in a bit of a rush, Caro. Haven't really had a chance to —'

'Don't worry, I'll go down.' From just inside the back door where Barbours hung in serried ranks above wellingtons, she snatched a pink jacket and hat, which she slung on now over her denim skirt.

'Keep them there for emergencies,' she grinned, deftly swapping her boots for slingbacks. 'Is your mother here yet? She was going to help me with the pigs.'

'Haven't seen her, but she did say she was going to—'

'NO, NO, THIS WAY!' she yelled suddenly. She ran towards the hedge, calling over it to some latecomers, who were hurrying towards the yard, the wives tripping in high heels, hanging onto their hats.

'Traffic!' they wailed.

'I know, dreadful! No, not through the yard, through the gate at the end of the lane, look . . .' She beetled off, running parallel with them by the hedge, arranging her face brightly and shepherding them in at the bottom.

I went inside to find Tim. Not in the sitting room, or in the study. In fact all was quiet downstairs, so I went up. The children's doors were open, revealing exploding bedrooms, unmade beds and still closed curtains. I went on down the corridor to Tim and Caro's bedroom door, which was shut.

'Tim?'

'Come in.' My brother's voice, subdued.

I poked my head round. He was lying on the bed in old jeans and a checked shirt. His gun was by his side. I stared, appalled.

'What are you doing?'

'Cleaning my gun. Why?'

'Oh!' I clutched my heart dramatically. Shut the door behind me. 'I thought . . .'

'What, I was topping myself?' He sat up with a struggle. 'Not quite there yet. But I can't even clean my gun without sitting – or lying down – now.'

'Oh, Tim.' I came and sat on the bed beside him: on the Jane Churchill bedcover they'd had for ever. I hadn't been in this room for a long time, but it struck me it had hardly changed since Mum and Dad's day. The faded chintz curtains still hung at the windows, the pale blue carpet underfoot.

'Is it very painful?'

'Very,' he said grimacing. 'But I'll get there. Hundreds of people walk around with artificial hips, don't they?'

'They do, but they don't farm.' I regarded him. He returned my look.

'I don't farm either, Evie. Oh, I've got a few cows, and we grow a bit of wheat and dutifully get it harvested, but d'you know how much I got for it this year?'

'How much?' I asked, not wanting to know.

'Twenty-three grand. That's my annual income. I have to pay Phil, obviously, because I can't do all the combining myself, and Steve, who comes to help in August, and d'you know what their wages come to?'

I didn't answer.

'Fifteen grand. Which leaves me eight grand to run the place and to feed a family of five for a year. Ha!' He threw back his head and gave a cracked laugh to the ceiling. I swallowed. Resumed my contemplation of the bedcover. 'D'you know how many acres I'd need to make a profit worth talking about?'

'How many?'

'Fifteen hundred. D'you know how many I've got?'

'Three hundred,' I muttered.

He nodded. 'Three hundred's not a farm, Evie. It's a fucking paddock. It used to be. You used to be able to make a living on a smallholding; seventy acres – less, even – but not now. Now you've got to own fucking Badminton.'

'Which is why Caro does all this,' I soothed, waving my hand out of the window.

He sighed. 'Yes.'

'And she makes a good profit?'

'She makes a profit. I don't know about good. But she's run ragged. And I feel—'

'I know,' I interrupted quickly. Before he said it. Impotent.

He gave me a twisted smile. 'It's not great, Evie, seeing your wife run herself into the ground, having your house overrun with people every weekend . . .'

'Well, not actually *in* the house.'

'Excuse me?' He cocked an ear theatrically. Voices drifted up from downstairs.

'They come in?' I boggled.

'To use the loo.'

'But the Portaloos—'

'Oh, they're not *supposed* to come in, we don't actually *allow* them, but the Portaloos get busy – or blocked – so they come up here. Don't forget, nearly everyone we entertain in our splendid house and grounds is pissed. They don't give a toss that it's your house.'

We heard the sound of a loo being flushed down the passage in the children's bathroom. Clearly the downstairs one was occupied. Then more footsteps tripped towards us and a loo seat banged down close by, next door, in fact, in Tim and Caro's ensuite, which could also be accessed via the corridor. I let my jaw drop incredulously. He raised his eyebrows back, told-you-so style.

'One Saturday I was watching the cricket in the sitting room, and a guy came strolling through the French windows, plonked himself down beside me on the sofa and asked me what the score was.'

'Bloody cheek.'

'I gave him a beer, actually. He was rather nice.'

I smiled. 'But things will improve,' I assured him. 'Your new hip will click in soon—'

'Like the bionic man.'

'Exactly, and then you can do more on your own. You won't need Phil.'

'And get to keep all of the twenty-three thousand pounds? Gee whiz.'

'Well, maybe – maybe wheat prices will improve? They said on *Farming Today* wheat prices were going up—'

'By two pence a ton.'

'And maybe the Europeans will have a terrible year and everyone will be gagging for English grain.'

'And maybe a whole heap of money will just drop out of the sky, just as if – ooh, I don't know, as if Dad didn't die intestate after all, and in fact the chunk he left to Felicity should have gone to me, to run the farm. Keep the place going.'

He gave me a steady look. I gazed back.

'Right,' I said eventually, averting my eyes. 'I wondered when we'd get to that.'

'You know?'

'I went to see Maroulla this morning.'

'Ah.'

Another silence prevailed.

'Ah well,' he said lightly, 'it's all been spent now, I imagine. So it's academic.'

'You think?'

'I don't know, Evie,' he said wearily.

'But I mean . . . is it legal?'

'This bit of photocopied paper?' He shifted on his side and brought it out of the back pocket of his jeans. 'Who knows? It doesn't exactly start, "This is the last will and testament of Victor Milligan."'

'Exactly.'

'And it clearly wasn't transcribed in a solicitor's office, and it's not on official paper—'

'But Mario and Maroulla witnessed it.'

'Yes.'

'And you only need two people?'

He shrugged. 'Dunno. Haven't made one yet. Got nothing to leave.' He hesitated. 'But, as far as we know . . . it was what Dad wanted. Which actually, is the point, isn't it?'

'Yes,' I said slowly. I paused. 'But . . . where's the original?'

'Well, somewhere along the line, someone may have . . .' he was carefully avoiding using Felicity's name, 'disposed of it, I suppose.'

'Not knowing Maroulla took a copy.'

We glanced guiltily at one another. Guilty, because we couldn't believe we were thinking it. Saying it. The loo flushed next door.

'Or,' I said quickly, 'Dad may have chucked it. Changed his mind.'

'Exactly. Didn't want to cut out his wife, which is quite a major thing to do, incidentally.'

'Well, quite.'

We regarded one another more equably.

'And on that note of finality,' Tim heaved himself suddenly off the bed, 'I shall place one end of this shotgun in my mouth like so . . .' He lifted it.

'Tim!'

'Joke,' he grinned, swinging it round and using it as a stick. 'Blimey, Evie, lighten up. I thought my nerves were bad.' He hobbled to the window. 'What's that godawful noise?'

A terrible banging was coming from the yard below where Caro had left her car. I joined him at the window as he flung it open. The trailer behind her car seemed to be bouncing about.

'What the . . . ?' Tim turned and marched, quite quickly for a man with a gammy leg, and using his gun to lean on, out of the bedroom, down the passage and down the stairs. He shot back the bolts on the front door and went out. I was on his heels. Something – or someone – was banging from inside the trailer, making a terrible din.

'Oh God – it can't be Caro's uncle, can it?' I gasped.

'Lionel?'

'Yes, she went to get him.'

'Did she? But why would he be in the trailer?'

'I've no idea, but she said he was in the back. Oh, poor man!'

Giving me a startled glance, Tim unfastened the clasp

and loosened the ramp. But before he could lower it, it came smartly down of its own accord, with a bang. An enormous, hairy orange pig stampeded down it, and raced past us.

'BLOODY HELL!' roared Tim, swinging about.

'What the . . . ?' I spun round.

'That's not Lionel, that's Leonard! The boar! Come to service the pigs!'

I clasped my cheeks in horror. 'Oh Christ!'

We watched, aghast, as the pig galloped joyously down the garden. It crashed through flowerbeds and made for the river, just as Phil, Tim's farm worker, giving the pig a startled glance, came running over the bridge and up the lawn towards us.

'There's a barney going on in the tent!' he yelled. 'You'd better come!'

'Oh fuck.' Tim started hobbling down the lawn. 'Phil! Get that pig!' he roared, as the pig, thwarted by the stream, veered left. Phil raced after it. 'Christ, we haven't even got to the disco yet, and they've only had one glass of champagne. The best man can't have plugged a bridesmaid already, can he?'

'Dad! Quick!' Jack, looking appalled but enthralled, was waving his father on with a huge arm from the mouth of the tent. We hurried across the bridge as Jack darted back in.

'Quick, Dad, before it's too late!' Henry ran out, distressed.

Too late for what? As Tim and I achieved the entrance to the marquee, it was to find a frustrating bank of backs blocking our way. The majority of the guests had shrank back to the sides of the tent to create a clearing on the dance floor. Not, we realized as we muscled through broad-shouldered men and women in hats, to give the happy couple room for a first waltz, or cut the cake, or make speeches, but for another couple, Caro and Felicity, the latter pale and trembling, the former the colour of her pink hat and jacket, to take centre stage. And the only speech being given, was by Caro. Her voice rang out, shrill and accusatorial, as she directed a ferocious diatribe at her step-mother-in-law, the gist of which, if one sifted through the scorching profanities, was that she considered her to be a dirty, low-down, conniving thief. Felicity's mistake, I gathered later from those closer to the action, was to interrupt, albeit in a low, quavering voice. At which point Caro took a swing at her. Felicity ducked, and Ludo leaped in to restrain Caro, with a half-nelson. At this identical moment, my husband made his entrance, seemingly from nowhere, but actually from the tent flap behind the disco. With a dramatic leap from stage to dance floor, his face an unfamiliar shade of white, he landed centre stage. He pulled Ludo off Caro, swung him around to face him, and landed his own punch on Ludo's jaw. It sent Ludo tottering back in astonishment and onto his bottom. As a collective gasp went up from an already captivated crowd, an unrestrained Caro found her own target, and delivered a mighty slap to Felicity's cheek. It was at this salient moment that the pig chose to enter the arena at racing speed. It stampeded through the crowd and sprayed guests left, right and centre as they ran, shrieking, for cover.

The pig continued to storm: he careered around the dance floor like a bull in a ring, knocking people off their feet, sending champagne glasses flying, upending tables and spindly gilt chairs at the fringes of the dance floor. Mouth gaping and barking loudly, he was huge, bewildered and terrifying. Women ran shrieking for exits, clutching their hats, and a huddle of bridesmaids who'd taken cover under a table rose up like a flock of birds as Leonard charged towards them, scattering them in all directions in a flutter of ivory silk. Men shouted orders to each other, to surround him, to corner him. One whipped off his jacket and fell on him, attempting to wrap the pig's head in his coat, to blind him. But Leonard was big, clever, and surprisingly nimble. Despite the fact that his trotters failed to gain purchase on the parquet dance floor and he slithered frantically, he still evaded capture; bucking like a bronco, tossing the coat off his head and the fifteen-stone man from his back, breaking out of the circle.

Through the mayhem I caught a glimpse of Felicity. She was looking dazed, sitting at the side of the marquee on a chair, for all the world as if she were watching the dancing, although her horribly shocked face and a huge red mark on her cheek gave a lie to that. Caro was sitting a few seats along from her on another gilt chair, slumped and spent. She was also staring into space, like a prize-fighter who's done her worst. She reached out and caught my arm as I ran past her.

'She took our money,' she muttered up at me, her eyes as vacant as a village idiot's. 'All of it.'

I shook her off and, ignoring the pig show too, raced to the scene of another crisis. Just to the right of the dance floor, amongst the round tables and chairs, my husband, looking nothing like his quiet, gentle self, was, to my horror, squaring up to Ludo again, fists, whilst not raised, still clenched. Ludo, meanwhile, back on his feet now, had his arms outstretched, palms up, doing his best to dissuade him.

'*Ant!*' I screamed, racing up.

As he swung round, even I could see I was the oil this fire didn't need. His eyes met mine with a glittering aggression I didn't recognize, and he turned, regenerated it seemed, back to Ludo. Happily, Clarence, on my heels, had sized up the situation, and in an instant had plucked me as a cat would her kitten, by the scruff of the neck, and flung me at Malcolm, whilst in another he'd got between Ant and his target. He took Ant's shoulders and walked him firmly backwards, eloquently suggesting over his shoulder to Ludo, in words of one emphatic syllable, that he might disappear, all the while making soothing small talk to Ant, along the lines of, 'Come on, Ant, that'll do mate. Calm down.'

Unfortunately, at this exact same moment, Leonard decided to leave the dance floor and pick a fight with Clarence. Clarence neatly sidestepped the charge on his legs, pushing Ant out of the way too, whereupon Leonard charged the top table instead. He bombed under one end, and as his trotters got caught in the long Irish linen, seamlessly performed the tablecloth trick, appearing out of the other end wrapped entirely in white, as silver, china, glasses and flowers flew up into the air, then smashed down onto the table.

'GET THAT PIG OUT OF HERE!' roared Tim, brick red in the face, glancing hopelessly at his wife, the only one sufficiently versed in pig husbandry to assist. She gazed blankly back as if to say – pig? What pig?

Meanwhile younger members of the male guests had taken up the challenge. Shimmying out of their jackets they hurled their coats at Leonard like matadors, and themselves after them, a strong smell of testosterone in the air. It was as if they sensed their moment had come: that Alice's wedding had to be rescued. Perhaps past beaus were amongst the gallant young men who attempted to rugby tackle the pig into submission, but Leonard was strong, and very angry now, and not even Clarence, who, having satisfied himself his antisocial and aggressive don was spent for a moment – arms hanging limply, shoulders hunched – could pin this boar to the floor. He slipped, he slithered, he evaded capture. And the awful thing was, he'd spotted the cake.

His little piggy eyes lit on it: three-tiered, white and gleaming, in splendid isolation on a table in the corner. One could almost see the thought processes whirring. Could something so tall, so white, so patently unlike swill in a trough, smell so delicious? Was his nose deceiving him, or was it really full of fruit and brandy and molasses and dripping with sugar? He cantered steadily towards it as yet more shirt-sleeved heroes flung themselves in his path; but every time he squirmed free, his eyes, beady and determined. He got up and made inexorably for it again, until, that is – a cry went up. Not a human cry, but a loud, desperate, porcine honk. It stopped him in his tracks.

We all swung around; Leonard too. There, at the entrance to the marquee, sat Mum, revving a quad bike. A small trailer was on the back, wire meshed, and once used, I recalled, for transporting chickens. Inside it now, honking her heart out, was a very horny Boadicea. She'd smelled Leonard, and she wanted him. Mum later told us she'd taken a small piece of wood from Leonard's trailer for her to smell. Boadicea had eaten it whole, as if demonstrating what she had in mind for him. For a moment Leonard hesitated. The cake was big, but this girl was hot; circling her cage, mad for him, desperate. And what's more, other potential girlfriends, who, after all, he'd come here with the sole intent to roger senseless, hearing Boadicea's cry, were baying for him in the background. Once more, the wheels of his piggy brain were visible. Food . . . or sex? Sex . . . or food? How many male hearts did not go out to him? Offer their sympathies?

Boadicea, sensing indecision, dug deep and gave one lusty primeval bark; a bark full of longing, a bark he couldn't resist. Leonard turned and trotted hypnotically towards her. He went to the back of the trailer, where Henry, Mum's accomplice, was poised, ready with the tricky little assignment of opening the cage door and letting Leonard in, but not Boadicea out. He hadn't grown up on a farm for nothing, though, and the operation went faultlessly. The pigs were united, in every sense. Within seconds, for the benefit of the entire wedding party, Leonard climbed aboard, and with his mouth hanging open, and with that glazed, faraway expression females of all species are familiar with, he jigged away making the two-backed beast, whilst Boadicea, now she'd got her man, looked for all the world as if she was quietly planning a dinner party.

The crowd went wild: cheering, whooping and clapping. It seemed Mum's inspired insight into the male psyche had saved the wedding. After all, the cake was still standing, only one tray of canapés had been eaten, the broken champagne glasses were quickly swept up, chairs righted. Leonard and Boadicea were driven away, up the hill to where the rest of the sows were waiting: not quietly, like ladies, but noisily, like ladettes, honking furiously, fighting each other tooth and trotter to be next, livid with Boadicea for stealing a march. Henry later told me, saucer-eyed, that as Leonard was shoed into the pen, the sows, real froth dripping from their mouths, reversed towards him – 'reversed, Evie' – and that, give the lad his due, he satisfied them one after the other, and sometimes twice, with the biggest bit of kit Henry had ever seen, 'shaped like a corkscrew!'

Meanwhile, back at the marquee, the wedding reception was recovering its equilibrium. Bridesmaids' tears were mopped, the top table was relaid with fresh china and glasses, and Alice, being a game girl, and no wuss, was encouraged to see the funny side. Was led to believe it was a wedding that would go down in the annals of history, one to be relived, reshown – had anyone got it on video? They *had*, well, there you are! And Alice, not being a dewy-eyed ingénue, but a cool and sassy twenty-six, rose to the occasion, and did not sob that her wedding had been ruined, but roared with laughter, along with friends, about what a hoot it had been; what a day.

My day, however, continued on its remorselessly un-amusing course. Ant, whom I'd taken my eyes off for one minute to watch the rutting pig show, had gone. I stood on the lawn outside the marquee, casting about frantically. I ran this way and that, cursing myself for being so stupid as to let him out of my sight. Then, suddenly I glimpsed him, sitting on the river bank, further downstream, beside Clarence. Clarence was in his shirtsleeves: his broad back harnessed by red braces, the gold clips glinting in the sun. Ant was a tall man, but he looked slight beside him. And beaten. Shoulders hunched, he was clearly giving a great deal of attention to what Clarence had to say as he contemplated the river. My instinct was to run to him, but sensibly, I hesitated. Gave them a few moments. Then Clarence saw me. He stood up and jerked his head meaningfully. I walked uncertainly towards them.

Clarence smiled down at Ant. 'He's all yours,' he murmured.

He sauntered away towards Malcolm, who, looking like he was welcoming back a conquering hero, was hurrying up the river bank towards us. Eyes glistening with pride, he was unable to resist hissing in my ear before he scooped his arm through his boyfriend's and swept him away, 'Did you see him? Did you see Clarence? Wasn't he *magnificent*?'

I sat down uncertainly beside Ant. He stayed staring at

the water, arms locked loosely around his knees. I too regarded the stream: fast and tawny at this point, rushing and tumbling around the smooth brown rocks. It occurred to me I knew every inch of this river. Every inch of this farm. The silence deepened. As it threatened to persist, a lump rose in my throat. Then Ant turned and gave me a lopsided smile.

'It appears I've made a complete tit of myself.'

I swallowed the lump and breathed again.

'Oh, I wouldn't say that,' I warbled.

'Those flowers. That note.' He shook his head, bewildered. 'I'm afraid I just saw red. I wanted to kill him. But Clarence says he just saw you through the bedroom window across the street. Saw you in your—'

'Yes,' I interrupted quickly. 'Let's not go into what I was in.'

'Still. Quite a familiar thing to write.'

'I know. I'm sorry.'

He shrugged. 'Not your fault.'

'Well . . .' I hesitated. No. Leave it, Evie. Not your fault.

'And then I rang Anna, to see if she knew where you were, and she was really upset. Said she'd seen you hugging some man at her gymkhana, some young chap with dark hair, and that one of the girls, the DC's daughter, had been spreading rumours that you'd been seen snogging him in a stable.'

'Oh!'

'I flipped, I'm afraid.'

'Oh no, Ant, it wasn't like that. I—'

'I know, I know,' he interrupted wearily, running a hand through his hair. 'Clarence explained that too.'

Did he? I boggled. Did Clarence know about that? Yes, I'd told him and Malcolm on the barge. Still, it took some diplomacy. Some explaining.

'I don't dispute that you are blameless, Evie,' Ant went on carefully, judicially even, as if I was the accused in the dock. I cringed. His eyes were still on the river. 'But the fact remains,' he turned to look at me and I felt justice approaching rather too fast, 'the fact remains that this man clearly has designs on you.'

I couldn't help but smile. At his appalled face. His horror. 'Is that so extraordinary?' I asked.

'Well, no,' he said, momentarily disconcerted. 'But – he seems to have pursued you relentlessly!'

'He has,' I agreed. 'But don't forget, Ant, at the time I had serious misgivings about where your own gaze was settling. I thought you were entranced by Bella Edgeworth.'

'So you encouraged him?'

'No, I didn't encourage him. In fact, if you ask Malcolm, I think you'll find I only agreed to work at the shop if our shifts didn't coincide. If Ludo wasn't there.'

Ant nodded gloomily. 'I know. Clarence said.' He brought his knees up to his chest. Hugged them fiercely. 'Ludo,' he spat. 'Stupid name.'

'Now you're just being childish.'

'And red roses. What a cliché.'

I smiled. 'That's how I knew they weren't from you.'

'I don't do clichés,' he said defensively.

'Or flowers, come to that.'

He frowned. 'Haven't I ever sent you flowers?'

'You picked me some buttercups, once. When we were in Devon.'

471

'I don't remember that.'

'I do.'

He blanched. Made a face. 'OK. Maybe I haven't been great in that department.'

'I've no complaints.'

'But . . .' he hesitated. 'A little bit of romance . . . ?'

'Is quite good for the soul,' I agreed softly.

He sighed. Narrowed his eyes up at the sun. 'And me, the big expert on the Romantic movement.'

'Oh, I think Coleridge and the gang would have been fairly horrified by Valentines and flowers.'

'It's almost an insult, don't you think?'

'What, to a woman's intelligence?'

'Let's see if she falls for this old chestnut?'

I shrugged, disinclined to put a stone in his sling. We sat there, shoulder to shoulder, gazing out across the river to the farmhouse, perched on the brow of the hill: solid, square and familiar. Comforting, somehow.

'So . . . were you tempted?'

I sensed an unusual desire in Ant, guarded and taciturn by nature, to get to the bottom of this.

'By Ludo?'

'Well, he's young, handsome, virile, no doubt,' he almost spat. 'And clearly besotted with you.'

'I was flattered,' I said finally. 'And I enjoyed that feeling. The feeling that I was being noticed.'

'But you didn't confuse it with anything else?'

'Oh, I didn't fall in love with him,' I turned, shocked.

He smiled. 'No, I can see you didn't. Although, I think he did with you.'

I blinked, baffled. 'God knows why. I mean, look at

him.' He followed my gaze to where Ludo, handsome, smiling and crinkly-eyed, was entertaining Alice's young friends just outside the tent. They swarmed around, flicking back their hair, laughing up at him. 'And look at me. A frowsty, middle-aged housewife.' I pulled at my billowing kaftan: laughed. 'Fading looks, marshmallow for brains—'

'Big heart,' he interrupted, giving me his steady look. I met his blue gaze, knowing he wanted to kiss me. But I had a confession – not of the Ludo kind, something else. I looked away.

'About my heart, Ant,' I said slowly.

'What about it?' He took my hand. I carefully extracted it.

'I think I should tell you . . . in fact, it's only fair to tell you, I've been very jealous of Bella Edgeworth. For all sorts of reasons. Brains, beauty, youth, of course, which we now know she doesn't have for much longer . . .' I paused. Pushed on. 'But the thing is, Ant . . .' I swallowed; licked my lips. 'Well, the thing is, I'm not sure that if Bella were to make a miraculous recovery, if a cure for her particularly virulent form of cancer were to be found tomorrow, and she was the first lucky recipient,' it was all coming out in a mighty rush now, 'I'm not sure I'd be so magnanimous. I have a nasty feeling that the reason I'm welcoming her daughter – your daughter – so graciously into my home is because her mother is not going to be around. I have an awful feeling I'm not a very nice person.'

There was a silence as Ant digested this.

'When you told me she was dying, a tiny part of me

473

felt sort of relieved. You should know that, Ant. You should know, before you wander round this city dewy-eyed and delusional, telling everyone what a generous, big-hearted wife you have, what sort of woman she really is. I'm no Bob Geldof,' I added in a small voice.

'I think we should also remember,' he observed at length, and was it me or did his mouth twitch, 'that only a very small part of you thought that.'

'Well—'

'And that many women wouldn't have admitted to it. Would have kept quiet.'

I struggled with this, tugged at the grass, tearing it up in handfuls, frowning. He wasn't going to let me have my hair shirt.

'You don't seem very shocked,' I muttered. 'I thought it was quite a confession.'

'I know you did. But let me tell you, Evie, if everyone held a mirror up to their soul like that, if everyone examined their motives so minutely, it wouldn't be a pretty sight. I too have a confession to make. If that man was found dead in a ditch tomorrow after his brakes failed on a sharp bend, I wouldn't be crying my eyes out either. In fact I might be dancing on his grave.'

Rather shocked, I followed his gaze to Ludo, who, back in brother-of-the-bride mode, was welcoming an elderly couple to the party, escorting them into the tent, but not before shooting an anxious glance over his shoulder in our direction.

'Instead of which,' Ant got to his feet, 'I have to go over and offer him my hand. Apologize for wrecking his sister's wedding. For hitting him.' He took my hand and helped me up too. 'It's not a question of being good, Evie, it's a question of behaving well. However bad you might think you are, however much you feel opening your home to Stacey is a knee-jerk reaction to what, in your eyes, could have been a far worse situation, you still did the right thing. It's what we do that counts; not how we feel. It's what makes us civilized people. Distinguishes us from the beasts. Nurture over nature, see Prospero on this.'

'Who?'

'Never mind. We can't control what goes on in our hearts, but we can help how we behave. And with that bit of cod philosophy out of the way, I shall go and shake the bastard by the hand.' He grinned sheepishly at his feet. Turned to go

'I love you, Ant.'

He turned back, surprised. 'I love you too.' His eyes widened. His arms opened too and I walked into them. 'More than you'll ever know,' he whispered.

We kissed, then, like lovers do. Not like a thoroughly married couple. And then Ant turned away and strolled along the river bank, back towards the marquee.

I crossed the bridge over the river and made my way through the long grass on the other side, and then up the lawn to the house. I appeared to be hugging myself, smiling foolishly at my shoes. Grinning even. I gave myself a stern little shake as I went through the back door into the kitchen. I was pretty sure this would have replaced the marquee as the venue for the continuing saga of any Milligan family dramas, and a euphoric, post-clinch haze, having effectively reaffirmed my wedding vows with husband, might not necessarily be what was called for right now. Sure enough, as I made my way upstairs towards Caro's bedroom, I met my nephews, quietly exiting it, shutting the door softly behind them.

'We took her a cup of tea,' whispered Henry, tiptoeing wide-eyed down the corridor towards me. 'Is it a nervy breaky, Evie?'

'Oh, no, she's just upset.'

'Still.' He glanced back, evidently disappointed, at his mother's door. 'She might need a couple of nights at the Priory, don't you think? If she's got issues? Maybe we should give her a laxative to calm her down?'

Jack snorted. 'Sedative, you mean. A laxative will give her the trots.'

'I'm sure she'll be fine,' I assured them, shooing them

downstairs and telling them to say as little as possible to Phoebe and Anna when they appeared. Although actually, I thought, as I opened the bedroom door and Caro rose, rigid from the waist from her pillows to stare at me, hair vertical, eyes seemingly rotating, a nice Valium sandwich might be just what my sister-in-law needed right now.

'She took our bloody money!' she blurted out, before I'd even shut the door behind me. 'I was in there,' she pointed a quivering finger to her ensuite bathroom, 'on the bloody bog, quietly minding my own business, when I heard you and Tim talking about it – couldn't believe my ears! I practically stopped mid-crap, froze to the loo seat. Couldn't believe you were both so calm about it. I wiped my arse and went straight down to knock her front teeth out!'

'You didn't, though, did you?' I said nervously, as I sat down on the bed beside her. I hadn't exactly had a ringside seat, what with muscling through all those hats. 'You only slapped her, didn't you?'

'Tragically,' she muttered, flopping back on her pillows. 'Must be my upbringing. Couldn't make a fist. I wish I bloody had, though.'

The door opened softly and Felicity stood in the doorway: very pale, very shaken, her hat at an unusual angle. I flung myself on top of Caro as she rose up from the marital bed like The Thing From the Swamp, all bared teeth and seasick-making eyes, a bit like Mr Rochester's first wife.

'*Arrrrghhh!*' she shrieked.

'Caro! Pull yourself together!' I yelled, pushing her

shoulders down forcefully, wondering if I should slap her myself. 'Felicity, I'm not convinced this is the moment,' I squealed over my shoulder.

Suddenly Caro went limp under my hands. Flopped submissively back into the pillows again.

'Let her come,' she said darkly, 'why not? Let's see what she's got to say for herself. Bring it on, I say. I hope you've got a good lawyer, Felicity. You'll need one.'

I cringed. Oh, this was horrible. Horrible. They were such friends. I wished I wasn't alone with them.

'Yes, you're quite right,' Felicity whispered, coming – rather bravely, I felt – to stand at the end of the bed. She looked almost unrecognizable. Her lipstick was smudged round her mouth, her pallor deathly, her eyes circled with grey. I saw her take a breath to steady herself. 'I will need a lawyer. Because I don't have any defence. I did take your money.'

Oh Lord. I crumpled inside. Felt Caro stiffen beside me, as, simultaneously, Tim appeared in the open doorway. He didn't come in, just stayed there, quietly propped on a crutch.

'But not immediately. I didn't know about that letter,' she glanced at me, then round at Tim, 'until well after your father died. Like you, I assumed he died intestate. After all, he hadn't told me he'd made a will, and we were happily married, so surely I'd know? Normally it's something husbands and wives do together, isn't it?'

I nodded. Yes it was. Ant and I had made one together. Relatively recently in fact, promoted by Dad's not doing so.

'First wives, perhaps!' snarled Caro, looking and sounding now like something out of Dante's upper circle of hell.

Felicity went on, ignoring her, 'Evie and I took that room apart, didn't we?' I nodded enthusiastically again; oh please, let this be all right. 'Drawer by drawer, file by file, box by box and we found nothing. And then I moved out and you moved in,' she looked steadily at Caro, 'because even though it wasn't written down that you should have the house, I knew it was what Victor wanted. He'd told me so. But I could have stayed. First or second wife, the house was legally mine. In a court of law it would automatically have gone to me.' Caro looked less sure of herself; glanced quickly at her husband. Tim's face was hard to read.

'So when did you find the letter?' I prompted gently.

'Almost a year later, when I'd been at my house in Fairfield Avenue for a good nine months. I went to MOT the car. Found the log book in the bureau, together with the grey plastic folder with all the documents. Inside was the tax certificate and the latest MOT, and tucked behind that, the piece of paper.'

I remembered Maroulla telling me she'd put it back when she'd copied it, not in Dad's messy drawer where she thought it would get lost, but in a very important-looking folder, with certificates. Birth certificates, she'd thought. I swallowed.

'It was a beautiful summer's day, I remember it vividly. I even remember what I was wearing – white trousers, pink shirt – and I was happy. I'd been deadheading my pots that morning, on the terrace – geraniums, stocks – and for the first time for ages, I felt my life was getting back on track. I had this dear little house, my job; I no longer had Victor, it was true, but I felt . . . I could do this. Go on without him. And I felt he was watching over me too, urging me on. Then all of a sudden, my life came to another juddering halt, just as it had a year before. I stood at the bureau and stared at the paper. I felt sick. I had to sit down. I went hot, and then cold. I was frightened.' She looked, for the first time, directly at Caro. 'I was nearly sixty years old. I was alone. I had no children, no family. And soon, no house.'

'You could have gone back into college,' Caro muttered, but less forcefully. 'Got a flat.'

'Could I? Those flats are fought over tooth and nail, as Evie knows, and in my college they were all allocated. Maybe I could have pulled rank, but how much rank did I have? I was no longer head of the department. I was a part-timer, working three days a week. I'd had my day. And I'd given up a flat once before, don't forget. Might the powers that be not gently suggest that actually, maybe I should think about retiring, instead?'

'Well, then you could have bought a one-bedroom flat off the Cowley Road!' said Caro savagely. 'Near the industrial estate. Lived according to your means!'

Felicity lowered her head. Didn't answer.

'What did you do with the letter?' I asked.

'Nothing, for a while. I sat and stared at it for ages, then I put it back, my hand shaking, I remember, in the top drawer of my desk. Under lots of papers. Buried it, like a dog would a bone. But almost hourly, I'd go back in the room, dig it out again, and stare at it. Have to sit down. Then quickly put it back again. It was dated six months before his death, but I couldn't decide what state of mind he'd written it in. I didn't know if it really was his last wish, or just a whim, late one night, after half a bottle of whisky. I didn't know if it was legal either, but that was irrelevant, really. What mattered was – had he wanted it to happen? If I'm honest, he'd said to me once that leaving Tim the farm with no money was a millstone round—'

'Of course it was!' shrieked Caro, rising up from her pillows again. 'It was like cutting his legs off! Like giving us the wagon without the wheels, the cart without the horse, whatever fucking farmyard analogy you care to mention! It left us impotent, and working so hard, *so* hard,' she quivered with rage, 'you've no idea. We had to keep the farm going by any means we could. We struggled day and night, while you sat watching, *knowing*, in your pretty Queen Anne house with its terrace and its wrought-iron railings, not only with your salary from the University but with Tim's inheritance as well!'

Felicity swallowed. 'Yes,' she nodded, 'yes, that's true. But my salary was my due, Caro. I worked for it.' Her voice quavered. 'And my husband's money, I'd *thought* was my due. We were married, after all. I was the wife, albeit the second one, who usually retains the estate when her husband dies. And as I said, I could, legally, have taken the house, the land—'

'Which would have been *entirely* against his wishes.'

'Exactly, so I didn't. But I *could* have. But we all agreed, didn't we?' She glanced around beseechingly. 'Tim and Caro should have the farm, Evie – well, not much . . .'

'I didn't need much,' I said hastily.

'And I'd receive whatever money—'

'But that was before you found the letter!' Caro exploded. 'And you say you didn't know how to read it – well, I don't believe you. I *know* why you went hot and cold, Felicity. You saw in that piece of paper that Victor Milligan wanted his son to carry on the farm for the next generation, for Tim, and then Jack, and then maybe Jack's son, to do the same. For not just four, but five, maybe six generations of Milligans to farm this land, as Victor's great-grandfather had done. You suddenly saw in a flash, in a tiny scrap of paper, that you weren't important in the scheme of things; that set against a barrage of history, against the pull of the land, you were nothing. You were just the wife!'

'And so are you,' said Tim, quietly.

It was the first time he'd spoken. Caro's eyed darted to him. She opened her mouth to object, but his face silenced her. He limped into the room.

'How much money did he leave? I forget.'

'Almost two hundred thousand,' said Felicity. 'Which I put down as a deposit on the house.'

'Not a great deal.'

'Not a great deal!' squealed Caro. 'Believe you me, my darling, two hundred thousand pounds would go an awfully long way to—'

'Not a great deal *in the scheme of things*,' he interrupted, deliberately using her words. She closed her mouth.

'But still, quite a lot for Dad to have?' I suggested. I remembered at the time being surprised it was there. But pleased for Felicity. 'Considering how broke we always were?'

'It was his sinking fund,' said Tim. 'I knew about it. Grandpa made most of it in the good days, but Dad never touched it. He lived pretty much hand to mouth, the idea being that one day, hopefully, he'd buy more land with it, make the farm viable. It was his contingency fund.' He turned back to Felicity. 'Did you ever consider showing us the note?'

'Many times. I often picked up the phone and thought – I must tell them, I must. I was in agonies. I knew it was deceitful, but as every day went by and I hadn't told you, as weeks, months … well, the awful thing was, it got easier. I still had to live with myself, of course—'

'But you had your charity works to salve your conscience,' Caro said bitterly. 'To make you feel better about yourself.'

'Perhaps,' Felicity agreed, miserably. 'Trying to be the person I knew I wasn't.'

'But not a bad person, Felicity,' I said quickly. She shot me a grateful look. 'I'm not saying I'd have done the same,' I said, as Caro shot me a venomous one. 'But – who knows? All I'm saying is I can see how it happened, how Felicity got herself into the pickle. No one knew about it, she was the only one who had the letter—'

'Apart from Maroulla, as you discovered when you went to see her in the hospice, which must have given you a *really* nasty shock,' interjected Caro. 'But then again, Maroulla was dying, wasn't she, Felicity? So soon, no one would know. Marvellous.' She folded her arms grimly.

There was a silence as we digested this. But I could feel my blood rising.

'OK, Caro, tell me something.' I turned to her. 'If you

found a letter – not even a proper letter, a scrap of paper – in the study, tucked, ooh, I don't know, behind a picture maybe, that one of Grandpa Milligan over the fireplace, written in Dad's hand, saying that actually, he wanted to leave the whole shooting match to Felicity, that there was no point struggling on with the farm any more, that Tim would be flogging a dead horse, what would you have done? How quick would you have been to call a family pow-wow? Hand your house back to Felicity and move back to the leaky little bungalow in Rutlers Lane with the fungus on the kitchen ceiling? And let's, just for the sake of argument, say that as you stood in front of Grandpa Milligan at the fireplace reading the letter, the fire was alight? In the grate? What would you have done, Caro?'

I fixed her with my eyes. She looked back defiantly, but nevertheless, her gaze was guarded. I knew Caro. Knew she'd protect, not just her own interests, but her family's interests, her children's, at all costs. I knew about the indomitable strength women have in that department, their intractability, their tenacity when it comes to family. Had felt it myself very recently. If she saw something precious begin to slip from where she'd hung it so carefully, boy, would she hook it back up again.

'Well, I'd like to think——' she began disingenuously.

'*Bollocks!*' I roared.

There was a silence. Caro and I glared knowingly at each other. She looked away first.

'I'll give it back, of course,' said Felicity quietly. 'I'll sell up, and then you'll have your money, Caro. Every penny.'

Tim cleared his throat. 'Felicity——'

'No,' she held up her hand; shut her eyes, 'I mean it.

It's what I should have done years ago. And, you know, it'll be a relief. I haven't enjoyed living like this. The guilt has weighed very heavy on my shoulders. I'm glad you all know. And I'm very, very sorry,' she added in a faltering voice. 'The house is as good as sold.'

We all looked at our hands. Even Caro had the grace to look uncomfortable.

Tim spoke first. 'Thank you, Felicity, but there's no need. Even with the money, it's still not enough to keep us going here. We'd still have to sell up.'

I glanced at him, shocked.

'We'd already decided that, hadn't we, darling?' he said gently, turning to his wife. Caro didn't speak. Her face was very pale. She looked in real pain now. Suddenly I understood where all this anger had come from. And possibly been misdirected.

'Look at me,' he appealed to us, holding out his arms crucifix-style, his crutch hanging from his wrist. His legs, we knew without looking, were splayed from various operations. They might meet at the knees, but you could kick a football through his ankles. 'This isn't a farmer. This isn't a man up to working the land.'

Even his wife didn't have the gall to gainsay this. Even Caro, who'd been in denial for years, kept her counsel, her eyes on the bedcover.

'This is a man who needs a desk job,' he finished bitterly. 'A man who needs to stop wincing every time he goes to work in the morning. I can't do this any more.'

He limped to the window and gazed out, perhaps to hide his face. He leaned heavily on his crutch. As he stood there looking out, it occurred to me that no amount

485

of money would have found a way around this. We all, Tim included, had fumbled and fudged our way round this for years, around what was essentially a disability. Felicity's money wouldn't have helped, and looking at Caro, I felt she knew this too. Her eyes were less bright now; no longer burning with injustice. There was a resigned inevitability about the slump of her shoulders on the pillows, as if the fight had gone out of her. I also believe, in her heart, she knew that even if Felicity *had* come round in a panic, waving the scrap of paper, Tim, whose call it was essentially, would have screwed it up, said – forget it, Felicity, it's not worth the paper it's written on. We can't possibly take your money on the strength of this. What's done is done; we are where we are – silencing, in one glance, the protests of his outraged wife. I don't say that simply because I know my brother, because he's a nice guy, but because it seems to me that if people behave well, it encourages others to do the same. Who knows, maybe even Caro might have been impressed; wrong-footed.

Yet when people behave badly . . . I looked at Felicity. She was not one I'd associate with human frailty, but fear is a powerful motivator, and once it had gripped her, once she'd found herself looking into what seemed like an abyss, her whole future dropping away from her, and once she'd given in to the vertigo, failed to rush round here, or pick up the phone, I could see how it became harder to inch towards the edge again. Much easier not to. And as the months and the years slipped by and no lightning bolt struck her from the heavens, no divine finger pinned her wriggling to the floor, as the world, in effect, revolved as usual, as she'd given her lectures, done her meals on wheels, pottered at home in her garden, as life went on, so the whole wretched business would have faded into the background. But maybe as she climbed the stairs to bed one Sunday evening, after lunch here at the farm, cooked by Caro, haggard with the perpetual motion that was her life, and maybe around the time Henry had been bullied at school and his parents had tried but failed to afford a private one for him, maybe as Tim had come in from the fields, yet again well after dusk, shattered, maybe the guilt had closed in on her then and she'd had trouble going to sleep. Maybe after all, as she'd said, it hadn't been worth it.

Footsteps padded down the corridor and the next face to pop round the door, wreathed in smiles, was Mum's.

'Oh, *here* you all are. I wondered where you'd got to. There's a terrific band playing in the marquee and Alice says we must all come and dance. You're missing all the fun.' As her eyes swept round the room, over our faces, her expression changed. It occurred to me she'd missed Caro slapping Felicity, because she'd been dealing with the pigs. She knew none of this.

'What's going on?'

I saw real panic pass through Felicity's eyes. She glanced fearfully at Caro. Felicity valued Mum's high opinion very much. Her best friend. A woman of integrity. A woman whose moral rectitude could not be questioned.

Caro got off the bed.

'Nothing,' she said shortly, smoothing her skirt down. 'I just felt a bit peculiar and came up for a lie-down. Then

Tim came in bellyaching about his hip, and the next thing I knew, the whole bloody family was in here.'

Three people flashed her grateful looks. It seemed to encourage her, spur her on. She dug deep and found more. 'Now come on,' she said briskly, finding her shoes under the bed and shoving her feet in them. She threw on her jacket, looking much more like her old self, 'we've got tea and cake to serve yet. And what a relief we *have* got cake, thanks to you, Barbara, and no thanks at all to Leonard.'

'Yes, although thanks to Leonard,' said Mum following her out, 'all your sows have now been serviced.'

Caro stopped in her tracks in the doorway. 'All of them?' She turned aghast.

'Yes, why?'

'I was going to separate them. Let him have two at a time.'

'Ah, I wondered. That's what I used to do. But Henry said no, Mum wants them all done at once.'

'Did he, by jingo? Which means in six months' time six sows will produce up to fifteen piglets apiece, which means . . .' she paused to do the maths, 'ninety piglets. Oh, splendid.' She looked a bit faint. Then something in her face lightened. She threw up her arms. 'So what? What the hell do I care? It certainly won't be *me* sloshing the swill in the trough, will it?'

And flashing us all a final defiant glance, she marched off down the corridor.

## 33

Bella Edgeworth died in March. The funeral was held in the tiny village church next door to her house in York- shire, and the Hamilton family were amongst the mourners. Initially I'd hesitated, wondering if perhaps just Ant and Anna would be more appropriate, but Stacey rang and said please all come, so we did.

There were so many cars outside the church that day we had to park right at the far end of the village and walk. As we made our way, the three of us, on that breezy spring morning, a mixture of flashing bright sunshine and hurrying clouds, the bells tolling slowly and relentlessly, getting ever louder as we approached, it turned into one of the longest walks I'd ever taken. We arrived in silence, along with other equally hushed little groups of dark- suited people. My throat was so constricted I could barely breathe. Stacey, however, at the church door with Ted beside her, greeting everyone, was having none of that. She was wearing a floaty white skirt and a pink camisole and cardigan, and her blonde hair fell in a shining sheet around her shoulders. It occurred to me she looked like an angel. On receiving our hugs and whispered condol- ences, our voices catching, she thanked us, but we were told firmly as she handed us the order of service: 'This is a celebration of her life. Mum and I had a lot of time to plan this, and it's what we both wanted. I'm fine.'

I suspected she wasn't, but she was doing a good job of hiding it. And if we could help by belting out 'All things bright and beautiful' and not, I noticed, 'The Lord's my shepherd', then we jolly well would. The tiny church was heaving; people were standing outside in the churchyard too, and we fairly raised the rafters. Then we listened as two of Bella's best friends read: first from Genesis Chapter One – Bella's choice; nothing tear-jerking about being in the next room waiting, just a factual account of how God made the world in seven days – and then her favourite Shakespeare sonnet, the one about the darling buds of May. She'd been thinking of Stacey, I thought as I listened. Didn't want anything that would set her daughter off. Just a few gentle reminders of what a beautiful world it still was out there.

Stacey didn't read, but back at the house, where we all gratefully went for tea and sandwiches later, much needed after the burial, she got up on a kitchen chair and said a few words. Blushing to the roots of her blonde hair, even her scalp turning pink, she stammered to begin with, but she got those words out: about how her mum would have liked to see everyone in her kitchen like this, eating her home-made jam and the scones she'd made herself and put in the freezer. How pleased she'd be to see us admiring her garden, how thrilled she'd be that the magnolia was out. How Stacey wished she was here, but knew she was very much amongst us, smiling and happy, no longer in pain, and that, however sad it was to lose her, she, Stacey, was glad she was no longer suffering. Those of us who'd held it together in church for Stacey's sake completely lost it now, myself included. I'm not sure there was a dry eye in the house.

Ted, beside me, mopped furiously with his huge white hanky, pulling faces to stem the flow, but Stacey ignored our blubbing. She looked her grandfather firmly in his damp eye and thanked him for all he'd done, for the rock he'd been. Then, to my surprise, she introduced Ant as her father, Anna as her half-sister and referred kindly to Anna's mum, who'd offered her a home in Oxford. It wasn't, she went on, that she was deserting her Yorkshire friends and family: her roots – her heart – she insisted, would always be in the High Peaks, she'd always be a Yorkshire lass, it was just that her mum, Bella, had wanted her life to move on: for there to be a natural progression, and for her to get to know her father properly. It was a straightforward, upfront little speech, one she'd clearly practised in her bedroom a few times, maybe even in front of her mother, but it told everyone precisely what the score was. It didn't exactly spare Ant's blushes, who, as everyone turned to peer at this Johnny-come-lately, went puce. It ended with a glass of champagne raised – 'To Mum. The best a girl could ever have. My world. My everything.' This last bit, I suspected Bella hadn't heard, and it was the only bit where Stacey's voice cracked.

'To Bella!' we all roared, to cover it, as she was helped down from her chair by Ant. Then the tea cups were put away and out came the wine and the drinking started in earnest.

Stacey was hugged by school friends with whispered assurances she'd done 'really really well', then, likewise by teachers, and neighbours and friends of Bella's. I felt very proud of her. I waited for my turn to come and told her so.

'Was it OK?' she asked anxiously. 'Not too schmaltzy? Mum and I felt something should be said before I just sort of – disappeared; thought it would be a good moment with everyone gathered. We also thought it might stem the flow of – oh, didn't you know?' She folded her arms and leaned on an imaginary garden fence, broadening her accent: 'There's a father. Oh, aye, 'e's finally cum out the woodwork. Didn't want to know 'er when she was a bairn, but now she's going to college, now she's proving herself to be an asset . . .' She rolled her eyes meaningfully. I laughed.

And actually, we had a few laughs that day, which made it a very different wake to the only other one I'd been to, my father's. But then Dad had died so suddenly, no one had been in any way prepared. Whereas Bella's death, although at a much younger age, so therefore more tragic, had been foreseen, so that now people were moving about her house remembering her fondly, picking up photographs, reminiscing about the good times, whereas at Dad's we'd all been white-faced and stricken. I remembered the shock, the pain. Knowing surely took the shock away? Although, I realized, looking at Ted, who was chatting away gamely but there was no disguising the grief in his eyes, it didn't do much for the pain.

Despite Stacey's brave words, it was surely the longest day of her short life too, and towards the end of the afternoon she looked very tired. There were more brave words though, as we said goodbye.

'I thought I might use Anastasia when I'm at Oxford. What d'you think?' She coloured up as she said it.

'I think it's a good idea. It's a lovely name. What did your mum think?' I could have kicked myself. Already looking for back-up, the first time she'd turned to me.

'It was her idea. But I don't know. I don't want people to think I'm . . . you know, reinventing myself, or anything.' She chewed her thumbnail.

This time I didn't miss a beat. 'That's just another word for taking life by the scruff of its neck. And there's absolutely nothing wrong with that.'

She looked pleased, and relieved. 'Although,' she hesitated, 'I might still be Stacey at home.'

This last word wasn't lost on me either, and as we drove away from that mellow stone house, up the snaking lane that wound through the green valley to the top of the hill, I felt moved and humbled beyond belief. What a privilege it was going to be to have her, I realized. To know her. To make her part of us. As I looked out of the car window to the huge shifting sky, the rushing clouds above, I made a silent promise to her mother. I know she's rare and valuable. I know what we have here. I shall cherish her accordingly.

Six months later and Stacey was beside me again. Yet again we were surrounded by bottles, yet again we were preparing for a party, only this time, it was of a very different nature, and she was the one helping me. Together we heaved clanking boxes into the boot of the car outside the farmhouse, preparing to take them to an occasion I don't think any of us had seen coming.

'Beer, d'you think?' I paused, resting a box of glasses on my knee. 'For the men? Or will they be happy with Pimm's?'

Stacey looked doubtfully at our groaning boot. 'Isn't there an ad where they load the truck with beer and then some Aussie says what about a bottle of sherry for the Sheilas and the whole thing collapses?'

'And I don't want a collapsing car, so let's forget it. The boys can drink Pimm's and lump it. Where's Anna?' I turned to look back at the house as I slammed the boot shut. Stacey grinned and got in the front seat.

'Still dithering about what to wear.'

'Come *on*, Anna!' I yelled back at the open front door. 'We're going!' No response. *'Anna!'* Eventually she appeared at the doorway with a big box of Hula Hoops, her only responsibility.

'And don't forget to lock the door,' I called to her.

It was odd, I thought, how, since Stacey had arrived, Anna had slipped effortlessly into the role of little sister. I watched as she tried to lock the front door whilst balancing the box of crisps on her knee, too lazy to put it down and do the job properly. She seemed happy to let Stacey play the part of elder statesman, whilst she, rather refreshingly, became the hopeless kid; the one Stacey and I exchanged indulgent glances about. We traded just such a look now as, predictably, Anna dropped the whole lot. Loads of little shiny red packets burst out of the box onto the yard.

'Sorry!' She looked up helplessly as Stacey and I went to help.

Happily the packets weren't too disgusting as the yard

494

had recently been resurfaced, and we brushed them down and slung them back in the box. Yes, amazing what half a hundredweight of crunchy gravel did, I thought as I followed the girls back to the car. Amazing what had happened to the farm full stop, I reflected as I got in and pulled my seat belt across. I glanced up at the crumbling façade, already covered with scaffolding, repointing work scheduled to start next week.

Ah yes, the farm: which had to be sold, that much was certain; everyone, even Caro, agreed. And she hadn't messed about. A frightfully upmarket estate agent called Peregrine had appeared at the double, with matching Volvo and wellies, and after lots of tutting about rising damp and dry rot, admitted it was worth a fortune, Mrs Milligan. Pound signs rotated in Caro's eyes as she personally, elbowing Peregrine out of the way, oversaw the bidding war that got underway. The victor, Mick Arnold, a local property developer, eventually paid way over the asking price.

'Twenty-five per cent more!' squeaked Caro excitedly when I popped round one morning for a coffee. 'Which means we can afford the house I've seen with the walled garden. Six bedrooms! *And* a Chalon kitchen.'

'Good.' I was thrilled for her. Knew it was genuinely what she wanted now. Knew that, when she'd crossed the line that meant leaving the farm, she'd done it in a leap. Landed on the other side without looking back. It was what Tim and the children wanted too, had wanted, probably for some time, and there'd been a collective, almost audible, sigh of relief.

'Have you seen the new house?' I asked the children

now as they lounged across the kitchen table, methodically stripping a bunch of grapes Caro had just put in a bowl in the middle.

'Not yet. But I know where it is,' Jack told me with his mouth full. 'Miles Jackson lives in the same road.'

'Oh, it's terribly convenient,' gushed Caro, pouring out coffee at the Aga as Tim came in. 'The children can even walk to school.'

'And the shops,' Jack reminded her, spitting pips into his hand. 'And the cinema.'

'And Ladbrokes,' added Henry, who nursed private aspirations to become a gambler. His father aimed a mock swipe at his head as he passed.

'It's literally just off the Banbury Road, in Westgate Avenue,' Caro told me happily.

'Oh, we looked there.' I turned, surprised, as she delivered a mug of coffee to me over my shoulder. 'But Ant thought it was too grand.'

'Not for us it's not,' snorted Caro, sitting down at the far end of the table with an enormous Designers Guild samples book. 'But you're right, it is grand. It's much bigger than your house, Evie.'

I laughed and picked up my coffee. 'Good old Mick Arnold.'

'And look what he's doing to the place,' said Tim in awed tones, unrolling plans and spreading them on the table in front of me. 'Look at this!'

I moved my mug and dutifully inspected.

'All the barns are being converted,' he explained, running his finger across the drawings, 'and they all look out onto a courtyard in the middle, here.'

I went cold. 'What – you mean like a sort of complex?'

'Well, there'll be six of them in all, oh, and a couple of flats. Tiny gardens, obviously.'

'Right.' I swallowed. 'And the farmhouse?'

He unrolled another sheet. 'Oh, the *house*. Blimey, Evie, you've no idea. It's going to be tarted up beyond belief. Every bedroom gets an ensuite, and then they're digging down to make an indoor cinema, can you believe it? And there's going to be a huge extension at the back, with a gymnasium and a sauna.'

'Christ. And what's this?'

Tim peered. Turned his head round to get a better view. 'Not sure. Think it's a fountain.'

'It is,' affirmed Caro, glasses perched on her nose, flicking efficiently through pages of stripy wallpaper. 'They're doing a sort of mini Versailles in the yard. Very tasteful, apparently; water sprouting from cherubs and all set in a cobbled circle.'

'Yuck.'

Tim grinned as he rolled up the plans. 'Yuck, but he's paying through the nose for it, Evie.' He looked me in the eye. 'And it's only a pile of bricks and mortar, after all. Not hearts and minds.' He gently jerked his head to his children at the other end of the table, all leaning eagerly over Caro's shoulder, picking wallpaper for their teenage bedrooms off the Banbury Road.

Yes, it was only bricks and mortar, I thought as I left that day. Before I got in the car, though, I stood in the yard where the fountain would be. Gazed at the barn where Grandpa had stacked hay for a herd of eighty Guernseys, Dad for twenty, and Tim for a couple of token gestures. Rusting machinery crouched there now, looking out impotently at the three hundred acres of very average land, which no doubt would be parcelled up too, eventually, and sold as individual plots for yet more desirable homes; more ribbon development in the Oxfordshire countryside. My hair whipped around my face as I narrowed my eyes to the familiar view: the rolling hills, the swaying chestnuts, no longer with a marquee flapping in the foreground. I supposed they'd still leave the willows standing, and the river would still run through the valley as it always had done – you can't stop a river, can you? I wondered nervously. But around it would be Willow Close. Or Riverside Walk. Yes, and why not? I thought, swallowing. I walked quickly to the car. People had to live somewhere, didn't they? Why shouldn't it be in my backyard?

I said as much to Ant that evening, with forced jollity: telling him about mini Versailles; making a joke of it as Caro had. I told him about the barn conversions, and how, if they played their cards right, that little community could go up to the tarted-up farmhouse and watch a movie in the sunken cinema of a Saturday night; take a bag of popcorn. Told him progress was good, and it was time the farm moved on.

'What, and become unaffordable executive housing?'

'Well, affordable to some.'

'Yes, but not the people who live in the village who need it. Not Madge and Tom Ure's children, who are desperate to stay. Londoners, second homers. City boys with fat bonuses, that's who'll be swelling the ranks of the village. And you call that progress.'

'Well, anyway,' I laid the table with something of a clatter, dropping the knives, 'it's all going through, and Tim and Caro are thrilled.'

The following day Ant came home from work looking thoughtful. Anna and Stacey were in the sitting room next door watching *America's Next Top Model*. He shut the kitchen door softly on them.

'Would you hate to live at the farm again?'

I turned slowly from the sink where I'd been washing up.

'No. I wouldn't hate it.'

'Could you even entertain it?'

My heart began to pound. 'Yes. I could.'

'The girls could too, I'm sure.' His eyes were overbright.

I took my hands out of the hot water, wiped them deliberately and turned to face him, clutching a tea towel.

'You're not seriously suggesting . . .'

'Why not?'

I sat down carefully at the table. 'Move from here? To the farm?'

'We could do it up. Make it – not chichi – but comfortable. Put a new kitchen in, solve the damp, redecorate. What d'you think?'

I thought a lot of things. But I didn't want to get excited.

'Can we afford it?'

'Yes, but not easily. Mick Arnold's offered a fortune, and we'd have to match it.' He was talking quite fast now. 'This place will be worth quite a bit, though, being so central, but we'd probably need two salaries. So in answer to your question, yes, we could afford it, but only if you work. Which is what you tell me you want to do.' He gave me a steady look. I returned it equally evenly.

'I do,' I said soberly. Then blinked. 'Gosh. Sounded like a vow.' And in a way, it was. To begin a new life. 'Oh Ant,' I breathed, gripping my tea towel, hardly daring to believe it.

He looked at me, surprised. 'I wasn't convinced you'd want to. You're such a townie.'

I laughed, taken aback too. 'Yes, I am, aren't I? But not always. I mean, once I was a farmer's daughter. And you know what they say: you can take the girl out of the country . . .' My eyes slid away over his shoulder. Then came back. 'And d'you know what, Ant? I've done the city. It used to hold me in such thrall, Oxford. It was such a challenge. Always there when I was growing up, a few miles away, goading me on, those flipping dreaming spires waving at me over the tree tops – come on, Evie, d'you dare? But I feel I've got to grips with it now. I've made my peace with it, and I'd like to go back to the sticks where I belong.'

It was a surprise to hear myself say it, even though I'd been thinking it these past few weeks, but it was true. And I no longer felt a fraud here, either. No longer felt I was travelling on a false passport. I'd fought my battles in this town, and now I was very much looking forward to going home and curling up in the window seat with a box of lime creams and a Georgette Heyer. My eyes widened in surprise, but I felt my heart swell too. I wondered if Caro felt that way about going back to town. Tossing her swill buckets over her shoulder and kicking off her wellies as she went.

'Caro—' I started.

'I know,' said Ant quickly. 'We'd be doing everything to the farm they'd ever wanted to. I know, Evie, that bothers me. We'd have to square it with them first, obviously, and I'm not sure—'

'No,' I interrupted impatiently, shaking my head, 'I mean yes, we will have to square it with them, but I didn't mean that. I don't think it will be a problem. Actually, I think she'll be fine.'

'You do?' Ant looked surprised, but I didn't just think, I sort of knew. Ordinarily I'd break out in hives at broaching such a conversation with my sister-in-law, but . . . well, it was a funny thing, life. What was that Chinese proverb? Be careful what you wish for. Perhaps Caro and I had both wished for too much. With maturity comes a certain wisdom, definitely, but also an ability to live in the moment, which, let's face it, is more restful than constantly striving to pin down an endlessly shifting future. It was over fifteen years since Caro and I had been passionate about our futures, and over time, I believe those passions had hardened into positions behind our backs. Our ancient desires had become unrecognizable, even to ourselves. I'd seen Caro turn round and blink in astonishment at her old self the other day as she'd flipped through her decorating book, as she'd glimpsed her new self in her lofty, spacious, state-of-the-art kitchen; in fact, I'd seen her gawp. It seemed to me it wouldn't matter how many terracotta tiles we put down in that farm, how painstakingly we restored the beams that Tim cracked his head on, she still wouldn't want it. Odd, I mused, that Caro and I had both reached that same place at about the same time: reached a tranquil state of acceptance of ourselves. But not that strange, really. Over the years, we'd done an awful lot together.

'I'll ring her later, sound her out. But as long as *you're* sure, Ant.' It was my turn to interrogate him. 'You're a real town mouse, and it's further into college —'

'I know, but I'm working at home more now. Doing more writing.' He walked round the kitchen, jingling coins in his pocket. He looked young, excited. 'I can work in your father's old study. French windows open to the garden, the stream . . .'

He turned. His eyes caught sharply on mine.

'No, no demons,' I said quickly. 'You?'

'No. Not now. Too long ago.'

Our eyes silently communed for a moment. I gave a small smile. 'So . . . not all progress is bad, perhaps?'

He gave a small smile back. 'No, not all.'


Which was how, some months later, I came to be standing in the not so muddy yard of my childhood, waiting for my girls. Happily they'd been enthusiastic about the move, planning bedrooms rather like their cousins, talking parties in barns, barbecues by the river. It also had the added bonus of giving both of them a fresh start, rather than just Stacey. A shared experience. They'd already worked out the buses into town, one of which, these last few days, Anna had started taking into school. Stacey, meanwhile, was still enjoying the end of her last, long, seemingly endless summer holiday, waiting for her new term to begin.

She'd been allocated a room at Balliol, which we'd all

been to see. We'd clattered excitedly up number two staircase, the four of us, throwing open her window over the quad, admiring her new quarters, but she'd told us, as we clattered back down again, that she thought she'd meet Anna at the bus stop on a Friday evening, and come back to the farm for the weekends. We'll see. I was already privately preparing myself, just as I was getting so fond of her, to see less of her as she joined in university life, went to parties, stayed in town at the weekends, although she insisted she wouldn't: was convinced she'd want to spend every spare minute with us.

'You're such a loser,' she told Anna now, who was giggling uncontrollably as she trailed yet more packets of Hula Hoops out of a box that had clearly burst its bottom. Stacey scooped one up and threw the trodden contents in a handy bucket. 'Shame the pigs have gone. They'd love these.'

Ah yes, the pigs. Happily no longer with us, and happily, not ninety of them either, only eight. Leonard, as is so often the case with rippling fecund males, turned out to be all gong, no dinner, and only Boadicea, the first recipient of his gifts, produced a litter. Caro – who had indeed kicked off her wellies with alarming alacrity, making it quite clear she considered any farm business our business now – had disclaimed all responsibility. She had, however, been kind enough to tell us about a lovely little slaughterhouse near Thame, which absolutely everyone went to – rather as if she were recommending a new bistro – and where a delightful man called Trevor would to do the business in seconds flat with a very sharp knife. Before I knew it, they'd be sausages.

'Oh!' I felt faint.

'Unless you want to do it yourself?' she demanded.

'Excuse me?' I gaped.

'Pack the sausages. You can, in a pork-packing unit in Ipswich. Or Trevor will do it for you in what looks like his garden shed. I wouldn't share that with the Environmental Health Officer, incidentally.'

'Um, Trevor,' I muttered, shaken, but much relieved: for the piglets were very much pigs now, up for having their own sex lives and babies soon, and I wanted shot of them.

I'd reckoned, however, without Anna and Stacey, who, despite eating a great many bacon sandwiches, had not found this plan acceptable. Whilst happy for the mothers to go to market – this, apparently, was entirely within the natural scheme of things – not so the piglets, and they'd sold them on eBay, using a photo of Boadicea surrounded by cute, suckling babies, taken quite a while ago. Eight deluded new owners arrived clutching it, with no idea they were about to collect a huge, ten-ton Spawn of Leonard. I needn't have worried, though. Amongst the smart county set, pigs were the new must-have: the Chanel bag. 'Darling, haven't you got a pig? Oh, you *must*, they're heaven.' They all went.

So, no pigs now – even Harriet, Caro's blind pig, had passed away in her sleep one night – but lots of restful sheep, thanks to Ed Pallister next door, who was leasing the fields, pathetically grateful for the extra acres. We didn't sell the land to him, though. Ant and I owned every blade of grass, and in a ridiculous, romantic way, I wondered if Tim's boys might want it back one day.

When Ant and I were old and grey and needing somewhere smaller? Perhaps a Sunset Home for the confused and bewildered.

Caro, naturally, was keen on this idea. She'd gripped my arm, eyes shining. 'Oh, *yes*, wouldn't that be wonderful? I mean, obviously I'm thrilled you've got it and not Mick Arnold with his repulsive Victorian lampposts and busy Lizzies in all the troughs, but if Jack could have it back one day . . .'

She'd been showing me round her new house at the time, and the children were with us. Jack, who'd recently confided his ambition to be a wealthy stockbroker and live in a flat in Docklands with a horny blonde, shot me a horrified look.

'Henry, even,' she mused happily, as Henry, behind her, slit his throat with his finger and fell quietly to the blond wood conservatory floor. It passed her by and I didn't rain on her generational farming parade. To be honest, she'd been a bit of a star, recently.

Yes, I reflected, as the girls and I finally set off with our booze-laden car towards town; once the stress of the farm had been removed, Caro had indeed become a different person. When Felicity, determined to redeem herself, had sold her house and taken a year's sabbatical at the University of Toronto, where her sister lived, writing Tim and Caro out a large cheque, Caro had promptly stuck it in an envelope, determined to return it. Tim and I, with a lot of eye rolling, had snatched it back and dissuaded her.

'It's what she wants, Caro. Don't throw it back in her face.'

'I'm not! But I feel awful!' she wailed.

'Bit late now' sprang to mind, but I didn't say it.

'We're not farming now, we don't need it. We're not short of money, she should have it. Oh God, what a mess.'

I sighed. 'Look, Caro, we are where we are. Take the money and have done with it. Write Felicity a big thank you, with an offer to come and stay whenever she's in Oxford. You've got six bedrooms in that house. Tell her one of them's got her name on it.'

'Yes. Yes, I will.' Her face lit up like a born-again Christian's. 'One of them *will* be hers for ever.' She turned to Tim and me with bright, shining eyes. 'I'll put "Felicity" on the door.'

Tim and I exchanged weary glances. So exhausting when everyone wanted to be good.

She wasn't through, either. Two days later, she and Tim came to see me.

'OK, we're keeping the money, but we're sharing it with you.' She handed me a cheque.

'He was your father too,' said Tim firmly, as I opened my mouth to protest. 'It's your inheritance as well. Fair's fair.'

I shut my mouth. If I'm honest, it had quietly occurred to me. I gazed down at the cheque in my hands. 'Thank you.' It also occurred to me that I'd never had money of my own before. Only my husband's. I looked up at them, a slow smile forming on my lips. 'Thank you very much.'

# 34

As I pulled up outside the shop, parking defiantly on the yellow lines and putting the hazard warning lights on, Caro was waiting for us. She shot her hand in the air and waved as she saw us. She looked stunning in chocolate linen trousers and an ice-blue cashmere wrap top, happily not stick thin any more, but with a wonderful curvy figure and fuller face. Tanned from a recent holiday in Italy, her bronzed, and not insubstantial, bosom jingled with jewellery as she hastened towards us.

'You're early!' I wailed, as I got out.

'I know, but I thought I'd help you set up.'

'You're a guest, Caro, you don't have to do that.'

She bustled round to open the boot. 'Nonsense, many hands and all that . . .'

Old habits died hard, I suppose, and actually I was glad of her: as we unloaded the contents of the boot onto the pavement I realized I needed muscle.

'Where's Tim?'

'Here,' she jerked her head as he came down the road. 'He went to park the car. What about Ant?'

'He's got a meeting, but he'll be along later.'

'Now, what can I do?' Tim appeared, rubbing his hands.

'You could set up the trestle table at the back of the shop — I've left it leaning against a wall in there — and take some boxes in. Girls, go with him and line up the glasses on the table.'

'Can we make the Pimm's?' asked Anna.

'You can, but don't put the ice in yet.'

'Cloth?' said Stacey.

'Good thinking.' I reached into the boot and handed her a white linen one.

They disappeared, the three of them, carrying a box of booze apiece, and then Tim came back for more, carting them back and forth; nimbler on his pins these days now he wasn't on them twenty-four hours a day, and without that look of continually suppressed pain about him.

He was selling agricultural machinery now, a rep; getting out to all the many farms around here, and indeed the whole of the southwest of England, which, as he said, meant 'seeing all my mates but not doing the sodding donkey-work. I wave bye-bye as they stand in the shit admiring my company car.' He pointed it out to me now as he came back for the final box of lemonade, parked just down the road: a brand-new silver Saab. I saw Caro smile as she shut the boot, and we listened as he eulogized about the turbo charged something-or-other, the fuel-injected what-not.

At the back of the shop the girls had laid the table with the cloth and were lining up glasses. Caro was paring a cucumber like a demon, and Stacey was attacking the lemons.

Mint?' She glanced up.

Oh. I darted back to the car. As I came back with it, though, I paused a moment midway through the shop;

took a second to gaze around. Yes, the duck-egg blue really *had* worked, I decided. Cheered the place up no end; made it – all due respect to Malcolm and Ludo – less like a gentleman's club, and more feminine; more sophisticated. But not remotely intimidating. I'd been nervous of going down that route, since that was something it had never been in Malcolm's day, and I certainly didn't want to alienate his old customers. I needn't have worried. As the door opened behind me, I turned to see a clutch of his elderly regulars come in, bang on the dot of six o'clock. I spotted Joan of the long brown coat and Spearmint smell amongst them as they hurried past to the back, keen to be the recipients of the first drink. I followed with the mint. Anna and Stacey were going to have to pour fast.

The cousins were next, strolling nonchalantly in from just around the corner. They instantly installed themselves with the girls on bar duty, where, I noticed, tasting was *de rigueur*. A few more early birds appeared, looking around in wonder, exclaiming, and then the man I was most worried about, who breezed in on a gust of wind with Clarence.

'Darling!' He sashayed across the room to kiss me, then clasped his hands in delight. He spun around, tossing a blue velvet scarf over his shoulder as he twirled. 'What a triumph!'

'D'you really think so, Malc?' I said nervously. I followed his gaze, fearful of his censure. More and more people were coming through the door now, Ant and Mum amongst them. They gave me a wave.

'Not too girly?'

'Oh, it's *girly* all right, but that's what makes it work, don't you think, hon?' This, hon, not directed to me, but to Clarence, smiling indulgently at Malcolm's over-camp style, whilst remaining resolutely straight himself.

'I agree – thank you.' He took a drink from Stacey, who'd approached with a tray. 'You've done a superb job, Evie. I hardly recognize the place.'

I relaxed: these boys had taste, and I was pretty sure I'd know if they were fibbing. Pretty sure I'd know if they hated it. I enquired about London life, which, they assured me, was working out well. Some months back, Clarence, having completed his sabbatical at Magdalen, had headed back to the smoke, to take up the reins of his legal department at King's, leaving Malcolm desolate. Until Clarence had asked him to come with him, that is.

'What, to visit?' Malcolm had told me how the conversation had gone. Malcolm was a very good mimic and he'd acted out the parts, jumping to one side to be Clarence, and affecting his deep, treacly tones, then jumping back to play himself, in a high, silly voice.

'No, to live,' Malcolm growled, a.k.a. Clarence.

'What, with you?' (High squeak).

'Unless there's someone else you'd like to live with.' (Low growl.)

'In your house?' (High squeak) 'In Little Venice?'

'If you can bear it.'

'But . . . what about my boat?'

'It's not called Little Venice for nothing, Malcolm. I'm sure a mooring can be arranged. If not, it can stay in Oxford and be our country retreat.'

'Can Cinders come too?'

'Sooty would be distraught if she didn't.'

Malcolm, adopting an even higher falsetto: 'You're asking me to move in with you?'

'That's . . . the general idea.'

Quite a lot of jumping up and down on the spot was re-enacted for me then, together with excited flapping of hands, and then smothering of fictitious Clarence with kisses, which I eventually had to ask Malcolm to edit out as he wrapped his arms around himself and really got going. Besides, there was more.

'But what about the shop?' squealed baby bear, stepping back from the embrace, panting and blinking rapidly.

'Ah, the shop . . .' More treacle.

'Quite a commute.'

'Hell of a commute.'

'Which is where you come in, flower.' Malcolm had turned to me then, in something more like his normal voice. 'Ludo wants to sell up too. He's going back to journalism.'

'Is he?' I'd flushed at his name.

'Oh, yes, didn't you know? He's going back to be our fearless, war-torn reporter in Afghani . . . Isbeki . . . somewhere, again. Says he's stultified his mind for too long. Needs to get back to where the action is. He went back to London last week.'

'Oh.' I felt a pang. Of regret, I suppose; but I was pleased for him too.

'It's the right thing for him,' I told Malcolm.

'Of course it is. He was wasted here. But the *shop*, dear heart . . .'

*

The shop. I moved around it now, feeling strangely weightless as I skirted groups of people, as if I was moving clear of the ground. The place had filled up quickly and everyone was chatting and laughing, exclaiming as they recognized old friends. I looked beyond them to the gleaming spines I'd lined up yet again this morning, making sure they were all neatly aligned, and a fastidious inch from the edge of the shelves, which I'd also had painted the same very pale blue of the walls. I nervously rearranged the flowers in the corner on the table, fanning out the sweet peas, then moved on to smooth the cream calico of the sofa and armchairs I'd had re-covered as I passed. Surely all bookshops didn't have to be dark green with leather chairs? Up above, spot lighting, which I'd put in to make it brighter, twinkled down like so many tiny stars, and underfoot the prohibitively expensive limestone flooring – I'd almost shut my eyes as I'd written out the cheque – felt smooth and cool. Restful. All of which had been paid for with Dad's money, of course. Would he have approved? I gazed round. I think so. The money wasn't going to support the farm any more, but it was going to support a family business, and that, I believe, would have pleased him. Oh, it could have gone straight into the bottomless pit of renovating the farmhouse, could have been poured effortlessly into the roof, for instance, or the dry rot, but Ant had said no. Use it for something definitive, something to remember him by: something for you. Use it to take out a mortgage on the shop. My shop.

'What d'you think?' I asked him now as he approached, even though he'd seen it dozens of times in its new incarnation. Even though he'd had to approve every colour swatch, enthuse about every lick of paint.

'Terrific.' He smiled down at me. 'You're terrific.' He bent his head to kiss me, and at that moment the door opened again, and Ludo walked in, together with Alice and her husband, Angus, and a very beautiful Asian girl.

'Ludo!' Ant and I said simultaneously and perhaps over-enthusiastically, springing apart like deflecting magnets. He and Ant lunged to shake hands, again, somewhat over-heartily, and then Ludo and I pecked cheeks as if we were encountering molten metal.

'Hi.' He stepped back smartly as I did too. 'This is fantastic.' He gazed around. 'You've done a very good job.'

'You think?' I wasn't really listening: I was looking at the fashionably crumpled linen jacket, the crazy red and white print shirt, which had replaced the enormous tweed overcoat and the loosened collar and tie.

'For sure. It's taken it out of the last century and brought it hurtling into this one. I always thought we were a bit nineties in here, but I couldn't work out why.' He saw me clocking the new wardrobe. 'Oh. Sunita bought me these.' He grinned, that lovely old tigerish smile that made his eyes crinkle at the edges and all but disappear, and then with a deft arm around her waist, drew the dusky beauty into the circle. Her hair hung like a long sheet of mahogany silk, her cheekbones were high, and when she smiled, her eyes and teeth dazzled.

'Sunita – Evie,' Ludo said. 'Sunita wanted to bring me out of the last century too.'

I laughed. 'About time too. It's lovely to meet you, Sunita.'

'It was nice of you to invite me,' she said with a secret smile, and I knew, in an instant, she knew. Had been told, maybe in bed last night, or maybe in the car on the way down; Alice perhaps leaning forward from the back seat to divulge more information: I once had a crush on this girl. Might he have said she brought me back to life? No. But Alice might have done. And I caught a glimpse of surprise in Sunita's eyes now. Girl? Woman, surely. Ah, but you see, Sunita, I thought, excusing myself politely and moving on, you don't have to be a spring chicken to make hearts beat faster. It helps, of course, but it's not mandatory.

I moved on around the room: being the party-giver and the jug-bearer gave me a delicious freedom and I greeted my guests here, accepted compliments there, exclaiming at people I hadn't seen for ages, revelling in being amongst friends, family, on this, my opening night; a blissfully balmy, late summer's evening. I spied Ted, talking to Stacey in the bay window, and went to say hello.

'You're sweet to come all this way,' I said, pouring him a drink.

He knocked it back in one. 'Don't be soft, I wouldn't have missed it for the world. Blimey, what's this, luv, horse piss? Got any beer?'

I laughed. 'No, and you can blame me and your grand-daughter for that. We didn't think we'd need it.'

'Granddad, it's Pimm's. You'll love it!' Stacey was indignant.

He made a face. 'I might like it better without the fruit salad. Get us one without the gubbins in it, eh, luv?' He handed her his glass and Stacey, raising her eyes to the heavens, went off to oblige.

'What an occasion, though, luv.' He rubbed his hands together excitedly. 'The girls are thrilled to bits!'

I laughed. 'I know. I think they regard it as their own private bookshop. They're always in here borrowing, and I haven't even opened.'

'Ah, but you've encouraged that, haven't you?' He jerked his head meaningfully outside and gave me a conspiratorial wink.

'I have,' I admitted. 'Couldn't resist it.'

'Course you couldn't, and who can blame you? But you must get them to work for it too. Get them behind the till of a Saturday. Teach them you don't get owt for nowt.'

'Oh, don't worry, they've already booked their slots. And they want more than the minimum wage too.'

'I bet they bloomin' do!' boomed Terrific Ted, his face, I noticed, already the colour of the spotty red hanky he'd rather roguishly tucked in the top pocket of what looked like a new and dashing tweed jacket.

'Aye, luv, you've done a grand job here. And look at all the support you've got.' His eyes roved around, marvelling at what was now, indeed, quite a crush. 'If all these people buy their books here, you're quids in. You've got a heap of customers already!'

'Well, let's hope they do,' I said nervously. 'I'm rather counting on people's loyalty to their small, quirky, local bookshop, so handily located round the corner. Can't compete with the chains any other way.'

'Aye, well, as that lovely lady over there was saying

earlier, that's the charm o' the place.' He nodded across the room. 'Its quirkiness.'

'That's my mum,' I said in surprise. 'Weren't you introduced?'

'Not properly, like. I just muscled in the chatter, then someone else nabbed her. Your mum, eh?' He looked in surprise: from me, back to her. 'Oh, aye, I can see it now. Same smile. Same generous spirit too, I'll warrant.'

'Oh, no, Ted, she's much nicer than me. Come and meet her properly.'

I led him across the room and introduced them. Yes, Mum did indeed look rather lovely, I thought, as I left them chatting. The girls had persuaded her to cut off her ponytail and have her hair done properly, with a few highlights, which had been a huge improvement; made her look years younger. In fact, everyone looked lovely this evening, I decided. Anna and Stacey were with their cousins behind the bar – or trestle table – where they clearly thought their duty lay, laughing at Henry, who was throwing Hula Hoops up in the air and trying to catch them in his mouth, missing every time: the boys looking gangly and adorable, smart shirts hanging out over pale chinos, the girls, very grown up in short skirts, huge belts and make-up; Phoebe too. She saw me looking and smiled across. Then, after a moment's hesitation, she peeled off from the others; came over and plucked at my sleeve.

'Um, Evie?'

'Yes, darling?' I glanced around distractedly. Should I serve the sausages now, I wondered. Surely everyone was pretty much here?

'You know you said to Mum that one day Jack or Henry could buy the farm back from you?'

I turned to look at her properly.

'Yes?'

'Would you say the same to me?' Her colour rose up her neck. 'If one day I wanted to, would you give me first refusal too?'

I put my jug down. 'Phoebe Milligan.' I put my arms round her and hugged her tight. 'With the greatest pleasure.' I whispered in her ear. 'The *very* greatest pleasure. Don't you worry, Phoebe, that place has got your name on it, should you ever want it.'

'Thank you.' She beamed at me. 'It's just, I thought I might go to Cirencester after school. You know, agricultural college. Learn how to do it properly. And, who knows, one day . . .'

'Who knows in*deed*,' I said warmly. 'But I tell you what, Phoebe, in case you change your mind, I wouldn't let on to Mum yet. She'll be so thrilled you'll never hear the last of it, and then you really *will* have to have it.'

She laughed, and then slid back to join the gang behind the trestle table; still a bit flushed, and just briefly catching my eye again as she picked up her drink, secretly delighted.

It was warm in the room, and I threaded my way through the noisy, baying throng to the front to open a window. I propped open the double doors too, hooking them both back on the wall, then wandered outside. The sausages could wait a minute. I wanted to see something first. Out on the pavement, a few people had overflowed to stand with their drinks, one or two smokers amongst them, laughing and chatting, blowing their smoke in thin blue lines up into the dusty sky. They smiled and raised their glasses when they saw me.

'Cheers! Well done!'

I smiled and raised my glass back. 'Thanks.'

But I didn't stop. I wanted to cross the street; to be at a vantage point where I could look back and see it all properly. I strayed across to the other side of the road, weaving around a lone cyclist. The tourists were leaving now, and with the students yet to arrive, there was an exhausted feel to the city: a brief hiatus. The distant hum of traffic from the city centre was audible, and the subtle September breeze, warmed by its journey across hot pavements, scented by various bars and restaurants, filled my senses. As I turned on the opposite pavement to look back at the shop, my heart contracted a moment, then kicked in.

Brightly lit and buzzing, juxtaposed by its darkened, quiet neighbours, it looked quite the place to be this Friday night: quite the party of the moment. In fact, it verily hummed. Voices sang into the night, and now and again, the occasional shout of laughter broke out like a spark from a fire, cracking right down the street to the Bodleian Head, or up into the skyline of treacle-coloured Cotswold stone. My eyes roved critically over the shop front. Two shop fronts originally, of course, one Malcolm's and one Ludo's, with separate entrances, but now seamlessly merged by a set of double French doors. All the panelling, the woodwork, some of it carved and intricate, especially around the bay windows, had been painted off-white, the detail picked out in the same duck-egg blue as the interior. Quite a lot of discussion had gone into that blue. Quite a lot of colour charts spread on the kitchen table with plenty of opinionated teenage voices. The doorframes had been painted off-white too, and either side of them, on the pavement, sat two lemon trees in round, leaded pots.

'They'll get nicked,' Malcolm had warned, the moment he saw them.

'I'll bring them in at night.' I'd retorted.

'You'll get lazy, you'll leave them, they'll get nicked,' he'd repeated.

'We'll see,' I'd smiled, and he had too, at my enthusiasm. Naïvety, perhaps.

Behind the lemon trees the window displays continued what I felt to be a vaguely Tuscan theme: in each of the bays was a long, rather beautiful, bleached oak refectory table, a matching pair I'd found at a local auction and snapped up in triumph. Both were covered in books: some were propped up, some just lying flat, some in piles, and one or two were open as if still being read. On one table, atop a tome about Impressionist painters, was a Panama hat – I know, I know – and on the other, a large ceramic bowl of china oranges. Malcolm had smiled at these last two, muttering something about a cuddly toy, and then about dust, but I hadn't been able to resist. My eye travelled up now above the windows, to something that, as Ted had so rightly observed earlier, I hadn't been able to resist either. Across the hoarding, in pale lemon scroll – another colour that had been the subject of hot debate amongst the females of the family – the name of the shop had been picked out in bold, swirling letters:

## *Hamilton and Daughters*

I smiled. Raised my glass. 'Here's to us,' I said softly, into the night.